Mr S.V. Edw
14 Cae Ger
Ruthin

TAMAJAO 241

A POW CAMP ON THE RIVER KWAI

First published in 1987 by
Paul - Leagas Publications
42 Clifton Road, Ashingdon, Rochford, Essex SS4 3HJ

ISBN 0 9512706 0 5

Printed by Basildon Printing Company Limited
Heron Industrial Estate
Wickford, Essex, SS11 8DL England.

DEDICATION

To all who fought in the Far East and above all to those who were taken prisoner by the Japanese.

To all my friends and former comrades in Australia, the United States of America, Holland, and so many other parts of the world.

To the officers and medics from the R.A.M.C. and the Australian Medical Corps, who did so much to help the sick and to save so many lives that would otherwise have been lost.

To my many F.E.P.O.W. comrades here in the United Kingdom, especially those who were forced to slave on the railway in Thailand and Burma and who have received scant official recognition.

To a brave Thai underground agent whose real name I never knew. (In the book he is called Captain Ayut).

To all of you, this book is dedicated.

The years have passed. Time never stands still, but now, as then, the spirit lives on. A large part of my young life will remain with you all forever!

Ernest Warwick
(Ern boy)

Ashingdon, Rochford
Essex, England
1987

ACKNOWLEDGEMENTS

My grateful thanks are due to all my old comrades who have helped me to remember the details of certain incidents and also to my good friend Jim Nokes, who has worked hard to present my story in a more acceptable fashion. To Clive Pike of Basildon Printing Company Limited for his constructive help and advice.

CONTENTS

The story of the lives of the principal characters continues in Book Two, by the same author - "RETURN FROM TAMAJAO".

The photographic reproduction opposite has been taken from an original painting of the author created in a jungle prisoner of war camp in Thailand in 1944, by the camp artist, George Old. Under difficult conditions, using paper and other materials stolen from the Japanese, the artist made brushes with human hair. The author cut away his beard and trimmed his moustache with scissors borrowed from Australian medics. He shaved by means of an old ground down knife, without the luxury of soap or brush. Today the painting remains a treasured possession of the author.

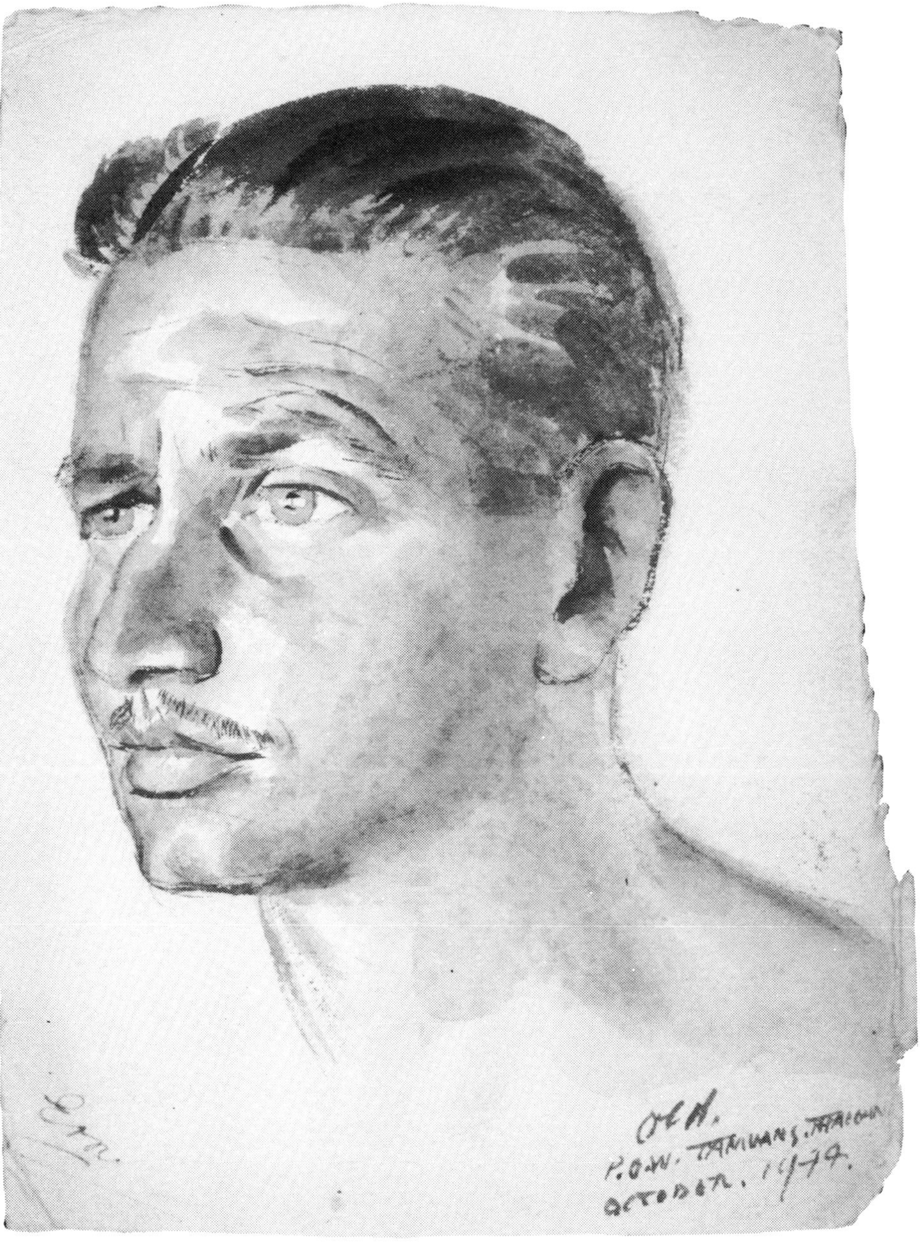
P.O.W. TAMUANG. THAILAND
OCTOBER. 1944.

PREFACE

It was never my original intention to use the secret notes I made while a prisoner of war as the basis for a book. The notes were written for the purpose of exposing to the world the unbelievable catalogue of appalling crimes, cruelty and brutality committed by the Japanese and Koreans against the many thousands of sick, starving and helpless Allied prisoners of war.

In August 1945, at the end of World War II, I dug up from where I had buried it for safety, a small metal box, inside which were my precious notes, written furtively on scraps of paper stolen from the Japanese.

It was with considerable difficulty and risk that I had managed to transfer these from camp to camp. It, therefore, seemed ironic that due to deterioration below the soil of Thailand, much of my writing had been obliterated.

However, during my enforced stay in hospitals in Burma and back home in the United Kingdom, with the scars still on my body and the nightmare event of three years and eight months of hell fresh in my mind, I attempted to rewrite the facts as I remembered them.

Although far from complete, these notes tucked away in an old wartime scrap box have now formed the basis of my story which contains so many of the grim facts. I can assure the reader that I have in no way over emphasized the brutal incidents, ugly situations, and sheer bestiality of the Japanese. On the contrary, and in order to spare the reader, I have in fact omitted some of the more revolting and sickening atrocities which I witnessed. For many long years I tried to shut off that terrible part of my life, but to no avail!

Forty years later, in 1985 on the anniversary of VJ-Day, in the lovely Suffolk town of Eye, I joined another Far Eastern prisoner of war, George Thurston, at the War Memorial where he had placed a wreath with a simple inscription: 'In loving memory of all our Comrades who died on the Siam to Burma Railway' signed 'From a Fellow Prisoner of War'.

It was a moving moment in my life, the past came rushing back to me; I wept unashamedly for my dead comrades. Afterwards I felt a compulsion to write the real story as I had experienced it.

Understandably, because of the war with Germany and the horrors revealed, Europe made the headlines and daily news; the Far East lay thousands of miles away, sometimes almost forgotten. Many questions are now being asked today as to what really happened: I sincerely hope my story will begin to enlighten those who are interested.

Memory tends to fade with time on smaller incidents and minor details, and I must apologise to all my comrades if my account does not tally with their recollections.

All the prisoners of war mentioned in the book are based on real-life characters, but I have deliberately changed their names to avoid any further unnecessary grief and suffering to the relatives of those who died. This was my paramount consideration whilst I was writing the book. I wish to emphasize that the main Japanese character, Captain Suzuki, was the real and brutal commandant of Tonchan camp. The other enemy names used have also been taken from real-life Japanese and Korean soldiers.

Except for Kwai-Tanu and Tamajao 241, all the POW camps in the book really existed. Kwai-Tanu has been based upon a camp near Kanburi, and there were in fact two Tamajao camps, no.237 and Wood Camp no.239. For the same previously mentioned and obvious reasons, Tamajao 241 camp was specially created by me. It follows, therefore, that any real life person mentioned can only be accidental or purely co-incidental.

This is a story primarily about the ordinary 'squaddies', and their appalling experiences at the hands of the Japanese. It is an attempt to convey to the reader the desperation of the thousands of helpless men faced with an implacable enemy, to whom their lives were wholly and utterly expendable in the service of the Japanese Emperor.

Every one of these men has a story to tell, this is but one of them!

Ernest Warwick
1987

CHAPTER 1

Incident at the Docks

The ropes used to tie the young British soldier to the tree didn't seem to hurt any more. Blood from his mouth had run down his neck on to his chest, drying fast in the hot tropical sun of Singapore. His fair hair was matted in dried blood from a wound on one side of his head caused by a blow from a rifle butt, although that didn't seem to worry him either. It was the ants, the bloody red ants crawling round his legs, upwards across his chest, up his neck to feast on his dried blood.

They were driving army Private Eddy Warton crazy. In desperation he tried to rub his head on his shoulders in a futile attempt to shake them off. Some thirty feet or so away, through his bruised eyes he could count eight Japanese guards, an evil-looking crew, talking, smoking and drinking bottles of captured British beer. That made him feel decidedly worse. Christ, he felt parched and he badly needed water. The Japs had erected a temporary wooden hut, from which on a pole hung limply the Japanese flag, the Rising Sun, a symbol of terror to all who fought against the cruel sadistic enemy in the Far East.

This was the beginning of April, 1942. Singapore had fallen some weeks earlier on the 15th of February. The dead had been buried, the city restored to some sort of order. Changi, the first large POW camp, had to send in daily work parties under armed guards, to continue to clean up the city and work in the docks. Also, about this time, the enemy were setting up new POW camps, such as the Bukit-Timah labour camp on the outskirts of the once lovely golf course and in swampy villages towards the causeway which joins the island to the mainland of Malaya at Johore Bahru.

Following the bloody massacre at Alexander hospital, where staff and patients had been bayoneted to death, Allied prisoners of war were experiencing and witnessing numerous atrocities carried out by the occupying Japanese force against the local inhabitants and Allied prisoners of war. Rape and looting were commonplace.

Out across the harbour, the Emperor's warships could be seen riding at anchor, flying the flag of terror. In the blue skies above, the Jap planes flew in V-formation flights of twenty-seven, typical of their blanket bombing methods which had done so much to destroy the city. In particular, the Chinese section suffered appalling damage and many thousands of innocent civilians were killed!

Allied troops felt very bitter about the almost total lack of air support. The enemy had thought long and planned well, his invasion coming at a time when the desperate battles for Europe and the Middle East were draining supplies of planes, tanks and weapons, thus leaving little to spare for the Far East!

Four days and nights had passed since Private Warton had whacked a Japanese soldier for committing an atrocity against an old woman. As he hung on the ropes he'd lost all count of time. Two of the guards armed with sticks approached him again, shouting abuse in Japanese, as they rained more blows on his body. It seemed almost with a feeling of relief that he slipped once more into unconsciousness, his body sagging limply on the ropes holding him to the tree. That hot day, as on others, many of the residents of Singapore hurried past the pitiful sight. Nearby stood a large notice in English, Chinese and Malay, warning all that death would be the penalty for anyone attempting to help the prisoner of war. No-one did!

On the fifth day, the heat of the sun revived Eddy Warton and he painfully regained consciousness. Through a misty haze he could just see and hear the Sons of Heaven chanting their daily monologue to the sun, bowing to the flag and to each other. His throat was swollen, dried up and parched beyond belief; his mouth was bloody and sore where it had felt the weight of a rifle butt.

Unexpectedly, a small captured British truck drew up and out stepped a Japanese major, complete with a large sword, accompanied by a Malay interpreter. Much bowing and saluting took place, and after some conversation, two Jap guards approached the prisoner and waited with knives in their hands.

The Japanese major was making some kind of statement; in turn the interpreter translated into English:

"You are being taken to another prisoner of war camp on the island, you will not be returning to Changi! You will appear seven days from now before the Japanese Camp Commandant for punishment of your crime. You will probably be executed."

Eddy felt bloody sick and although he could hear OK, it didn't seem to register, or even if it did, he was in no condition to react.

The Japanese officer spoke again, the Malay translated: "Our nation, under orders from our most wonderful and honourable Emperor has come to free this part of the world from the British and their Allies; do you understand?"

"Bullshit" thought Ed, as he nodded that he understood.

The officer nodded his head to the two guards who cut him free from the ropes. His legs gave way and he collapsed on the pavement. The two guards lifted him up and bundled him on to the metal floor of the truck. The tailboard was secured, and it sped off in the direction of the causeway.

Leaving behind the small village of Kranji, the vehicle swung left down a winding dusty dirt track leading to a large newly formed prisoner of war camp. After more bowing, the gates swung open and the truck drove hastily on down past a variety of different huts, coming to an abrupt halt outside a large wooden one, from which fluttered a Red Cross flag.

The two escorting guards, dropped the tailboard down, rolled the prisoner to the edge of the truck and pushed him out. He landed with a sickening thud as he crashed to the ground. Having lifted the tailboard up again, the guards climbed back into the truck, which raced away, leaving behind a giant cloud of dust. Two Australian medical orderlies (medics) came running from the hut and knelt down beside the crumpled body. A pair of blue eyes opened and gazed up at them.

"Bloody oath, he's alive", one of them exclaimed.

"Let's get him inside quick", replied the other.

Carefully, they lifted him up and carried him into the hut, where they laid him on a makeshift bed of boards and blankets.

"Water, water", croaked Eddy.

"OK, mate", replied one of the medics, as they efficiently set about the task of reviving the beaten prisoner of war.

Several hours later they had cut away his bloodstained shirt, shorts and pants, treated his wounds, and washed him from head to foot. They even managed to dress him in new pants, shirt and shorts, his own having been taken away for burning.

Private Eddy Warton was feeling a whole lot better.

"Look mate", said the Aussie medic, "Joe has fetched this special from the cookhouse". Greedily, Eddy devoured the boiled rice and dried fish, washing it down with yet another mug of weak tea. He felt like a king; bloody, battered and sore, but by Christ, yes, he sure felt like a king!

After he'd rested for another hour, the two Aussies returned to his bedside.

"Feeling better now, mate?" they chorussed.

"Sure do, thanks a lot" came the reply.

"Smoke?" asked one of the medics, offering a packet to Ed.

"Thanks, mate. You keep 'em, I don't smoke."

The Digger looked surprised. Ed grinned: "Well, I used to before I joined up, then some of us got the keep-fit bug, and we packed up smoking. I've never smoked since. Must say I did feel a helluva lot better at the time, that is, until I landed in this bloody awful place!"

The Australian replied: "Good on yer, mate. The Japs are issuing us with twenty fags a week until supplies run out." He grinned: "Mind you, they're our own bloody fags that they captured." He went on: "You're a bloody Pommie. aren't you? What's your name and where d'you come from then?"

"I'm afraid so. My name is Eddy Warton, I'm a private soldier with the Suffolks."

"Well, good on yer mate, my name's Bluey Longhurst, and my mate here is Joe Langton. We're both from Melbourne in good old Australia. Whereabouts in England are you from, then?" The questions came thick and fast.

"I'm from Southend."

"Where's that then, mate?" Ed explained: "It's a seaside town in Essex, not far from London."

"Look mate" said Bluey, we'll call you Ed, that 'right with you?" The three young soldiers shook hands solemnly.

At that moment an Australian Medical Officer arrived back in the hut, walked straight over to Ed and announced: "G'day, my name's Saunders, Captain Don Saunders from the 8th Army Medical Corps."

He was a tall dark good looking man with a big grin. "Been out visiting the sick - well really seeing what else we can pinch from the evil bastards. By the way, I'm in charge of this bloody so-called hospital."

He went on: "While I was out in the camp, word got around on the bamboo grapevine you were here, and that you'd been in trouble. Also, the Camp Commandant had me in to inform me that you have to appear in front of him in seven days time. Meanwhile, we have to get you fit again."

"He's a Pom" interposed one of the medics.

"That'll do, Bluey" answered Captain Saunders sharply. He grinned. "None of us can help what we are, all of us are in the same bloody war and as I see it, right now we're all up shit street."

"Too right" muttered Bluey, "Too bloody right."

The captain addressed Ed again. "I've had a word with one of our majors, Wrightner is his name. He was a solicitor in Sydney. Good bloke, he will represent you when you have to appear, OK?"

"Thanks Captain, but they've already said they may execute me."

"God man, what the hell did you do? I'll shut up now and you relate to me what happened, then I'll relay the information to the major."

"Not a long story really", replied Ed. "I came down from Changi with a work party to work in the docks the day it happened. We were having a break on the side which backs on to the public path and main road to Bukit-Timah. There are very wide iron railings all along the path, wide enough for a man to get through. An old woman came along the path with a basketful of sherpatties (rice cakes, baked). I had a few Malayan dollars left, and seeing the guards' attention was diverted elsewhere at the time I slipped through the railings, gave the old woman the money and was passing the cakes through to my mate Bill Slatoe. He's also in the Suffolks, joined up with him - blimey, where was I?"

"Take your time", said Captain Saunders, "What happened next?"

"Well," continued Ed, "Bill got the grub through the railings OK. The business was over, but before the old woman could run away or I could get back through the railings, a bloody Jap came racing down the path, waving a gun at us and shouting like a lunatic. We froze and thought it best not to make a move, although I shouted to Bill and the other lads to run like hell before they were caught, which they did. That left me and the old woman, held on the path by this evil-looking bastard."

Ed paused for breath, then continued. "The old woman was crying with fright. The Jap made her stand opposite me about five feet away, then he kicked her legs apart, made her hold both hands up to her shoulders, picked up a five foot iron bar that was lying nearby, pushed it into her hands and motioned her to hold her arms outstretched in the air above her head. She did try, but she couldn't stand the weight, brought her arms down and dropped the iron bar.

Holding his gun with one hand, the bastard unbuckled a wide belt he was wearing and slashed the old woman across the face. She screamed in pain, and blood spurted from her nose. I couldn't stand it any more, so before he could pull the trigger, I belted him hard, right between his slant eyes. He went down, out cold, the shitbag."

"Bloody hell" swore Captain Saunders, "What happened next?"

"Well" replied Ed, "I told the old woman to run like hell. D'you know, she said 'God bless you son', he reflected. "She must have been seventy or more, anyway she ran right across the Bukit-Timah road and disappeared safely in the distance!"

Ed paused again. "That left me with one hell of a problem and no time to solve it. My immediate reaction was to grab the gun and shoot the bastard. Then, I guess, to run for my life. Anyway, it all happened so fast, before I could do anything I saw armed guards running down the path towards me shouting and screaming. I thought 'That's my lot'.

"Go on" urged the Australian Captain, "Tell us the rest."

"Not too clear" replied Ed. "They tied my feet together with a rope, jerked me arse overhead on the concrete. That bloody hurt! Then they bashed me on the head with a rifle butt, dragged me across the Bukit-Timah road and tied me to a tree. Then they took turns to beat the shit out of me. The rest I guess you know."

Ed felt tired and mortally sick after having relived the first episode in his POW life. Little did he realise how lucky he was to be alive. He had much to learn in the years of horror which lay ahead.

"Have a rest now," advised Captain Saunders, "you'll be right mate. I've got to go and have a talk with Major Wrightner about your defence. Guess I'll catch you later."

"Ed" said Bluey Longhurst, "We reckon you deserve a medal, mate, not a bloody good hiding like you've had."

"Too right" echoed Joey Langton.

"By the way Ed, how old are you?"

"What's the date?" asked Ed.

"April 5th."

It so happens my birthday is April 12th. I'll be twenty-two" replied Ed.

"Reckon we'll celebrate that" answered Bluey.

Being young and fit, Ed Warton made a remarkable recovery from his ordeal, although the rope marks on his arms were to stay with him for months ahead.

The Australian POW camp in which he found himself, officially named 'Jurong POW Camp', had been dubbed 'We can do no wrong camp.' The reason for this was that the Aussies tricked, cheated and robbed the Jap guards of anything and everything, from stealing back captured British medical supplies (so urgently needed), to siphoning petrol at night from Japanese transport parked in the camp, and selling it through the wire fencing to a local businessman.

With the money made from these surreptitious sales, the Aussies were able to buy eggs for the sick, and other luxuries. The guards permitted these purchases from the Malays, who were allowed to call at the camp gates once a week under strict supervision.

Mr. Chong-Wang was the businessman who made frequent visits to the wire fencing on the east side of the camp to purchase the precious fuel at three dollars a gallon.

Unfortunately, the week before Ed's arrival, the petrol business had ceased abruptly when Mr. Chong-Wang's little baker's van was stopped and searched in the early hours by Jap guards. Instead of bread, they discovered twenty gallons of petrol aboard.

With his hands tied behind his back, one very distressed Mr. Chong-Wang was made to kneel before a Japanese officer, who swiftly executed him by means of the sword, neatly severing his head from his body. At the place of execution by the wayside, his head was then stuck on a pole, complete with flies. This was his punishment for stealing from the Japanese forces! Fortunately the Japs had not discovered the POW source of supply, although back in camp the Aussies heard the sad news the next day.

Now that lucrative source of income was closed, the indomitable Aussies were already planning other means of robbing the enemy.

Escape, the burning issue, haunted Ed's thoughts and plans. Escape was one thing, but tracking an Englishman on the run would not prove difficult on such a small island, swamped with Japanese troops and Far Eastern natives. With enemy ships patrolling the waters, now was not the right time for an attempt. That night, an Australian working party marched back into Jurong. By all accounts, they had been working in the city and had made contact with a British working party from Changi. The news was bad.

Six Britons and one Australian had escaped from Changi and eventually all had been recaptured. At revolver point, three British officers had been forced to witness the execution by shooting of the seven men! 'Murder by shooting', as it quickly became known, was a vivid and timely warning not to attempt escape!

Australian medical officer, Captain Don Saunders, had managed to keep Ed in his hospital hut away from the guards, in order to give him strength and protection prior to his trial.

On the fifth night since his arrival, with permission granted from Major Mizutani, the English-speaking Camp Commandant, the 'Diggers' were holding an unrehearsed concert on a stage made of bamboo in the centre of the area of dry dust known as the parade ground. Some of the Diggers had managed to hold on to various musical instruments, and as a result were making a terrific din. The audience were sitting in the dust, smoking, laughing and singing. They gave a particularly noisy rendering of the old army favourite 'Bless 'em all', ending with the words: 'You'll get no promotion this side of the ocean, so cheer up my lads, up 'em all!, clearly a message for the Japs!

Ed grinned. The words are the same, he thought. Even my mob couldn't have put it over any better. A loud rendering of 'Waltzing Matilda' followed, more applause, and then an announcement that Sid Johnson, from Berwick (near Melbourne), would sing the final number to conclude the concert. The guitars strummed softly as the young Digger began to sing: 'I'll be seeing you, In all the old familiar places...' He had a fine voice; in the background, it seemed the whole camp had joined in singing the well-known words.

Beneath the bright moonlight, it all seemed unreal. Two thousand Australian POW's sitting in the dust singing with all their hearts. Memories began flooding back to Ed Warton. He suddenly felt very homesick.

"Have a mug of tea, Ed", said Bluey. "Know how you feel, mate! Sort o' gets right to you. Still, we'll be all right, mate! Our turn'll come for sure."

Ed nodded in agreement, his thoughts at that moment very far away.

"Thanks for the tea, Bluey. Going to turn in now. Goodnight, mate!"

Day six: again hot and humid, as the sun blazed down relentlessly from the brilliant blue tropical sky. Major Leslie Wrightner arrived at the hut to interview Ed prior to the trial, due to take place on the following day.

"G'day, soldier. Wrightner's the name, major in the 8th Div.", announced the officer as he held out his hand and shook Ed's hand warmly. He was of medium build with fair hair, a youthful face, and piercing grey eyes. Ed thought he didn't look like a solicitor, not that it mattered anyway.

The major listened intently as Ed related the details of the events leading to his being there awaiting trial. They discussed various aspects of the case, and then the officer informed Ed that the Japanese Commandant had ordered the trial for 9 a.m. the next morning, April 12th. He concluded: "Be prepared for anything, soldier. Given a fair chance, I'll do my best and maybe things won't be so bad!"

He seems a bloody good bloke, thought Ed, as he thanked him when they shook hands again on parting. Ed began to feel hopeful.

The following morning, after a breakfast of plain boiled rice, washed down with a mug of tea, Ed made ready for his 9 o'clock appearance. He had borrowed a razor from a medic, shaved, washed and smartened himself up. Captain Saunders and the two medics shook hands with him and wished him luck. At 8.30, Major Wrightner arrived, accompanied by two armed guards.

Ed was ordered to march beside the major with the two guards bringing up the rear. They marched briskly down the dusty road, across the parade ground towards the commandant's hut. As they marched, the Aussie officer said: "These two guards can't speak a word of English. It must have been great to knock out a Jap, but these little bastards mean bloody business. They've already crucified one of our men at Changi. Things are getting worse, so if you want to stay alive, just say yes and no at the right time!"

"What do you think will happen?" asked Ed.

"Really don't know. We'll have to wait and see."

Outside the commandant's hut, two more scruffy-looking guards were on duty with fixed bayonets. Above them, on a long bamboo pole, hung the Rising Sun. The accompanying guards halted, and one went inside. A lot of talking in Japanese could be heard. The guard suddenly reappeared at the door and motioned the two prisoners to enter.

Seated at a large captured British desk was the English-speaking Camp Commandant, Major Mizutani, surprisingly tall for a Jap, clean shaven and dark haired. He was looking very serious, smartly dressed, with a row of medal ribbons across his left breast.

Major Wrightner and Private Warton both bowed. (as was required of all POW's). The two guards stood either side of the desk. Major Mizutani spoke first in fluent English. "You will remain standing. I have the details before me. Private soldier E. Warton, the British Army, Suffolk Regiment, for no reason at all you struck a Japanese soldier. You will of course plead guilty to this charge?"

Major Wrightner interrupted before Ed could reply. "I am here, sir, to represent the prisoner and wish to submit to you his defence."

The Japanese officer's face blackened with anger. He rose from his desk, walked across to the Australian officer, and slapped him hard across the face. The Aussie major did not flinch. The Jap resumed his seat, eyeing both men scornfully. He spoke in English again. Addressing Ed Warton, the Japanese officer was clearly in no mood for argument. "You are guilty as charged. The sentence is death by the sword."

The colour drained from Ed's cheeks, he felt weak at the knees and bloody sick. The Japanese officer grinned in fiendish delight at the effect of his words. "Do you understand?" he asked.

Ed couldn't speak, only nod his head in reply. Major Wrightner stood in stunned silence. There was an uneasy pause, then the Jap officer started to speak again.

"Today is a very special day. General Yamashita, our great and honourable Commanding Officer of all land forces, is visiting the island. I am to be decorated in view of our glorious victories in Malaya and Singapore", he boasted. "I wish to prove to you how generous the Imperial Army can be. Hear me, good English soldier, your life will be spared on this occasion. You are hereby sentenced to twenty-eight days on rice and salt, with a canteen of water twice a day, at sunrise and sunset. You will never return to Changi. Three miles from here we have a special punishment centre, where you will serve your sentence, after which you will be returned to this camp to prepare for our great task ahead. I will give you more information on that in a few minutes."

The Japanese officer continued: "We do not understand your offensive attitude to our friendly and helpful army. Any future attempt to strike a member of the Imperial Japanese Army will carry the death sentence automatically, do you understand me?"

Ed nodded, there was no alternative. Major Mizutani clearly felt very pleased with himself as he spoke again for the next five minutes.

'That's about the biggest load of bullshit I've ever had to listen to', thought Ed, although both he and the Aussie Major wisely remained silent.

"Later this year", the Jap went on, "Japan is to carry out a feat that other nations have tried to do for a long time, but have failed. To build a railway through Siam to Burma. Japan will do what all these other nations have not been able to do, in order to carry our troops and supplies to assist our most glorious Imperial Army. Our labour force will be drawn from Allied prisoners of war, as well as some native labour. That is all. This meeting is at an end. Major Wrightner, you may now bow to me and return to your quarters. The prisoner will wait outside in the sun until transport arrives to take him to the punishment centre.

How long he stood bareheaded in the hot sunshine, Ed never knew. He was on the point of collapse, when a small captured open-top British truck drew up. Two Jap guards ordered him to climb in the back and sit on the floor.

As the camp gates swung open, he could still see some POW's through the swirling dust, waving their goodbyes. The small truck roared away quickly, covering the short three mile journey to the Malay village of Cho-Kang. Half a mile further on down a long narrow dirt track the truck skidded to a halt outside a small Jap camp, which was heavily guarded.

Once inside the gates, Ed was instructed to get out by a Malayan interpreter, who accompanied a black-bearded Japanese captain, with a vicious looking face and a clear hatred of prisoners of war.

The captain barked out his orders, the Malay translated.

"You will use punishment box no.2, that's the one over there."

In amazement and dismay, Ed looked across to where the interpreter was pointing. The box (or cooler, as it later became known) was a corrugated iron contraption, around four feet high, four feet wide, and six feet in length; there was some sort of sliding door at one end. This was about three feet in height.

The bearded officer then began another statement: "You will not be allowed to leave the punishment box until your twenty-eight day sentence is over. You will have to make your own latrine."

"Bloody hell!" muttered Ed, as he was marched to the door. A sharp kick on his left shin was quickly followed by a second on his right one, causing him to fall to his knees. The door was slid open and Ed was made to crawl in on his belly. With a final kick from one of the guards, the light became darkness as the door banged shut behind him. He lay stretched out full length in the stinking heat. His thoughts were chaotic. He felt anger, frustration and hatred against the cruel, vicious enemy. Would he survive?

Ed clenched his fists. "You murderous evil bastards!" he swore. His misery complete, he gave an almost hysterical laugh. In the blackness the young Suffolk soldier broke down and began to sob.

There was no-one to hear him! It was April 12th., 1942. He had just become twenty-two years of age!

CHAPTER 2

North to Thailand

Days and nights blurred into one. The young British soldier had lived his life a million times over, his brain somewhat confused in the darkness. Twenty-eight days later, he was still in his metal tomb. Despite this, his strong constitution, determination and will to survive had kept him sane, while deep in his heart lurked a bitter hatred for his cruel captors.

Suddenly, the metal door banged wide open and an interpreter translated the order for him to come out.

Slowly, painfully, he crawled on his belly into the scorching sunshine which blinded him as he collapsed helplessly on the ground. A waiting party of four Japanese guards and a sergeant looked down on the pathetic figure. Amidst laughter and amusement, the sergeant barked out an order. Four guards lifted him from the ground into a captured British Army truck standing nearby. The vehicle then drove quickly out of the punishment centre en route for the POW camp whence he had come.

Outside the medical hut at Jurong, the truck halted, creating a swirl of dust. Ed's mates, the Australian medics, were allowed to lift him by stretcher into the intensive care section, where they promptly cut away his clothes and set about the task of restoring life and health.

* * *

Nearly three months had passed. Ed Warton was feeling good again. The Diggers had done a good job and Captain Saunders had managed to keep him in the sick bay out of sight and reach of the guards.

Then came the order for the whole camp personnel to be moved in stages to Thailand (then Siam). The Japanese told them that the sick who could walk must go on the wonderful journey to a land of plenty, where they would all soon recover! In point of fact, the real objective was to be the construction of the Siam to Burma railway, which Ed had already heard about from Major Mizutani's rantings.

By earlier orders from General Fuyure, Japanese Officer in charge of POW. camps, Allied prisoners of war had already been deprived of their free cigarette and tobacco issue. However, they were still able to buy from local native traders these very necessary items for the many smokers among them. The POW's were also allowed to keep and, on occasions, to play any musical instruments in their possession. The only restriction was on the playing of bugles. Whilst buglers were permitted to retain these military instruments, their playing was only allowed at the burials, of which there were to be so many in the years and months to come.

The Diggers' thieving committee had been successful in recovering a supply of captured British Army clothes from the dock area (This was to be their last supply for more than three years) and, newly kitted out in these, the POW's started on their long journey. The date was the 15th July, 1942.

Ed, feeling fit and well, marched with the medics towards Singapore station, carrying a haversack on his back. In it were two round containers of boiled rice. But what the guards did not suspect was that, hidden in a false bottom of one of these harmless-looking containers, was a miniature radio receiving set, operated by batteries. The false bottom would unscrew with a tap. These small sets had been prepared by skilled army personnel at Changi, shortly before the fall of Singapore.

The Australians had managed to obtain one of these somehow, and batteries were procured from the natives at a price. Operating the sets was a dangerous risk, with the Japanese ordering the death penalty to anyone caught operating or even being in possession of one. The sets were powerful enough to pick up news in English from transmitting stations in India.

Whilst in the sick bay, Ed had learned about the radio sets from a fellow patient, Captain Seaton, an Australian signals officer, who was being treated for fever. The young British soldier felt that he owed the Diggers a lot; he also hated the Japs enough to volunteer to carry the secret radio. Thus it was agreed and so it came about that Ed was the one with the set concealed in his backpack! Captain Seaton would also carry twin food containers, one of which would conceal earphones and batteries. The food containers were about two feet in height by ten inches in diameter; this was ideal for their dual purpose role.

About half a mile from the station the party was halted by the wayside, where three unfortunate Chinese subjects were kneeling down in the grass with their hands tied behind their backs. They were pleading with a Japanese officer and four other Japs for their lives. What their crime was, the prisoners of war never knew. One by one, their heads were severed from their bodies, decapitated by an almighty blow from the sword of the Japanese officer. It was a filthy, bloody ghastly sight that the prisoners were forced to witness in the scorching sun. They heard the last chilling scream and then absolute silence! The scene at the roadside resembled a butcher's shop or a slaughterhouse! Further orders were given and the POW party marched on in sickened silence. The Japanese had clearly enjoyed their brutal executions.

At the station, chaos reigned supreme: guards were dishing out orders, accompanied by much bashing of those unfortunate enough not to understand all that was being said or sign motioned. Finally, with thirty-two men and two armed guards to each truck, the train began to chug its way out of Singapore station.

The prisoners at that stage were carrying the bare necessities of life: mess tin, knife, fork, and spoon (gut irons), a blanket each and an army bottle full of water. In addition, the medics had been allowed to take along limited medical supplies.

The railway carriages were, in fact, simply large metal goods truck containers. The heat of the day made them bloody unpleasant, unhealthy and uncomfortable, whilst at night they seemed to transform into ice boxes. The only humid air came from the two big metal sliding doors, which had to be kept open at all times. Trying to sleep on metal floors, with arms and legs digging and poking into one another, was unpleasant and completely hopeless!

The sun shimmered on the cool water, which reflected its glorious rays as the train thundered across the causeway towards Johore Bahru, leaving the island of Singapore far behind as it steamed steadily north. A stop was made at Bata Pahat to take on water for the engine as well as chopped firewood to fuel the boiler. The prisoners used the break to urinate and defecate on the train wheels.

Steadily northwards for many hours steamed the train. At a signal box three miles south of Kuala Lumpur the train shuddered to a halt once again. Without waiting for orders, the prisoners alighted at great speed, anxious not only to stretch their legs, but also more importantly, to answer the urgent calls of nature. Those who had not been for the last eighty miles were bursting as they stood by the wheels of the train. Many urinated high into the blue sky, freely, as if there was no tomorrow. Modesty had long since passed them by. Others, needing to empty their bowels, took it in turns to do so on the rails amidst the flies, between the buffers of each container.

The Japanese guards were busy doing likewise, All were using wild leaves growing beside the track in lieu of toilet paper, a luxury long since past. One of the Diggers squatting low, holding firmly on to a buffer, started to groan. Then suddenly, and not quite unexpectedly, came a thunderous roar from his backside, rapidly developing into an almighty non-stop fart. Big Billy Foster, a countryman from the outback, was at it again.

In utter amazement, the Japanese guards looked and listened.

"Number one-ka" they chanted in wonder at Billy's fantastic performance, carried out with almost musical variation in the sound. It had lasted all of three minutes. Big Billy, fast running out of strength, grunted, stood up and grinned: "Bloody oath! That feels a helluva lot better, mate." he announced to the world. The Jap guards clapped their hands in delight, unaware that Big Billy had held the camp's farting championship for several months, his antics and accomplished performances being a never-ending source of amusement.

Bluey, who had just finished urinating against a wheel, turned to Ed, who was doing the same. "Christ Almighty, Ed", he shouted. "Good job he didn't drop that beaut' in the truck, otherwise we'd all be dead." Ed gave a big grin and nodded.

"All men line up for searching, all haversacks and possessions to be shown." came the sudden order, translated via the interpreter. The prisoners put down their few precious belongings at their feet, as a Japanese sergeant and two guards searched systematically through them. The Malayan interpreter accompanying them had a distinctly unfriendly manner.

"The food containers, the guards want to know what's in them." Ed held his breath, then answered: "Boiled rice, it's what we eat on the train, of course." He paused and went on: "I've just had them refilled over there", pointing to a makeshift cookhouse nearby that had been previously arranged by the Japs to supply boiled rice and water to guards and prisoners en route.

"Empty them out!", came the sharp order. Ed immediately did just that, promptly emptying both containers on to the ground.

One of the guards looked suspiciously at the containers, bent down and picked up the one with the hidden radio in it. Despite the heat of the day, Ed's blood seemed to freeze in his veins. The guard looked inside, smelt it, turned it upside down, threw it on to the ground and gave it an almighty kick. Still intact, it rolled to a standstill some four or five feet away.

"Speedo, speedo, fill it up! came the command. Breathing again, Ed knelt down and hastily scooped the rice - dirt as well - back into the containers. He had barely finished when two shots rang out from one of the trigger-happy guards. An agonised cry went up as a Malayan native, with blood pouring from two chest wounds, slumped to the ground. Apparently, he had been attempting to purchase a pair of boots from one of the Diggers. As he lay dying in the grass, the order was given with complete and callous indifference: "All men re-train." Once aboard, the helpless POW's looked out at the native lying alone, his bloodied body in stark contrast to the vivid green vegetation, blue skies and hot sunshine.

Gathering speed, the train roared on northwards, crossing the border into Thailand. A day or so later it rolled slowly to a halt at a small rundown station. "We're here, we're here. All men out", translated the interpreter. The total journey from Singapore up the Malayan peninsula had lasted some four or five days and nights of extreme discomfort.

Once more, in a terrible rush, the prisoners answered the calls of nature, in what had now become standard practice, under the interested gaze of the natives of Thailand. As far as the prisoners were concerned, these natives looked much the same as those of Malaya.

The excited Japs were preoccupied by a handful of pretty young native women engaged in prostitution, using nearby bushes as speedy bunk-up beds. After negotiating the rate for the job, the Japs were dropping their trousers like yo-yos.

"Hope they all get a dose of the pox and die slowly, a bloody long and painful death", remarked Bluey, with which Joe and Ed vehemently agreed.

Many a swift deal was carried out while the guards' attention was thus diverted. The Thai traders would purchase from the POW's anything from shorts to boots, rings and watches, the proceeds of which would come in very useful for the purchase of eggs, dried fish and fruit.

The shagging and trading session over, the order was given: "Fall in, all men march now." Wearily, they set off on what proved to be a two-hour march in temperatures of over one hundred and ten degrees, along dirt and dusty mud tracks. This led them finally to a staging camp bearing the illustrious name of Bampong. Not the expected base hospital in the land of plenty that the Japs had promised, simply a collection of squalid native huts, made from very large bamboo frames roofed in attap (giant dried palm leaves). With nothing but the dirt ground to lie on, it was in fact just a filthy native area covered in excreta and flies, which bred fevers, malaria, and dysentery at an alarming rate.

At the so-called cookhouse, six British prisoners had been retained to cook food for those unfortunate enough to be sent to Thailand. A ration of boiled rice, jungle vegetable stew (jungle juice), one mug of weak tea minus milk and sugar, and a refilled army bottle of water, were issued to each man.

Wearily, the new camp arrivals laid down their single blanket on the ground for the night; glad, so bloody glad, to rest their aching bodies and sore feet at last. Ed was still with the Aussie medics who were preparing to sleep, when suddenly he heard an English voice he'd have known anywhere in the world.

"Any bleedin' Englishmen amongst you lot?"

Ed leapt to his feet. "Bill, Bill Slatoe, you old sod", he shouted, "What the bloody hell are you doing here?"

"Ed boy, my old mate", replied Bill. "We thought you were dead!"

With the Diggers as interested onlookers, the questions flew thick and fast. Bill was still shaking Ed's hand warmly. He couldn't believe that his mate was still alive.

"Bloody hell, Ed", he exclaimed for the third time. "They said you were executed for whacking that bleedin' Jap bastard down the docks. It's bloody marvellous to see you're still alive. With a bit of Southend luck, maybe we can stick together now mate!"

Bill Slatoe was a good-looking young man (he always described himself as 'bleedin' 'andsome'), with a mop of dark hair, good teeth, laughing grey eyes, and roughly the same height and build as his mate Ed. They'd first met the day they had both joined the army early in the war. Coming from the same hometown, they'd immediately hit it off.

Back in civilian life, Bill had always been a hit with women, single or otherwise, and an unscrupulous rogue with it. Any kind of fiddling was his speciality. Somehow he always seemed one jump ahead of others.

Ed's Digger mates, Bluey and Joe, soon made friends with Bill, and talk of home and the events leading up to the war continued for another couple of hours. In answer to the Diggers' question, Ed explained that he and Bill had joined the army at the recruiting depot of the Essex Regiment at Warley. On completion of eight weeks basic training as combat soldiers, they were both drafted with hundreds of others to the Suffolks. Apparently, the War Office had decreed that raw recruits from Essex and other counties were required to make up the wartime strength of an East Anglian division of the British Army ready for active service. That's how it came about that they were sent to serve with the Suffolks for the duration of the war.

"How come you got left in this bloody hole?" Ed suddenly demanded.

Bill grinned. "Tell the truth, Ed, when we got here, my bollocks were so bleedin' sore and painful, the M.O. said I had to stay here until they improved."

"Changi balls!", exclaimed Ed. "Nearly everyone seems to have got 'em in one form or another, due to lack of vitamins and minerals and soddin' starvation. I had an attack in the cooler; bloody painful, itch like mad till you scratch 'em raw."

Bill grinned even more as he went on: "Listen, Ed. I've found a cure, and the way I see it, if we ever get out of this poxy hell alive, I've got a helluva lot of catching up to do. In the meantime, I've got to look after my chopper and my balls."

"Join the club", agreed Ed, and the Aussies concurred.

"Anyway", continued Bill, "the Japs told us this morning that we all march upcountry with the next party, sick or not, so I reckon we'll all be going together."

"All?"

"Yeah, I haven't had a chance to tell you, but over in hut ten are another twelve lads from our mob who'll be going with us."

"Like who?" queried Ed.

"Well, there's Dave Wandle, you remember him, Ed, the Cockney from Millwall. Foxy Wright, a good old Suffolk mate. He comes from a little village near Needham Market. Tony Smith, from Norfolk. Morrie Finestein, from Westcliff, and a few more you know. You'll meet them all in the morning."

"That's great news, Bill, but you still haven't told us how you cured your Changi balls."

The Aussies shifted forward. "Well, I'll tell you my secret", said Bill. "It's tea, mate, cold bleeding tea! You get a mess tin, half fill it with cold tea, then you just sit and dangle your cobblers in it for about half an hour."

His audience listened in amazement. Bill continued: "Blimey. it's a beautiful sensation. A feeling of utter relief, almost like some bird stroking 'em with cool fingers. Don't know what it does, but it's bleedin' wonderful! Morrie nicked a load of tea from the Japs. He flogs it cold at five cents a mug for your balls and ten cents hot for drinking. He's doing great business, only hope it lasts! Oh, by the way, Ed, the Japs say they are going to pay us ten cents a day for our labour. What a bleedin' insult!"

* * *

Darkness falls swiftly in Thailand. That night, above the miserable camp of Bampong, the tropical stars shone brightly. Prisoners of war from all walks of life and from different parts of the world found themselves thrown together against a cruel and vicious foe. For some in that strange unreal situation, lifelong friendships were formed with a handshake, while for so many others the shadow of death lurked upcountry in the valley where runs the river Kwai. It would transpire that for every railway sleeper laid, a prisoner would die!

CHAPTER 3

March to Hell

Three a.m. in the early hours, all hell broke loose. A series of shrill whistles, the Japanese signal for 'tenko', or rollcall, were being blown at random. Guards were screaming like lunatics in their efforts to arouse the unsuspecting prisoners from their uncomfortable sleep.

Many of their rantings were in broken English: "Speedo, speedo, all men hurry!" The replies of "Bollocks!", and "Piss off, you miserable sods!", were predictable and appropriate.

Further persuaded by a bang on the head or a punch in the face, the unfortunate POW's forced themselves to get up and find out what the hell was happening.

The interpreter Atwai stated that Captain Aha Watanbe, of the Imperial Japanese Army in charge of road construction, had ordered up many more Allied prisoners of war to expedite the progress of making jungle tracks into roads through the fever-ridden belts, prior to the construction of the Siam to Burma railway.

Back in Tokyo, Emperor Hirohito and his war lords were impatient and displeased at the army engineers' slow advance when there was so much slave labour available from the thousands of helpless prisoners of war. He decreed that the planned four hundred and fifteen kilometre railway must be completed rapidly, regardless of cost. Hence the urgent orders to get the railway started.

Assisted only by kerosene and bamboo flares to light the inky darkness, the POW's were ordered to the cookhouse to collect rations of boiled rice and to fill up their army water bottles, having already packed up their sparse but precious belongings. They were then to report to the parade ground. All this was achieved at an astonishing speed.

Some of the men were returning to the parade ground from the latrines (nicknamed the shit-track run), when a sudden cry went up: "Help, help! For Christ's sake help me!"

It was the unmistakable voice of the all-Australian farting champion, Big Billy

Foster. He roared loudly again: "For Chrissake hurry, I'm bloody drowning!"

Ed and the Diggers, followed by a guard carrying in one hand a flare and his rifle in the other, rushed back to the latrines to discover Billy floundering up to his shoulders in a slit trench. This was some seven feet in length, three feet wide, eight feet deep, filled with human excreta and seething with maggots!

"Bloody oath!" yelled one of the rescuers, "Let's get him out of there!"

The Jap guard, standing on the edge of the trench, thought the whole episode extremely funny, and started to laugh.

The two Diggers knelt down, grabbed Big Billy by the wrists, and shouted: "You climb as we pull." With a mighty heave, Billy made it to the surface, covered in muck and crawling fat white maggots. Shrieking loudly, he rushed off towards the wash-house area.

At the same moment, the earth on the edge of the trench beneath the guard's feet caved in, causing him to slide rapidly downwards. Quick as a flash, Ed grabbed his rifle, and battered him violently several times over the head without mercy. In the darkness amidst the filth, the guard choked on his own blood as he sank down below the seething maggots to his death. His rifle followed quickly, and the flare burned out.

"Back to the parade ground quick", gasped Ed. "That's got to be the best Jap bastard I've ever met!" he added grimly.

"Bloody oath, Ed", answered one of the Diggers. "Won't he be missed at 'tenko'?"

"No way. Several of 'em are still missing up the brothel in the village. How d'you blokes feel about it?"

"Aw beaut', mate. Best thing we ever saw. Makes us feel bloody great, real beaut', Ed."

Back on the parade ground, Big Billy rejoined his mates, still soaking wet, but glad to be alive.

"You OK?", asked Ed. "What happened, mate?"

"Bloody oath, Ed. When I got up, I had the urge to crap, and just as I was squatting over the slit trench, the bloody side collapsed under me. Thank Christ I got out of that!"

"Speedo, speedo," Once more the same old bullshit. "All men speedo." They were to be counted and searched yet again. It mattered not what unit or mob they belonged to. As Japanese prisoners of war they were just numbers, totally expendable.

Quick to take advantage of the situation Ed, together with Bill and some of their mates from the Suffolks and Norfolks, joined ranks with the Australians, including Big Billy, now fully recovered from his ordeal, who was still cursing the enemy in between farts.

After the final count, Atwai translated the order: "All men march now", and much to his own dismay, he was ordered to remain and march with the POW's.

Lieutenant Hai Usaka, the Japanese officer in charge of the march, was an ugly squat little man. His evil grin revealed one gold tooth, supported by a black one either side, which quickly earned him the name of 'Black Chops'. In common with so many more of his race, he was well known for his hatred of the British. Both Ed and Bill, along with many others, had at different times suffered beatings as a direct result of his orders. All the POW's were agreed that he was such a wicked little bastard that even his own mother must have hated his guts!

Atwai asked Black Chops where the men were going. The replies he received were not very encouraging. First they were making for a village northeast of Kanchangburi, a distance of some twenty miles, then lots and lots more marching into the jungle.

Despite sickness, starvation and cruelty, the Japanese were unable to crush the spirit of the POW's or their determination to survive. It was late August 1942.

The first streaks of dawn were breaking as the column swung out from the gates of Bampong, headed by two armed guards with fixed bayonets.

Ed was still carrying his two containers of boiled rice in his haversack. Apart from during the constant searches he hardly ever thought or cared about the hidden radio set. Captain Seaton continued to carry his share of the burden, always managing to stay within sight of Ed, both fully aware that in order for the operation to be successful at the final camp, it was essential that they should not become separated.

Following up at the rear of the column were four more armed guards and Black Chops, ready to deal with escape attempts or any unfortunate stragglers who might fall by the wayside.

Conversation finally petered out. After six miles of slogging with the sun growing hotter all the time, the order suddenly came: "All men 'yazume' (rest)." Everyone seemed to collapse where they halted on grass verges; hot, filthy, exhausted, drinking thirstily from their water bottles.

Dave Wandle, one of the Suffolks, glared defiantly at the guards sweating in the shade of a tree. Echoing the thoughts of all the other prisoners, he suddenly announced: "You evil bastards. We're roastin' in the bleedin' sun while you sit in the shade, you lousy fuckpigs!" His outburst went unheeded, which was just as well, as the guards were preoccupied talking noisily among themselves.

Fifteen minutes later came the order: "All men march, speedo, speedo!" Reluctantly, the POW's struggled to their feet. The column marched forward again with temperatures above one hundred and ten degrees. The march became a nightmare. Men fell to the rear, only to be spurred on with a clout from the guards' rifles. Finally, two men collapsed, unable to march any further.

Lieutenant Usaka was summoned to the rear by one of the guards. "Get up and march now!" he shouted. Captain Saunders made a quick examination. He explained that the two men were completely exhausted and could not possibly march any further.

An enraged Lt. Usaka whipped out his revolver pointing it menacingly in the direction of the exhausted men: "In that case other prisoners must carry them or I will shoot them now." He cocked the gun ready to carry out his terrifying threat.

There was no time to be lost in argument. Captain Saunders called for volunteers. Ed, Bill and the two Australian medics stepped forward, two stretchers were hastily improvised from bamboo poles thrust through four empty rice sacks. It was agreed that every two miles, four more volunteers would take over the task of carrying their sick comrades.

"Speedo, speedo!" snarled the hated lieutenant, still waving his revolver.

"You evil little black bastard", muttered Captain Saunders, as painfully the column got under way again.

By sunset, they had covered a distance of fifteen miles. The situation was becoming desperate when they came within sight of a large white Buddhist temple, situated amidst several acres of well laid out and cultivated grounds, the borders of which were surrounded by coconut palms and enormous clumps of bamboo trees. Dotted around in the gardens were clusters of rare and exotic tropical flowers giving off a profusion of beautiful colours.

The Japanese headed the column into the grounds, halting on the grass lawns some three hundred yards from the building. After a brief consultation with the Jap officer, Atwai informed the POW's that they were to spend the night there. Totally exhausted, they flopped down on the grass to ease their pains. They drank the little if any water that was left, and shared out the remainder of the stinking fermented rice.

Captain Saunders examined the two patients and solemnly announced that the lad they had learned came from the Beds and Herts regiment was dead, the result of a massive heart attack brought on by extreme exhaustion. The second man was not expected to live the night out.

A burial party was quickly organised. A hastily dug shallow grave was provided in the shade of the bamboo trees. With a brief ceremony, a few words from the bible, and the strains of the Last Post, the young soldier from Eastern England was laid to rest. He would suffer no more. Death was fast becoming a means of escape.

In the distance the yellow robed priests, with their close shaven heads, looked on in sympathetic silence. Later that evening, they placed fresh cut flowers beneath the crude wooden cross on the grave. The prisoners noticed that the Japanese kept well away from the Buddhist priests and did not enter into any conversation with them.

On the far side of the grounds, the enemy had set up a temporary cookhouse, where the prisoners were ordered to draw cooked rice and dried vegetable rations, and to fill their water bottles ready for the next day's march. Then they were told to sleep.

"Thank Christ for that", Ed commented to Bill.

"I'm bleedin' knackered", came the reply.

They lay down on the rock hard ground. Ed used his haversack for a pillow, his neck resting uncomfortably on one of the rice containers. From the Buddhist temple the sound of strange weird oriental music drifted through the air.

Ed had always loved music, soft beautiful music. In a moment he was fast asleep. He dreamed of home. It was magic. He was at the front garden gate of the family home in Southend, His mum was saying: "Take care, son. Come home safe, we all need you. Your dad would have been proud of you, Ed, Dear me, it's nearly seven years now since he died. I've packed you some sandwiches. I know you'll get hungry on the journey."

Ed put his arm gently round her shoulders. "I'll be all right, mum. Honest I will. Look after the kids." A swift kiss on the cheek, as his mother blinked back her tears. They watched him to the top of the road. Ed paused to smile and wave to brothers, sisters, and to dear old wonderful mum. Another wave, and then he turned the corner and disappeared.

He moved his body slightly and was jolted back to harsh reality by an uncomfortable stone that was digging into his side, sharply reminding him where he really was.

For a while, he lay awake thinking and listening to the oriental music still coming from the temple. It seemed to go on for ever, sounding some sort of warning not to enter the steamy jungle ahead in the valley of death. Ed resolved that night to escape somehow, sooner or later.

Early next morning, the POW's were awakened by the ever haunting sounds of the Last Post, sounded by a bugler from the Norfolks. This could only mean one thing.

As the notes faded away, they were replaced by the shrill whistles of the guards, and the all too familiar sounds of another day in the hands of the Japanese.

Captain Saunders announced: "There's nobody to carry today. You lads did a great job, but sadly it was all to no avail! The other young fellow died a while back. The medics and I buried him alongside his mate. Sorry, fellows!"

"Speedo, speedo", yelled the guards.

"Same old bollocks", muttered Bill, as he lined up with Ed and the rest of the men, ready to march again.

The morning sun was breaking through as the column marched from the grounds of the temple. As they passed the two fresh graves, Captain Saunders gave the order: "Eyes right!" As he saluted, every prisoner of war sharply turned his head in a final and silent farewell to their brave young comrades.

CHAPTER 4

Kwai Tanu

Later that day, the scenery began to change. Made up roads trailed off into dusty unmade dirt tracks winding and twisting towards the fringe of the tropical forests on the outskirts of the fever ridden jungles of Thailand.

Mainly in silence, the POW's marched on in surprising good order. Singing and whistling had long since ceased. Man was helping man despite his own problems. As with every other seemingly endless day, the tropical sun blazed down mercilessly from the brilliant blue sky above, adding to the many difficulties of the forced and continuous marching covering so many miles for hours on end.

Throughout the appalling march, the medics shone through as cheerful as ever, with many an encouraging word as they went about their frequently unpleasant and distasteful tasks of tending the walking sick. Without their devotion and help under the worst possible conditions, many more would have died. At some time or other, in the grim time ahead, all prisoners of war would have good cause to be grateful to the medical officers and their loyal team of medics.

In the distance could be seen the outline of the old city of Kanchangburi, shortened to 'Kanburi'. Their destination was another five miles north east, close to the village of Rhanon Thuan, situated on the banks of the Moe Khlonge, a tributary of the mighty river Kwai.

Less than half a mile from the village, the dusty bedraggled column headed through the gates of a staging camp known as Kwai Tanu. At first glance, the camp appeared merely to be a repetition of the foul and squalid camp at Bampong, but there was one miraculous difference: a river flowed freely along the southern boundary.

The waters sparkled as the rays from the sun danced on the surface. Without waiting for orders, almost as one the POW's dropped everything where they stood, stripped naked, and rushed across the camp. Down the steep muddy banks into the cool inviting refreshing waters of the Moe Khlonge the prisoners poured in an unstoppable horde. Many of the guards followed suit.

It was noticed that resident guards were manning machine gun posts at strategic points on the river banks against the possibility of anyone attempting an escape.

Many miseries of the prisoners seemed to vanish temporarily. Feelings of freedom and intense relief swept over them as they drank and bathed in the cooling waters.

To the surprise of some Ed, Bill and Morrie smothered themselves in mud from the river bed, rinsing off in the clean water. Several others did the same.

"Better then soap", yelled Ed. "Used to do this for fun when we were kids back in Southend."

Half an hour flashed past: whistles were sounded for all to return to the camp and get on parade. Reluctantly, the men dried quickly in the sun, and climbed up the slippery banks with considerable difficulty. Collecting their belongings, they returned to the parade ground area for counting and searching again.

Before the parade was dismissed, Atwai announced that six Thai traders were being allowed inside the camp gates that evening for the purpose of buying or selling, if anyone had any money, or goods left to barter.

Captain Saunders was pleased to learn that his small group of medical orderlies were to be reinforced by four prisoners from the British Royal Army Medical Corps. They had been left behind for some obscure reason. An attap roofed hut served as a temporary sick bay, and it was here that introductions were made, while they pooled their meagre medical supplies.

The camp's star turn was Morrie Finestein, who had successfully nicked more tea from under the noses of the Japs. He was still carrying on his profitable business. He had set up a small stall in the camp, supplying his wares to soothe thirsty throats and Changi balls. Even the Japs tended to grin and ignore him. Morrie boasted about his uncle Sidney who owned half of the Southend Kursaal amusement park. Ed reckoned that true or not, his uncle Sidney would have been very proud of him today, with the business acumen he was displaying.

There was a commotion at the river bank as a barge load of fresh Japanese and Korean guards arrived. There were twelve Japs and eight Koreans under the command of a Japanese captain, of whom the prisoners were soon to learn a lot more.

'Tenko' was suddenly called again. In the centre of the dusty parade ground, the guards had erected a small wooden platform, complete with six steps up from the ground. Standing in the centre, accompanied by Atwai, was a short dark haired squat faced Japanese officer with thick horn rimmed glasses, smartly dressed and wearing a large sword hanging from his waist.

Silence fell as he started to speak slowly and deliberately to allow time for Atwai to translate.

"My name is Captain Suzuki, of the Imperial Japanese Army. Tomorrow we march to Wampo, a distance of twenty miles. After an overnight stay, we shall continue to march to a new camp, Tarsoe." The captain paused, and then went on: "When that section of the railway is complete, we will build a new camp many miles to the north. That will be called Tonchan, and I am to become the commandant of it. After that, as the railway continues, we shall build further camps right up to and through Three Pagoda Pass into Burma. You will all have to work very hard. Those who are sick will only get half rations."

He continued contemptuously: "You have all disgraced yourselves by becoming prisoners of war. Japanese soldiers are brave, you are not. The Kempi Tai (secret police) will visit from time to time to search and question. Anything discovered such as cameras, radios, or documents will result in death, as will any attempt to escape. Is that clearly understood? Death by execution!"

The news was received in stony silence. Captain Suzuki spoke again: "Tomorrow we enter the jungle. Do not fall behind. Long live our Lord and Master, the glorious Emperor of Japan. All men now dismiss!"

As the men left the parade ground a buzz of conversation broke out. "What do you know?" questioned Ed. Bill shook his head. "Sounds like it's going to get bleedin' worse."

At that moment Dave Wandle joined them. "Got some news", he confided. "Atwai just told me that Black Chops and the new bloke Suzuki are going up the local village brothel tonight. Hope they get a dose. At least with them out of the way, it might be a bit easier to nick some gear from the guards."

With that, the meeting broke up. Ed turned to Bill: "Listen, I've got an idea how to get a bit of our own back on these bastards. While they're busy buying and selling, we can carry out a reconnaissance of their ammunition dump. It's all stored in a large tent towards the main camp gates. We can count the distance in paces from the trees to as near the tent as we're allowed to go. Got the general idea?"

"OK, Ed."

It was agreed the two would meet up later to discuss the plan Ed had dreamed up.

* * *

As always, there were several bonfires in the camp. Seated on the ground round one of them were Ed and Bill, the Aussie medics, Bluey and Joe, and several others. Conversation started inevitably with food, women, or what the Allies should do to win the war. This night was no exception.

"I'm bloody starving. How would you all like a real Australian steak, garnished with onions and loads of fried spuds?" said Big Billy. As if to emphasise the point, he let rip one of his special farts.

"No offence, mate", he grinned to Dave Wandle. who was unlucky enough to be in the direct line of fire.

"I think you're a big stinking git", retorted Dave. "Bet you never went to bleedin' school anyway. Right now, I'd settle for a big plate of chips, eggs and bacon!"

Everyone groaned. The more stinking boiled rice with little else that they had to eat, the more they talked and dreamed of food. They agreed however that the subject was a non-starter due to their acute hunger.

"How about a good bunk-up? suggested Bill. "Cor, I remember the little widow I had the night before we left Hereford."

His audience leaned forward expectantly in eager anticipation of Bill's sexual prowess. They had heard lurid details of his sexual conquests before; A never failing source of entertainment which sparked their imaginations.

"Bloody hell", Bill continued wistfully. "She couldn't get enough of me, loved it, she did!" Further explicit details followed, much to the delight of the men gathered around the fire.

Not to be outdone, Bluey joined in. "Mind you, mate, we've got some real beaut' sheilas back in Aussie. Me and Joe had a couple the night before we left, in a nice house I know right on the city limits of Melbourne. That was one helluva night, right Joe?"

"Hell, yes. They were real beauts. Wish to Christ I was there right now!"

As the general conversation continued, Ed Warton's memory flashed back in time to the night before he'd left the U.K. Clearly, he remembered the fair, blue-eyed A.T.S. girl of eighteen. That also had been a helluva night! The frustration of the situation in which he now found himself as a prisoner of war suddenly reacted on him and made him angry.

"Listen, you blokes", he interrupted. "Let's face the cold facts. We're all bloody starving, 'cause we can't get enough to eat, we can't get any women either. So what about doing something to upset these evil bastards?"

"Like what?", came the chorussed replies.

Ed was growing more and more angry. "Like blowing up their soddin' ammo' dump that's over by the main gate."

There was a short silence. Then Foxy spoke up: "Bloody good idea, Ed, but there is a problem. How the bloody hell can you or anyone else do anything like that without weapons?"

"Daft as it may seem, there is a way it can be done, and somehow I'm going to do it!"

"Listen, Ed, you can't operate a one-man bleedin' war!"

"That's true, but if we can inflict some damage on them, we'd all feel a whole lot better, wouldn't we?"

Everyone agreed.

"OK, then", Ed went on. "I've got a plan which I don't want to discuss right now, but pass the word around for everyone to keep well away from the guards' hut and the ammo' dump tonight."

"OK, Ed, we wish you luck!" said the Diggers.

Morrie was worried. He thought a lot of the lad he had joined up with. They'd been good mates a long time. "If it goes wrong, Ed, you know what the penalty will be?"

"Yeah, Morrie, only too well do I know. It's the Japs' soddin' answer to everything - death by the sword! Well mate, it won't go wrong, I promise you."

"It's not worth it, honest it isn't", Morrie pressed. "Anyway, how are you going to do it?"

Ed looked hard at Morrie, then at Bill and Foxy. "It's best I don't tell you at the moment. See you later."

With that, he disappeared in search of Captain Seaton. He found him talking with Captain Saunders and the small group of medics.

"Everything OK?" he asked, with reference to the secret radio.

"Yes, everything is OK", replied the captain. "But you must appreciate we have to be patient and wait until we reach a permanent camp before we can risk listening in."

"That's understood", answered Ed. "Can I speak to you in private?"

"Of course." Captain Seaton walked with Ed a few yards out of earshot of the others.

Ed outlined his scheme. The captain approved. "But where is the necessary explosive coming from?" he asked.

"Simple."

Ed explained in strict confidence that he knew of a certain small wooden medicine chest with a false bottom, which contained six hand grenades, treasured and preserved for an emergency.

Ed pressed home his point. "I only need one. I won't miss!"

Captain Seaton capitulated. "Call back to the medical hut in half an hour. In the meantime, I will confer with Captain Saunders."

Ed rapidly rounded up Bill Slatoe and Foxy Wright. Ed had already told Bill of the plan, and when it had been outlined to Foxy, he too was all for it. Anything, however small, as long as it injured and delayed the enemy, just had to be a good thing.

The agreed reconnaissance was carried out and the three met up again. With the aid of a small stick to draw in the dry dust on the ground, they accurately pinpointed the entrance to the Japanese ammunition dump. This showed the placings of the sentries and a vital tree under which Ed could shelter and make good his escape. All was set!

Ed returned to find Captain Seaton waiting for him. "We think it's too risky, and you're bloody crazy. If anything goes wrong, you're on your own. Understand?" Ed nodded his agreement.

The Australian signals officer continued: "Against our better judgement, we have agreed. Ah, shit, man, here's the bloody grenade. Good luck, mate. Don't forget, it has got to look like an accident in case of reprisals, OK?"

An excited Ed nodded and taking the cold hand grenade he placed it firmly under his left armpit and quickly disappeared into the darkness of the night.

Foxy and Bill were anxiously waiting for him. "All set?" he asked.

"All OK!" Stealthily, the three men set off in the direction of the ammo' dump. Minutes later they arrived at the arranged spot behind a tall palm tree. They lay flat on their bellies and waited.

Shortly they heard the men back at the bonfires, led by the officers, commence a hearty singsong. "She'll be coming round the mountain when she comes!" A popular number that the Jap guards always requested.

Foxy and Bill, who had been scouting out, reported back to Ed that the guards on the main gates were preoccupied with four local whores.

"Stay here!" hissed Ed. "Keep your bloody heads down, OK?"

He crawled forward on his belly. As he neared the target, to his surprise he saw a light from a coconut oil lamp shining in the tent. He could also see a number of guards playing cards on a large box of ammunition. 'What an excellent state of affairs', he thought to himself.

He made it to the tree selected for cover, which was but fifty feet from the entrance. The hand grenade felt strangely comforting. He grasped it firmly in his right hand.

In the distance, the singing seemed to grow louder. Ed knelt up, and holding his breath, he swiftly pulled the safety pin out, keeping a firm grip on the lever. With a deliberate and powerful aim, he hurled the grenade directly into the shaft of light: the guards never knew what hit them!

Ed lay flat on his belly behind the tree, as the first explosion ripped through the air. To the accompaniment of screams of pain and horror, there followed a series of much larger and more devastating explosions, which reverberated around the camp in the night air.

Ed slithered rapidly backwards until he reached a safe area, where he got up and raced away, colliding with Bill and Foxy.

At that moment, there was a final enormous bang, and the whole area seemed to be alight, with screaming and hysterical guards running around in circles.

The singsong had suddenly turned into wild cheers. It had to be the best thing yet for those in captivity.

The three men rejoined the cheering crowd. Ed reported to Captain Seaton: "Mission accomplished OK, captain."

"Great, man, just bloody great! Did you hear those bastards screaming?" shouted the elated Australian officer.

"At least, we've got one back at 'em", replied a delighted Ed. "And this is only the bloody beginning!" he added, with conviction.

The surviving guards were shocked and stunned by the event. The two Japanese officers rushed back from the whoreshops in the village. They were informed by the sentries on the main gates that six Japanese and Korean guards had been playing cards and smoking in the ammunition tent, and nobody really knew what had caused the series of explosions.

Nevertheless, at precisely 2 a.m. that morning, all POW's were awakened and ordered to the parade ground for searching and checking yet again. Of course, nothing was found. Nobody could connect the events of the evening with the prisoners.

Atwai informed the men that, owing to an unfortunate accident, there had been explosions which had totally destroyed an ammunition dump and resulted in the death of six Japanese soldiers. with ten more seriously injured.

"What a bleedin' shame", came the sarcastic reply from Dave Wandle. "It's a pity the whole fucking lot didn't die", he said, echoing the thoughts of all the prisoners.

Atwai continued: "A party of prisoners will be required to dig graves in the morning. Understood?"

"Yes, we understand", replied Captain Seaton. "We will carry out orders and bury the dead with the greatest of pleasure, I assure you."

"All men dismiss", came the order. At long last the POW's were able to rest their weary heads and relax with a feeling of satisfaction. Finally, the tables had been turned just a little.

Before sleep overtook him, Ed Warton pondered hard. He had travelled a fast road from a young civilian to soldier and to Japanese prisoner of war. Now a trained killer, deep in his heart he knew there was much to do. He was no longer afraid. Suddenly, he was asleep.

CHAPTER 5

Tonchan via Tarsoe

At the crack of dawn the POW's were aroused and ordered to report for 'tenko' on the dusty parade ground, where they were lined up, counted and checked ready for the day's march.

Captain Saunders had requested permission to speak urgently to the Japanese commandant, who was standing on the platform in the centre of the parade ground. Captain Isu Suzuki looked down contemptuously and arrogantly.

The young Australian medical officer stood to attention, made the compulsory bow, and addressed the Jap commandant in the strongest possible terms, protesting that there were many very sick men who could not possibly survive another day's gruelling forced march. He mentioned also the fact that the medical team was desperately short of supplies.

In rapid Japanese, Suzuki snarled out an order. Immediately two well built guards stepped forward and proceeded to beat up Captain Saunders, who somehow still managed to stay on his feet, with blood pouring from his mouth where it had felt the weight of a rifle butt. Suzuki spoke to him:

"There is only one law here, that is the law of the Imperial Japanese Army officers, who will be obeyed at all times. Japanese soldiers are not sick. The Japanese remaining in this camp will bury their own dead. All men march, means just that. All men march. All prisoners must understand that!"

Captain Saunders, still standing to attention, wiped the blood from his mouth with the back of his hand. There was nothing to say.

The camp gates swung open. Once more the POW's marched forward, accompanied by millions of flies, mosquitoes and beautiful exotic butterflies swarming around in great abundance.

Shortly the terrain changed. The trek became increasingly difficult as the jungle paths narrowed down. Jagged spikes from bamboo clumps caused cuts and scratches, which rapidly grew into tropical ulcers due to the lack of treatment.

As the men marched on into the thick green vegetation they could see overhead schools of chattering monkeys swinging through the trees. They heard shrieking baboons and every now and then slimy snakes would slither rapidly past.

Hampered by the thick creepers and the ever stinking heat, progress was slow, much to the displeasure of the guards. All day they slogged on; those unfortunate enough to fall to the rear unable to march a step further promptly received the barbaric treatment of being beaten over the head by the guards, and left to die at the fangs of wild animals which roamed the jungle at night.

For the last few painful miles, Geordie Smith was carrying Jimmy Thomson on his back. On arrival at the staging camp at Wampo, Captain Saunders examined Jimmy and gently told Geordie that his mate was dead. On hearing this news, Geordie Smith, who had so gallantly struggled on despite his exhaustion and distress, collapsed. About an hour later he joined his comrade!

They were both laid to rest at a small cemetery created by an advance party of guards and prisoners, who had already constructed the camp and were now clearing jungle areas and making dirt roads.

By dawn the next day, one British officer and six other ranks had also died. The situation was deteriorating fast. The dead men were left for fellow POW's at Wampo to bury, as Captain Suzuki and his henchmen were anxious to march on again.

Another grim day passed. Five more men had been beaten unconscious and left to the mercy of the wild animals.

As sunset approached, they reached another new camp which was to become as notorious and horrendous as the others. It was called Tarsoe, and was situated on a level area of ground, bordered on the south side by steep banks leading down to the river Kwai.

At sun-up the next morning the men were put to work under the supervision of Japanese engineers and fresh armed guards, all of whom had been transported upcountry in barges manned by Thai natives.

The prisoners were divided into separate work parties to continue building the camp site, and to clear and make roads, clear the jungle vegetation from the surface area over which the railway was to be built. They also had to dig latrines and construct special huts for the Japanese officers and men.

One hut, a hundred and fifty feet long with an attap roof, was quickly and specially constructed ostensibly to be used as the camp hospital. In effect, it was simply a place to fight for life and to die with dignity.

Colonel John Harvel, of the Royal Army Medical Corp, was the principal officer. Many times since being captured he had been beaten and yet still stood up to demand more medical supplies for the sick, while steadfastly refusing to send dying men out to work on the railway. Paradoxically, the Jap senior officers seemed to respect the British colonel, whose strength and resilience in the face of adversity was an inspiration to all.

Out on the hillside some five hundred yards away overlooking the broad waters of the river, stood Tarsoe cemetery, which daily grew in size. Taffy Jones was in charge of the small mortuary, situated just outside the cemetery gates. It was his task to close their eyes and cover the dead in rice sacks, and to confer with the padre to plot the area in which the bodies were to be buried.

Owing to the large numbers of sick in camp, it became a routine task for the daily work parties to bury their dead comrades when the day's work was over.

One evening, four weeks later, another unfortunate column of prisoners of war arrived in the camp. There was always news to exchange, and some of the men met up with mates who had become separated.

It was with surprise and delight that Ed, Bill, Foxy and co. discovered that among the newcomers were several men from the Suffolks and Norfolks. There was Alan Pottel from Ipswich, Ticky Lone from Sherringham in Norfolk, Bill Lewis from Colchester and several others. In addition, there were ten American POW's who had been captured in Java, fifty white Dutchmen and two hundred natives from the Dutch East Indies, now known as Indonesia.

POW news was disseminated quickly. The newcomers were shocked and saddened to learn of the deaths of so many of their comrades and alarmed to hear of what lay in store on the railway.

That evening, when all else had been completed, the prisoners sat around giant bonfires talking and getting to know some of the new arrivals. Ed, Bill, and Foxy were sitting alongside two Americans, who were fascinated by the different English accents as the men talked. They introduced themselves:

"Hi, pleased to meet you guys. My name's Baker, Elmer Baker. My buddy here is Smith, J.W. We're both from Texas."

Ed introduced his mates, then asked: "What's J.W. stand for?"

"Hell, I don't really know", came the reply. "My grandaddy was always called J.W., my daddy was called J.W., so I guess when I arrived, my momma just called me J.W. That's my name, Y'all call me J.W., OK?"

Ed, Bill, and their mates took an instant liking to J.W. Smith and his buddy.

When there was a lull in the conversation, J.W. looked across at Elmer. "What y'all thinking about?"

Elmer grinned. "Well, I'll tell you man. Ah was thinking what I'm gonna do when this goddamn war's over and we're back home in the States."

"How'd you mean?" questioned J.W. Elmer Baker was a six foot Texan who had an insatiable appetite for any pretty woman who performed well in and out of bed. He paused for a moment before replying:

"The way I see it, I figure that I ain't never gonna work again. Guess I'm just going to do a little huntin', a little fishin', and one hell of a lot of goddamn fuckin'. That's what I aim to do, all day long. The way I figure it, that's got to be the best way to go. Better then being killed by these evil bastards!"

"We all go along with that", replied J.W. "What say you guys?"

"Sounds like a splendid idea", answered Ed.

Bill groaned. "Out there somewhere in this bloody world there's all that grub, bags of crumpet, and we're stuck in this poxy hole. It's all bloody wrong!"

At that stage in the conversation, Captain Saunders, accompanied by Captain Seaton, arrived and joined the men around the bonfire.

"Any news yet?" asked Ed, referring to the hidden radio.

"It was my intention to set it up with your help", replied Captain Seaton. "But we've just had a buzz from Atwai that the Kempi-Tai may be paying us a visit soon. Also we may be moving upcountry again to Tonchan, so I thought it wise to wait a little longer."

Ed agreed that it was best not to take unnecessary risks while there was a possibility of a visit from the Japanese Gestapo!

In the early months the railway route had been surveyed and mapped out by Japanese engineers. They were now busy using dynamite and other explosives, blasting their way through yellow rock-hard formations in the hills.

Allied prisoners of war slaved on daily, with back-aching tasks. They carried, cleared and broke up solid rocks, preparing the path that the railway lines would take, mercilessly driven on by beatings and torture from the brutal and fanatical armed guards.

Elephants played an important part also in hauling enormous teak trees into positions ready for bridge construction across the broad river and its surrounding hills. Controlled by Thai natives, these elephants were an accepted part of the industrious scene.

At the close of the working day, they became bathing partners to the prisoners, washing themselves in the river alongside the POW's, who gave them affectionate names such as Ellie, Olly and Fat Cow. There was always a danger that one might roll over in the water in order that its Thai master could wash the top of its giant body with a large brush. Because of this, most of the men kept a respectable distance at bath times.

Morrie reckoned that the large turds they dropped would be worth a fortune in the market garden business back home, while Big Billy figured that if he could get one back to Aussie he'd make quite a pile. He reluctantly admitted that even he could not compete with the force ejected from an elephant's behind. As there was so little to laugh at in captivity, when Olly farted below the water line, as she did very often, the result was always a fountain of water shooting some five feet up in the air, to the accompaniment of roars of laughter from the prisoners.

Always the comic, Dave Wandle would shout at Big Billy: "Top that if you can, mate!"

* * *

The Asiatic labour force, made up in the main of Tamil (Indian) natives, increased almost daily as the death rate soared. They were made to live in camps of their own, near the POW areas. Their lower standards of hygiene made the foul and squalid camps a breeding ground for the tropical diseases and worm infestations. Because of the Japs' fear of catching diseases, the prisoners were forced into the distasteful and unenviable tasks of burying the dead Tamils, whose bodies were thrown into communal graves.

The majority of Allied POW's were now without socks, boots, or clothes of any description. The Japanese solved this problem by issuing each man a crude form of loin cloth to cover their private parts. Needless to say, they quickly earned the well deserved title of 'chopper covers', or 'Jap-happies'.

Some ingenious souls made crude wooden clogs, being held on the feet by a strap of cloth which fitted between the big toes. Most, however, preferred walking barefoot. After the initial soreness and cuts, in time feet became toughened up and the prisoners got used to the idea.

This lack of clothing only caused discomfort at night because, strangely enough, in contrast to the heat of the day, night-time in the jungles of Thailand became quite cold. Some men still had one army blanket but the majority made do with empty coarse hessian rice sacks, of which there were always plenty available.

To date, the rains had not yet arrived, although it was with some alarm and dismay that the men discovered from Atwai that the monsoon season usually started in June and continued through until October. This was still, however, five months away.

Colonel Harvel, the medical officer, was busy doing his morning rounds of the sick and the dying. At great risk, he and his loyal team of R.A.M.C. medics had skilfully managed to negotiate with certain Thai traders for a quantity of drugs and medical supplies, with a promise of more to come. These drugs had enabled the medical officer to stop internal bleeding in some cases of dysentery, directly reducing the daily death rate. These traders came upriver on the ration and supply barges. Some were friendly and helpful, while others were not to be trusted. There was therefore always the risk of betrayal, with death the penalty!

On completion of his rounds, the Colonel informed Captain Saunders that fifteen more had died overnight, with a distinct possibility of several more before the day was over.

Captain Saunders was taking the camp sick parade that morning. As usual, there was a large number of patients to be seen. In his private opinion all the men were far too ill and quite unfit for work, but he had an extremely difficult daily task trying to persuade Major Toyoda, the unpleasant English-speaking Japanese medical officer (nicknamed 'Doctor Death'), who would review the sick parade and send unfit men out to work.

Due mainly to the fact that, as POW's, most men considered themselves equal, and also because of the tremendous Australian and American influence, the word 'sir' when addressing officers, had almost disappeared from the British POW vocabulary. Upcountry, medical officers did not object to being called 'doctor' or 'doc'.

The first man in the queue was Big Billy Foster. He complained miserably: "Got the shits, doc." At the same time he did not see fit to inform the M.O. that his Australian pride was being sorely tried by cattle farmer Lou Palmer from New South Wales, who was fast moving up the scales to challenge him in the Allied farting stakes.

"For Christ's sake, doc, give me something", he pleaded.

Captain Saunders was indeed sympathetic. He also possessed a rugged Australian sense of humour. Whilst on the one hand he was unable to prescribe medicines that were unobtainable, he managed to resist the grave temptation of suggesting to Big Billy that perhaps, just maybe, the only other solution would be to shove a bamboo cork up his backside and hope for the best!

In the event, it was as well that he did not propose such a dramatic remedy, because not only would it have been unthinkable and unethical, but also Dave Wandle had already told Big Billy quite bluntly what he should do, all of which had left Big Billy wholly miserable, as he held on to his belly and raced for the latrines for the twenty third time that morning.

Ironically, Dave was next in line. "What's your problem, soldier?" asked the

Medical Officer.

"It's me arse, me bleedin' arse", wailed the unfortunate Cockney. "Feels like its got a million fish hooks in it, tearing' me to bloody pieces!"

"Sorry, we've got nothing to help you at the moment. As you know, we're waiting, hoping and trying bloody hard to get more medical supplies. When we get lucky, we'll let you know."

Unhappy and disgruntled, Dave ambled painfully away. Captain Saunders was desperately worried about the general situation. He resolved to tackle Major Toyoda again that morning.

The sick parade revealed fifty men going down with malaria and fevers, eighty in the first stages of dysentery, and forty five with serious leg ulcers.

In the early hours of the next morning four large Thai barges, loaded with various supplies including many sacks of rice, tied up to the mooring posts down the river entrance to Tarsoe. The main tracks led up a steep manmade dirt road bordered with thick green jungle vegetation leading to the Allied POW cookhouse and then further along, to the Japanese cookhouse, some fifty yards to the east.

At 'tenko', a special work party was quickly selected for the ration run, as it had become known. This party comprised Ed, Bill, Foxy and Morrie, two Americans, three Dutchmen, and another Suffolk soldier, Alan Pottel. These ten men were lined up and marched down the slope with a single armed guard in charge.The enemy needed every available guard out at the railway site, and they were confident that nobody would attempt to escape into the surrounding jungle.

Ed thought that this was an excellent state of affairs, and Bill agreed. The party arrived at the river bank and stopped while the guard went on board the first barge to converse with the Head Thai in charge of all the four barges.

The party waited on the bank. They could observe three or four natives on each barge, as well as three Thai women. This was not unusual. Invariably, the Thais would have womenfolk aboard. Two of the women were middle-aged, but the third looked a well endowed young woman in her early twenties.The sex-starved prisoners could only stare, longing and lusting in vain.

The Korean guard climbed off the barge clutching his little Jap-English phrase book in one hand. Reading and indicating in broken English, he recited: "All men now work hard!"

Ed, Bill, Foxy and Morrie clambered aboard the first barge. The Korean signalled to the remainder that they should start to unload the other three boats. He then sighted the younger Thai female. Waving, he indicated for her to come ashore. She did not hesitate, and the guard was soon preoccupied.

Ed whispered to the head man: "Speak English?"

The Thai looked furtively around and nodded. Ed knelt down beside a sack of rice.

"We need all kinds of drugs and medical supplies urgently. Many, many men are dying. We can get you Thai dollars." Ed whispered quickly to Bill: "Make a start on unloading and cover for me, will you, mate?"

Bill nodded his agreement and began his task.

To Ed's surprise, the head Thai also kneeling down, whispered in clear

English: "I am Ayut. I work for the underground in Bangkok. We hate the Japanese and Koreans who have invaded our country. Please, no money will be wanted. We have come prepared to help."

Ed could hardly believe his ears as Ayut continued: "In rice sacks marked 4, 6, and 8 there is quinine and other supplies. Inform your cookhouse corporal so that he knows what to do. Your Colonel Harvel is a very brave man."

Suddenly it dawned on Ed that there was already in existence an underground link from Ayut the Thai via the POW cookhouse to Colonel Harvel and his medics in the hospital.

The Thai went on: "Do not trust anyone on these barges. They will betray you. The girl is a whore and a decoy. She will keep the guard busy while you hide extra sacks of food in the jungle. Your name?"

"Ed Warton, from England."

"Go now. We will meet again in other camps upstream. I will remember you."

Ed's brain raced. Grabbing up sack number 4, with sweat pouring from his brow, he struggled uphill with it on his back to the cookhouse, where Ron Hunter, the corporal in charge, was waiting anxiously for news. Ed conveyed his newly-acquired information. Corporal Hunter grinned and replied: "Thanks, mate. OK, we know what to do. Leave it to me, I'll contact the medics. Careful how you go. Ayut works with us and he's our only link with the outside world. We daren't risk his life, OK?"

Ed nodded and started off down the hill, joined by his mate who had been waiting for him. As they walked, Ed informed him what had transpired. Bill found it hard to believe, but like Ed, he was delighted.

They were not unduly surprised to find the Korean missing when they returned to the barges. The Thai girl's giggles in the nearby bushes betrayed their particular whereabouts.

There was no time to lose. With incredible speed, produced only by the sheer desperation of their position, the POW's were spurred into rapid action. They quickly stashed away two sacks of dried salted fish, two sacks of dried vegetables, and one sack of dried meat. All was safely hidden out of sight in the thick green jungle foliage near the top of the hill. From his position on the barge, Ayut watched with approval. Hard times and starving prisoners meant desperate chances had to be taken. It was planned that they would collect their loot after darkness had fallen.

They carried on with their toil. As the Korean emerged from the bushes, G.I. Elmer Baker was returning downhill, passing close by the spot where the guard stepped out. "OK?" said Elmer.

"OK-ka", came the surprised answer.

Feeling encouraged, Elmer persisted: "You number one OK, my turn now. I'll give that bitch a real one." He looked across to the young Thai girl who was washing her body in the river without any sign of shyness or embarrassment. Her small well shaped and completely naked breasts were clearly visible for all to see. Elmer was instinctively inflamed and aroused with passion.

The Korean did not seem to understand the meaning of Elmer's excitement. "England number one-ka?" he queried.

"No buddy", came the swift reply. "Me good old United States. Uncle Sam number one-ka, OK?"

Abruptly, the guard's attitude changed. Becoming extremely angry, he yelled: "Japan number one-ka, you number ten-ka." As he spat at the American, looking dangerous, he stuck his rifle and fixed bayonet in front of his chest. Then he forced him to stand to attention on the side of the hill in the blazing sun, where his passions quickly cooled. Ed reckoned that Elmer had to be the most disappointed G.I. in the entire United States Army that day.

In his disappointment and frustration, Elmer Baker yelled out: "You goddamn stinking sonofabitch. I hope your cock drops off and you roast in hell!"

Fortunately, the Korean did not understand Elmer's outburst though he again pointed his rifle menacingly and snarled: "You no speak!"

J.W. Smith, becoming alarmed, called: "Cool it Elmer. For Christ's sake, just bloody cool it and shut up."

Elmer did not reply. Four hours later, he passed out from the heat of the sun, whereupon a large tin of river water was thrown over him. On revival, once more he was forced to stand to attention. Some hours later, he was allowed to rejoin the working party, just as they were finishing emptying the last of the barges.

Because of the guard's now alert attention, there was no way that Ed could converse again with the Thai Ayut. He remembered his words with satisfaction and felt sure that somewhere upstream they would meet again...

Back in Tarsoe that night, after helping to dig graves for another twenty men, Ed and Bill, together with Morrie and Foxy, reported the day's events to Captains Saunders and Seaton. The latter were happy to tell the men that in addition to the medical supplies which had been received via Corporal Hunter and his cookhouse staff, with the help of Colonel Harvel, Captain Saunders had managed to obtain a further small but vital quantity of medicines from the Japanese M.O., Major Toyoda.

After dark, a party of men led by Ed and Bill set off to retrieve the stolen sacks of food. These were then safely installed in Corporal Hunter's cookhouse store, to be shared out the next day by all, with particular benefit for the very sick.

It had been another hard day in Tarsoe. The men slept, exhausted. What sort of hell the dawning of the next day might bring was anyone's guess!

CHAPTER 6

Tonchan Camp

The date was the 15th. February, 1943. One year had passed since the fall of Singapore, and the invasion of Thailand and Burma. Thousands of miles across the China Seas on the islands of Japan the warlords were meeting at Imperial Army General Headquarters in Tokyo. The Emperor of Japan was in attendance.

There had been lengthy discourse, with much disagreement. The warlords were worried and Hirohito in particular was gravely displeased by the staggering amount of shipping losses taking place in the Straits of Malacca, the Gulf of Siam, and the Andaman Sea leading to the Indian Ocean. The British Royal Navy was hitting back ferociously, thus posing a considerable threat and a real and dangerous problem on the vulnerable sea route to Burma.

There was, however, complete agreement that the slow progress of the planned overland railway link must now become an urgent military matter of top priority. The Emperor was at a loss to understand any reason for delay. To make matters worse, the solid stand being made against their troops in the jungles of Burma by the courageous British Fourteenth Army and their Allies was giving them cause for grave concern.

The war they had started was not proceeding as planned! At the conclusion of an unpleasant meeting, urgent messages were dispatched to Thailand to commanding officer, army engineers and officer in charge of all prisoners of war camps, Major General Fuyure. The text read: "You will issue strict instructions immediately to staff officers Colonel Wasake, Major Sudo, and Captain Watanabe, and via them to all camp commandants. The construction of the railway must be speeded up regardless of cost in life or money."

Meanwhile, back in Tarsoe, Captain Suzuki, on receipt of orders, acted immediately. Instructions were issued for his mixed unit of Allied prisoners of war to march north at dawn. Those who died on marches upcountry and those who had perished at Tarsoe were replaced from the most recent POW arrivals in camp.

As darkness gave way to the first streaks of dawn, 'tenko' was completed and the men marched forward mostly in bare feet, with their few pathetic belongings. Captain Seaton and Private Warton were still carrying the containers with the hidden radios.
Two more days of misery and slogging followed before they finally arrived at another position close to the river, which was to be called Tonchan, a camp destined to become another jungle hellhole on the railway, where thousands more POW's were to perish. They had now marched in stages upcountry a distance of 139 kilometers from the base at Non-Pladuck and Bampong.

News from downriver had reached them that the first wooden bridge at Tamarkan had been completed, six miles north of Kanburi, and that rail lines were being laid at astonishing speed from Wampo towards Tarsoe.

On the newly made dirt roads, Japanese transport was now almost through to Tarsoe POW camp. The enormous project was gathering momentum, yet still the enemy were not satisfied with the rate of progress.

Tonchan soon proved to be even worse than Tarsoe. Absolute priority was given to the building of comfortable huts for the Japanese officers and their staff. These were furnished with camp beds complete with mosquito nets. After this, the men were set to work to build the long hospital hut (nicknamed the 'chamber of horrors'), soon to become a familiar place to so many sick prisoners. A few hundred yards away, the burial ground was established, to become a resting place for the numerous prisoners of war who but for the Japanese brutality might well have been expected to return home at the war's end.

Suzuki, firmly established as camp commandant, was ably assisted by a fresh replacement of Japanese and Korean guards, who had been transported upriver on Thai barges. The POW's believed, with some justification, that these guards had been specially selected on account of their sadistic and totally uncivilised barbarism towards them.

Among the more notorious of these were Lieutenant Takasaki (the Rat), Sergeant Yamanoto (the Pig), Sergeant Noro (Baldy), the Koreans Kaneshiro (the Undertaker), and Chiba (the Singing Master), to name but a few of them.

The new prisoner of war arrivals included five officers: Major James Wystock-Hall, the bamboo pipe smoker from the Indian Army, Captain Tim Thursted from the Norfolks, Lieutenant Reg Ashdown of the Suffolks, and Lieutenants Eric and Alan Hazel, two brothers from the Malayan volunteer force who were working as rubber planters at the time of the Japanese invasion. To complete the new intake was another mixed number of British and Australian other ranks.

More by luck than judgement, Ed, Bill, Morrie and Foxy Wright had managed to stay together, along with Alan Pottel, Dave Wandle and a few others. Strictly keep-fit enthusiasts prior to being captured, the gang of four - as they became known - were non-smokers. Therefore the lack of cigarettes and tobacco did not affect them as it did the smokers in the camp.

Captain Suzuki was very fond of alcohol, frequently making a pig of himself on Japanese saki, a form of rice whisky. True to form, he was luxuriating in a specially built hut, designed to give him the maximum of comforts, as befitting one convinced that not only was he the Emperor's right hand man, but second only to God!

The bamboo hut in which he resided was crowned with the Rising Sun, and overlooked the large area, cleared and levelled to form the parade ground. In the centre stood Suzuki's specially built wooden platform with four steps leading to it from the ground.

To Suzuki this was no ordinary stand. Not only was it an essential base for preaching Japanese propaganda at 'tenko' and other important times, but here also was the dais which, owing to its superior elevation, had the effect of raising Suzuki's eminence until he overflowed with patriotism and ambition for his country. Indeed, with the aid of his maniacal imagination, he convinced himself that the Japs would eventually rule the world.

Meanwhile, the engineers were swiftly blasting at the yellow rock again at a cutting in the hills half a mile from Tonchan. At around one o'clock, the Japanese major in charge of that section of engineers announced: "All men now yazume." Wearily, the sweating POW's threw themselves down to rest in the shade by the sides of the track, thirstily drinking from their army waterbottles river water which had been boiled before leaving camp, and hungrily eating their small ration of cold, boiled rice, A number of beatings had already been given to sick men, who, in the opinion of the guards, were not working hard enough in the blazing tropical sun for Nippon, as they sometimes chose to call their country.

Fifty yards away a number of guards sat huddled together, smoking cigarettes and vile-smelling native cheroots. They were all laughing and talking. High up on the banks, machine guns glinted in the midday sun, manned by the ever-watchful guards.

Conversation between the prisoners was desultory, ascribable to the general exhaustion which was exacerbated by the intense heat. One of the Suffolks, Doug Pardy, needed to answer the call of nature; he had a sharp pain in his guts. He approached the guards and bowed. "Me benjo?" he requested. One of the Koreans looked up, blowing a cloud of blue smoke through his black teeth. For a moment he hesitated and glared at the prisoner. "OK-ka."

Doug dived desperately for the nearest green bushes. On his return he committed the unpardonable offence of passing the group of guards without stopping to bow. Korean Chiba - the 'Singing Master' shouted: "Halt!"

Standing him to attention in the sun, he promptly struck him hard across the face. The other guards grinned, sensing some further amusement was about to take place at the expense of the unfortunate prisoner.

Not satisfied with the punishment, Chiba barked out an order in broken English: "You sing song!"

Doug's mates had long since informed him that he had a voice like a frog, a fact of which he had even then been aware. Besides, no songs would come to mind.

Gallantly he stood up to the 'Singing Master'. "Singing nei-ka" (no), he answered truthfully. That got him another stout smack across the face which rocked his head.

The thickset and stocky Chiba was growing angry. "I speak, you sing song", he screamed. Nearby, Ed and Morrie sensed the situation was getting dangerous.

"For Christ's sake, sing something!" called out Ed.

"I can't, I don't know any bloody songs", wailed Doug in reply.

Chiba's normally ugly face was now contorted in a paroxysm of rage. Morrie, in desperation, shouted out: "Try 'God save the King'."

Ed and Morrie listened in amazement at the appalling rendering of their National Anthem. To make matters even worse, Cockney Dave Wandle looked across in horror and muttered: "I don't believe it. Christ, it's bleedin' terrible!"

Chiba's features suddenly transformed, lighting up with pleasure. He clearly did not understand the words or the tune, which was indeed fortunate for the unhappy British soldier. The other guards clapped their hands in approval. The listening POW's thought the whole situation was hilarious and some doubled up with laughter.

Doug finally finished, feeling very relieved. Chiba announced: "Gelta-ka (very good). I speak, you sing song."

"I've just bloodywell sung it!" replied an indignant Doug Pardy, glaring at Chiba. "Nei-ka!"

"I speak. You sing song!" shouted the Korean again.

Reluctantly, a very non-musical and miserable prisoner of war commenced to give another awful rendering for the 'Singing Master', who was clearly delighted with the tune. The other guards also thought the incident highly amusing, blissfully ignorant of the meaning of the song.

By now, the 'Singing Master' was completely carried away. Suddenly he spun round to the laughing prisoners. Waving his arms in the air to conduct and shrieking with delight, he shouted: "All men sing song, I speak!"

Much to the relief of the solo singer, all the prisoners burst forth into song, rendering a noisy, hearty, well intended version of the National Anthem, sending it echoing through the valley.

The 'Singing Master' was so pleased with his ability to make the men sing, he walked up to Doug Pardy and offered him a Japanese cigarette. "Me presento you smoke." After resisting the great temptation to tell him to shove it up his arse, Doug accepted the fag with a curt "Aringato" (Thank you).

The shrill whistles sounded. Yazume was over. "All men work hard, speedo, speedo!" Everything was back to normal.

Back in Tonchan that night, they wearily lined up for their ration of weak tea, boiled rice, and jungle juice. The meal over, they went down to the river to wash after digging twenty more shallow graves for the men who had died that day. Finally, they sat down on the ground around the nightly bonfires.

Captain Seaton, accompanied by Lieutenant Ashdown, came over from the officers' hut and joined Ed around the fire. "We need to talk", said the Captain.

The three men went for a walk out of earshot of the others.

"It seems as though we're going to be stuck in this hole for some time. The heat is off and the Kempi-Tai search didn't materialize", advised the signals officer. "Tomorrow night, come over to the officers' hut, as I'm going to set up our radio. I hope like hell it works after all this time."

A few more words were exchanged, then the two officers returned to their hut.

* * *

As darkness fell the next evening, Ed made his way over to the officers' POW hut. It had been arranged at the first sign of danger that Lt. Ashdown, patrolling outside, would whistle 'Auld Lang Syne'. All was set. At the far end of the bamboo hut, by the dim light of a coconut oil lamp, the two men carefully tapped around the base of the rice containers. The ends unscrewed with ease, revealing their secret compartments. The men back in Changi had done a good job.

The batteries were wrapped in a special insulating cover and in the airtight container had remained amazingly fresh. The miniature radio set and the plug-in earphones were still intact. The Australian captain grinned at Ed. It was an exciting moment as he quickly connected everything together. He positioned the strap holding the earphones over his head and fiddled with the controls. Nothing came through; the set was dead.

The officer looked puzzled for a brief moment, then pushed a small red wire further into the set. Suddenly, he gripped Ed's arm excitedly, nodding frantically as he rotated the tuning knob.

Captain Seaton could hear music, which stopped abruptly to allow for a news broadcast in English from Radio Calcutta in India. It was a breathtaking moment. He listened intently, then passed the earphones over.

Ed was spellbound as he listened to a repeat announcement of news in English. It was an unforgettable moment as the words came through clearly from the free world: "British Broadcasting Corporation from Radio Calcutta. Today South East Asia Command announce the sinking of four Japanese cargo ships and two destroyers by the Royal Navy in the Straits of Malacca. The Royal Air Force has again bombed Rangoon. In the Pacific Ocean, the United States Air force has bombed bases in the Philippine Islands, scoring many direct hits on units of the Japanese fleet. Further details will be given in our next bulletin."

"United States marines have landed successfully and recaptured two islands in the Solomons group. After a fierce battle, the Japanese garrison surrendered."

There were further items of news and then the news bulletin finished.

Carefully, the officer dismantled the set and returned it to the rice containers. Looking squarely at Ed, he declared: "Ed Warton, you're some soldier. When we get out of this it's my intention to see you are rewarded for risking your life to help me!"

Ed laughed. "That's all right, Captain. After what the bastards did to me on Singapore, to help our own is the least I can do. Speaking personally, I'd settle for a good dinner right now!"

Later that night, Ed returned hurriedly across the camp to where his mates were seated around the bonfire, anxiously awaiting news. Excitedly, Ed passed on all the information he had received. The men were delighted. These were not rumours but real news from the free world. It was a great morale booster.

"Perhaps the war will end soon", some wishful thinker suggested. At least it was a thought for a moment. Little did they know that, having been captives for just over one year, the war was to continue for another two years and eight long months.

"Hungry, Ed?" asked Morrie.

"Christ, I'm starving!"

Morrie was apologetic as he opened a small metal container. "Sorry Ed, couldn't get fish and chips tonight, they're not frying", he grinned. "But I managed a bit of boiled rice, cold, and a nice piece of boiled snake, cold. Bought it off one of the Dutchmen for fifty cents. We've all had a bit, that's your share."

"Thanks, Morrie, you're a good mate", replied Ed as he rapidly devoured every morsel.

"Don't know what we'd do without Morrie", declared Bill.

"So far we've all managed to stick together", interposed Foxy. "Let's hope like hell we'll still be able to, though we thought we'd lost you in Singapore, Ed."

"Well fellows, here's a present from good old Southend", said Morrie with a big grin. "Not a stick of yer bleedin' rock, but a mug of char, no sugar or milk and a bit weak, I admit. Best of all, no charge to me mates."

Dave Wandle looked longingly as the mugs were passed round. "Got a mug of Rosie Lee to spare, Morrie?" he asked. "Ain't got no bleedin' money, though."

"Christ Almighty, blokes like you ruin my business" Morrie grinned. "Here you go, mate", handing a hot metal mug to Dave.

"Cor, ta, mate", replied the grateful Cockney. "You're a right thieving sod, bet the bloody Japs don't know you nicked it from their cookhouse!"

"Must never discuss the source of supply", chirped Morrie. "That reminds me, I know that a lot of us don't smoke, but for the benefit of those poor sods who are dying for a fag, tomorrow I'm getting hold of some native cheroots for sale real cheap. Pass the word around, mates."

The small amount of tea available only slightly flavoured the hot boiled water, but to the prisoners gathered around the bonfire in Tonchan that night, it was as if they were drinking champagne, the finest in the world, whilst they talked and dreamed of home and their loved ones many thousands of miles away.

At 'tenko' next morning, Ed and Foxy both felt ill. They wondered if it was the portion of snake they'd had the night before.

"By Christ, I feel bloody cold", said Ed.

"So do I", replied Foxy. "I'm bloody freezing."

Corporal Jack Linton of the Beds and Herts said: "I reckon you two should go over the hospital bay and report sick."

"Guess you're right", replied Ed. "Come on, Foxy." The two men then joined on the end of a queue of fifty waiting to see the Medical Officer.

By the time they were seen, both were icecold and their teeth were chattering noisily. Foxy was first to reach the M.O. In his broad Suffolk accent he spluttered: "Am I gonna die from the snake I had last night?"

"No, I don't think so yet", replied Captain Saunders. He grinned at Ed. "You and your mate are both going down with malaria, so I'll have to keep the pair of you in the sick bay for a few days."

An R.A.M.C. corporal showed them to a place on the ground inside the hospital hut. "You'll be all right there, lads, until the M.O. comes round to sort you out, OK?"

"G'day, mate", greeted Ed and Foxy as they looked up at the faces of Bluey Longhurst and Joe Langton, the medics from Aussie. "Got malaria?" queried Joe. "Me and my mate Bluey will look after you no problem. You'll both be all right, mate."

They were interrupted by the arrival of Major Toyoda, the English speaking Japanese officer, accompanied by a single armed guard and a protesting Captain

Saunders. Toyoda stopped by the two sick Suffolks. "Their names and rank?" he demanded in good English.

"Privates E. Warton and F. Wright", came the answer.

"Ah, these men don't look sick enough to be in hospital. They must report for work at once", ordered Toyoda.

"They've got malaria", replied the Aussie M.O.

"Japanese soldiers do not get malaria or dysentery. Your men always have something wrong with them."

"With respect, Major, Japanese soldiers have boots, protective clothing, mosquito nets, good food, anti-fever injections, quinine and other drugs; also they do not have to work like starving slaves in loin cloths!"

Major Toyoda's mind was already made up. Suzuki had warned him that the railway must not fall behind schedule. He listened to the outburst, then announced: "You have made your point. You have said all these things before. You forget we are at war. These men must report for work at once. If you refuse, then I shall further restrict your medical supplies. My guard will make sure they return to work."

The situation was not new, but it could not have been worse if the Jap officer had been holding a loaded revolver at the head of the Australian medical officer. "Sorry men", he apologised. The sick men staggered to their feet and shuffled outside with several others.

The main work party had already left for the railway cutting half a mile from camp. A total of twenty five sick men were given heavy iron crowbars to carry. Then, escorted by two armed guards, they stumbled through the gates of Tonchan along the jungle paths in their bare feet.

On arrival at the work site they were assigned to loading large wicker baskets with broken flints and rocks, using their bare hands. Every two men would have to carry a heavy basket between them a distance of sixty yards, empty them down an embankment, and then return to load up again. This process was repeated by a long chain of POW's for the purpose of clearing the way for the railway track.

By midday several of the sick men had been beaten across the backs with heavy sticks, to the never-ending chanting of: "Speedo, all men speedo." Sergeant Yamanoto (the Pig) was in charge of the sick gang, assisted by the 'Undertaker'.

Ed felt desperate as his icecold body suddenly changed to a burning, raging heat. He was pouring with sweat, his head was thumping and spinning. He swayed as if to fall and, despite his own similar condition, Foxy put out his arm to steady him. The two men staggered on.

The Pig ordered them to halt. He stood in front of the two sick men. "I speak. Speedo, speedo!" he growled.

Ed tried to protest: "Taxan malaria."

The Jap sergeant's face was black with anger. "Malaria nei-ka, you speedo."

Ed could take no more. "You fucking black git!" he yelled. The enraged Jap started raining blows on his body with a pickaxe handle. In seconds Ed heeled over, mercifully unconscious.

Foxy Wright had also broken into a raging fever and sweat. He was next in line for the same brutal treatment. Within minutes, he also lay unconscious alongside Ed on the hot ground in the blazing sun.

Next was the turn of a fair haired twenty two year old from Suffolk. Normally a happy youngster with a ready smile and a cheery word, at that moment he was in great pain with dysentery. The internal blood his body was discharging from the back passage ran down his legs to his feet, forming a grotesque and unpleasant pattern. Multitudes of flies were attracted by this. The 'Undertaker' approached him wielding a stout stick: "Speedo, speedo!" he cried.

Weakly, the sick prisoner replied: "I can't, I've got a terrible pain in the guts."

The Undertaker's reaction was predictable. He began to rain blows with the stick on the helpless victim.

Other prisoners working nearby were filled with horror and revulsion at the sickening spectacle. Two young soldiers from the Norfolks could stand it no longer. They stopped work and rushed across to the Korean in a threatening manner. "Leave him be, you fucking maniac!" shouted one, the other waving his fist angrily at the Korean.

Sadly, it was too late for the Suffolk soldier, who was already lifeless on the ground.

Sergeant Yamanoto and four other guards rushed to the scene. All the prisoners had stopped work, standing still and looking on silently, as if frozen in their tracks. The machine gunner on the high bank swung round, pointing the gun barrel directly towards the prisoners. The atmosphere was charged with danger.

Yamanoto barked out orders in Japanese. The Korean savagely struck the two Norfolks with the stick, his face filled with anger and hatred. The two men were then isolated from the others, and forced to stand to attention bareheaded in the sun.

The Japanese Major in charge of that particular section of engineers arrived. Without ceremony, he whipped out his loaded revolver, pointing it menacingly towards the stationary prisoners: "All men work now!" The men shuffled away to their allotted tasks.

The two men standing to attention were only too aware of the penalty of trying to help a sick comrade.They stood together, proud and defiant, as Sergeant Yamanoto and Kaneshiro set to work with pickaxe handles. They did not whimper or cry out in pain.

In a few short minutes it was all over. Crushed and broken, their young bodies lay dead in the midday sun. Other prisoners working close by turned their heads away in revulsion, frustration and despair. Under the Japanese rule of the gun, death was never far away.

At the end of the shift, the prisoners rallied round to carry their shattered comrades back through the jungle paths to the POW camp.

The young soldier from the Suffolks and his two brave mates from the Norfolks were taken to the mortuary hut to await burial later in the evening alongside fourteen others, who had died in camp that day.

Still unconscious, with dangerous high tropical fevers, the other two Suffolks, Ed Warton and Foxy Wright, were carried to the hospital hut to fight for their lives.

It had been another black day in Tonchan!

CHAPTER 7

A Place to Die

In the long unpleasant-smelling bamboo hospital hut at Tonchan, that night, as on every other night, the medics worked through in ten hour shifts, tending the sick and dying. Some weeks earlier, they had, with the aid of a few walking sick, managed to construct a number of bamboo platforms some two feet off the ground, in bays of around six feet in width and seven feet in depth. Each bay could accommodate four or five prisoners, and although rough and extremely uncomfortable, it was considerably better than lying on the ground; at least it boosted their morale.

Through dysentery and weakness a number of men were totally unable to control their body functions and, in between long bouts of coughing, violent farts would erupt, accompanied by dull explosions from stomachs which in turn only added more stench and misery to the discomforts of the other patients.

Cries of pain and despair could be heard amidst the constant pleas of: "Orderly, orderly, bring the bedpan", swiftly followed by: "Too late, bring the shovel!"

From the adjacent annexe, men in the ulcer ward could be plainly heard in anguish, sounding off intermittent screams, as they rolled on or accidentally touched the long open and gaping wounds on their badly ulcerated limbs. During the medical officers' daily rounds, it was not unusual to hear a man plead for the amputation of a leg or an arm, to relieve the burning agonising pain. Others would break down and sob in despair at the sight and stench of their rotting flesh.

Bluey and Joe had just started a duty shift. They were particularly concerned at the plight of Ed Warton: the friendship they shared went back to their days in Jurong POW camp on the island of Singapore, where they had first picked him up out of the dust a year earlier.

Worried and anxious, Bill Slatoe and Morrie Finestein had visited Ed late that night. He was lying motionless and still unconscious; there had been no movement or change in his condition. In fact, there was no news for the visitors;

they looked at each other despondently. Foxy Wright had regained consciousness, but was rambling incoherently; unable therefore to talk, in despair the two men left the hut.

In the early hours of the next morning, the high fever raging through Foxy started to subside. The Aussie medics felt confident that given time, he would pull through, despite having been badly beaten up. Suspecting among other things a fracture, and without the vital assistance of x-ray equipment, as a precautionary measure they had put his left arm in splints.

Early the next morning before 'tenko', Bill and Morrie raced to the hospital. On arrival at the entrance they stood aside silently and in dismay as they counted three bodies being carried past them to the nearby mortuary hut.

"Christ Almighty", muttered Bill, "Will it ever bleedin' well end!". Morrie did not answer.

Bluey and Joe were on duty and informed them that Ed was still unconscious; there was no change!

"Anything that we can do?" asked Bill.

"Not really", came the reply. "Though it's possible we might need some blood later on." Almost as if one person, Bill and Morrie offered to give theirs.

"Got to wait for the M.O.", said Joe, "But we can take a couple of blood slides for checking in case we need to call on you." a quick prick in the fingers and the two slides were completed.

Sergeant Les Thomas from the R.A.M. Corps was in charge of the precious microscope. All cross checking on blood groups and the task of diagnosing tropical germs was left in his skilled hands. A blood sample was taken from Ed Warton to check on the suitability of the donors. At that moment, the shrill whistles sounded for 'tenko'; the two volunteers left to report for another day's toil on the railway.

After the daily sick parade was completed, the Australian medical officer set about his morning round of hospital patients. He was concerned over the condition of Ed Warton; the first angry flushes of malaria had died down, but he also had been savagely beaten and showed no signs of rallying round. Captain Saunders made a thorough examination, stepped back into the gangway looking grim. His two medics looked at him questioningly.

"There's a Pommie with bags of guts. Put him on the danger list", came the stern order. The M.O. continued, "God knows he suffered enough on the island. Remember 'Kwai-Tanu'? The bloody animals in the jungle behave better than these evil bastards!"

Turning to his patient again, he muttered, "He's lost a lot of blood from the wound in his neck. I'll watch him through the day; might need a transfusion later. We'll see how it goes."

Bluey informed him that two volunteers were ready when they returned from work. Medic Joe Langton commented, "If only we had more supplies and equipment things would be one helluva lot better."

"Too bloody right", replied the M.O. "Although you know that's just wishful thinking. The bastards won't give us enough of the anaesthetic or drugs that we so badly need!" The officer continued, "I've questioned them about medical supplies, feeling confident that through the International Red Cross, the Allies would have despatched large quantities of medical gear to us."

"Any luck, Captain?", questined Bluey.

"Luck?", came the answer. Suzuki and Toyoda thought my questions were bloody hilarious. I'm suspicious about that. There's something wrong somewhere. I'm sure maybe we'll find out more later on. Meanwhile, Christ knows what the hell we are going to do. Makes me feel desperate. Still we mustn't give up." He gave a weak rueful grin."Soldier on regardless, isn't that what the Pommies say?"

Later in the day, the M.O. again checked on the two Suffolks. Foxy had quietened down and was thirstily drinking pints of river water, which had been boiled (as a precaution against the dreaded cholera germs), and then cooled for drinking. By the end of the day he was able to manage a few intelligible words in between bouts of delirium.

That evening, Bill and Morrie visited again. Captain Saunders, accompanied by the medics, was checking Ed's condition. While they waited, they managed to exchange a few words with Foxy, which helped to cheer them up. Suddenly, the medical officer looked up. Addressing the two Suffolks, "We need two pints of blood immediately. It's urgent. There's no time to lose if your mate's going to survive. We've got to act now." There was a sudden flurry of activity. The R.A.M.C. sergeant had said that, by a stroke of good fortune, their blood groups matched.

Without any ceremony, Bill and Morrie sat on the ground in the gangway as the two medics searched for veins, inserted needles, and commenced to extract blood through a fine thin rubber tube into clean bottles. It was soon over. They waited. Morrie felt horribly faint as the medics swiftly hung the first bottle on a bamboo support. Another fine rubber tube transferred the blood in a steady drip into Ed's bloodstream. A grim looking medical officer checked everything carefully. Sensing the drama, Bill and Morrie watched anxiously, looking despairingly at the M.O.

"Sorry fellows, he's got a fifty fifty chance tonight. The crisis is close." At that moment, the officer was called away to examine another patient further down the hut.

Bill Slatoe's eyes were moist as he reached out and took Ed's limp hand in his. "Don't die, mate", he whispered, "For Christ's sake don't die. We bloody need you!" Bill brushed away the tears hastily with the back of his grubby hand.

"See you outside, Morrie", he muttered, as he hurried away, overcome with emotion.

Morrie was unable to contain his feelings; tears began to trickle down his young face. He felt choked and lost. In sadness, he took hold of Ed's hand "Listen, Ed, there's no way we're going back to Southend without you. Perhaps you can hear me but can't answer. I owe you, mate. Remember when I was being done over, 'cause I couldn't finish my stint of bloody rock breaking, you finished the bleedin' lot and saved my life."

Morrie paused to brush away the tears blinding his eyes. He tried again, "Ed, mate, what I told you about my rich Jewish family in Westcliff, it's all bullshit. Honest, we're bleedin' poor, just like you. We work the markets, do all kinds of things to make a few bob. What a stupid git I was, pretending all that. Well, now you know the truth, Ed. I'm just the same as you. For Christ's sake, don't leave me, mate. I'll be back later."

Morrie looked hard at his unconscious mate. There was no response; the blood continued to drip steadily into Ed's vein. Trying not to let anyone see the tears, he gently let go of Ed's hand, brushed his eyes again, and walked quietly away from the hospital hut. Sad at heart and in a daze, Morrie wandered aimlessly around the other huts in the camp. Like Bill, he did not want anyone to see his tears; it was not considered manly to cry.

Twenty four hours later, Foxy was making steady progress towards recovery. Despite weakness, he was at last able to eat and to talk. Still lying next to Ed on the bamboo platform, he felt relieved and excited when Bluey had told him that Ed had survived the crisis OK. That evening, Bill and Morrie had just reached the entrance to the hospital hut when they froze in horror.

The medics were lifting a body from the bay in the vicinity of Foxy and Ed. They remained stationary as the medics carried the corpse past them. They could see a mop of ginger hair hanging limply out of the end of a rice sack covering the soldier's face. Almost as one, they breathed a sigh of relief: It was neither Ed nor Foxy.

The two men walked cautiously towards their sick mates. The medical officer was about to leave. He paused, looking directly towards the two visitors reassuringly, he smiled, "Your mate's out of danger. A bloody survivor if ever there was one. He'll be OK."

With that message of hope, Captain Saunders was called sharply away by one of the medics. Three bays down, a twenty two year old from Blackpool lay dying. The end was close as the M.O. held the thin wrist to feel for a pulse. The bright blue eyes opened wide in their hollow sockets; the youngster was still conscious.

Through his parched lips feebly he begged the question, "Am I dying?"

"No, you'll be right, soldier", came the untruthful answer. His bony fingers suddenly gripped the M.O's hand tightly. His head slumped forward; the fair crinkly hair flopped down over his forehead. He had died with dignity, without a fuss. It was almost as if he had known! The Captain nodded.The medics laid his head back and gently closed the lids over the bright blue eyes. The young soldier from Blackpool would suffer no more. They covered him in rice sacks and carried his body out to the mortuary hut.

Foxy was sitting propped up, talking cheerfully in his broad pleasant Suffolk manner to Bill and Morrie. "Did you blokes hear what the doc' said. Ed's gonna be all right. He's gonna make it!" The three men from the Suffolks looked intently at their sick friend. There was a slight movement of his head and the eyes opened slowly. They could see clear signs of recognition in them. Although unable to speak, it was a tremendous moment. Ed Warton was returning from the brink of death.

* * *

Camp commandant Suzuki was easy to corrupt, having received from special agent Ayut, officially 'Head Thai' trader, a massive bribe of whisky, cigarettes and tobacco, plus importantly, one week's free services of a shapely young Thai whore, to perform with him in his comfortable well-furnished hut.

In return, he had agreed to permit the traders to resume calling at the camp by barge. Suzuki decreed that, under strict supervision of armed guards, one special traders barge - in addition to the normal supply barges which arrived daily - could call twice a week in the evenings to allow Japanese and Koreans to purchase whatever small luxuries they required, followed by prisoners of war who still had goods to barter or money to spend.

* * *

Outside the hospital hut, an excited Morrie grabbed Bill by the arm. "C'mon, mate, we're going shopping. The barge is due in tonight."

Bill gloomily replied, "Got no money."

Morrie laughed. "Forget it, mate, I've got some stashed away. Let's go back to the hut and collect it!"

Down at the river bank, being the business expert he indubitably was, Morrie haggled well and finished up with six eggs - at a premium price. Two pineapples, a bunch of bananas, a pomelo (a kind of grapefruit), and a packet of brown sugar.

The two men returned triumphantly to the hospital hut where they were delighted to find that Ed had fully regained consciousness. Dumping the purchases on to the bamboo platform, Morrie proudly announced, "They're for you and Foxy", despite the fact that they were starving themselves!

Ed grinned weakly, whispering his first words since being beaten up. "Thanks, mates, let's all share." In point of fact, Ed was unable to eat anything at that stage, although Foxy was ravenous.

Bill rushed out and boiled the eggs in a billycan on the nearest bonfire. On his return, they rapidly devoured the goodies amongst them, leaving the two hard-boiled eggs for Foxy to share with Ed the next day. For a few magical minutes, they could have been sitting dining at the Ritz Hotel in London or Sydney, instead of in the miserable hospital hut at Tonchan!

Two weeks had passed. Australian Captain Don Saunders and his team of medics were rightly pleased at their patients' progress. Ed and Foxy were regaining strength rapidly. They were now able to walk to the latrines and back, also assisting with others worse off than themselves. Above all, was the joy of being able to converse freely with each other. News from down country was that newly-made dirt roads were now almost through to Tonchan and Japanese transport lorries would shortly be bringing up additional supplies of explosives and various other items required for the engineers working on the railway. Further news was that the line at Wampo was complete and the first train would shortly reach Tarsoe.

A few miles north, new POW camps had been established at Kanu and Kanu II. Beyond them lay jungle camp 203, Hintock, Brankassi, then Rintin.

Atwai, the interpreter, was thoroughly disillusioned with the Japanese Greater East Asia Co-prosperity propaganda. Added to the fact that, being unable to return to his native Bam-Pong, he also was virtually a prisoner, however, because of his knowledge of languages, he was well treated and trusted by the Japanese officers.

This was a serious mistake on their part, because Atwai had turned pro-British. Therefore, he was always ready to pass on any vital news and scraps of information that he learned from the enemy.

It was from this useful source of information that Australian signals officer, Captain Seaton, had learned of the possibility of a move from Tonchan to a new location much further north, towards the Three Pagoda pass, a few miles short of Konkuita. This bore the grim-sounding name of Tamajao, which the survivors of Tonchan were destined to learn a lot more about in the months ahead!

Daily contact was made on the railway with work parties from the Kanu camp. Stories of Lieutenant Usuki (the Kanu kid), the Korean Kumdiet (the Bombay duck), and their appalling atrocities brought no new fears to the unhappy inmates of Tonchan. The utterly inhumane and brutal ill treatment was a common feature, regardless of which camp the men were imprisoned in!

To the complete surprise of everyone, Major Toyoda had issued a batch of white postcards to Captain Saunders and the other Allied officers in the camp. Instructions were given that every POW should write on one side the address they wished to send it, and fill in details on the reverse side. The cards were to be completed and returned to Major Toyoda the next morning. Time proved that for those working on the railway, this was to be the first, last, and only communication allowed during their long years of captivity.

Foxy studied his card carefully. There had been a big rush to borrow pens or pencils. He read it at least five times before returning to Ed. "To hell, man", he remarked, "Suppose we'd better sign it. Never know, it might reach home, then at least they'll know we're alive."

Ed read his card and agreed. In the top left hand corner was painted a small dove of peace, followed by Japanese writing, which the two men presumed meant, 'International Red Cross'. One of the medics lent him a pen. Slowly he printed the full address, underlining the district Southchurch, Southend-on-Sea, Essex, England.

Turning the card over, he was surprised to find written in English, in large black letters right across the top 'IMPERIAL JAPANESE ARMY', followed by printed messages which read:

"I am a Japanese prisoner of war."
"I am very happy."
"I am working for pay."
"I am not in hospital."

and finally,

"I am being very well treated."
"Signed.............."

Ed signed his name and returned the precious pen to the medics.

The next morning, all the cards were collected and returned to Major Toyoda, who assured the officers that through the 'International Red Cross'. The cards would eventually reach their destinations in different parts of the world.

Later on in the evening, Morrie, Bill and Dave Wandle visited Foxy and Ed. They were squatting on the bamboo slats as they talked. Dave, thinking about the printed messages on the postcards, suddenly laughed.

"Something wrong?", asked Foxy.

"Christ, no", replied the Cockney lad. "I was just thinking about them bloody postcards. I mean, mate, wot a lot of old bollocks that is, I ask yer!" He went on, "Arf the bleedin' camp's dead, we're all bloody starving, I mean to say that if my old lady really knew she'd go mad!"

"That goes for all of us", added Morrie. "Wonder if those bleedin' cards will ever reach home though." (Strange to relate, most of them did reach their destinations.) He went on, "What'll happen after the war when the folks find out that thousands of 'em who sent cards are dead. They will never go home."

No-one answered!

Next day, Foxy was lying on the bamboo platform still alongside Ed. The sick had been talking at length about home. A wave of nostalgia seemed to sweep through the hospital hut. Ed had managed to persuade Foxy to give the lads some of his expert farmyard impersonations, ranging from cockerels, ducks, cows and many others, plus his incredible bird calls and whistles. The Aussie medics reckoned that Foxy should have been on the stage; his performances were that good!

"What about the jungle animals? asked Bluey, who had just come on duty.

"You mean like this?", answered Foxy.

He then set about imitating monkeys, baboons, tropical birds, and even an elephant call. When he had finished, all the medical staff together with the sick patients burst into a hearty round of applause. The good hearted country lad from mid Suffolk had become a star in his own right at the dreadful hospital hut, where he gave the sick a laugh when there was really nothing to laugh about.

At that moment, Ed Warton realised what a valuable asset Foxy's talent could prove, particularly at night in the jungle in order to fool the Japs into a false sense of security. Having survived so far, and looking towards a grim future, in Ed's mind it was an exciting prospect. For the present the all important thing was for Foxy and himself to become as fit as possible.

* * *

Foxy had lived with his parents in a small cottage close to the tiny village of Creeting St. Peter, approximately three miles from the bigger village of Needham Market, and around three miles from Stowmarket. At times, when the mood took him, he would talk at great lengths about the beauty of the Suffolk countryside, market days at 'Stow' and Bury St. Edmunds. On special days, for a visit to the seaside, he would bike with his pretty young girlfriend, Emma, to Felixstowe and back, a distance of some 24 miles each way.

Often in his quiet moments, he would dream and think about the 18 year old petite lass who worked as a counter assistant in the local general store in the main street of Needham Market. She lived with her parents and younger sister Rose in a modest house just off Barretts Lane. There was never anything really said about being serious or getting married; rather, some sort of understanding that one day it would happen!

Foxy turned to Ed, who was lying looking up at the beautiful deep blue tropical sky, which shone through the entrance of the hospital hut.

"Think that's a nice sky up there, Ed. Ever been to Suffolk, mate?"

Ed shook his head.

"This time of the year, everything comes to life. Springtime, the hedges open up their green foliage, the birds really sing, the meadows turn green, dotted with buttercups and daisies. In the country gardens the daffodils and tulips are really beautiful. It's a wonderful time!"

Foxy paused for a moment, overcome with nostalgia. He continued, "Then there's the fishing, from the winding old river Gipping, to the many lovely lakes tucked away in the thickets and meadows. Promise me, Ed, if we ever get out of this bloody hell, you'll come and stay with me in Suffolk. You'll really love it." Dreamily, Ed promised he would.

The next day, Ed asked Bluey if he could scrounge an old metal box from somewhere. Unfortunately there wasn't anything suitable. Undaunted, Ed asked Morrie and Dave Wandle if they could oblige, plus some scraps of paper and bits of pencils.

"What's it all about?" asked the lads.

Ed looked at them intently, then replied, "The way I see it, these bastards are murdering and torturing our mates and I think we should keep a record of it all, which I can bury and dig up from time to time to update."

He continued, "You boys get me the gear, and I'll be responsible for recording important events. Then, after the war, we can use the evidence to see these bastards are punished."

Morrie said, "Whilst I agree, Ed, it's too bloody risky. If you're caught with that kind of evidence then you know only too well what the penalty will be."

"OK, so I know", replied Ed. "It's what our officers would call a calculated risk, and I'm going to take a soddin' chance!"

The next night, Bill Slatoe turned up with a neat light metal box about ten inches long, five inches wide and three or four inches in depth.

"Ideal", beamed a delighted Ed. Morrie and Dave had managed to obtain a few small scraps of thin plain paper as well as three half pencils.

"Really excellent", Ed thanked them. "Where did you nick the gear from?"

The lads just laughed. "That would be telling", said Dave, "You want it, we nick it, mate! That's our share, OK.? Where it came from, well Ed, I reckon that's our bleedin' problem."

With Foxy keeping a good lookout, the next day Ed started to record the main dreadful events of recent weeks. On completion, he dug a hole in the ground with his bare hands, sank the box and covered it carefully with loose soil. At last he was able to record some of the enemy's many crimes.

He slept better that night!

CHAPTER 8

Carnage

Two weeks later, Foxy and Ed had made remarkable recoveries. Captain Don Saunders and his gallant team of medics managed by devious means to keep them in hospital as long as possible and away from the Japanese medical officer, Major Toyoda. However, the daily situation was becoming more difficult. As a result, they were due to return to work in the next few days.

Ed had managed to update his brief notes, and keep them safely hidden in the soil below where he slept. By now, in the special hut reserved for them, there was a total of seventeen Allied officers, led by Major James Wystock-Hall. Atwai, the interpreter, visited them in the morning, to warn them that there was a real possibility of a sudden move out of Tonchan, up country far north.

He also informed them that, because of the ever-increasing death rate, in order to prevent work on the railway falling behind schedule, two fresh batches of POW's were planned to be sent up from Changi on Singapore island. They were to be known as 'F' force, followed later by 'H' force, in addition to thousands more native labourers. These, and other moves, the enemy hoped would be completed before the start of the monsoon season, which usually arrived around the beginning of June!

Two days prior to this information, the first Japanese lorries had begun to arrive in Tonchan. The dirt road was continuing on towards Tonchan North, and the equally infamous camps of Kanu, and Kanu II. Further information was that the enemy had set up a vast hospital camp down south, to be known as Chungkai where, among other things, the amputation of limbs was to become a regular daily occurrence, of which more was to be learned at a later date.

During mid-afternoon, an agitated Atwai hurried into the hospital hut to speak urgently to Captain Saunders. Something had gone badly wrong: the Kempi-Tai (Japanese Gestapo) were in camp, and were holding all the Allied officers for questioning prior to a full-scale search everywhere.

The news travelled like wildfire. Captain John Seaton, the Australian signals officer, and Lieutenant Reg Ashdown from the Suffolks, had been isolated, and were being tortured Kempi-Tai method to make them talk. The situation was ugly and deadly serious.

Atwai had discovered that the Secret Police had been watching a certain unnamed Thai trader for some time. Down by the riverside at Tonchan, they pounced, torturing him until he had betrayed these two Allied officers, informing the Kempi-Tai that he had been supplying them with radio batteries.

Having obtained this information, they promptly made him kneel before them with his hands tied behind his back, whilst they executed him by means of a swift blow from a sword.

On learning the news, Ed quickly smoothed the loose soil covering the small metal box, which housed his records of atrocities. He then prepared to sweat it out. There was not long to wait. Two uniformed members of the Kempi-Tai arrived to search the hospital hut, its staff, and patients. Ferocious looking and armed with revolvers, at first glance they appeared much taller than the average Jap or Korean. Methodically, they searched through all the medical equipment, drugs, and boxes as well as the few pathetic belongings of the patients. Those sick who could stand in the gangway, were made to do so, and to remove their loincloths, to stand completely naked for inspection.

Finally, one of the Kempi-Tai called in a Korean guard with a rifle and fixed bayonet, and ordered him to dig at random in the loose soil beneath the bamboo platforms. Digging the bayonet wildly, he approached the area of the hidden box. Ed froze inside as he glared at the Kempi-Tai officer, who was intently watching the guard at work. Abruptly, the guard grunted and moved on. By a strange quirk of fate, the box had been missed: Ed breathed easy again.

"Fucking hell!" exploded a very relieved Foxy, as the Kempi-Tai left the hut. "I thought that was your bloody lot, Ed. Someone up there must like you!"

"To be honest", came the answer,"so did I!"

At that moment, three terrible piercing human screams echoed grimly across the camp, followed by an almost uncanny silence. The torturers were at work, using the dreadful expertise copied from the German Gestapo. It worked: the two officers cracked, and the Kempi-Tai discovered the radio!

On returning to camp, outside work parties were greeted by more armed guards, and marched directly to the dusty parade ground where they were made to form up on three sides, in long ranks of three deep. The men immediately sensed something wrong! The only POW's not required were the medical officer and his staff, hospital patients, and cookhouse staff.

The giant parade was counted and checked at least three times. Fifteen Allied officers, flanked by four armed guards with bayonets fixed, were made to stand in front of the other ranks, about twenty five feet to the left of Suzuki's vacant platform. A glance upward to the four corners of the camp, at the twenty foot high gunposts, told the all familiar story. Each machine-gunner looked down menacingly, pointing the barrels of the deadly weapons directly towards the helpless prisoners of war.

The tropical sun blazed down relentlessly from the vivid blue sky above on to all assembled. Four thousand prisoners standing barefooted with but a scrap of loincloth to protect their genitals: the atmosphere was electric, tense, and deadly.

From out of his comfortable hut strode the black-haired arrogant camp commandant, Captain Isu Suzuki, looking fresh and resplendent in a cool clean white open-necked shirt and full military regalia, complete with a row of medal ribbons on his left breast. As usual, he had been drinking sake (rice whisky). From his waist belt dangled the traditional sword. The slant eyes were bloodshot behind his thick horn-rimmed glasses, which glinted in the sun.

Unsteadily, he climbed the four steps to his platform, followed by an officer from the Kempi-Tai, Major Toyoda, and interpreter Atwai. The four men bowed low to the Rising Sun, suspended above them on a long bamboo pole attached to the platform. For a brief moment there was a deadly silence.

Gripping the surrounding handrail for support, Suzuki barked out an order. The guards jumped rigidly to attention and bowed. The prisoners stood silent and motionless. The commandant started to speak, pausing for Atwai to translate, despite the fact that Major Toyoda could speak fluent English.

"Today the Imperial Japanese Army has executed a native trader who was captured with radio batteries in his possession. After investigation (torture), he betrayed two of your officers, who were persuaded to confess to the hidden whereabouts of the forbidden radio.

Obviously enjoying every minute, Suzuki continued coldly and deliberately, "You have all been warned in the past. You must realize that we, the Japanese, are the master race. We rule. You will obey. If anyone wishes, at this late hour, to confess to any other radio or secret documents, speak up now, and I will be lenient!"

Needless to say, there was no answer, no movement, only silence.

From behind Suzuki's special hut marched four members of the Kempi-Tai with two Allied officers roped together between them. They halted a few yards in front of the platform. Each man had his hands tied behind his back.

From where Morrie and Bill were standing, it was quite obvious that the officers had been tortured and were still in pain. Eyeing them suspiciously, Suzuki started to speak again.

"We have before us Captain Seaton of the Australian Army, and Lieutenant Ashdown from the British Army. For concealing and operating a radio set, they are guilty and have confessed. As a final warning to prisoners, I intend to make an example of them before their execution by shooting!"

Despite their pain and despair, trembling visibly in distress, the two young officers tried hard to stand to attention, glaring back defiantly at Suzuki and his henchmen; it was terrifying and desperate.

Following the grim words of the death sentence, it became horribly real as two of the Japanese Gestapo stepped forward armed with pickaxe handles. They set about the two defenceless officers, beating them to the ground unconscious. Men turned their heads away in utter revulsion at the sickening scene. Many were physically sick where they stood.

Blood gushed from the two bodies, turning the hot dust of the parade ground into scarlet mud!

From the front rank nearest the nightmare, someone yelled out, "Stop, stop, you fucking animals. For Christ's sake, stop it!"

Other prisoners joined in, screaming obscenities. A number of them broke ranks, and surged forward in anger and frustration in a futile effort to prevent the brutal murders taking place before their eyes.

Suzuki signalled the machine-gunner in the right-hand corner post. Rapidly, he opened fire with a short sharp burst. A hail of bullets cut down those who had surged forward. Several fell dead, and a number of wounded were screaming and rolling in pain and agony.

The parade ground had become a blood bath. Other prisoners remained frozen with fear, tensed and frightened! Death was close at hand! Suzuki surveyed the slaughter with much satisfaction. Prisoners of war were expendable, anyway. The important matter was that Japanese law had been maintained by the rule of the gun!

Suzuki ordered the fifteen Allied officers to remain on parade, then dismissed all other ranks. He also instructed a guard to inform Captain Saunders to send a full team of medics immediately to remove the dead and wounded, including the bodies of the two young officers brutally murdered. The firing squad would not now be required!

As the bulk of the parade dismissed, for a moment Suzuki looked down with hatred at the fifteen remaining Allied officers. Then his ugly squat face broke into a grin of amusement at their plight. It appeared simply part of the Japanese way of life to laugh while prisoners died!

Major Toyoda and the Kempi-Tai officer had left the platform to take drinks and refreshments in the commandant's hut. A surprising feature of the dreadful events had been the attitude of Major Toyoda, who, despite his high education, knowledge and ability to understand the English way of life and their language, had apparently enjoyed the slaughter and the sight of the Westerners' ultimate humiliation at the hands of the Kempi-Tai!

Captain Suzuki addressed the officers, with Atwai translating: "As from now Allied POW officers will be segregated from all other ranks. Tonight you will be marched to a new camp for officers, where you will be forced to work! You have all been lazy and looked down on our Japanese officers, who are far superior!"

Suzuki paused, then continued: "Only medical officers and padres will be allowed to remain in camps with all other ranks. Is that clearly understood?"

There was no reaction or answer from the Allied officers. They simply remained silent. The commandant curtly dismissed the parade.

Two hours later, they were being marched out of the gates of Tonchan for what was then an unknown destination. Twenty five kilometers away, this camp was to become known as the 'Allied officers only' POW camp.

At the final count, including the two murdered officers, eighteen men had been killed. Twelve more were wounded and taken to the hospital hut, where two died shortly afterwards. Another twenty six men had died from starvation and tropical diseases that same day. In all, a total of forty six prisoners of war were laid to rest in Tonchan cemetery late that night!

As the strains of the 'Last Post' died away and night became darkness again, Bill and Morrie related the horrors of the day to Ed and Foxy in the hospital hut.

Ed said he ought to enter the essential details in his notes. Morrie became angry. "Don't be so bleedin' stupid. It's far too bloody dangerous with the Kempi-Tai in camp. Listen, Ed, my memory will last for ever. You can record it another time, when it's safer!"

Ed's face was grim as he agreed: "Christ, I hate those evil bastards", he swore.

"Don't we all, mate", replied Bill. "As I see it at the present time, we can't do sod all!"

Morrie and Bill were unaware of Ed's narrow escape that afternoon. He and Foxy had earlier agreed that it was best not to mention the search in view of the dreadful events of the day.

Looking very serious, Captain Don Saunders entered the hospital hut, not to examine patients, but for the purpose of a general discussion with the men. "As you know, lads, I'm the only officer left in camp apart from Padre Hall. What a hell of a bloody day! Looks as though we've got to be prepared to move again. Atwai tipped us off earlier, so we'll have to be ready for anything now!"

As the conversation dwindled, Ed looked up at the tall young Australian medical officer. "Captain, have we still got five hand grenades left?" he demanded.

Captain Saunders replied with a rueful grin, "Yes, we have, Ed. I know how you feel, but mate, there's no way we can usefully handle them at the present time!"

"Maybe not", came the reply, "but we've got to have a go at these bastards somehow."

Morrie was getting worried. "Not now, Ed, for Christ's sake!"

The medical officer interrupted, "When the time is right, we will know. Till then, in view of what happened today, stay bloody patient, OK?" Ed did not answer.

Two days later, against the protests of the medical officer, Major Toyoda ordered ten more sick patients to return to work, among them Ed Warton and Foxy Wright.

Nothing had changed. As they lined up for 'tenko', ready for their return to the railway, the usual counting and checking was carried out. Then, as they prepared to march off, Korean Chiba (the Singing Master) isolated the last ten men in the batch for the daily ration run from the river.

At least, it made a change. Today's party consisted of Ed, Bill, Morrie, Foxy, four Australians, Dave Wandle and Doug Pardy. With only the Korean to guard them, the men were marched down the steep dirt slope to the river bank, where four supply barges were tied up to mooring posts in the swirling early morning mist. As the party drew near, two guards emerged through the now rapidly clearing haze and indicated to them to 'yazume' or rest.

The ten promptly sat down on the river bank to wait while Korean Chiba went on board the first barge to speak with the head Thai, as was the custom. They talked among themselves, glancing idly around. On the decks of all four barges there were two or three middle aged and elderly Thai women lazily chewing bright red betel nuts.

Bill pointed out to the lads a younger shapely Thai female on the fourth barge. In the distance her jet black hair framed an attractive face of light coffee coloured complexion. She was colourfully dressed in a pretty clean blue and white sarong. Ed and Bill laughed, and waved to her. To their surprise, she gave a dazzling smile, displaying her lovely white teeth as she laughingly waved back. At this, the other eight members of the work party also laughed and waved, whilst making suitably salacious remarks with much wishful thinking. The young nubile female could obviously not undertstand what was being said. Bill and Ed reckoned that GI Elmer Baker would have loved to have been on the ration run that morning.

At least the minor incident, brief though it was, tended to brighten up their day. The surrounding deep jungle vegetation ran alongside the winding river banks as far as the eye could see, contrasting with the deep blue sky above. By now, the morning sun was already hot and uncomfortable. The waters of the river Kwai looked, as ever, tempting and refreshingly cool.

From the river, looking up the dusty dry dirt slope towards the cookhouse area, the bordering tall jungle grass seemed like an emerald necklace. All around flitted myriads of large beautifully coloured butterflies, accompanied by the rarest of exotic deep multi-coloured tropical birds, winging their way freely over the valley. In the distance, a troupe of monkeys could be seen displaying the most fantastic acrobatics, as they swung high in the trees.

The conversation was completed on number one barge, the head Thai bowed to Korean Chiba as he stepped ashore. Looking very pleased with himself, with a gift of Thai cheroots, he quickly selected the first four men to go on board. Knowing the drill, Ed and his three mates had made sure that they were the first to start work.

"All men must now speedo very hard", grinned Chiba, as he escorted the remaining six to barges number two and three. On the way, he was explaining in broken English that when barges one, two and three had been emptied, all ten men would have to work on the fourth barge. The explanation was totally unnecessary, because at some time or other, all the prisoners had worked on the ration run and so they knew the drill. That was one way that they had learned to become experts at thieving from the enemy.

The Singing Master had good reason to be pleased, for it had now become an established practice for guards on the ration run tasks to receive free cheroots and tobacco from the head Thai. But, more importantly, they also enjoyed the services of a young Thai whore without any charge. The Korean Chiba was excited at the prospect, and seemed scarcely able to contain his lustful desires.

Aboard the first barge, with great relief Ed and Bill recognised agent Ayut, officially the head Thai in charge. He indicated that Ed should kneel down behind a pile of rice sacks out of sight. The other three mates in the gang were excited. Bill bent low and said: "Carry on, Ed. We'll make a start on unloading and cover for you. Find out all you can, mate!"

Korean Chiba was busy distributing labour and organising the unloading of the other barges, after which he was carried away with the young female. He talked coaxingly, with the object of getting her ashore and into the bushes, but she appeared to be playing for time.

Ed Warton and Ayut took swift advantage of the situation. In excellent English, Ayut spoke first: "At last we meet again. Your name I remember, Ed Warton." Ed nodded as he listened. "Many bad things have happened. Four of our members from the Bangkok underground movement have been tortured and executed by the Kempi-Tai. I still have a lifeline of supplies and information to Colonel Harvel at Tarsoe!"

Ayut continued: "We know of the murders and bloodshed in this camp three days ago! The Japanese are a very cruel and harsh enemy!"
Ed interrupted: "Have you any information about when and where this camp will be moving?"
The agent replied: "There are thousands more prisoners of war coming up from Singapore. Any day now the first party should arrive. This camp is due to go farther north toward the Three Pagoda pass, which leads to Burma. It's difficult, mountainous, and dangerous. I shall be taking supplies to all camps. The Japanese think I am a sympathiser and they trust me!"
He paused to look over the rice sacks and observe the Korean trying to persuade the girl to come ashore. He smiled at Ed. "It never fails. Whores have more than one use. She will keep him occupied for some time yet. As you English say, that's the object of the exercise!"
Ed thanked Ayut for his valuable help and the risk he was taking. The agent smiled again, replying:
"It is the least we can do. They have invaded my country. We Thais want rid of them, so you see, my friend, we are your Allies!" He added: "Because of shipping losses, the enemy have started to move bargeloads of ammunition by night up from Bangkok to the Burma borders. It then goes by Jap transport over dirt roads to the railway at Thanbyuzayat!"
Ed answered: "All information is vital and important to us prisoners. We may be helpless now, but our turn will come." He had a sudden thought: "If we need them can you get explosives to us upstream where we're going?"
Ayut paused in thought for a moment, then replied: "It would be very dangerous indeed, but yes, we can do it by arrangement. As most of the camps are by the river, we will be in contact again!"
"We're bloody desperate to escape."
Ayut interrupted him: "Too many have, and all have died or been recaptured and executed. In the jungle there's nowhere to go, especially at night. When the time is right, we will do all we can to help. We cannot talk any more now."
Ed nodded. He fully understood. Ayut concluded: "To help you all, I have deliberately tricked the Korean guard about the numbers of sacks on this barge." He looked carefully across the stacked rice sacks, noting to his satisfaction the young Thai girl, holding the guard's hand, disappearing into the thick undergrowth.
Ed grinned. "It worked OK."
Ayut laughed. "Go now, as you did before, and hide two sacks of rice, two sacks of vegetables, and a sack of dried fish."
Morrie, Bill, and Foxy had just arrived back on the barge. Together the four men did (as Dave Wandle put it later that night) "The fastest fallen off the back of a lorry job in the world."
With the stolen goods stashed safely away, the hard work of emptying and carrying the rest of the heavy sacks uphill to the cookhouses continued until Korean Chiba crawled out of the bushes, happily boasting in broken English: "Tokyo number one plucka!" Then he sat down in the shade and promptly fell asleep.
The ill-treated prisoners of war gazed in amazed disbelief at the guard, now

lying on top of his rifle and bayonet, mouth sagging wide open, flies still undone, snoring like a pig.

They could quite easily and cheerfully have murdered him, and then escaped into the thick surrounding jungle. They were, however, only too well aware of the almost inevitable consequences, which would have cost all of them their lives. They knew from bitter experience how the Japanese would have revelled and relished more such senseless slaughter!

To escape successfully in the jungle would need to be carefully planned. As yet no-one had escaped and made it! As the party again moved down the steep incline towards the barges, almost as if reading their thoughts, the Korean grunted, sat upright, and grabbing his rifle, shouted sleepily: "All now speedo. Now, I speak!"

"And bollocks to you, too!" muttered Dave Wandle as very reluctantly they carried on with their backbreaking work.

CHAPTER 9

Before the Rains

Five days later in the evening, as the burial party returned from the cemetery, unexpectedly the guards started blowing whistles and screaming like maniacs in an effort to urge the reluctant POW's to get on parade without delay. Something was up: Captain Saunders and Padre Hall were also required to report.

Captain Suzuki, Major Toyoda, and the interpreter Atwai were already standing on the platform, waiting impatiently as the prisoners manoeuvred into position. The usual three ranks were lined up on three sides, where they were checked and counted. A sudden long shrill blast on the whistle given by Sergeant Yamanoto quickly silenced the whole assembly.

Yamanoto bowed low to his master, Suzuki, who appeared agitated as he launched into his speech. Doubtless, the warlords in Japan had again been despatching urgent messages to Thailand concerning the railway. "Tomorrow morning at dawn, all prisoners in this camp will march north in stages of twenty miles, with overnight stays in staging camps. There is a long journey ahead." He paused, looking round for any reaction to his words. There was none. The captain continued: "Imperial Japanese Army officer commanding the march will be Lieutenant Kokubo. You will obey his orders!"

"When you arrive at your destination, we will be there to meet you!"

"Christ!" muttered Ed to Bill, "That's bloody bad news." It could only mean that Suzuki, Toyoda and several others were going upstream by barge.

Suzuki concluded: "A final word of warning. If anyone falls behind, you all know the consequence!"

Through Atwai, Captain Saunders requested permission to speak. Suzuki curtly agreed. The young Australian medical officer stood to attention and bowed: "Sir, what do you intend to do with the very sick men, the crippled and the dying. It is a matter of the most urgent importance. I must stress that those men cannot be left without medical aid!"

Captain Suzuki scowled, but acknowledged the question by answering. "Major Toyoda will deal with that problem. Our task is to speed up the progress of the railway into Burma."

Speaking in clear English, Toyoda replied: "Padre Hall and two R.A.M.C. medics are to remain with the sick. During the course of tomorrow, Japanese transport lorries now reaching this camp will return them to Tarsoe or further downriver to Chungkai!"

Before Captain Saunders could answer, Suzuki spoke again: "New arrivals from Singapore will take over this camp and also the Kanu Camps. As your march progresses north, men from other jungle camps upstream will be joining your column. At 208 jungle camp, there is a small team of medics with a surgeon in charge. They are also joining you and will assist with any medical problems. There can be no further discussion on the matter."

Abruptly the commandant barked out an order in Japanese. The guards immediately sprang to attention and bowed. Suzuki smartly saluted them, glared sullenly round the assembly, then dismissed the parade. As the prisoners left the dusty parade ground, a buzz of noisy conversation broke out.

Bill Slatoe's reaction was much the same as many others. "What a load of old bollocks!" he exclaimed. "Nothing ever changes." Dave Wandle, walking alongside Ed and Morrie, grimaced as Ed remarked: "Looks like another middle of the night start!"

Bill replied: "Like the rest of us, you don't have a choice, mate!"

Doug Pardy, walking with the group, had 'Happy feet', severe pain from dry beri-beri. "How's your plates of meat (feet)?" asked Dave.

"Bleedin' 'orrible", came the swift reply. "To think we've got to march more and more bastard miles in bare feet. Christ Almighty, will it ever bloodywell end?"

There was no answer to that!

Later in the evening, Captain Saunders held a series of short meetings with NCO's and men. There was much to discuss, and precious little time to confer. General agreement was quickly reached on the main objective: survival, to stay alive, somehow or other!

* * *

Back home in Melbourne, the newly qualified Don Saunders had, in a short space of time, established himself as a popular young doctor. He possessed all the right qualities, graduating with full honours. Tall, dark, goodlooking, a rugged all round Australian with clear blue eyes and a balanced sense of humour.

Although he was now looking a whole lot thinner and gaunt, he had proved himself a true leader of men. In times of stress, 'a bloody good doc' was how the POW's fondly referred to him.

Because of the events on Singapore island and at the camp at Kwai-Tanu, Ed Warton had developed a special kind of understanding with the captain. The question of rank had never arisen.The two men from different countries possessed a great deal of faith and respect in one another's ability.

Without ceremony, Ed managed to speak to the M.O. out of earshot of the others. It was quickly agreed that, as there was no longer a radio, he should now carry, in the special haversack sling, the small medicine chest with the cleverly concealed secret compartment which still contained five live hand grenades. It could also hold his hidden notes!

At the conclusion of the general discussions, the captain summed up: "Listen, blokes. All we can do is take one day at a time. Try not to do anything bloody stupid if you want to stay alive!" He gave a sheepish grin. "I guess we've all done stupid things in our time, but we know the score. There's no point in being a dead hero!"

The medical officer paused, and then continued: "Things look as if, I'm sorry to say, they will get worse with the monsoon season not far away. Get yourselves ready for the move out at dawn. Stick together, fellows." Again he smiled: "Specially for you Poms, as we say in good old Aussie, Give it a go, mates. Good night!" With that final remark, the officer disappeared in the direction of the hospital hut in order to conduct a last check on his patients.

The first light of dawn was just breaking when the guards commenced blowing their whistles, shouting and yelling in their usual manner to arouse everyone ready for 'tenko'. Many of the men crowded the hospital hut to bid goodbye to their mates. Foxy and Ed were among them. Sadly, only a very small number were destined ever to meet again!

Padre Hall, a short kindly man, who never really seemed to understand what was happening, shook hands solemnly with as many as possible. "Say one for me", bawled Dave Wandle. "I'm gonna bleedin' well need it!" The padre promised to pray for everyone though what bloody good that would do, Ed and Bill couldn't make out.

As the last of the men left for the parade ground, Captain Don Saunders stood in the centre of the squalid hospital hut to give a forced cheerful farewell to his patients. There were 210 very sick with a wide range of tropical diseases, plus 80 more in the ulcer hut, lying in agony.

"Goodbye and thanks, doc", they shouted. "Aw, c'mon you blokes, you'll be right", he replied. "You Pommie mates come on down to Aussie when this bloody war is over. Don't forget, now, guess I'll see the rest of you back home. Good luck, men!"

Feeling choked, he bent down and picked up his haversack of medical supplies, well aware that several of them would die before the day was over. Without a backward glance, he strode from the hospital hut for the last time towards the parade ground where he lined up with the mixed team of R.A.M.C. and Australian medics.

As daylight finally broke, all was ready. Camp commandant Suzuki, ever arrogant and evil, was already standing on the platform. After the customary counting and checking, followed by the traditional bowing, he returned the salute of Lieutenant Kokubo. In turn, orders were issued to the POW's to pick up their few belongings and march forward through the gates of Tonchan and into the jungle.

Atwai was a very unwilling and unhappy interpreter. He had protested in vain to Suzuki that he should be allowed to return to his native Bampong. Instead, he found himself marching alongside Captain Saunders and his medics to the rear of the long column.

Barefooted, almost silently, their path led them around the perimeter of the cemetery. As they filed past the entrance shrouded in the early morning mist, each man turned his head to the left in a final farewell to their sleeping comrades.

As they left Tonchan behind it was the fourth day of April 1943. Marching along the dirt track leading past the camp of Kanu in the direction of Kanu II, the miles seemed to get longer. The conversation grew less and less, petering out altogether as the golden haze of the morning sun turned into the burning tropical heat to which they had become accustomed.

Ed Warton felt the weight of the medical chest in the sling on his back growing heavier. Gritting his teeth, he consoled himself with the knowledge that the hand grenades and notes were still intact. Captain Saunders had warned him earlier of the risks involved. Being stubborn, he was adamant that this was what he wanted to do.

With few exceptions, the guards on this march were a fresh bunch who had been brought upriver by barge in order to escort the POW's further north.

*   *   *

Seven days later, as sundown approached, wearily moving like slow mechanical toys, the POW's entered the gates of Hintock camp, where they were to spend the night.

Although a much smaller camp, Hintock proved to be no better or worse than any of the other POW camps dotted along the banks of the river Kwai. The usual arrangements prevailed for feeding: boiled rice, jungle juice vegetables, and quantities of boiled water for drinking, for which the overnight arrivals were extremely grateful.

From the unhappy residents, a warm welcome was extended. Ed, Bill, Morrie and Foxy met up with a handful of Suffolks they knew. There was Les Ardwool from Woodham Ferrers, Smithy from Dagenham, as well as Joe Levy, a young Jewish lad from Hackney, and Chalky White from Yarmouth. The Diggers were also meeting up with lost mates from down under.

Prisoner of war news was rapidly exchanged. The joy of meeting up with old mates was overshadowed by shock and sadness on learning of the appalling deaths other comrades had suffered. The lads in Hintock were due to march north at dawn with the new arrivals.

Duly at sunrise, the enlarged column set forth again. A couple of miles on, Bill Slatoe informed Ed that by his bamboo stick calendar, he had figured out it was the twelfth day of April. "Happy birthday, Ed. All the best, mate!"

"Christ, I'm twenty three today. Bill. What a way to spend a birthday! Only too well, I remember what the bastards did to me on my twenty second!" he reflected as they marched on. "Wonder what's happening back in Southend right now? Perhaps they don't even know whether we're dead or alive?"

Bill half wished he hadn't brought the subject up. Ed was a sentimental sod. "Bet Ma Warton and the family won't forget your birthday, Ed", he added. Ed did not reply. For the next few miles, he marched in silence, his thoughts revolving around home. Every barefooted, painful step he took didn't seem to register. On and on they plodded, mile after mile! Suddenly, there was a shout which passed right down the line. "Yazume (Rest)" At last!

As one, the POW's slumped to the ground, exhausted and almost too tired to drink from their water bottles. Big Billy Foster found a shady spot to lie in, near to Dave Wandle and Russ Damoned. Billy took a large greedy swig from his water bottle, belching and farting violently at the same time. Dave Wandle was too tired to protest. The best he could manage was: "You're a stinking bleedin' pig. Why don't you sod off!"

Billy eyed Dave innocently before replying: "Cause I've got nowhere to go, mate" he grinned. "But, bloody oath, that sure feels better!"

A few yards away, there was a sudden shout of pain and fear, followed by a cry for help. One of the lads from the Norfolks had been bitten in the thigh by a deadly short snake, similar to the Indian or Malay krait. Two of the medics went to examine the leg to see if they could cauterize the bite area. It was too late. A vein had been punctured by the snake's fangs.

They called for Captain Saunders, who promptly arrived and examined the young man's thigh with a sinking heart. One of the many medical supplies they lacked was any form of anti-snake venom. In a flash, he knew that the victim had less then one hour to live!

Through Atwai, the medical officer explained the grim situation to Lieutenant Kokubo, who was in no mood for delays, whatever the reason. His reply was predictable. "Either he stays here, or you carry him" The M.O. realized from past bitter experience that it would be useless to argue with a Japanese officer. He appealed that the soldier had not long to live. Could he delay the column for a time?

Lt. Kokubo's reaction was swift. Whipping out his revolver, he cocked the catch. Ordering the medics to move away, he promptly and cold-bloodedly fired three shots directly into the stricken man. As they echoed strangely in the jungle, the horrified medical officer needed only a quick glance to confirm that the lad was dead. Amidst the stunned silence, Kokubo grimly announced: "Your problem is solved, Captain. Yazume is ended. All prisoners will march now!" The guards started to sound their whistles and shout their orders.

"Can we bury our comrade?" requested Captain Saunders.

Kokubo was enraged as he snarled: "I order all men march now. The vultures will take care of the body. March now!" he repeated, still waving his revolver towards the men.

Toughened as they had been by their many ordeals and privations at the hands of their vicious captors. the POW's still felt a sense of shock and outrage at this latest example of Japanese brutality. Silently, they gathered up their few belongings and marched forward as ordered. They were all bitterly aware that they could not strike back or argue with the rule of the gun, so vividly demonstrated.

Overhead in the clear blue sky loomed the vultures, screeching in anticipation of their prey. Hardly had the long winding column of tattered prisoners disappeared from sight when they swooped low to feast on the bloodied body of the murdered Briton.

*   *   *

Ten days more the prisoners had marched. Totally exhausted, they stumbled into POW Jungle camp 208, a few miles short of the notorious Brankassi camp. When they left again the following morning at dawn, they had been joined by the inmates of camp 208. With them were a British surgeon and four medics, who struggled to carry among other things, a large folded mosquito net, used as the basic cover for their makeshift operating theatre.

Major Ray Boone was the M.O. and hailed from Aldeburgh on the Suffolk coast. Barely thirty years old, he had joined the Territorials just before the war had broken out. Of medium height, slim build, with flaming red hair and bright blue eyes, he was a jovial type with a good sense of humour. Whenever he spoke, there was always a hint of Suffolk dialect, which became more pronounced when he swore about the Japanese!

Captain Don Saunders and his medics quickly teamed up with the British surgeon. It was a strange beginning to a friendship which was to survive the grim times ahead. They pooled their meagre medical supplies and marched together with the medics, assisting the sick along the way.

* * *

Several more days passed. The terrain became even more difficult. In the distance, a range of mountains stood out in stark contrast against the blue skies. Deep down in the valley, the river widened, running through a short series of rapids, as it continued to flow swiftly southwards. The dark green jungle vegetation remained as thick as ever, highlighting the brilliant colours of the wild, exotic and tropical flowers growing in abundance throughout the whole area.

At Tamajao 237, there was an overnight stay. In the morning, the column bypassed Tamajao 239 (the wood camp), heading between the mountains in the direction of Konkuita. At this stage, the POW's were now a distance of over 240 miles from Bampong. They marched on, passing a large filthy Tamil camp on their right.

Three miles further on, they rounded the foot of a mountain and could see the huge bamboo gates of what appeared to be a newly created POW camp, still a long way off. Carrying their sick comrades somehow, and stumbling, falling, and dragging one foot behind the other, the weary, exhausted and bedraggled column of prisoners approached the entrance of what, unbeknown to them at the time, proved to be their ultimate destination.

CHAPTER 10

Tamajao 241

This, then, was the grim jungle Japanese prisoner of war camp. Almost a replica of Tonchan, everything seemed to follow the familiar pattern, except for its enormous size. Well guarded on three sides, the fourth was bordered by the swift flowing river.

High above in their specially built tall bamboo guard huts, the machine gunners looked down as the long pathetic column approached and entered the open gates. It was the evening of May 4th, 1943. The sun was still hot and the atmosphere humid. The rainy season was but three weeks away!

The new arrivals were marched to a vast dusty parade ground, along one side of which stood the specially constructed and well built officers' huts. In front of these was the inevitable Japanese camp commandant's platform complete with hand rail and a bamboo pole. Atop of this fluttered the Japanese flag.

The POW's later learned that Tamil labourers from the camp they had passed on their forced march had been brought upcountry by barges a few weeks earlier in order to prepare the site as the basis of a new POW camp. Despite what had been achieved the camp, as yet, was less than half constructed. There was still much work to be carried out.

A prolonged whistle sounded, bringing silence. Captain Suzuki, followed by Major Toyoda, walked briskly from the hut, looking cool and refreshed in clean white open necked shirts and smart officers' uniforms. They climbed the four steps to stand on the platform. Atwai, the interpreter, pushed his way forward to the front rank, but Toyoda indicated that his presence was not required on this occasion!

The camp commandant addressed the POW's, translated by Major Toyoda. "Now you have arrived this camp will be known as Tamajao 241. We are not many kilometers from the Burma border. You can see there is much work to be carried out to complete the camp. Tomorrow morning at 'tenko', you will be divided up into work parties and given different tasks." Suzuki paused, looking round for a moment at his large weary audience, then continued: "Priority work will, of course, be the railway. There must be no delays! You may now rest. Eat the rice that has been prepared by the Japanese cookhouse staff. Your own cooks will build and operate your cookhouse in the morning."

Captain Suzuki then turned to address the medical section standing to one side, headed by Major Ray Boone and Captain Don Saunders. "The two medical officers and their staff will find a new hospital on the far west of the camp. This is still in the process of construction. You will occupy the building tonight and then tomorrow assist in its completion. More POW's will be arriving in the next few days from other camps downriver. I understand that there will be a padre among them, an Australian. For the moment, that is all. Our glorious army is continuing its wonderful victories in Burma. Long live the Emperor. Parade dismiss!"

In the chaotic conditions of the new camp the remarks of the prisoners followed a by now predictable pattern. Absolute weariness had, however, taken, its toll. For most it was enough to grab the meagre ration of boiled rice, drink their boiled water and collapse on the hard ground, exhausted beyond belief. Morrie, Bill, Ed, and Foxy were soon sleeping the uncomfortable sleep of those in captivity.

That night, Ed dreamed of his home in Southend. He was walking in the grounds of the local Southchurch Park. It was springtime; by a footbridge over a lake, he paused to look at the beautiful flowerbeds of tulips and daffodils. The sun was shining in the blue sky and over the other side of the footbridge he could see a pretty young woman he knew. She waved, laughed and began to cross the bridge to meet him.

Suddenly the whole scene vanished. He awoke with a start. Cold and disappointed, he realised that he had been dreaming. That's all it had been, a brief beautiful dream. An escape from the living hell of the prison camp! Uncomfortably, he pulled up the rice sack that was covering his cold bare feet and legs. Amidst the snoring of his mates, he rolled over and fell into another restless sleep.

The two medical officers and their teams of medics looked aghast at the new hospital, referred to by Suzuki. In actual fact, it was merely another hut, with attap roof and sides, except that it was some 160 feet in length, 14 feet wide, but more to the point only half built! Although they themselves were completely exhausted, they tended the many sick, who had fallen along the wayside during the nightmare journey and had just made it into camp with the help of their comrades. Finally, they settled down to rest. Tomorrow there would be another long day ahead.

*　　*　　*

Ten days later, the camp hut building programme had been completed. There were now two hospital huts able to accommodate over three hundred sick. Each hut comprised a number of two foot high bamboo platforms in bays of six. A special annexe had been constructed for ulcer patients, which was in reality just a third bamboo hut complete with attap roof and sides, boasting the luxury of an extremely large mosquito net, beneath which stood the makeshift operating table.

This was simply a very uncomfortable bamboo platform, on which the helpless patients had to lie. They often had to be strapped down tight, due to lack of any anaesthetic whilst being operated on by Major Boone, who performed the many amputations of limbs daily!.

The Allied POW cookhouse had been quickly established high on the banks of the river. A distance of two hundred yards separated it from the Japanese one, and between the two a narrow dirt road had been cleared leading down to the river, to facilitate the unloading of the supply barges which tied up there regularly.

The usual slit trenches for latrines had been dug to a considerable depth, and within hours were seething with fat white maggots. The pride of place went to the newly created urinals, dreamed up by Joe Pithey, who back home had worked for the urban council. These consisted of one upright hollow bamboo pole about six inches in diameter, and around three to four feet in height with a special rounded out section at the top into which to direct the stream of urine.

These numerous smelly poles stuck in the ground always attracted millions of flies, but soon became popularly known as pissaphones. In turn, this created a new sport called 'Direct hit'. Competition was fierce as the competitors directed their choppers at the correct angle and aimed. The winner out of six was the fellow who could successfully urinate directly into the rounded out section without touching the sides. There were no prizes, only roars of laughter. Foxy stayed champion for a long time.

* * *

He reckoned that when he was a boy of twelve at the local village school he had plenty of practice, because the urinal the boys used had no roof and the kids would take it in turn during the dinner break to see who could urinate the highest. Boasting the biggest weapon in the school, he was invariably the winner.

Despite his local fame, Foxy sadly recalled the day when he proudly broke all records and successfully went right over the top of the urinal wall to the wild cheers of his school chums. Unfortunately for him, the headmaster, one bald-headed Hector Cecil Thomas, was passing close by at that precise moment. To his surprise and horror, a mighty hot spray descended on his very bald head and ran down his neck!

Being completely devoid of any sense of humour, the headmaster had caned Foxy until the cane broke in his hand. By then, he had so many weals on his behind that it was several weeks before he could comfortably sit down again. It was small wonder that Foxy held the Tamajao pissaphone championship for the year 1943.

* * *

Outside the camp gates across a new dirt road one hundred yards to the left, in the shadow of the mountain was the cemetery of Tamajao. The thick jungle vegetation had been cut back and the site cleared to allow for the ever increasing number of dead POW's to be buried in neat rows with crude wooden crosses, from which hung their identity discs. On average, twenty a day were being laid to rest before the rains and cholera struck.

The very Reverend Mick Schofield had arrived with a new intake. A middle aged Australian volunteer from Toowoomba in Queensland, he quickly took up his many duties as camp padre: praying for the dying, conducting daily funerals, and comforting those many sick who requested his assistance.

Rev. Mick was a plain spoken likeable character, who would steal from the Japs without batting an eyelid. He would swear with the best and often did. Not in any way religious themselves, the Southend lads would admire and laugh at the antics that the padre performed.

He reminded Ed and Morrie of the pre-war preacher on Southend seafront, 'Happy Harry', a real character who would finish every short sermon with the hymn: 'Bringing in the sheaves, bringing in the sheaves, we shall come rejoicing, bringing in the sheaves', at the same time as his little old lady assistant would be going round with the collection bag for the offering from the listening public. As soon as the hymn had finished, Happy Harry would shout excitedly, pick up the collection bag, and rush for the nearest pub to refresh himself.

In some ways, there was a striking likeness between the two. The result was that as the word got around the camp, the Very Reverend Mick from Toowoomba quickly became 'Happy Harry' from Tamajao.

From downcountry, more POW's had arrived to swell the numbers. At one time it was estimated that the camp contained over fourteen thousand Allied prisoners of war, predominantly British and Australian.

News filtered through to the prisoners that an embankment had slipped as the first train had reached Tarsoe, and wrecked the track. This caused the unfortunate POW's in that sector to work in sixteen hour shifts so that the line could be restored.

The nearby Tamil camp held several thousand natives. In addition, they had set up two more new camps about a mile down the track from Tamajao.

Out on the railway, progress was fast. Jap engineers were busy blasting cuttings through deep yellow rock formations, whilst thousands of POW's slaved on the many and varied tasks. Apart from the daily beatings for not working hard enough, there were always other casualties. Crushed fingers and hands as well as the many painful and jagged cuts on legs and arms, caused by sharp splintered flints which spun off the sledge hammers and drills. For these wounds there were no bandages or cures. In a short space of time most of these injuries would fester into tropical ulcers, rapidly becoming extremely painful and dangerous!

Many of the familiar enemies from other camps were on the railway line daily, among them Sergeant Yamanoto (the Pig), Korean Kaneshiro (the Undertaker), Korean Chiba, and several others. In addition there was a large number of fresh guards who, in every way were equally as cruel, brutal and inhumane. Intense hatred and brutality were always the order of the day. Death was the only final escape! Small wonder that many POW's lost their reason and in some cases committed suicide by leaping off the cliffs and crashing to a welcome death on the rocks below.

One young lad, suffering acute agony from leg ulcers, hobbled with the aid of a stick to a large bonfire. To the horror of the onlookers, he hurled himself into the centre of the inferno to die, in a rapid and bizarre manner. Someone remarked:

"What a bloody way to go, but at least he's out of his misery!"

Dave Wandle, the lad from Millwall, found himself in the ulcer hut alongside a Jewish lad, Nat Ruben, from Bethnal Green. They soon became pals, and had much in common as Dave said cheerfully: "You'd know a bleedin' Londoner anywhere in the world, mate."

Dave had an ugly gaping ulcer, resulting from a kick in the shin from Kaneshiro's hobnail boot. Nat Ruben had two rock flint cuts which had struck like shrapnel, opening his left leg to the bone. That also had turned into a giant ulcer and was causing intense pain and distress.

Every night, when all other work was finished, Ed, Bill, Morrie, and Foxy would visit their mates in the hospital hut and the ulcer annexe. Despite their own sufferings, the four lads would volunteer to carry up cans of water from the river to be boiled outside the hut. When cooled sufficiently, this was then used with a minute quantity of stolen salt to help cleanse the stinking ulcers of pus, after they had been scraped clean by the medics, using a small kind of tablespoon.

Often the lads would help hold down a patient during this extremely painful and terrifying ordeal. With the greatest courage, they suffered the burning pains which were almost indescribable. The dressing was old bits of cloth or tattered wornout bandages, which had been washed and boiled a thousand times. Quite often, all that could be provided were large banana leaves tied on with raffia twine in a desperate attempt to keep the flies off!

One evening about a week before the monsoon, Morrie confided to his three mates that he had learned, through the bamboo grapevine, that of all things the camp commandant was having certain livestock brought upriver to supplement the Japanese rations. There were wild pigs, yaks, cows and chickens, which were going to be placed in a specially built stockade close to the camp's eastern boundary. The gang of four quickly decided that a reconnaissance was necessary without delay.

The same night after the camp bonfires had been lit, the lads set out to assess the situation. They had decided that the only safe route would be down by the river bank. Cautiously, they set off. Ten minutes later they had made it safely out of the camp and were following a narrow jungle path, which led them to the outskirts of the stockade.

Excitedly, in the bright tropical moonlight, they counted ten yaks (oxen), four cows, twenty fat pigs, and numerous chickens. There was no-one on guard at all. The four starving POW's gazed in awe. Here at last was food! Real live bloody food! Morrie whispered nervously: "Now we know. Let's withdraw and make plans to rob the bastards without getting caught!"

Stealthily and quietly they returned via the jungle path to the river bank, where they managed safely to re-enter Tamajao. The next hour was spent discussing and weighing up the possibilities of how to steal some of Suzuki's livestock and escape without getting caught. Finally, they agreed on a plan of action to be put into operation twenty four hours later.

The next evening, Bill kept a lookout whilst Ed hastily updated his notes on stolen Japanese paper. Carefully, he returned them in the small metal box to the hole in the ground below where he lay. Covering well with loose soil, he then spread out a rice sack, on which he placed his old army haversack, as well as his water bottle - an extremely uncomfortable pillow - so as to hide all trace of the hole. Like all the other lads, Ed had another flea-ridden rice sack to cover over himself, since the Thailand jungle had proved to be a very cold place at night!

Later in the evening, the four men started out, avoiding the areas lit by bonfires. They had armed themselves with two Japanese spades and a sledge hammer stolen from one of the two small tools stores situated in one corner of the large camp, which surprisingly had been unguarded at that stage. Dangling from Foxy's waist on a thin strip of rope, courtesy of the railway engineers' survey group, was a long bladed and dangerous looking knife, nicked by a clever ruse from the Japanese cookhouse. It was neatly sheathed between two flat thin pieces of wood with a convenient small hole drilled in the handle. With surprising speed, they made their exit from the camp via the riverbank as on the previous night, taking the same jungle path. After a few minutes, they arrived at the edge of the animal stockade. There was not a guard in sight, which proved to be an excellent situation. A few yards from the boundary, the four prisoners took it in turns, as frantically they dug a large hole in the ground two feet below the surface.

"That'll do", Ed whispered. "OK, fellows, in we go for the kill!"

Crawling on their bellies beneath a hollow in the ground underneath the thicket hedge, all four emerged safely inside the stockade.

They were glad of the brilliant moonlight on this occasion. To their utter amazement, standing quite motionless swinging his tail right beside the spot they had emerged from, stood one of Suzuki's ten yaks. In a flash, Ed knew what he had to do. There was no margin for mistakes. Gripping the sledge hammer tightly, and holding a deep breath momentarily, he swung the hammer through the night air to land an almighty crushing blow between the eyes of the yak. The animal heeled over unconscious without even a murmur.

Swiftly all four went into action, dragging the beast below the hedge over to the newly dug hole. He fitted into it beautifully! Knife in hand, and using all his country expertise, Foxy knelt down and neatly slit the yak's throat at the vital spot. He watched the blood gush out into the soil for a short period. "OK, lads", said Foxy quietly, "he's well dead. Let's get him covered over with dirt and camouflaged before the bastards get searching!"

It was a matter of minutes before the yak completely disappeared from sight, well covered with jungle soil and vegetation. So far, so good, thought Ed and Bill, when Foxy whispered: "Hang on a bloody minute." He again disappeared into the stockade, only to reappear in less then three minutes, much to the relief of the others. He was proudly waving two dead chickens.

"Christ Almighty", uttered Bill. "That was bloody quick!"

Foxy grinned. He had no trouble killing chickens. The only problem was, as Dave would say, "Where to bleedin' well find 'em."

Foxy carefully replaced his knife in its sheath. Ed carried the sledge hammer, Bill and Morrie a spade each. Quietly they retraced their steps along the narrow track to the river bank.

Before they emerged from the thicket, they observed two Jap guards talking and smoking at the foot of the dirt track leading uphill into the camp. Ed signalled for the lads to stay low. Foxy crept a few yards away unseen, but closer to the Japs. He cupped his mouth with both hands and let forth a very realistic imitation of a tiger growling. It worked fast as the delighted POW's observed the two guards beating a hasty retreat up the hill.

After that it was a matter of minutes before they were all safely back in their own hut. The two chickens were plucked and gutted with astonishing speed, the waste being disposed of on the bonfire. One hour or so later, four starving POW's were making short work of Suzuki's two chickens. It had been a good night's work in Tamajao!

The next day, as predicted, the guards made a systematic search throughout the camp for Suzuki's yak. Many questions were asked. The only suggestion that the puzzled POW's could make was that, presumably the yak must have escaped from the stockade on its own accord and got lost in the jungle.

* * *

Three days had passed and the matter had died down. It was only then that the four lads commenced nightly raids to their secret hiding place, bringing back a different joint on each occasion. After carefully washing the meat in the river all went well. Nothing was wasted and a fair proportion was distributed among their sick mates.

On the first day of June Ed, Morrie, Bill and Foxy were hard at work with thousands of others on a new embankment about one mile north of Tamajao. It was late afternoon, many beatings had taken place, the mood and temper of the guards indicated that something was wrong.

Suddenly, as if a miracle had been created, the intense heat of the blazing tropical sun was blotted out. In the distance the sky looked black. There was an uneasy and strangely chilling atmosphere in the air!

There was a shout from a Jap machine gunner perched high up on a bank of earth. As the prisoners of war looked down the valley across the broad river, in the distance they could see what appeared to be a dark wall rapidly approaching. In seconds, it had arrived. The sunshine of Thailand was completely blotted out and the tropical rains poured down in their fury. All hell broke loose.

The monsoon season had arrived.....

CHAPTER 11

Monsoon and Cholera

By the time the railway work parties paddled back to Tamajao in the ice cold torrential downpour, the jungle tracks and paths had become a morass of mud. In bare feet, the prisoners found the going slippery and tough.

Back in the camp, the returning workers had to report to the Japanese guardroom. Once there, to their complete surprise, each man was issued with an old British army type gas cape, doubtless from captured British stores in Malaya. The capes had obviously seen much better days, but still, anything was better than nothing. There were, however, no capes issued to the sick and the other residents of the camp.

On the other hand, the Japanese and Koreans were well kitted out in waterproofs and rubber Wellington boots. In addition, a neat row of fourteen waterproofed tents had been miraculously erected that afternoon, well to the rear of the camp commandant's hut. These were, of course, not to look after the luckless prisoners of war, but solely for the purpose of protecting the guards.

The two Allied medical officers had sought a meeting with Major Toyoda, and through him had protested in the strongest possible terms to the camp commandant about the appalling lack of medical supplies. They had pointed out the imminent danger of cholera and the urgent need for vaccines and protective clothing for all the POW's.

In effect, Captain Suzuki's final and totally predictable answer came as no surprise to the Allied officers.

"At the present time, there can be no additional medical supplies or anything else for that matter. Every item is needed and must be sent to the brave Nippon troops fighting in Burma!"

In conclusion, the commandant wished to make it quite clear that, despite the monsoon, Japanese engineers and soldiers would continue to work on the railway as normal.

"There must be no delays and all prisoners of war will also carry on working daily on the railway line. Those reporting sick will only receive half rations of rice, and some will die! OK-ka. There are plenty more prisoners to take their place!"

As far as Suzuki was concerned, that was the end of the matter!

The untold misery that followed was unbelievable. All the while it rained and rained. It was always raining! The men went to sleep wet! In the darkness at 6 o'clock each morning, they would slither to the nearest maggot-filled and overflowing latrine to empty their bowels. From there, they would line up at the cookhouse to receive their morning dollop of soggy rice. Sometimes, as an alternative, it had been ground down into a vile mess of rice pap, with a terrible taste. A mug of boiled water was issued at the same time, and the army water bottle was also filled ready for work.

Breakfast over, they would then report to the muddy parade ground to be counted, checked and divided into various work parties. After this, tools would have to be drawn from the Jap stores before the prisoners began their unhappy way to the railway site, slipping and sliding through the mud.

Once there, they were met by Japanese engineers and allocated their tasks for the day. This usually involved hard, demanding, and often dangerous work, particularly if they were directed to bridge building.

Despite the tropical rains, the construction of the line continued relentlessly. There was no let up. Backbreaking tasks became increasingly more difficult, due to the mass of sticky mud, where once there had been light soil to dig. No longer did anyone pay attention to the daily and hourly beatings. It was only if an unfortunate prisoner suffered broken limbs or was rendered unconscious that the other POW's bothered to take any notice. This was not out of any callousness on their part but was born out of the sheer hell and misery of their daily efforts.

The river curved around the side of the mountain thus causing another all wooden bridge to be built. It was now in an advanced stage: the giant teak upright poles had been hauled to the edge of the river, using Thai elephants. From then on, these poles were manhandled into position by POW's using stout ropes and chains with crude block, tackle and pulley equipment, then pile driven from above by other gangs. When this had been done and the uprights were in place, they were firmly secured by a maze of criss-cross supports.

Across the top of the uprights was built a rough wooden jointed surface which would eventually hold the sleepers. The last stage was the laying and spiking of the rails themselves.

Under normal conditions, such difficult bridge building would have proved a daunting and dangerous task. With the almost nonstop rainfall, the whole project became a nightmare. Sixty or seventy feet high above the rocks and the torrential rushing waters of the river, daily the fantastic semi-circular wooden monster grew. It seemed to clutch hold tightly to the side of the craggy limestone mountain, almost as if afraid to let go!

Working on top in bare slippery feet or crossing over with nothing to hold on to was a nerve racking business. Seven prisoners of war had already slipped, instantly plunging to their death on the rocks below. The only reaction from the

Japs being: "Speedo, speedo, plenty more men!".

About mid-day, the rain stopped for a while and the guards then ordered a yazume for dinner break. Escorted by two armed guards, four POW's had just returned from the camp cookhouse with the men's rations. This consisted of hot boiled rice in several huge metal dixie pots hanging from poles slung from the shoulders of the struggling POW's.

Their bodies filthy dirty and glistening with sweat, many covered in sores or jungle ringworm, the young men wearily lined up for their totally inadequate and pitiful ration. No-one complained, no-one seemed to care anymore, as they hungrily devoured the precious rice. Without warning, the skies opened up and the rain poured down again in all its fury. It continued to rain nonstop for the next 24 hours!

Ed and Bill had been working on the bridge that day. Foxy and Morrie had been with a different party, building a new embankment further up the line. In the evening, they met up again by the weak flickering glow of the half coconut oil lamps, dotted around the bamboo dishing-up table in the cookhouse. The meal of the day was, as ever, soggy rice, a ladleful of jungle juice and boiled water to wash it down.

Despite their own misery, after eating and washing in the swollen river, the four made their way to the hospital annexe to visit Dave Wandle and Nat Ruben in the evil smelling ulcer hut. Dave's leg was extremely painful and clearly getting worse, Nat however appeared to be improving.

Conversation was sparse. What the hell was there to talk about? The lads spent an hour trying in vain to cheer up their sick mates, during which time two more men died in the hut.

"Fuckin 'ell", groaned Dave. "I begin to fink those poor bastards are better off out of it all. Me bleedin' leg, it hurts like bloody 'ell!" No-one answered.

In the darkness and in an unhappy silence, they returned to their leaky attap hut, accompanied only by the ceaseless chant of millions of bullfrogs.

Since the start of the rains, in an endeavour to get off the smelly wet ground, the POW's had made up platforms on which they slept. Wearily, they climbed up on to their bed spaces, pulling the damp rice sacks over their bodies in a vain effort to keep warm and sleep.

By this stage this was inevitably the restless haunted sleep of the semi-starved, sick and physically exhausted!

* * *

Another three weeks of unending rain had passed. Many more of their comrades had died. More unfortunate prisoners fresh up from Singapore, known as 'F' force, had passed through Tamajao. These were followed by 'H' force. On their terrible march even further north into Burma, these men were horrified and frightened at the sight of the travesties of the men they met. Little did they realise that, within a very short space of time, they were destined to become the same skeletons that they now felt pity for!

One morning during the fourth week of the rains, something seemed amiss. At 'tenko', the Japs and Koreans appeared subdued and uneasy. It wasn't long before the POW's discovered what was wrong. Hastily, four special parties were made up, each comprising six POW's and two armed guards. At the stores, they were issued with spades and chungkals (digging tool), and then marched out of camp, bare footed and soaking wet.

Koreans Kaneshiro and Okawa were in charge of the first party, made up of two Australians, Sergeant Reg Farqual and Bluey Johnson, Ed, Bill, Morrie and Foxy. Once outside the camp gates, the party was led in the opposite direction from the railway, down the muddy road towards the Tamil camp. As they neared the entrance, the reason the Japs were uneasy became abundantly clear. Across the road in a small stream which ran out of the side of the camp, five Tamil natives were lying dead in various positions.

The two Koreans hung well back. "Christ Almighty!" muttered Bill. "What the hell is this?" he demanded glaring at the guards.

Suddenly, it dawned on them that the dreaded disease had arrived. "I'll tell you what it is mate" announced Bluey Johnson "It's cholera. Bloody oath, that's what it is!" The shocked burial party looked hard at each other. No-one spoke. Each man had despair in his eyes!

Shouting and waving their guns, the two evil Koreans indicated that the party should start digging a large communal grave. They set to work beside the mud road, taking out an area about 12 feet square. All the guards would allow was a depth of two feet or so. Then came the grim task of removing the bodies from where they were lying in the stream and placing them in the grave.

The Koreans prevented the men filling in the shallow grave until they had completed a search of the immediate vicinity for other Tamils. Apparently, when the pains had struck their stomachs, the natives had run in sheer panic and terror into the jungle to die alone. A rapid and horrible death! As they searched, and despite the rain, overhead flew the ever watchful vultures, banking and wheeling in large circles waiting to swoop on the human flesh!

Fifty yards or so into the jungle, the burial party found three more natives. One was already dead, the other two were foaming at their mouths in the last throes of death. They looked a frightful and hideous sight, their large eyes staring, bulging almost out of their sockets in fear. The two guards shouted and motioned for the burial party to remove them into the nearby open grave. Reluctantly they carried the bodies, placing the two they thought were still alive on top of the others.

Suddenly to their horror, the two Tamils struggled weakly to sit upright in the shallow watery grave. Clearly, they were still alive. Korean Kaneshiro yelled "Speedo, speedo", indicating that the men should now fill in the grave.

"Not soddin' likely!" shouted a defiant Ed "They're still alive!". The other men in the burial party stared fixedly as though mesmerised.

Bill Slatoe glared through the rain at the Korean. "Neika (No)", he shouted. "They're not dead yet, you wicked bastard!"

Kaneshiro's face blackened. He was enraged, but obviously very scared of cholera. He rushed forward, snatching the spade out of Ed's hands. The men were then forced to witness a sickening spectacle as he swiftly and mercilessly battered the heads of the two natives. In seconds they fell back, brutally murdered.

"All men speedo, speedo, I speak", he raged. Silently, the burial party began to cover the sodden earth over the corpses. As the rain beat down, it washed some of the mud away forming a ghastly and grotesque sight. There were two more similar burials that day before the party returned to Tamajao. As they left, the vultures began to dive ....

* * *

There was a lull in the rain for a couple of hours. This enabled the men to wash the filth from their bodies in the swollen river, using the mud in place of soap. In case of cholera germs, they took great care not to drink any of the water. After the usual rice ration session, they all went over to the hospital hut to report the details of the day's events to Captain Saunders, who was not unduly surprised. He had long since come to terms with the brutality and inhumanity of the enemy.

The medical officer informed them that, whilst they had been out working, there had been a new intake of 500 white Dutch prisoners of war. With a senior medical officer in charge, Major van Gazell, they were originally from Java and Sumatra. Apparently, they had been brought in from a camp near Niki-Niki. Fifty per cent of them had already died from tropical diseases. They were busy building new huts in the eastern section of Tamajao, which rapidly became known as: 'New Amsterdam'.

On arrival, they had brought alarming reports of outbreaks of cholera. There had been many deaths in the camps to the north. Cremations had been necessary to prevent any further spread of the dreadful disease, which strikes without warning in the guts of man, causing dreadful pain followed by violent vomiting as flesh shrinks visibly from the bones. Without medical aid, nothing can really be done to help the unfortunate victims. The result is invariably a quick death.

Within a few miles of Tamajao camp, only a tiny handful of survivors from cholera lived to tell the story!

* * *

Two days later, one of the young Dutchman became the first at Tamajao camp to die of cholera, swiftly followed by seven British, five Australians and two Americans. It was a black situation which had taken a turn for the worse. Outside the camp gates beyond the fast growing cemetery, a special area of jungle was cleared for the bonfires which would glow nightly as the bodies were cremated.

There were no bugle calls and no burial rites! The pitiful bodies were just picked up and hurled into the flames like bundles of sticks. Several of the pall bearers also picked up the infection and within 24 hours were themselves being cremated.

In the distance, other fires could be seen through the darkness of the night at camps wherever cholera was present. The death toll rose at an alarming rate. Still it continued to rain through until early September when the monsoon petered out and the warmth of the tropical sun returned to the jungle of Thailand.

The thick green vegetation grew again at a staggering speed. The animals seemed to come alive. Rare wild exotic white orchids bloomed along with many other multi-coloured flowers, which seemed unreal in their fragile beauty against a background of vivid dark green. Birds and butterflies reappeared as if by magic. Life, after the long rains, was once again returning.

When the Allied prisoners of war were captured early in 1942, they were fine young healthy men, one hundred per cent physically fit. They were aptly described as the cream of the nation, a fighting force to be proud of.

By September 1943, most of the survivors looked almost unrecognisable. Skeletonlike, they were reduced to relics of humanity, with bones protruding through parched skins, hollow cheeks and socketlike sunken eyes. Most of them now weighed no more than seven stone, and were suffering from all kinds of tropical diseases. Although still alive, it was with despair and heavy hearts that the prisoners reached mid September.

*　　　*　　　*

Ed and Bill had been down with malaria and amoebic dysentery a number of times. Foxy and Morrie had suffered just as badly but at least they were all still alive.The art of survival and the will to live still burned deep within them. In various forms, they all had leg ulcers.

Sadly, so many of their mates had died. Dave Wandle, the lad from Millwall, was happily still alive, however. Although in a bad way with his giant sized ulcer, amazingly even at this stage he still retained his marvellous cockney sense of humour.

Nat Ruben had been very ill, but was now back working on the line. His leg ulcer had fortunately healed. Dave badly missed his mate from London in the ulcer hut, but Nat and the other lads would visit him regularly to cheer him up.

Full of hope for the future, Morrie from Westcliff and Nat, from Bethnal Green, would spend much time discussing ways of making their fortune back in the U.K. Bill and Ed reckoned the only way they would ever get any money was by robbing a bank. Foxy never agreed with any of them on the subject of money.

"Wanna' do what I do, boy", he would say in his likeable Suffolk way. "Work on the farm, lads. Be happy and healthy, with plenty of good country grub and a glass of beer. Can't wait to get back to it all", he would add wistfully.

"For Christ's sake, don't talk about grub!" pleaded Bill. "But we'll all come up to Suffolk, mate, after this bloody war's over, and eat all the good grub you talk about!"

*　　　*　　　*

Out on the railway, the first train had reached Tamajao across the almighty wooden bridge curved round the side of the mountain at the edge of the river. The bridge had creaked and groaned under the enormous weight that it bore. To the wonder and amazement of the POW's, it held as the train, overloaded with Japanese troops, had trundled over. Once across the other side, these troops promptly detrained and had to finish their journey to Burma overland, since as yet the railway was not completed.

Two miles inland from Tamajao, and linked by dirt roads from south to north, the enemy had built a vast transport camp, which housed hundreds of Japanese and Korean troops. Half a mile down river to the south, six new railway sidings had been built so that once the railway line was in operation, military trains could carry troops, ammunition and other supplies up to Burma and on the way back accommodate the Japanese wounded.

Now the weather had changed, Captain Suzuki resumed the daily 'tenko' and used the familiar platform for his rantings as before. It was during one of these unpleasant sessions that the POW's learned that the railway was scheduled for completion in October. If that came to pass, what then? No-one could possibly know the answer to that question in advance.

The camp commandant, having been bribed again, had consented to Thai traders resuming their business from the river barges in the evenings. Japanese and Koreans had first choice, after which the POW's were able, under the watchful eyes of armed guards, to negotiate and purchase any goods, provided they still had money.

Morrie quickly made good use of the situation, using some of the money he had carefully hidden away. Once again, he was able to haggle, which he loved to do. Taking shrewd stock of the potential for business and in the light of his previous experiences, he purchased duck eggs, brown sugar and fruit, which he readily shared with his mates. Morrie's only real stumbling block was the lack of supplies. Unexpectedly luck was on his side, when he discovered that the new Japanese sergeant, in sole charge of the cookhouse and stores, was none other than the former Corporal Chida who had recently been promoted.

They had previously met in the camp way back in Bampong, where business had been carried out before. Sergeant Chida had put on a lot of weight and Morrie had become horribly thin, nevertheless they immediately recognised each other, Chida was easily one of the most dishonest Japanese around. A quick furtive deal was struck and Morrie was soon back selling hot sweet tea and occasionally coffee, happily nicked from the Japanese stores.

Most of the business was transacted in the late evenings. Nat was enlisted to help Morrie promote sales, and things were looking up for them. Ed, Foxy and Bill carried out some hair raising raids at night on Suzuki's private farm. His chickens tasted much better than the usual rats, lizards, snakes and other wild stock. On pieces of curved tin or steel scrounged from the Japs, the POW's had long since learned how to make and fry rice rissoles or dovers in coconut oil, also nicked from the Japs. At least, it helped to vary the menu a little.

Ed and Bill had been on the ration run several times, making contact with the secret agent Ayut. He helped the POW's in many different ways, especially with drugs for the very sick. Also, he was able to pass on a lot of useful information about the movement of enemy troops and supplies. By this means they learnt that four barges, fully loaded with ammunition, were being towed up river. Led by a powerful motorised army barge, this convoy was scheduled to pass near the Tamajao camp area around midnight in two days time, en route for the Three Pagoda Pass, beyond which lay Burma!

Ed, Bill and Foxy discussed the vital information in detail and were in complete agreement that there was nothing they would like better than to have a go at the ammo barges. They formed a plan. Of necessity this was a plan full of danger. The other three felt it best not to inform Morrie of their daring scheme, mainly because he had a heart of pure gold and was already taking considerable risks in his own way with the business. Morrie had more than enough to worry about and so the other conspirators agreed to tell him afterwards. That way, they would not add to his concern.

After all they had been through, was it worth the risk? Strangely the question didn't arise. Each man justifiably hated the enemy to such an extent that, in any way that they could, they would take the slightest opportunity to hinder, wound, or even kill him.

In the event, there were only twenty four hours in which to prepare and take action......!

CHAPTER 12

Sabotage

Late into the night, the three men thrashed out the plan. They agreed that the five hand grenades the medics had safely hidden away would not be safe to use, because of the danger of immediate flying shrapnel. There was not sufficient hard tree shelter on the edge of the water, only soft undergrowth. So there was no point in offering the plan to Captain Saunders, who had more than enough problems with the sick and the dying. It was finally decided they would take their chance and go it alone.

The question of how to obtain and use explosives was discussed in detail. The POW's were well aware of the position of the dump used daily by the Japanese engineers. This was situated less then 500 yards beyond the northern boundary of Tamajao.

From every day experiences lugging heavy boxes of dynamite, guncotton and other explosives to and from rock blasting sections of the railway route, they knew exactly the spot and which jungle path to take in order to reach the dump. The problem was undoubtedly it would be guarded. The barges were due at midnight 24 hours later!

There was no time to lose. One hour after midnight, the three men crept silently from their attap hut, moving in the direction of the river. The dying embers of the nightly bonfires still glowed as they moved swiftly past. Five minutes later, they were padding along the edge of the river bank. There was no guard in sight as they escaped safely beyond the northern boundary.

Stealthily, they made their way forward down the twisting jungle path towards the dump. The earth beneath their bare feet felt cold and clammy. Foxy was carrying his ever-sharp killer knife at the ready in case of emergencies. Ed had earlier spent hours making a belt and carrier bag out of raffia, which he was now wearing. In his hand he carried a three foot length of light tough rope, which he had managed to acquire from the Jap engineers. If things went wrong and the situation warranted it, he might just have to use it round an enemy soldier's throat! Bill was carrying a knife also, by courtesy of the Jap cookhouse.

Hopefully, it had not been missed!

Each man was silent and tense. The brilliant rays of the tropical moonlight filtered through the thick undergrowth, forming strange eerie and uncanny patterns. The only noises came from the nocturnal animals of the jungle, who never sleep, as well as the ceaseless chant of the bullfrogs.

As they approached the large attap hut which housed the explosives, in the distance they could just see two lighted cigarettes glowing in the darkness. The men crept closer and clearly observed two armed Jap guards, smoking and talking idly. According to the pre-arranged plan, Foxy moved through the undergrowth to the right in front of the hut. Well concealed, Ed and Bill moved in as close as possible to the edge of the clearing. They lay on their bellies, breathing hard and waiting. It looked like a twenty yard dash across to the back of the dump.

Suddenly, the night air was shattered by three loud roars and a growl, uncannily resembling a wild tiger, coming from somewhere in the direction of the front of the hut to the right. Foxy was performing brilliantly. The guards were alarmed. Hastily they stubbed out their fags and looked uneasily in the direction of the noise. Two more loud roars ripped forth, causing the two Japs to run quickly to the front of the dump. Ed touched Bill's hand to signal he was going forward. Swift as an arrow, he covered the twenty yards to the back of the hut. Lifting up a section of the light attap covering, he disappeared inside.

As he waited, Bill Slatoe gripped the knife in his hand firmly. The seconds ticked away slowly. Each one seeming like an hour, but in point of fact it was a little over a minute. Ed knew what he was after and exactly where it was in the dark. Meanwhile, Foxy had backed off from where he started and let forth another roar. One of the guards cocked his rifle, looking uneasily towards where Foxy was lying. He could see the two guards silhouetted against the moonlight quite clearly. He realised that at any second they would panic and fire. He rapidly withdrew further back into the undergrowth, preparing to rejoin Bill.

By now, Ed had packed into his raffia bag all that was needed. The guards were still up front as he emerged from the back of the hut. Glancing round the open space, he sprinted the distance back to the undergrowth in record time. Bill breathed a sigh of relief as Ed knelt down triumphantly beside him. There was a slight rustle nearby as Foxy arrived back.

Not a single word was spoken as they backed off a few yards deeper into the bush. They could hear the two guards calling to one another. Strangely enough, no shots were fired. Now a safe distance away, the three men stood upright, following the twisting jungle path back to the river bank. Undetected, they quietly re-entered the POW camp without difficulty.

Inside the camp, it was only a matter of minutes before they arrived back in their own hut. Morrie, who slept on the right of Ed, was wide awake and very concerned. He had got up to go to the latrine and discovered that his three mates were missing.

"Where the bloody hell have you lot been?" he demanded quietly. "What's bleedin' going on. Are you fellows all right?" Both Ed and Bill assured Morrie that all three of them were OK, promising to explain everything in the morning.

Before climbing on to the bamboo slats to sleep, with their bare hands they dug a hole below their beds, large enough to hold their bag of loot, and carefully smoothed back the soil over the top, to hide all traces of their digging. In the darkness, Foxy grinned. He never dreamt that his farmyard impersonations could be turned to such an advantage in the jungle. To be able to fool the Japs at night was almost hilarious. Ed and Bill, no longer tense, were feeling exhilarated as their grim dull lives had suddenly become exciting. Surprisingly, they slept well that night.

Early next morning Morrie wanted to know the full details of the previous night's escapade. Taking him to one side, Ed, Bill and Foxy explained their exploit. Morrie was not pleased with his mates.

"After all we've bleedin' well been through", he exploded. "You must all be soddin' mad. Anyway, why didn't you tell me?"

"Because we didn't want you to worry about us", answered Ed.

Morrie felt hurt. "Well, I do worry about my mates. I'm like my ma. I can't bloodywell help worrying. Anyway, if your minds are made up, I can't stop you. When are you going to carry out the attack?" he demanded.

"Midnight tonight", came the answer.

"Bloody hell", exclaimed Morrie. "I think you fellows should cancel the whole bleedin' thing!"

Bill suddenly interrupted: "There's no way we're gonna back out now, mate! It's something we've got to do, so there's no point in bleedin' arguing about it!"

Morrie looked at his mates for a moment, then he grinned. "OK if I go along with you, then?"

"It's difficult", said Ed, "it only needs three of us. So why take an extra risk?"

Morrie was not to be put off. "Listen for a moment", he argued. "You said there's four bloody barges. Well, I'm coming anyway!"

They all knew Morrie well enough to know that he meant what he said. The three nodded their heads in agreement. "OK, Morrie", said Ed. "You're in! Be ready at midnight!"

Suddenly, the whistle sounded for 'tenko'. All four of them walked together towards the parade ground, ready to be divided up into work parties for the day's toil. They lined up at the end of the long row of other POW's in a three deep formation.

After being counted and checked, Korean Chiba (the Singing Master) isolated ten men for the day's uphill slog on the ration run: three English-speaking Dutchmen, three Australian, and the gang of four, Ed, Morrie, Bill and Foxy.

"That's bloody useful", muttered Ed to Bill. "We'll be able to get the lie of the land ready for tonight!" Korean Chiba proved to be the only guard in charge which was also a fortunate situation. The men's spirits were high as they were marched across the camp, between the POW and Jap cookhouses perched high up on the river bank, and down the dirt road to the river's edge. The barges were already tied up to the mooring posts.

The Korean indicated that all men must sit and 'yazume', whilst he went on board to converse with the head Thai. The POW's knew the drill only too well. Ed and Bill strolled casually several yards along the bank, to where the river began to bend. Morrie and Foxy walked in the other direction, curiously watched by the natives on the waiting barges. There was no time to waste and the four POW's quickly weighed up the layout, and then returned to the other prisoners sitting by the mooring posts. They had previously agreed to make a more detailed reconnaissance during the midday 'yazume', when they were quite sure that the guard would be in the bushes enjoying his Thai whore for a second time.

As the men waited, two of the younger Thai girls on the third barge were waving and making obvious sexual signs to them, inviting the POW's to come on board and help themselves. In the circumstances, the offer was regretfully and politely declined, despite the men's deepdown natural instincts. Bill Slatoe grinned. "What a waste of crumpet, mate!" he remarked to Ed.

"Dunno", replied Ed, "Reckon they look all right, but no doubt they're poxed up to the eyebrows, anyway!" Foxy and Morrie grinned. Foxy looked at the sexy, dark haired girls still trying to attract attention. "Bloody hell!" he exclaimed, "it's a good job GI Elmer's not here right now, 'cause pox or no pox, he would shag himself to death with them two little beauties!"

Unfortunately or otherwise for Elmer Baker, he was with J.W. and many others on bridge building work that day. Suddenly, the Korean emerged, shouting excitedly: "Yazume all finish. All now work, speedo speedo!"

The gang of four boarded the first barge, whilst the guard, clutched his free Thai fags and cheroots, guided the remaining men to the other barges. Having set them to work unloading supplies, predictably the Korean rapidly disappeared into the undergrowth by the river bank with the younger-looking, sexy and scantily dressed Thai girl, who had been waving to the prisoners earlier.

This gave the work party the opportunity they needed to stash away stolen bags of rice, dried fish and vegetables in the long jungle foliage on the other side of the hill to be collected after dark. Judging from the suggestive squeals coming from the nearby bushes, the guard Chiba was very happy with his extra bonus ration of crumpet. This gave Ed the chance to discuss with Ayut, the head Thai, the movement upriver of Jap troops and military supplies. The Bangkok underground was emphatic about the impending shipment of ammunition upstream by barge and that it was scheduled to be passing the vicinity of Tamajao camp around midnight that night.

In his turn, Ed explained that they had a plan in mind, although he did not enter into details. Ayut was a native of Thailand with a lot of courage. He looked at Ed and cautioned him to be extremely careful, because of the cruelty and callousness displayed by the enemy to anyone falling foul of them. Only too well were the prisoners aware of these and many other grim facts.

The day's toil ended as all others. After darkness had fallen, the ration gang met up again and once more successfully recovered the hidden sacks of food, which were shared out among the prisoners.

Later on that evening, after the dead had been buried and all the other chores were finished the POW's, as usual, gathered in small groups around the nightly camp fires. This night, the gang of four isolated themselves from the others and were earnestly discussing the final details of their plan. Drawing on their experiences when working with Jap engineers on blasting various rock formations, Ed and Bill demonstrated how to deal with the explosives they had stolen. This they did, using a small stick and marking in the dust where to insert the primer and detonator into the slabs of guncotton, which they had also managed to acquire in the recent raid.

There were four slabs of guncotton explosive, about six inches in length, four inches across and two inches thick. In the centre of each was a small round cutout, into which would fit the primer. In the middle of the primer was a smaller hole, where they would have to insert a cigarette-sized red-coloured detonator before throwing at the target.

"What then?" asked Morrie. Bill replied: "At the very last moment, you shove in the red detonator, aim and throw. Then you run like hell. These Jap ones have a thirty second time delay built in."

"Christ Almighty", groaned Morrie. "You mean to say we've only got half a minute to move?" Bill grinned: "That's your lot, Morrie mate. Half a minute or else." Morrie wasn't very happy, but he'd volunteered, and that was that!

The lads went over the plan in detail until all was clearly understood. Foxy would make three clear sounding noises, like a tailless gibbon. That would be the signal to push in the detonators, throw and run!

Provided the explosive landed on the barges OK, the sharp severe cutting power should prove more than enough to detonate the ammunition on board. This, in turn, would set off a highly dangerous chain reaction. As anticipated during the midday 'yazume' break, they had been able to select the ideal spot. In order to avoid rocks on the far side and in the centre of the river, the convoy would be forced to pull over. This would bring it close to the camp side at the point where the sweeping bend of the river led to the final curve at the wooden bridge.

The attack positions chosen were about thirty five feet apart. The rendezvous was behind a broad teak tree, where they could shelter from the shrapnel before withdrawing back up the hills into the deep undergrowth. They figured that, by moving fast, they could all make it to this spot before the first explosions went off. There was no thought given to the possibility that something might go wrong. Desperate situations called for desperate chances to be taken!

The lack of a time piece had been solved a few days earlier, when a Japanese engineer, Lieutenant Osato, had foolishly taken off his wrist watch for a few moments prior to setting off a rock blasting operation. On his return, the watch had completely vanished, by courtesy of Bill Slatoe. As it happens, the watch was an English one which no doubt had been obtained from some unfortunate prisoner of war in the past.

Morrie felt excited and very proud. He had been put in charge of timing and tonight was wearing the watch on his left wrist. All was finally understood and ready.

During the course of the evening, Foxy obtained four empty rice sacks from behind the Japanese cookhouse. With his deadly knife, he cut crude holes in the top and sides. "There you go, mates", he grinned, "four ready made pullovers, a bit rough but they'll help to keep us warm. It's so bloody cold at night."

Crude they were, but anything was better than nothing, and the other lads were grateful for Foxy's efforts, despite the lice in the seams.

About ten thirty, Ed uncovered the hole below the bedspaces, removing his raffia carrier which contained the explosives. He undid a small round tin which held twelve red detonators. Extracting four, he resealed the tin and reburied it in the ground only a couple of feet from his hidden notes.

While they waited, the four lads sat on the bamboo platforms and checked their gear. The four slabs of guncotton were carefully primed by Bill. The four primers coming from the same source fitted the centre of the slabs perfectly. Morrie was to carry the four detonators separately. From Ed's waist hung the raffia carrier holding the slabs of explosives. In his hand, he carried his light short length of killer rope. Morrie was equipped in the same manner. Foxy and Bill were armed with knives. Precisely at eleven thirty Morrie gave the signal. Without a word, the four slipped quietly from their hut.

Moving across the camp near the hospital area, they could plainly hear despairing cries of agony from their mates in the ulcer annexe. Carefully, they bypassed the Jap cookhouse, proceeding downwards towards the river. In the thick undergrowth on the right hand side of the dirt road near to the bank of the river, they could hear the voices of the two Jap guards who were talking and smoking close by the mooring posts. The four paused for a moment, listening intently. Still well concealed, they moved sharply to the right of the guards, following a rough track close to the water.

Rounding the first bend, swiftly they arrived at the area chosen for the attack! The bright intense rays of tropical moonlight reflected on the fast running shimmering waters of the river Kwai. Across the far side, distant rocks visibly jutted out as the waters dashed over them causing enormous jets of foaming spray. It was an ideal spot as the rock formation would force the convoy inshore at this point. The undergrowth hanging conveniently low way out into the river, afforded excellent cover.

They waited beneath the foot of the large teak tree nearest the water. This was their agreed place of rendezvous. Once back there, they would be safe. Checking the time from Lt. Osato's luminous watch, Morrie whispered: "Five minutes to midnight." Apart from the rushing swirling waters and the wild jungle night life all was still. Midnight came and went. It had been previously decided that they should not take up final positions until such time as they could hear the motors of the towing launch and were able to observe the convoy. Fifteen minutes past midnight. Still nothing!

Morrie was getting uneasy and anxious. He seemed fidgety. "What's wrong?" whispered Bill.

"Don't reckon they're coming", answered Morrie. He added: "I'm bloody cold standing here just waiting. It's five and twenty past twelve, for Christ's sake!" Ed was straining his ears. Suddenly he hissed: "Keep bloody quiet. I can hear something." The other three were instantly alerted. Sure enough, in the distance were the unmistakable sounds of diesel engines labouring under heavy load.

There was no mistake. The engine noises drew closer and closer. Their miseries were temporarily forgotten as tension mounted and excitement grew. From their vantage point looking down river, outlined in the moonlight they could clearly see a large and very powerful looking diesel motor launch chugging slowly upstream with four barges in tow, lying low in the water.

As the convoy drew closer, Bill questioned Ed: "Hadn't we better get ready?"

Ed looked intently across the river before replying: "OK, fellows!" The time had come. He handed each man a slab of primed guncotton. Morrie gave out the small red detonators. Ed had the last word. "Don't forget to wait for the third ape call from Foxy. Shove in the detonator, aim and run like hell!" As he spoke, the convoy chugged closer still. "OK, fellows, into position. For Christ's sake, don't miss. There's no second chance!"

The distinct noise from the diesel grew louder as the four moved speedily into their positions, roughly thirty five feet apart. With ease, they slipped into the edge of the water, standing waist high and keeping the contents of their hands well above the water line. Concealed by the shelter of the overhanging undergrowth, they waited tense and ready.

The sudden coldness of the water didn't shock them. Subconsciously, they could feel the tropical fish nibbling at raw ulcers on their legs. That didn't even bother them as they prepared for action.The brilliant moonlight gave them a perfect view of the vessels as, avoiding the jagged rocks, the powerful large motor launch swept away from midstream in the direction of their hiding places. Intently, they watched as the bows of the launch nosed to within twenty feet of the bank before turning and heading upstream again.

The towing barges swung in a curved line towards them, straightening out behind the launch. Enemy troops on board could be seen smoking and talking as the stern of the boat passed the spot where Ed and his pals lay in wait. Above the noise of the diesel engine were heard three loud distinct cries of the gibbon ape. Instinctively, each man inserted his time delayed detonator into the explosive. Almost as one, they aimed from their different positions and raced from the water, reaching their rendezvous in seconds. They flung themselves flat on their bellies, panting wildly and breathless, safely behind the base of the large teak tree!

Ed and Foxy were confident that their deliveries had landed squarely on the decks of the leading and second barge. Morrie and Bill felt sure they had made the target on barges three and four. The convoy still chugged upstream. It seemed as if for some unknown reason their mission had failed!

Then suddenly, the first loud explosion ripped through the night air, followed in quick succession by three more almighty bangs. As predicted, in turn they rapidly set off a seemingly never ending chain reaction from the stored enemy ammunition.

Shrapnel flew through the air like ten million cutting knives whistling through the trees above them. Running from tree to tree, the gang of four made their way safely halfway up the hill to a spot from which they could look back and observe without danger to themselves.

The explosions continued. Vivid flashes were illuminating the giant curved bridge in the distance. A whole section of the river appeared to be on fire.The motor launch had blown up and sunk immediately. Screams of pain, terror and cries for help could be heard in between the bangs. It seemed to go on for ever. With a final almighty blast, the whole episode was over. All four barges and their contents, the launch and its passengers had all been blown sky high and completely destroyed.

Ed whispered: "We've done it, lads. We'd better get back right now, before the bastards miss us!" The four men made their way through the jungle undergrowth as if walking on air. Morrie was elated. "At last we've got one back at 'em, the poxy bastards!"

Bill added: "It did my heart good to hear those bleeders screaming in the water." These sentiments were shared by everyone. They made tracks for their hut. The whole camp was wide awake. Wild rumours were running rife. The general opinion being that at long last, our Air Forces had started bombing. In reality, it was to be a long time before the start of Allied air attacks!

Captain Suzuki and every available camp guard were out in force, screaming hysterically as they raced down the hill to the river. There they found only a handful of badly wounded survivors. The river explosions would prove a night to remember in the vile history of Tamajao.True to form, as anticipated, dawn was breaking when the first whistles sounded for 'tenko'. The guards shouted, hollered, kicked and screamed in their efforts to get the POW's out of their huts and on to the special parade. As each hut was vacated, the contents were unceremoniously and speedily searched. Fortunately, it was not so methodical or thorough as it might have been and nothing of interest to the Japanese was found.

By the time the entire camp had been paraded, Atwai the interpreter was already waiting on the platform for the camp commandant to appear. After a few minutes delay, Captain Suzuki emerged from his comfortable hut. Looking dishevelled and untidy, he was followed by a visiting Japanese officer, one Lieutenant Sejuki. As the commandant of the Kinsyok POW camp, he was notorious as a Jap with strong anti-British feelings and a firm reputation for his hilarious laughter when confronted with the daily death roll.

Commandant Suzuki first called for a complete rollcall, and a double check on every POW in camp. This was duly carried out. Despite his suspicions, everyone was present. In the hospital huts, the sick were checked, and the cookhouse staff also. A lot of bowing and saluting took place, after which Captain Suzuki commenced to speak. "No doubt you all thought that your Airforce had made an attack on the railway last night.That would be stupid on your part, as Nippon has already captured all of Burma and is about to invade India. Therefore the Allied Airforces have been rendered quite ineffective."

He paused to gaze round the mighty parade, hoping that his propaganda was helping to demoralise the POW's. To the contrary, the men were so used to these useless speeches that the natural reaction was: more bloody Nippon bullshit! Suzuki continued: "Unfortunately due to the carelessness of a Nippon soldier, who will be executed, there was a serious accident on the river involving some of our vessels. The matter has now been resolved. The railway must go on. You will all start earlier today!"

Sergeant Yamanoto bowed to his master, followed by all the other guards. Suzuki saluted and dismissed the parade. The men broke ranks to collect their mess tins and water bottles. Then they lined up for their breakfast ration of rice before reporting for work. Ed and his three mates were feeling very confident that there was no way the Japs could connect the night's events with the prisoners of war. Feeling justifiably pleased with themselves they breathed easily once again.

Mixing with the Japanese officers Atwai managed to obtain some details resulting from the attack. It emerged that a military motor launch and four barges containing important supplies of ammunition, destined for the troops in Burma, were completely lost in the river. Forty three Japanese troops had been killed, four more were still missing, and fourteen survivors had been taken to a Japanese hospital a few miles away in the transit camp.

The news was received with great pleasure by the inmates of Tamajao. Captain Saunders sent Bluey Longhurst to look for Ed Warton. He caught him just as he was leaving the hut with his mates to report for work on the railway. "G'day, Ed" grinned the young Australian. "Captain would like a few words in private with you tonight after you return from work. OK, mate?" Ed grinned. Captain Saunders was no fool. "Tell him I'll be along, Bluey. OK!"

"Good on yer, Ed. By the way, did you and your mates have anything to do with last night? That was terrific."

Ed replied: "Why do you ask?" Bluey glanced round to see if anyone was listening, and then replied: "The Captain said it has the hallmarks of an Ed Warton Pommie attack!" He went on: "Besides that, mate, I came looking for you about midnight, 'cos I was on nights and Dave Wandle wanted you to come over and talk. His leg's bloody bad! But you and your three mates were missing. Doug Pardy said he thought you'd all gone walkies down the riverside!"

"Speedo, speedo", yelled a guard, walking quickly toward them, waving his arms and a big stick. "Got to go, Bluey. Tell Dave we'll be over to see him tonight. I'll see the Captain then." "G'day, Ed", grinned the young Aussie, as he walked quickly away towards the hospital hut.

CHAPTER 13

Jungle Operating Theatre

During the course of the day, the men out on the railway made contact with other POW's, working south from Konkuita. The news was bad. Their terrible conditions and death toll were much the same as those in the other grim camps, upcountry on the Kwai. News from Niki-Niki, the camp above Tamajao, was that a sergeant, corporal, and four privates from the Suffolks had escaped. They were being hunted by Japanese search parties!

Ed and Bill had been separated, as was also the case with Morrie, Nat and Foxy. This was not unusual with the work parties. In any event, they would all meet up on their return to camp in the evening. Bill Slatoe and several others were digging soil from a bank of solid earth, using their spades and chungkals.

Taking advantage of the nearest Jap guard's back being turned, Bill decided to take a rest and lean on his spade for a minute, blissfully unaware that another guard was watching from a higher position on the embankment. To his complete surprise, he felt a sudden blow across his back from the weight of a heavy stick.

"Christ Almighty" he yelled, as he stumbled forwards into the earth. He stood up to be confronted by a squat faced, black whiskered grinning Japanese guard, who shouted at him in Japanese. Bill had learnt enough to know that the guard was asking "What do you think you are doing, yazume nei-ka!"

Bill was hurt and angry. "You stupid little sod, I'll tell you what I was doing" he replied. "Waiting for a bleedin' bus!"

The guard looked puzzled "Bus-ka?" he queried. "Yeah" retorted Bill "I'm going down the bleedin' sea front at Southend!"

This remark brought laughter from the lads working with him. Bill thought it was funny himself and gave a large grin. It was extremely fortunate for Bill Slatoe that the Japanese guard couldn't speak a word of English, although he was clearly suspicious as his expression changed to one of anger. Sensing real trouble, Bill started to dig at the soil again. The guard lashed at him with the stick and indicated for him to stop work and stand to attention a few yards away in the blazing tropical sun. The first guard had now returned to the scene. Pulling his English-Japanese phrase book from his tunic pocket, he glared at the unhappy Bill.

"I speak. Who number one-ka?" he demanded. Bill knew what he said but pretended he didn't understand the question. "No understand", he answered, shaking his head. The two guards looked angry, then one of them spoke again. "I speak. Who number one-ka, Churchill Lonn-donn?" Bill suddenly understood. "Churchill number one London" he proudly announced. That reply brought him a resounding smack across the face.

Again the Jap repeated the question. Not intending to be caught a second time, Bill brightly spoke up: "Tojo (Jap Prime Minister) No.1!" His reward was a swift whack across the shoulders with a stick "You can't win with these bastards" groaned Bill. At that moment the Japanese engineering officer in charge of the section arrived, making it plain to the guards that he also hated all prisoners of war. "Now is the time for work, the railway must not be delayed." They bowed low to the officer. Much to Bill's relief, he was then allowed to resume work.

Ed was passing nearby, carrying a box of dynamite for the blasting engineers. He was closely followed by an armed Korean, when he stumbled. Catching his bare foot on a sharp flint caused him to fall flat on his face. Before he could pick himself up, he received at least half a dozen hefty kicks in the right thigh from the Korean's heavy hobnail boot. As he slowly struggled to his feet, the blood trickled down his leg. Retrieving the box of dynamite, he proceeded painfully on his way.

It was obvious that a desperate push was on to complete the railway in October. Many beatings took place that day before the toil was completed. It was with no small measure of relief that the POW's collected their tools to return to the stores and begin their barefooted trek back to Tamajao camp, only to learn that another twenty comrades had died that day!

At rice ration time, the lads met up again. They sat on the ground eating their meagre portion and washing it down with boiled water. As they ate, the events of the day were discussed in detail. Nat Ruben commented drily: "Good job it wasn't detonated Ed." Bill laughed. Ed replied with a grin: "Have they got any more daft sods like you in Bethnal Green?" Not to be outdone, Foxy added: "You bloody townies would do well to come and live with us swede bashers after the war. Still you ain't a bad lot altogether."

Later in the evening, they made their way over to the hospital hut to visit their many sick mates. They took with them precious small gifts of eggs, fruit, dried fish and pomelos to help in some small way, despite the fact that they so badly needed these items themselves. In the main hut, most of the sick were lying helpless on the bamboo slats. Their emaciated bodies were covered with filthy lice ridden hessian sacks as, without hope, they waited for death to release them from their living hell.

Alongside the main hut, in the vile evil smelling ulcer annexe, the lad from Millwall, Dave Wandle was in a bad state. His ulcerated leg gaped wide open, showing the white shin bone, from the knee to the ankle. The young cockney was writhing in agony. Tears ran down his hollow cheeks as he spoke to his mates.

"Should feel better tomorrow, the Major's going to chop this bleedin' leg off above the knee."

His four mates looked on in silent despair. They had witnessed it all before. Many amputations had already taken place. Some patients had survived limbless, but many had died from their weak condition. In view of the state of Dave's leg, they realised there could be no alternative if he was to survive. For a few seconds no-one said anything; it was an awkward situation.

Dave looked at his four mates, blinked back his tears and spoke again: "Captain Saunders has been a bloody hero, but he said if I wanted to go home, me leg, it will have to come orf! Major Boone's been to see me. He's a bloody nice bloke, speaks all posh like. He said I won't know anything about it, 'cos he's got enough anaesthetic from Dr. Death to do six of us tomorrer!"

Ed spoke first: "Don't worry Dave mate, we'll look after you OK." The others nodded in agreement. Morrie added thoughtfully: "Sergeant Porter's a bloody good carpenter. He makes crutches and peg legs." Dave quickly wiped the tears from his eyes with his hand. Even against such tremendous odds his cockney spirit was still alive.

"I'll tell yer mates, wot I'm really worried about is my old lady. She'll do her nut if I turn up with only one bleedin' leg. 'Sides, that there Dolly, that's me girlfriend, bit of a snooty cow she is. Don't reckon she'll want me like that. I mean to say, 'alf a man. Christ, I made a funny. Don't none of you bastards call me Arfur". He bravely gave a weak grin!

Bluey Longhurst, the young Aussie medic, appeared with a small metal bowl and a painful cleaning out spoon. "You'll be 'right mate. Don't worry Dave, We'll look after you." While Bluey set about the horrendous task of scraping the wound clean, the lads promised to return later, and went on to visit other mates in the main hut. Ed excused himself in order to visit his trusted friend, Australian Captain Don Saunders, who was now installed in a small attap hut adjoining the hospital.

Used as office and personal quarters, he shared this with a senior Dutch medical officer, Major van Gazell, Major Ray Boone, RAMC and Padre 'Happy Harry' from Australia. The four had crude made-up bamboo beds, a small table and four bamboo chairs. When Ed arrived, all four officers were present, involved in a game of bridge with a tattered pack of cards. The hut was lit by six crude lamps made from old tins containing coconut oil and a wick.

"G'day Ed", said Captain Saunders. "Grab a chair, we've got a lot of news to catch up on. Firstly, let me introduce you to my fellow medical officers. You already know our padre." Ed nodded. "This is Major Van Gazell, Dutch Army Medical Corps, and this is Major Ray Boone, R.A.M.C. We are very fortunate to have their assistance in this bloody hell hole. Now gentlemen, let me introduce you all to Private Ed Warton from the Suffolks. Under the circumstances, we've cut out all the formalities. We all know him as Ed!"

Each officer shook hands with Ed. Major Van Gazell sat on his bed in order that Ed could sit on one of the bamboo chairs. "Let me explain, Ed", said the Captain, "As officers, amongst ourselves there are no secrets. We can talk safely and openly. Van Gazell originates from Amsterdam. He was captured in Java and speaks fluent English. Atwai has given us all the details of the night's events on the river, as well as the enemy casualty figures. I must confess we're all very happy about what happened!"

Don Saunders looked intently at Ed Warton, then went on: "You know well enough we are not so gullible as Nippon. You and your gang were missing on the night. It all adds up, so I think you can really let us in on what happened. We're all very keen to know."

Ed grinned. "OK, Captain." The other three officers leaned forward in eager anticipation. "I suppose I had better explain. With respect, we didn't contact you for two reasons. Firstly, because the five hand grenades you've still got only have a five second delay. If we'd used them, we would have all been killed. Secondly, quite frankly we thought you all had more than enough to worry about with the sick and the dying." The four officers remained silent, listening intently.

Ed Warton proceeded to outline the whole operation in detail, starting from the time they stole the explosives, right through to the attack and the results. When he had concluded, the Captain replied: "I knew it. I told my fellow officers that those explosions were no bloody accident!" Major Boone was enthralled. "Bloody good show, man!" was his immediate reaction. Van Gazell said quite simply, "It's almost unbelievable!"

"Brave but dangerous" were the padre's terse comments. Captain Saunders was delighted. He grinned broadly: "Simple, effective, altogether in my opinion a brilliant operation and it came off. You all got away with it, and the bloody fools never found out. Amazing! Congratulations to your team. We're proud of you all!"

In a more serious vein, the M.O. continued: "Listen, Ed, really you and your mates are fools to take chances after what you've all been through. It begs the question, mate, is it worth the risk?" He smiled again. "I thought us Aussies were stubborn and tough, but you Poms never cease to amaze me!"

Ed made ready to leave. Captain Saunders thanked him for calling, asking him to keep in closer touch. Noticing the persistent flies on his leg, he had a look at the Korean's handiwork, and told Ed to report on sick parade in the morning. "No need to worry about Doctor Death. He's going up on a day trip to Konkuita by lorry. There's now a dirt road through the jungle connecting the camps. So we'll have a good look at that leg tomorrow." "OK, and goodnight Captain", replied Ed, as he left the officers' hut to return to his mates.

After he had left, there followed a lengthy discussion among the officers concerning the young private soldier. Padre Thorpe remarked: "I've seen that young fellow about many times while I've been visiting the sick. He and a gang of three or four others often carry up water from the river to wash their mates. Also, they take them in precious food that they so badly need themselves. Despite all that, from what I've learned tonight they've still got the guts to have a go at the enemy. My fellow men never cease to amaze me!"

The padre studied the faces of the medical officers, then continued: "Must say I never see any of them at prayer meetings. Perhaps they're not religious." He smiled: "But sadly neither are so many others." He gave a resigned sigh. Captain Don Saunders grinned at the padre.

"Well, padre, it takes all sorts you know to make this world of ours. All I know is that Pommie and his mates are the salt of the earth. After what they've suffered, their kind of courage - I'd say guts - is quite unbelievable, especially when you think of all the other poor devils who have just given up! Whether they choose to follow God, or are simply heathens is in my opinion, their own free choice."

Major Ray Boone diplomatically interrupted with: "I think it's time for lights out gentlemen. Goodnight everyone." So saying, and before anyone could disagree, he got up and extinguished the coconut oil lamps.

Next morning at 'tenko', Ed reported sick and joined Morrie who was also on parade suffering from the runs. There was the usual long column waiting to see the M.O. Big Billy Foster was in front of Morrie.

"G'day Billy", said Captain Saunders.

"G'day Captain", replied Billy.

"What seems to be the trouble?" came the question.

"Well I can still fart OK, but my bloody feet ache so much I don't know what the hell to do with them!"

Morrie was standing next in line, and he muttered to Ed: "And I've got a bleedin' heart, but it don't get you anywhere!"

The M.O. examined Billy's bare feet. "Looks like you've got dry beri-beri. At present I'm afraid we've got no vitamins to help you." Billy was in pain, fed up and unhappy.

"What am I gonna do, Doc?" he pleaded.

"Take the day off sick and stick your feet in a tin of cold water!" came the answer.

G'day Morrie, what's your problem?"

"Got the shits, Doc", replied Morrie.

"Got nothing to give you yet. Keep off work and rest up. Sorry!"

Morrie rushed away to the nearest latrine.

"G'day Ed. Lets have a look at your leg." The M.O. studied it closely.

"The bastard gave you a good kicking. Better get Joe Langton to clean it up. I'm always afraid of new ulcers, as sometimes these things turn into blood poisoning, ending up in great big jungle carbuncles. Stay off work. If it gets worse, report sick again. By the way Ed, can you give me a bit of moral support for DaveWandle this morning. Poor bloke, he's going to need all the help he can get!"

Ed thanked the Captain, promising to go and see Dave before the operation. Then he made his way over to the long queue that Joe Langton was dealing with. In between rushing to the latrine, Morrie decided shortly after to join Ed, who was patiently waiting. A few yards away, they noticed a tall fairhaired man sitting on a bamboo bed, wearing on his arm the traditional white band with a small red cross in the centre. He was one of Major Boone's medics that Ed had not met before.

The man appeared to be drawing. Morrie and Ed were puzzled. There was still a long wait for treatment, so being curious, they decided to go and look at what he was doing. There was room on the bamboo platform, so they sat down beside the medic. He looked up, grinned and said: "Good morning."

"Hello and good morning, mate", replied Ed. "What are you up to? The young man with sharp blue eyes put down his drawing before answering.

"Just trying to sketch some of the lads in the sick queue. "Look, you two lads are there."

Morrie and Ed looked at the pencilled drawing in amazement. It was very good, realistic and impressive.

"You an artist then, mate?" Morrie asked.

"Well, I was going to art school before I got called up." He smiled thoughtfully. "I was just 21 years then". Ed and Morrie looked at the long queue, waiting for the medical orderly to clean up and attend their wounds. There was plenty of time.

"Look mate", said Morrie, "What's your name?"

"George Bold", came the answer. The artist grinned at the two lads. "Looks like you have got plenty of time to talk today. I've been on duty all night, so I'm off now. It's so hot I didn't feel like sleeping yet. So what's your names? Tell me about yourselves. There's precious little else to talk about in this bloody hell hole. I like to know people, I find them interesting."

For the next half hour they conversed. Ed and Morrie outlined their backgrounds, where they came from and some of their grim adventures to date. In return, George Bold explained that he lived with his parents at Romford in Essex. On his call up he found that he was to serve with the Royal Army Medical Corps. Being in the same East Anglian Division as Ed and Morrie, he'd also been captured at the fall of Singapore.

"Where d'you get your materials from to make your drawings?"

George smiled: "With considerable difficulty", he replied. It's the old POW story. I pinch a bit here and there from the Japs. Use my own hair to make brushes when I paint and so on."

Morrie interrupted "Your problem's over, George. Me and my mates have various ways of getting all kinds of gear. All you've got to do is tell us what you want, and we will get it, OK?"

George Bold was suitably impressed. He thanked the two men, and went on to explain that he did paintings as well as drawings.

"Don't the Japs mind?" asked Ed.

"Funnily enough", came the answer, "they sometimes have a look at what I'm doing, but they don't seem to take any notice of portraits of people and animals, things like that. In fact, every now and then, a bloody off-duty guard or officer wants one done of himself. They supply the paper and materials, and I get paid in fags. I do like my fags!" he added.

George continued: "Mind you, beneath all this is a more serious aspect." At that moment, Morrie had to rush for the latrine: "Back soon", he gasped.

"Don't understand", answered Ed. The artist went on: "Well, in confidence, when I can get hold of the right materials I make paintings of the more gruesome sights - in particular the amputations carried out by Major Boone. We fully realise that the enemy wouldn't like this positive evidence used against them so we have to be very careful when I carry out that type of painting. And believe me. Ed, Major Boone keeps them well hidden. We're trying to compile some sort of pictorial record that will expose the terrible horrors and experiences undergone during our lost years!" Morrie returned from the bog. "Christ, I feel bloody awful", he moaned.

"Stay and talk to George", suggested Ed, " 'cause it's now my turn in the treatment queue, OK!"

"Feeling rough, Morrie?" asked George, "Have a fag, chum. It'll make you feel better." Morrie was grateful for the offer, but explained that, like his mates, he didn't smoke. "Well, bully for you lot", laughed George. "I'm afraid I'm like a lot more. I can't bloody well live without my fags."

Over in the treatment queue, Aussie medic Joe started to clean up the congealed blood and mess on Ed's thigh, using a weak mixture of yellow antiseptic. "It's the best we can do, mate", he smiled. Ed winced in pain. "Bloody oath Ed, you've got the makings of a bad leg there. Looks like three beaut's coming up in a row."

Ed pulled a face. "They throb like hell, mate. What d'you reckon they are?"

"The beginning of three jungle boils, mate", came the reply.

Ed grimaced. "Thanks a lot, Joe. See you soon, I reckon." He got up and limped away to rejoin Morrie.

Taking leave of their new found friend, George Bold, the pair of them decided to visit the ulcer hut, to see Dave before his operation. As they entered, young Joe Levy was just leaving for the theatre. He stopped to speak.

"Good here, ain't it. I've got to walk to the bleeding theatre. 'Spect you've heard, they're gonna take my hand off. Guess they'll have to carry me back 'cause I'll be bloody knackered."

There was silence. The lad from Hackney was justifiably depressed. His right hand had been crushed two weeks earlier. A Korean was savagely beating him across the back, which caused him to slip forward just at the very moment when a heavy baulk of timber fell backwards and trapped his hand. He was fortunate to escape with his life!

Dave gave a weak smile "Right bleeding pair we'll look Joe. You wiv' no hand, and me wiv' no bleeding leg. Never mind, mate, at least we're still alive!" Joe did not reply as he left the hut. The two medical orderlies arrived, carrying on a stretcher a young Australian patient, blissfully unconscious.

"That's Johnny Thompson. He lives near Melbourne", said Dave. "Just 'ad his leg orff." Gently they transferred the Aussie from the stretcher back to his uncomfortable bamboo slatted bed, covering him with two dirty hessian sacks. On their way out, they stopped by Dave, who looked up anxiously.

"When we bring back Joe Levy later on, it'll be your turn", said one of the medics. "The M.O. said, when there's more room in the main hut, we'll transfer you blokes out of here. See you later." As they left, the hut reeked with the strong odour of anaesthetic, contrasting strangely with the vile stench of rotting flesh.

Dave looked at his two mates. "Thanks for coming, me old chinas."

Morrie said. "Sorry Dave, got the shits again. Gotta go to the bog, then I'm going back to our hut 'cause I feel bloody rough, OK!" In a flash, he sped from the hut, holding his belly with both hands, sprinting towards the nearest latrine. Ed sat on the bamboo platform, talking to Dave. Morrie didn't return. The time dragged on. "Feel sorry for old Joe", said Dave, "I mean ter say, 'e was only married for eight weeks before we were sent abroad. I know he fink's the world of Minnie. Never stops talking about 'er. What a bleedin shame!"

In his mind, Ed contemplated for a moment the sheer courage of his cockney mate. About to face a terrible ordeal under dangerous and appalling circumstances, he was making out he wasn't scared, and finding in his heart pity for his fellow man! An hour passed. Conversation dwindled. Then suddenly, the two medical orderlies returned with the stretcher bearing the unconscious Joe Levy. As they lifted him on to the bamboo platform, Dave reached out, instinctively gripping one of Ed's hands. The time had come!

"Right" said the first medic, "You're next."

They lifted him on to the stretcher. "Ta for comin', mate. Are you gonna walk down to the theatre wiv' me?"

Ed looked down sympathetically. "Sure I'm coming, Dave, and when you come round, I'll be there to say hello. As I'm off sick, I've got the time."

They carried him across the ground to the operating theatre, an impressive name in the jungle. This consisted of a large bamboo framework with an attap thatched roof. Suspended from its beams was the enormous two-in-one mosquito net, that the medics had struggled to carry upcountry on the forced march. In the centre, rigidly hammered into the ground was the crude bamboo surfaced operating table with a solid timber framework, locally known as the chopping block. Across the upper end was a specially fixed small teak hand rail, well known as the agony bar. This had been cleverly thought up by Major Boone for patients to grip hold of for minor operations, since these were invariably performed without the benefit of an anaesthetic. Desperately needed for major surgery, there was a grave shortage of the necessary drugs, as these were tightly controlled and strictly limited by the enemy. This was the source of many bitter complaints by the Allied medical officers who were constantly battling with the Japanese commandant for more supplies of the urgently required anaesthetic drugs. More often than not these battles proved to be of no avail!

When operations were in progress, outside the theatre was a continually burning bonfire, in order that the medics could boil old tin cans of water, constantly required for washing and sterilising surgical instruments. A large old metal bowl was always at the ready for the surgeon and his two assistants to scrub up in. In addition, there were other cans of hot water to wash, boil, and re-boil old used bandages and pieces of rough canvas over and over again. These were required to cover the worst of the wounds from flies and germs.

Anyone who was so inclined could stand outside the giant mosquito net and watch the surgeon at work. It was not unusual to find off-duty guards standing around in morbid curiosity, smoking, drinking, watching and often laughing as amputated limbs were incinerated in the bonfire.

One of the medics already inside the hut lifted a corner to allow the stretcher to enter. The cockney lad had the final word: "You know I'll be glad to get rid of this bleedin' leg", he called out as the net dropped back. Seconds later, he was being lifted on to the operating table. Ed watched anxiously as the medic prepared to administer the anaesthetic.

Major Ray Boone was a highly skilled surgeon, but he was hampered by a frustrating lack of important medical equipment and supplies which were contantly disappearing en route to the camp. Most of these missing supplies had been sent but had never arrived. At the time, the Japanese were blamed for stealing them and diverting them up the line to their own medical corps. When the war ended, it transpired that this was precisely what had occurred.

Along with so many other POW's, the medical officer was making do the best way possible. The scalpel he used was adapted from the padre's open razor. One of the medics had laboriously ground it down to the required size on a slab of hard rock.

Always the surgeon, today he looked as bright as ever, proud of his tattered old white coat and apron, which he had managed to retain through thick and thin. It gave him a clinical look, which inspired confidence in the team around him. Though his clothes had been boiled many times over, faint red blood stains still showed through the front of the apron. His flaming red hair proved a vivid contrast, and his blue eyes still retained a twinkle. Smiling and looking horribly thin, the major welcomed his patient with a few reassuring words. In a few short seconds, relieved of his agonising pain, the youngster from Millwall lay mercifully unconscious. The surgeon commenced to amputate the rotting right leg above the knee. This was the third operation that day, and there were still more waiting!

Ed sat on the ground outside the theatre for a while. The never ending flies were bothering his injured leg. Angrily, he brushed them away. One of the medics emerged from under the mosquito net, carrying a metal container which held the amputated leg. He walked to a second bonfire at the rear of the theatre, where the diseased limb rapidly withered in the flames. Ed felt sick!

Bluey Longhurst emerged from the mosquito net. He had been assisting Major Boone. He walked over to scrub his hands in the bowl of water. "G'day, Ed. That's more or less over, mate. He'll be taken back to the hospital hut shortly. He'll be right." As an afterthought he added: "Mind you, he's gonna find the going bloody tough!"

"We'll do all we can to help, Bluey", replied Ed. Bluey grinned.

"Knew you would. Good on yer, mate." Major Boone arrived, looking more like a butcher in his freshly bloodstained apron. He proceeded to wash his hands in a businesslike manner. (Rubber gloves were non-existent.) Wiping them carefully on rough shirt strips torn and boiled for the purpose, he walked over to where Ed was sitting.

"One of the Suffolks - your chum, I imagine?" Ed nodded. The major smiled: "With a bit of luck, he'll make it alright. Not a bit like our hospitals back home, is it?" Ed got up from the ground before answering: "Damn right, major. Not like the old Southend General at all!" As he spoke, the two stretcher bearers left the theatre to return his unconscious mate to the hospital hut. Feeling very despondent with the day's events, Ed slowly walked along behind.

CHAPTER 14

End of the Line

Late that afternoon, Dave Wandle gradually regained consciousness. Ed was resting by his side on the uncomfortable bamboo slats, using the place vacated by a young Dutchman who, following amputation of a foot earlier that day, had died from cardiac arrest.

Dave slowly opened his eyes. Ed spoke first: "It's all right, Dave. It's all over, you're gonna be fine." The lad from Millwall was still under the influence of the anaesthetic. Faintly he asked: "Get me some water, Ed, me lips are bleedin' parched." Ed reached over for Dave's water bottle. Holding the spout up to his lips, Dave sucked, taking down a small amount. He was very weak. "Christ, that feels better, mate."

Breathing heavily, he laid his head back on the hard rough haversack he used as a pillow. "Ed," he whispered, "I 'ad this most wonderful dream. There I was, sittin' down in the kitchen wiv' me old lady. Me old man's bin dead for years." He gave a weak grin: "Would you believe it, mate, I'd just finished a bleedin' great plate of dog and chips, beans and all. Ma said: I suppose you're going to the match 's afternoon. Have another cuppa char son. You know, you get more like your Dad each time I see yer." He took another sip of water. "What d'you know Ed, Millwall were playing Souf'end! Of all bleedin' teams! Well, I ask you mate, as I was walking down the road, there was all these Jap bastards walking towards me with guns. I went absolutely berserk, then I woke up and its all gorn'. Me old lady, though, she looked the same as I remembered 'er!"

Ed did not answer. Only too well was he aware that dreams in captivity were so vivid, almost uncanny at times, and were unfortunately followed by shattering disillusionment on awakening to the grim reality of still being a prisoner of war of the Japanese.

Dave took another sip from his water bottle.

" 'Ad a look at me stump, mate?" he asked. Ed glanced down at the rough hessian sacks. They had slipped off to reveal the heavily bloodstained bandage and canvas strips covering the stump.

"Not yet, Dave", he answered.

"Don't bleedin' hurt any more, mate. I'm telling you, it's a bloody relief", sighed Dave. In his weak condition, he closed his eyes and fell asleep again.

Joe Levy was fully conscious, although not talking. Ed observed him staring intently at the package of canvas strips at the end of his right arm. Tears were trickling down his thin face as Ed got up and quietly left the hospital hut. With his leg getting more painful by the hour, slowly he made his way back across the camp to find Morrie was a little better, but a long way from feeling well. It was now evening time. Foxy and Bill were just finishing the last precious grains of their rice ration. Ed and Morrie had yet to go to the never ending queue at the cookhouse to collect their portion. Almost as one, they posed the question: "How is he?" Ed explained the events of the day.

"What about Joe Levy?" asked Morrie.

Ed replied that he thought that Joe was taking it hard, but seemed to be pulling through OK.

Later that night, Morrie and Bill managed to get some eggs from the Thai trader's barge. Hastily they boiled them, ate one each, and reserved two, one for Dave and the other for Joe. They all three set out to pay a visit to see their mates in hospital. Morrie explained that he might have to dash off to the bog. Ed's leg was getting bloody painful. In comparison to Joe, Dave and several others their problems were only minor.

* * *

Six days later, Ed had to report to the theatre for minor operations. The surgeon was going to open up three giant abscesses on his right thigh and one on top of his right foot. Painfully, he limped his way over. When he finally arrived, he found Bluey on duty. "G'day, Ed", he laughed.

"Hi ya, Bluey", came the answer. "How long have I got to wait?" he questioned.

"Aw, not long, mate. Major Boone is just coming over. Today it's all the minor ops., and you happen to be first on the list." Bluey looked down at Ed's leg and foot. "Bloody oath, mate!" he exclaimed. "They look real angry and painful." Ed assured him they were.

The bonfire supplying the boiling hot water was well under way when Major Boone arrived and came through the mosquito net. A few minutes later, he looked out and smiled reassuringly. "Right, Bluey. Bring in the first patient, please." Somewhat apprehensive, burning with pain, Ed hobbled into the theatre. "Hop on the table", said the Major. The two medical assistants gave him a hand and laid him down on his left side. The surgeon made a close inspection and then told the medics to clean up the area on the right thigh and the right foot. The major commented: "Have to explain, old chap, we cannot spare any anaesthetic for this type of operation. As I am sure you are well aware, we are desperately short of medical supplies. I suggest you hang on tightly to the bar above your head. Try not to move. If you shout out, we're used to it. If you faint, then of course there's no need to worry. Do you understand, OK?"

Ed nodded that he understood.The two medics strapped down the injured leg with canvas straps, securing it tightly to the bamboo slats so that it could not move. With a cheerful smile of encouragement, the surgeon picked up the make-do scalpel. "Be as quick as I can, old chap. Just relax and hold the bar tightly."

Bluey grinned: "You'll be right, mate." As he looked upwards and outwards at the bright blue sky shining through the green mosquito nets, Ed Warton did not feel happy. Suddenly, he felt the first incision of the open razor. It seemed like a white hot knife was slowly carving through his bare flesh. Twice each way in the form of a cross. Three times in all on his thigh. Then a repeat performance on his right foot. In reality, it was but a short space of time, but to Ed, sweating and gripping the agony bar, it seemed endless. At last it was over! He felt horribly faint. The medics were busily cleaning out the pus, waste matter and dark filthy blood that gushed forth. Christ, it all felt on fire, raw and agonisingly painful. He was quite unable to move. The major came over to talk to him: "That wasn't too bad, now was it?" Ed nodded, as if to say that was a matter of opinion. Finally, it was all cleaned up and a weak mixture of antiseptic was applied.

"Got a problem over a shortage of bandages", said Major Boone cheerfully. "So we'll have to use banana leaves, tied on with raffia, to cover the wounds. At least it will keep the flies away."

The medics unstrapped Ed's leg. "You can get down now, but you'll have to stay in hospital for a few days, till we see which way it goes. Bluey and Joe will carry you back on a stretcher. Captain Saunders will be in charge of your case and he will let you know when you can return to your mates."

Ed mumbled: "Thanks, Major", as the medics lifted him from the table to a stretcher and returned him to the hospital hut. The blood still trickled down his leg!

* * *

Two weeks had passed. It was the beginning of October 1943. The railway was scheduled for completion any time now and the Japs were getting desperate. The engineers and guards had reached the stage of hysteria in their efforts to extract more work from the helpless prisoners of war. Working through from Thanbyuzayat on the Burma side, the same desperate situation prevailed as the push towards the link-up at Konkuita accelerated. Daily, more and more sadistic and brutal beatings were heaped upon the heads and bodies of the luckless prisoners of war. Due to a shortage of labour through chronic sickness, even some of the medics were put to work on the railway.

* * *

Back in the hospital hut at Tamajao camp Ed's wounds were healing fast - by a stroke of good fortune and thanks to his strong constitution. He was already walking again. Compared to the terrible plight of others, Ed felt almost ashamed of his minor injuries. Dave was slowly coming to terms with the grim fact that his right leg had been amputated. Joe Levy was sometimes cheerful, but often depressed, particularly when he spoke about his young wife, whom he obviously adored.

There was a strong rumour that, once the line was complete, the enemy might move the disabled and very sick prisoners downcountry, to the so-called base hospitals of Chungkai, Kanburi, and Tamuwang. As yet, it was still only one of a thousand rumours that daily ran rife. The most popular one, of course, was that the war would soon be over. Up to this time, there hadn't even been one Allied air attack on the line, despite intense enemy activity. There was a continuous movement of troops by dirt road and by river upcountry through the Three Pagoda Pass into Burma.

Nightly, Bill and Foxy used to visit Ed, Morrie and their other mates in hospital. Morrie seemed to be drying out, as he put it. He was anxious to get back in business. Ed reckoned that any day now he would be able to return to the hut. Each time he saw Captain Saunders on his daily rounds, he would ask if he could leave the hospital hut and rejoin his mates.

Bill said that Atwai had told them that the railway would be completed about October 11th. or 12th. It was now the tenth. So it came to pass that the last section of the line was laid and the final spike was banged home early on the morning of the twelfth of October 1943. The Siam to Burma railway was finally completed at a terrible cost in lives!

Word was that the main pressures were off and that the enemy was making preparations for a special ceremony to be held to officially open and celebrate the completion on the 25th. October, when high-ranking officers of the Imperial Japanese Army would be in attendance. It was even rumoured that the enemy would declare a day's holiday for all POW's. That remained to be seen!

Meanwhile, outside work parties were still required daily for quarrying, maintenance and strengthening existing embankments. Captain Saunders was officially informed that the disabled and chronic sick were to be evacuated downcountry in stages by barge and by train. He was informed that he would be contacted through Major Toyoda before the evacuation was due to commence.

On the morning of the 15th October, the Japanese medical officer visited the Allied medical officers in the hospital hut. He informed them that Captain Suzuki had issued orders for all very sick and disabled POW's to be dispatched downcountry by river barge and by open goods train and that this would commence next morning to base camps of Chungkai, Kanburi, and Tamuwang. At 'tenko' next day, stretcher bearer parties were selected. By devious means, the gang of four made sure they were on the party conveying the limbless down to the barges, which the previous day had brought up rice, and were still moored at the river bank. The hospital evacuation was supervised by Major Boone and Captain Saunders, whilst the Dutch medical officer and the very reverend "Happy Harry" were left in charge of the remaining patients.

Working in teams of four bearers to each stretcher in that order, Ed, Bill, Foxy, and Morrie were able to stay together. In a second team were Doug Pardy, Nat Ruben, Les Ardwool, and Tony Smith. There were two other teams, one of four Australians and the other of four Dutchmen. The first twenty patients were taken on board and settled uncomfortably on the wooden decks with their few pathetic belongings. In addition, they had been given one portion of rice in their old army mess-tins, and one army bottle of boiled water. It was understood that they would be calling at camps downstream for further rations when required.

Two armed Japanese guards were allocated to each barge. No medical supervision was allowed, despite the brave arguments put up by Major Boone and Captain Saunders. Thai natives were manning the crafts. The loading of the last barge was almost completed when the four Suffolks, carrying the stretcher holding Dave Wandle, made their way down the dirt road on to the barge. Gently they lowered him down beside Joe Levy.

Despite his courageous Cockney spirit Dave, like so many others, looked very ill. Captain Saunders stepped on board. Dave looked up gratefully. " 'Bye, Captain. 'Fanks for saving me life. You 'n the Major, that is." The tall Australian medical officer knelt down and shook the lad's thin right hand.

"G'day, mate", he smiled. "We'll meet again when this bloody lot's over."

Dave tried to grin: "You're a bleedin' good doc'. Wish you were coming wiv us, Captain Saunders." The question of rank did not even occur. Everyone was a comrade on equal footing.

"Aw, you'll be right", came the firm answer. "I've got to stay up here to look after all these other blokes and all you bloody Poms." Dave gave a weak smile. After shaking hands with several more, the Captain rejoined Major Boone on the bank. Ed and Bill knelt down on the deck, as did Morrie and Foxy. It was a moment of strange sadness.

"Time to say goodbye, Dave" said Ed. They all shook hands. Joe Levy bravely held up his left hand, which was warmly accepted. "Don't forget, Dave", said Bill, "We wanna see you in Southend when this bleedin' war's over." For a brief moment Dave looked intent.

"You bleedin' lot 'ave got to come up to Millwall. You know the bloody address. Don't forget to tell me old lady it wasn't my fault losin' the leg! I mean to say, Foxy, you bleedin' swede bashers, you're the bloody best. Ta-ta, mates!"

As the four men jumped ashore, the guards were shouting. The barge slowly began to move into the deeper water of the river. As it swept downstream, the men on the bank waved their final farewells to their comrades. They watched the barge until it vanished from sight round the first wide bend in the river. It was as if something had suddenly gone out of their lives!

The stretcher bearers trudged back up the dirt hill towards the camp in silence. "Gonna miss old Dave", remarked Ed. No-one replied. Unaware at the time, they were destined never to meet again. Dave died suddenly from a blood clot on the way down river. Ironically his body, along with seven others, was put ashore at Tonchan for burial in the vast jungle cemetery outside the evil camp they had all hated so much!

Back in camp the guards called a welcome 'yazume' for the midday rice ration. While they were eating, from the hospital hut they could hear a wild noise like the howling of a dog. From the hut a wreckage of human being appeared, tripping over, falling flat on the ground, and screaming like a madman. Two medics rushed forward and forcefully escorted him back, still screaming!

The men carried on eating as though nothing had happened. They had seen and heard it all before. Like others in different stages of jungle fever, this one had cerebral malaria. Within two hours, mercifully he was dead! 'Yazume' over, the whistle sounded for work.The task was to carry the very sick half a mile to the railway line. This process was to continue for the next three days. That afternoon, the first open topped goods truck was loaded with its human cargo, hopelessly overcrowded, and extremely uncomfortable, with forty to fifty per truck. The two guards escorting the stretcher bearers called for a 'yazume'. Wearily, the exhausted bearers threw themselves on the ground, so glad of a rest in the shade of the nearby trees.

Ed and Bill were seated alongside Morrie and Foxy. The two guards had seemed strangely indifferent as the lads had bid their farewells to those that they knew and to many others they didn't know. It made no difference who they were or what they were: they were all prisoners of war in the hands of the Japanese. As such, there existed among them a spirit of comradeship, born in captivity, where man was to face the toughest test of human endurance. They became a special breed burning with the spirit to fight on and to survive. Despite their own sufferings and miseries, there was room in their hearts for compassion for their fellow man. As they rested and took account of the surroundings, the tropical sun of Thailand blazed down on the jungle, highlighting the bizarre scene before their eyes.

Bill looked around and spoke to Ed: "It's almost unbelievable, mate." Ed nodded his agreement.

Foxy looked up: "I thought we looked bloody skinny, terrible in fact, but, Christ Almighty, it's hard to believe even now."

Morrie felt choked. Bitterly he commented: "Take a bleedin' good look at what the Emperor's bastard army has done to these poor sods."

Ed spoke for them all as he answered: "You know, my old ma, she never brought us eight kids up to hate anyone, but that night I heard those bastards screaming in the bloody river, I'll be honest, it made me feel good. Christ, how I hate the Japanese!" "So say all of us", echoed Bill.They looked at the revolting sights among the sick men waiting patiently in the goods truck. It didn't seem that long ago - or was it years - they were all fine healthy young men. Today they had been reduced to living skeletons, several of them barely alive. Many would not survive the journey downcountry. Bodies covered in jungle sores of all kinds, ringworm, ulcerated legs and arms which looked little more than bones covered with dry skin. Large hollow sockets where once shone bright eyes. Over them hung the spectre of death. It was hard to believe they were human beings.

The Emperor and his warlords were not only guilty of starting the war in the Far East. Through their brutal representatives during the construction of the Burma to Siam railway, they were wholly guilty of one of the greatest atrocities committed against mankind in World War II.

By nightfall on the third day, despite many deliberate delays, the main evacuation of hundreds of the chronic sick was completed. As the medical officers had anticipated, many perished on their way downcountry. Frequent stops were necessary to offload and bury the dead. The survivors were indeed grateful to reach the so-called hospital base camps of Chungkai and Kanburi. Some even reached Tamuwang. They were received with all kindness by Allied medical officers and orderlies, who did everything within their power to share their meagre food and medical supplies, and to make life more bearable once more.

At 'tenko' on the morning of October 24th., large work parties were formed up and allocated the unenviable task of visiting three squalid evil-smelling Tamil camps in the area. From the interpreter Atwai, it was learned that several high-ranking Japanese officers would be travelling upcountry by train the next day for the official opening and celebration ceremony, due to take place where the two sides had met at Konkuita. Furthermore, it was suggested that tomorrow may be a complete day of 'yazume' for all prisoners of war!

All day the outside parties worked hard, cutting fresh bamboos from the giant clusters where they grew in abundance, as well as many other tropical ferns and trees, which contained lots of deep green foliage. These were to form huge screens along the railway track where it ran close to the native camps, presumably so that the exalted Imperial Japanese officers would not be offended and would be spared the revolting sights of these native camps.

Returning to Tamajao, conversation was sparse. The men were starving and weary, so much so in fact that they were even looking forward to their small ration of rice and jungle juice. There had been some speculation among them because word was that the camp commandant was calling a special 'tenko' parade that evening.

The young fair-haired lad from Westcliff, Doug Pardy, was trudging along in his bare feet, like the rest. He caught the big toe of his right foot on a hard piece of rock jutting out of the ground. Normally quite a happy youngster, he provided his mates with a short burst of amusement as he proceeded to outline what he would like to do with all Japanese and Koreans, commencing with: "The poxy bastards, I'd make them walk barefooted slowly over a bleedin' bonfire, and then spend hours hanging them from jungle trees." He grinned: "On second thoughts, that's much too bloody good for 'em." Sentiments shared by all. Morrie had been thinking about the giant screens they had built.

"You know", he remarked to Ed and Bill, who were plodding along with Foxy and Tony Smith, "I've been thinking. The silly bleeders think the top brass won't see the Tamil camps. Maybe that's so, but there's no way they can hide the bloody stench. Anyway, it don't make any difference to us."

The work party entered the tall bamboo gates of Tamajao 241, expecting to be dismissed in order to return to their huts before collecting their rice ration and washing themselves in the river. To their surprise, they were marched directly on to the main parade ground where most of the camp were already assembled. Suzuki's platform was vacant. Most of the POW's were sitting in the dust, as the guards paraded around.

Sergeant Yamanoto (the Pig) appeared from behind the commandant's hut, blowing his whistle in between barking orders to the guards, who bowed low, then immediately commenced shoving, pushing and shouting in order to get the prisoners into orderly ranks. Atwai walked from the commandant's hut, followed by Major Toyoda and finally, Captain Suzuki, obviously the worse for drink.

Missing the first step on the platform and tripping over his large sword, he fell flat on his ugly face in the dust, to the great amusement of the POW's and the consternation of his guards.

Bill whispered to his grinning mates: "Pity he didn't break his bloody neck."

Sergeant Yamanoto was in such a hurry to reach his master, he also caught his foot on the lower rung and sprawled over Suzuki, whose esteem and dignity was sorely tried. Toyoda rushed down the steps to help. The POW's fell about laughing! It was like a scene out of the 'Keystone Kops'. Atwai tried hard to look serious.

Captain Suzuki was enraged. On being helped to his feet, he promptly smacked Yamanoto a hard blow across the face, cursing him in Japanese. The sergeant wasn't used to being on the receiving end, but resisting the urge either to reply or to retaliate, he bowed low to Suzuki, who kicked him straight under the jaw, causing him to fall over backwards. There was a spontaneous burst of applause from the POW's. They hadn't seen anything so funny in a long time!

With help from Major Toyoda, Captain Suzuki finally made the four steps to reach the top of the platform. Leaning heavily on the handrail, he commenced to speak. As usual, Atwai translated.

"Tomorrow will be a holiday for everyone. It is a day of great honour. At Konkuita, high-ranking officers of the Imperial Japanese Army will arrive by train to officially open and celebrate our great historic achievement, the completion of the Siam to Burma Railway." The whole POW assembly listened in complete and utter silence for the next few minutes as Captain Suzuki poured out Japanese propaganda, which even a child would have known was a complete load of rubbish. At the end of this diatribe, he had the effrontery to read extracts from a letter sent by POW Group Commanders, thanking all Allied POW's for their co-operation in the building of the railway, and pointing out that, now that task was finished, they must be prepared to work hard at new projects Nippon was planning.

The camp commandant swayed unsteadily as he gripped the wooden handrail surrounding three sides of his dais. His bloodshot eyes glared like tiny beads from behind his thick hornrimmed glasses. Regaining his breath, he started to speak again: "In keeping with the generosity of Nippon, we are going to issue a special ration of extra food tomorrow. This will take place at 'tenko' in the morning."

Finally, it was all over. Wearily, the prisoners made their way to the cookhouse to queue for their rice and jungle juice before washing in the river, lighting the nightly bonfires, and visiting any sick comrades left behind in the now half empty hospital huts.

That night, Ed and Bill sat talking round a large bonfire. Foxy, Tony Smith, and Doug Pardy were also gathered there. Assisted by Nat Ruben, Morrie arrived with hot sweet coffee and iron mugs of weak tea. Dear old Morrie was back in his beloved business, nicking from the Japs, buying from the Thai traders, and flogging the gear all round the camp, with no charge to his own mates.

Later that night, business completed, Morrie and Nat rejoined their mates. They sat down to talk. Nat had an idea for tomorrow night.

"For a real bloody change", Nat said, "How about a bleedin' concert?"

The other lads looked at one another in the glow from the bonfire. For a few moments there was silence, then Foxy spoke up.

"A bloody good idea, Nat", was his first reaction. Bill thought so too. Morrie and Ed agreed. The more they talked, the more they liked the idea.

Ed and Bill suggested they should discuss the matter with the medical officers and also get permission from the camp commandant through Atwai in the morning. After 'tenko', they talked late into the night. Tomorrow would be a busy day.

Next morning after 'tenko', an issue was made to each POW of one small tin of Japanese pilchards, complete with key, plus another tin of fish. Tinned milk had been sent to the cookhouse with a large issue of Indian tea, extra rice and vegetables as well as a quantity of dried salted meat. With all that extra food, it would be a day to remember for the hungry prisoners of Tamajao.

Breakfast proved to be a sheer delight with the helpings of boiled rice stirred up with pilchards, plus two mugs of unsweetened tea, beautified by the luxurious addition of powdered milk. A breakfast fit for a king. Maybe not, but the lads in captivity thought so!

Shortly after breakfast, Ed and Bill met Major Van Gazell and Captain Saunders. Major Boone was over at the theatre, where he had some minor operations to perform. The padre had gone to visit someone in the hospital hut who hadn't long to live. Captain Saunders was very pleased that 'Doctor Death', the Japanese medical officer, had issued urgently required and long overdue medical supplies in sufficient quantities to last for another two weeks. Among the most important were: quinine tablets for malaria, and precious grains of emmetine for amoebic and bacillary dysentery. He was at a loss to understand why the supplies included anti-constipation tablets. The medical officer had yet to meet a prisoner of war who was constipated. Perhaps they were meant for Suzuki!

Atwai was passing by. Captain Saunders called him over to explain that the men wanted to hold a concert that evening. Could they get permission from the camp commandant? Atwai replied that he was on his way over to visit Captain Suzuki and he would explain and make the request and then report back. Inside half an hour, Atwai returned to say that Suzuki had given the OK. A camp concert could be held that night.

Captain Saunders grinned with delight. "Away you go, lads", he laughed. "Get it organised, and don't forget, I want a front seat!" Nat laughed: "It'll be a bit bleedin' hard on the ground." Captain Saunders wasn't bothered.

"I still want a front seat. The ground won't hurt my arse." The lads laughed. "There's one thing I should mention to you blokes before you go." They looked puzzled. "Padre Schofield", replied the M.O. "He'll be there for sure. Now, I know you blokes can swear with the best Diggers in the world, but I should tone it down a bit. I don't think the padre will approve!" Nat laughed: "What, old 'Happy Harry'. He can swear as good as anyone I know in Bethnal Green."

The atmosphere of the dreadful camp suddenly became alive. Word travelled at an amazing speed throughout the entire camp. A bloody concert. Of all things, what an exciting prospect in the middle of the Thailand jungle, not far from the borders of Burma. Ed and Bill did not ponder over the problem of how to get it organised. The talent was there, the spirit was strong. Morrie and Nat were born organisers. Foxy was a star in his own right. Excitedly, the men dashed about the camp rapidly, talking to different groups here and there. The twelve Americans could only raise a couple of mouth organs, but anything was better than nothing.

At least, they were keen!

Four young Scottish lads offered to help. Two of them still possessed their old battered guitars, which they'd hung on to through thick and thin. With the Dutchmen, the lads struck oil; no less than two of them still had their old piano-accordions, and one still had a guitar. Things were looking good. The Diggers had not got anything in the way of musical instruments, and they were bashful about singing. Big Billy Foster was adamant that there should be a farting contest, as a major event.

The camp carpenter always had a ready stock of flutes fashioned, which played extremely well. The only problem was that there would be no time for rehearsal. All day the excitement grew.

It was generally acknowledged that the show would start about seven o'clock, in the Dutch area of the camp where there was a convenient mound of earth elevated high enough to make a stage. So everyone went to work with great enthusiasm. Only men in captivity could have produced so much, at such astonishing speed. In hours, a stage had been created; the prisoners' ingenious imagination was absolutely astounding.

With true nationalist spirit, Taffy Thomas, from the Signals, was desperately rehearsing a Welsh choir, although being a bit short on true Welshmen, he had to content with swede bashers, Cockneys, Geordies and a Scotsman. All of these had suddenly decided they could sing, except for Doug Pardy, who had given his all at the solo performance of the National Anthem back at Tonchan.

*   *   *

Meanwhile, out on the railway, a small train was puffing its way past the camp over the treacherous bridge and round the foot of the mountain. On the way it had passed several filthy native camps, camouflaged on one side by their newly created high screens. Each open topped truck held a specially constructed bamboo framework, which supported an attap-thatched roof, a sort of hut on wheels. High ranking Japanese officers, smartly dressed in their dark green tropical uniforms and polished boots complete with ornamental swords, could be seen seated in chairs. The last goods truck in the convoy contained members of a small military band, who were clutching their instruments as the old steam engine, fired by wooden logs, chugged its way steadily northwards to the site of the ceremony at Konkuita.

It was strongly rumoured that a senior British officer had been invited to attend, but it had been explained to the Japanese, quite simply, that there was no way that either he or any other Allied officer would attend such a ceremony or associate themselves in any way with such an occasion. Had he still been alive, Dave Wandle, in his true Cockney way, would have put it to the Japs far more bluntly: "Get stuffed, you wicked bastards!"

Captain Suzuki had already left, to travel by lorry up the winding dirt road to the ceremony at Konkuita. Atwai said that when he had left Tamajao, he was already half drunk. Had the prisoners busy organising the concert been at all religious, they would have prayed for the lorry to plunge over the cliff and for him to be killed outright. As they were not religious, they just hoped the bastard would slip on his sword and die very slowly anyway.

*   *   *

By four o'clock that afternoon many things were under way. There was much argument about the presentation, the compere, and who would do what. At the same time, several serious rehearsals were taking place in the blazing afternoon sun. Taffy Thomas was reaching stages of hysteria, conducting his newly created choir, who were standing in their bare feet and loincloths, doing their damnedest to "Keep a welcome in the hillside". If nothing else, the forthcoming concert excitement and nerves were reaching fever pitch.....!

CHAPTER 15

Jungle Palladium

Taking full advantage of the fact that their commanding officer had gone upcountry to Konkuita for the day, most of the camp guards seemed more relaxed. After all, they had been promised free drinks that night in celebration by Sergeant Yamanoto, who promptly assumed the role of God in the absence of Captain Suzuki and Major Toyoda. They had been informed by the commandant that permission had been granted for the forthcoming concert among the POW's and given instructions that they were not to interfere. However, they seemed somewhat disenchanted with the war in the jungle and appeared disinterested in the internal affairs of Tamajao, much to the relief of the POW's.

During the course of the day, Ed and Bill, ably assisted by Morrie and Foxy, had been extremely busy stealing various little items required from the Japanese and with Morrie's financial interest influencing the Jap cookhouse Sergeant Chida to provide amongst other things a large empty coconut oil barrel. This was to form an important part of the band.

It was intended for the Aussie from the outback, Big Billy Foster, who felt that his real talent lay in being not only the accomplished and consummate farting champion, but also that of a jazz drummer. So most of the day he had been practising with a couple of small sticks and a shaped out block of wood. He even dreamed of playing at a famous opera house, as he banged away wildly to his heart's content. Billy was really keen to perform.

The entire camp had suddenly caught concert fever. Everywhere became a hive of activity. For the moment the presence of death and suffering was pushed to one side as the lads set about turning into reality the enthralling prospect of a concert in the wilds of the Thailand jungle. In civilian life, young Nat Ruben had done all kinds of things, from nicking cars to window cleaning. A typical Eastender with a great heart, a lot of old chat, and a likeable character, he often produced short bursts of humour at the very time when it was so badly needed. Today Nat, along with Doug Pardy, was rushing around the camp to organise and liaise with the many volunteers who were busy rehearsing their acts. It had sure got the adrenalin flowing. Excitement was in the air! At one stage, after talking to some of the Dutch residents, Nat really got carried away.

Turning to a grinning Doug, he confided that when he returned to Civvy Street, he wouldn't now be going into business with Morrie.

"Bethnal Green won't be big enough to hold me!" At last Nat had found his true vocation. "I'm going to be a bleedin' impresario, mate", he announced decisively.

Doug was puzzled: "What's that mean, Nat?" he asked innocently.

"I don't bloodywell know!" came the swift reply. "But it's got something to do with theatres, I think. Anyway, sounds posh to me."

Led by Sergeant Porter, the camp carpenter, a gang of no less than fifty volunteers were hard at work, rapidly erecting large bamboo frames, complete with an attap roof, to form the basis of a crude theatre. Empty rice sacks had been split down one side and hung in position with raffia ties. These provided excellent cover for the stage sides and for the artistes. After considerable discussion, it had been decided that Morrie Finestein, with his personality and natural 'gift of the gab', would make the ideal person to compere the show. It was far removed from the stalls in the market back home, but Morrie was quite confident, and readily agreed to the daunting task of trying to make thousands of toughened POW's laugh.

The evening meal had been brought forward an hour and the POW cooks did the camp inmates proud on this occasion with an extra helping of boiled rice, a full ladle of green vegetable, and two small pieces of boiled dried meat, plus a mug of tea, again treated with powdered milk. After this sumptuous repast, it was a quick bath in the river, and then all was set for the final preparations.

From around six o'clock onwards, scores of men were already sitting in the dust, smoking, talking, and waiting for the big moment. On top of the level mound of earth a big bamboo frame had been constructed, adorned by hessian sacks. The whole scene began to look like something resembling a stage. It was a far cry from the dear old London Palladium, but it seemed that in a remarkably short space of time a miracle had been created.

The few men who somehow or other had managed to hang on to their battered old instruments were seated to one side, with Big Billy and his oil drum. Between them, they made up the camp band. They had been rehearsing enthusiastically all the afternoon. Some of them were due to go on stage also as solo acts. As the time for the curtain up approached, excitement mounted. Captain Saunders and the padre arrived, taking their seats on the ground. They were followed by Major Boone and Major Van Gazell, the Dutch medical officer.

The huge audience was fast growing still larger, and getting impatient. Morrie had an attack of stage fright when he saw the size of the crowd. He suddenly became more nervous than ever before in his life. It wasn't a bit like being back home on the old market stalls. "I can't do it, Ed", he wailed.

Nat, who was hovering around like a blue arse fly, interrupted: "Don't be bleedin' daft, Morrie. You've got to bloodywell do it now! 'Sides that, we ain't got nobody else!" The audience began to slow handclap. That made Morrie decidedly worse.

"Christ, they're taking the piss", he groaned. 'That's all I need."

To add dignity to his role of compere, Morrie was wearing a somewhat tatty pair of shorts, homemade by the courtesy and help of Foxy, who was definitely not destined to become a tailor in Civvy Street. The pair of them had created this wonder of needlework from an old rice sack. Well, on one hand they didn't look that bad, but on the other hand, they didn't look that good either! What really bothered Morrie was the lice in the seams, nibbling first at his testicles and then at his backside. It could all prove most embarrassing for a compere.

Too late now, the Tamajao orchestra was already playing the opening number, 'Here we are again, happy as can be, all good pals and jolly good company'.

He was due on the stage any minute now. By Christ, his behind was really beginning to itch. Morrie wished like hell that he'd kept his 'chopper cover' on. As the band ceased, amidst a loud burst of applause, Morrie emerged. As the evening sun blazed down, he walked somewhat awkwardly to the centre of the stage.

In desperation, he looked out. Bloody hell, there were thousands of them, sitting there just waiting expectantly. His throat felt dry and lumpy. His backside itched like hell. Trying to smile, despite his feelings, and assuming the poshest voice he could muster, Morrie commenced the opening lines: "It's my pleasure to welcome you all to the Jungle Palladium", he stuttered. "Hope you're all going to enjoy yourselves and join in the fun and singing. Have a good time."

From way back in the huge crowd, a Cockney voice bawled out: "Stop scratching your bleedin' arse, and get on wiv it."

Morrie was wounded and stung to the core by this crude interruption. He rose to the occasion magnificently by retorting loudly in his best market voice: "You can shut your fuckin' row to start with." The audience fell about laughing, and burst into a round of wild applause. The ice had been broken. Morrie's stage fright disappeared in a flash. Full of confidence, he went into action with all his old chat. As Nat said afterwards: "Like a true professional, mate."

"Introducing on the harmonica - I mean mouthorgan really - our friends from good old USA, Elmer Baker and J.W. Smith from Texas. They're going to play a cowboy number, 'Home on the Range'. That's the only bleedin' number they can play, so don't ask for an encore." Amidst howls of laughter, Morrie added: "I'm only kidding. Here they are, the cowboys from Texas." Morrie walked off, as the two G.I's took the stage, wearing cowboy style hats, made from old bits of wire and palm leaves. They played remarkably well. In seconds, they had the lads singing with them, as they played through six numbers. It ended in a great burst of applause as they walked off stage to rejoin the band.

Morrie returned full of bounce and cracked a couple of jokes. Then he introduced Johnnie Leaton, a fair-haired youngster from Beeston, Nottingham, who spent the next ten minutes impersonating film stars. He followed that with a one man take off, recalling when His Majesty the King had visited the battalion prior to embarkation for active service. The whole act was received with admiration. Johnny concluded by adding, "That night in the Officers' Mess, it was rumoured that the colonel would never again wipe his arse with the hand that shook the hand of the King." The audience went into fits of laughter and called for more. As an encore, Johnny gave a quick take off of German radio's Lord Haw-Haw giving a propaganda talk to the Japanese camp commandant on how to hate all prisoners of war. Then taking off Captain Suzuki, he replied, "I know it all, I hate all plucking prisoners, anyway." With a final bow and to roars of applause, Johnny Leaton left the stage.

In between acts, Morrie had shed his lice ridden shorts, and donned his Jap happy chopper cover. He was now in his element as he related the story of the young Jewish cabinet maker, up before the beak for nicking door handles from the furniture factory in Tottenham, where he worked. Asked if he had anything to say, the lad plunged into a longwinded tale of how he hadn't been married very long, things were hard, they had just moved into a new house and needed some door handles. He had helped himself but he was sorry 'n it was a foolish thing to do. Feeling by now that he had won the sympathy of the court, he stood humbly to attention as the judge began to speak.

"Being newly married does present one with many difficult financial problems. This court understands that. But the law requires you not to steal. Clearly you are guilty, but before I pass sentence, I feel it is my duty to express the court's surprise at the number of doors in your new home. Four hundred and seventy eight, to be precise. You will go to prison for six months!"

There was only light ripple of laughter, but not put out in any way, Morrie continued, "So you don't think that was funny? Neither do I. What about: The boy stood on the burning deck, his feet were covered in blisters, he aimed a sausage at the cat and hit it on the whiskers." They laughed and Morrie grinned as he introduced his mate from Southend, Ed Warton, to sing the wartime number made famous by Issy Bonn. The guitars strummed, and Ed started to sing.

"When the gang meets again on the corner in my home town, we were friends in the past and that friendship will last, till the curtain of life comes down.....!"

The crowd yelled for an encore, Ed sang 'Old Mammy Mine' followed by 'For all we know we may never meet again'. The audience sang along, that's what it was all about. There were many moist eyes in the crowd, as Ed took his final bow, amidst a generous burst of applause.

Next on the programme were four G.I's, performing a singing act. They took off the famous American prewar group 'The Inkspots'. Harmoniously, they sang their most popular number, 'Whispering Grass'. This was followed by 'The touch of your lips' and 'Pennies from heaven', amidst wild shouts of: "More, more!" and "Encore!" They grouped together again to sing 'When the deep purple falls', concluding with a touching rendering of 'Smoke gets in your eyes'.

Bursting with confidence and excited enthusiasm, Morrie came back on stage. Proudly he announced, "Now for a surprise act. Something you lot out there never dreamed of. George Bold, the camp artist, has gone to a lot of trouble, to scrounge materials for the next act and he has made them all look bloody beautiful. Two Diggers, two Pommies, a Dutchman and an American. I present to you our own, undreamed of bevy of beauties, the 'Tamajao Dancing Girls'!"

The band played Hawaiian numbers, starting with 'Aloha', and 'Sweet

Leilani'. The audience gasped in amazement, bursting into spontaneous applause, as six females appeared on stage, waving their arms and swaying their hips seductively to the rhythm of the music. It was hard for the prisoners to believe their eyes, as the 'dancing girls' pranced around in short grass skirts, rice sack bras stuffed with half coconut shells. Somehow or other they had all been clean shaven. Their colourful makeup was staggering. Even tree roots had been utilised to obtain colours. To the credit of George Bold, their long hair had been combed out, and from a distance they really could have been mistaken for girls.

Some of the audience were getting quite excited. Wolf whistles, wild waves, and very indecent suggestions were shouted out as they danced, waving and making eyes at the lads. Undoubtedly they were one of the big hits of the evening. The crowd went wild, yelling for more. The 'girls' obliged again, finishing with the Maori farewell song, 'Now is the Hour that we must say Goodbye'. Bill Slatoe and Elmer Baker were quite carried away. "Makes you think of all that bleedin' crumpet back home", muttered Bill wistfully. Elmer's reaction was more to the point. In his rich Texan drawl, he announced: "Can't wait to fuck me'self to death, man!"

Next on stage were four Dutchmen, who gave a really good song and dance performance, which earned them rapturous applause. These were followed by the MacGregors of the Highlands, a group of six Scottish lads who cracked jokes, danced and sang. They concluded with 'Maxwelltown Braes' ('Annie Laurie') and 'You'll tak' the high road'. The audience participated and gave them yet a further tumultuous round of applause.

* * *

Over in the guardhouse by the camp's main gates, Sergeant Yamanoto was making a pig of himself on rice whisky. ('The Pig' had been the nickname given to him by the prisoners of war back in Tonchan camp. It was a good choice and absolutely appropriate). His cronies, Korean Kaneshiro and Chiba, were also busy getting roaring drunk. As they were off-duty that night, they felt they had nothing to fear from their master, the treacherous Captain Suzuki, who had still not yet returned from the ceremony at Konkuita.

The camp concert proceeded, blissfully uninterrupted by the enemy. The prisoners were now being entertained by Sergeant Rank, who hailed from the popular pre-war East Coast seaside resort of Yarmouth. The sergeant was a wizard with the cards and clever with his conjuring tricks. These completely bamboozled most of the audience, and earned him well-deserved appreciation from the POW's.

Morrie had been driven potty by Taffy Jones, who was of the opinion that his Welsh choir would be the star turn and should have been on stage far earlier.

"Listen, boyo", he said angrily to Morrie, "I've worked bloody hard to rehearse my choir."

Morrie grinned: "OK, Taffy, mate", he replied, "You're on next. Get 'em ready. I'll go on to announce you all." Taffy beamed with delight. His moment of glory had arrived. He quickly ushered his choir into the ready position.

Morrie finished his announcement. Excitedly, Taffy Thomas gripped the short bamboo cane that he had fashioned as a conductor's baton, and stepped on to the stage. Unfortunately, much to his embarrassment, he missed his footing and fell flat on his face in the dirt, amidst roars of laughter from the crowd, who thought it was a comedy act. Dusty, but undaunted, Taffy recomposed himself. As the laughter died down, he raised his hands high into the air, and began to conduct his choir for their first number. This was warmly received by the attentive audience.

Taffy bowed humbly in acknowledgement, poised his stick ready for 'When you come home again to Wales' which was surprisingly good. In all, the choir rendered six vocals and were well applauded. Taffy Thomas felt justifiably proud of the choir's performance and the exceptional reception from the prisoners of war.

With the depression and misery of captivity temporarily pushed aside, Morrie felt elated as he took the stage again to introduce, 'Flash Roberts and the village idiots'. A comedy group of POW's made up of men from all over Suffolk, Norfolk, Cambs, Beds and Herts, Diggers and Dutchmen, they commenced with a sketch about the beginning of the war, where they were being taught how to make 'Molotov Cocktails' (petrol bombs) out of beer and lemonade bottles, filled with petrol, a cork and wick. The object of the exercise was for an assault platoon to ride up on a shining new bike, knock politely on the side of an enemy tank, wait till the lid opened, light the wick and drop the bomb inside the tank, thus exterminating the enemy.

The whole camp fell about laughing at the antics of the comedy act. It had to be the funniest thing they'd heard and seen for some years. All too soon the comedians finished and it was time for the star turn of the evening. Proudly, Morrie introduced: "The master of all voices, my old mate from Needham Market in Suffolk. I give you Foxy Wright." Since his first days in the army, like so many more, the young Suffolk lad had blossomed out considerably. He could quite easily take off his London mates, or revert to real deep country dialect. He was indeed a man of many talents.

Full of confidence, he walked on to the stage to begin his act. Skilfully using the wooden flutes and whistles which the camp carpenter had created much earlier, four of the lads in the band were playing 'In a Monastery Garden'. Foxy whistled his way through with fantastic renderings of English birds, ending with the long trilling of the nightingale. The applause was deafening. He bowed and grinned: "I'd like to take you all on a walk through an English farm to meet some of the animals, starting with the cockerels."

Foxy continued brilliantly, including most of the more widely known animals in his repertoire. "What about the jungle?" shouted someone loudly.

"No problem", and Foxy promptly provided some hair raising jungle calls. When he had finished, the applause went on for ages and was seemingly nonstop. Foxy was enjoying it all.

As the sound died away, he put on his deep Suffolk dialect and announced: "For a change, I would like to talk to you about the way things were when us old swede bashers met them townies for the first time." Playing all the parts, Foxy proceeded to give a hilarious account of past events, ending with a little piece about Big Billy, the Digger from the outback who was sitting with his oil drum in the middle of the band with tears of laughter running down his cheeks as Foxy concluded: "Been nice knowing all you Poms. G'day, mate, and g'night!"

The crowd was still applauding and calling for more as Morrie walked back on stage. "That was our final item in the show, and I know how you enjoyed it. For the rest of the night, it's sing-song time. The band's now coming on stage. I hope you all forgot your troubles for a few hours. One day soon, it's all going to end." With the cheers ringing in his ears, Morrie left the stage, as the band commenced with a World War I number, 'Roses are shining in Picardy'.

The camp bonfires were ablaze. No trouble from the guards. It was midnight as the last song echoed across the vast jungle prisoner of war camp. Thousands joined in singing 'Goodnight, sweetheart, all my cares are for you'. It had been a brief escape from hell. Many had been able to laugh for the first time since being captured. Most had enjoyed the good sing-song. Others were overcome with nostalgia as they wended their way back to their lice ridden bamboo huts and grim reality of their continuing captivity.....!

CHAPTER 16

Escape?

It was now mid-November 1943. Completely unknown to the captives of Tamajao, in the outside world beyond the Thailand jungle, many important gains were being made by the Allies.

In Southern Europe, following the occupation of Sicily, and on the same day as the Allies began the invasion of their mainland, Italy signed an armistice agreeing to the unconditional surrender of all her armed forces, leaving the Germans to fight it out alone. The British Royal Navy again held complete mastery in the Mediterranean, and the Red Army was pushing the Germans back relentlessly, inflicting upon them unparalleled losses in both men and material.

In Russia, the enemy everywhere was beating a hasty retreat, which was proving to be a costly one too. In the toe of Italy, the Fifth Army, mainly Americans, but including some British divisions as well, had made new assaults on the beaches south of Naples, at Salerno.

Meanwhile, in the Far East, hard fighting by the Australians had taken place in a series of brave landings in New Guinea. The bases of Salamana and Lae, having been captured, the campaign in the South Pacific by the Americans resulted in the recapture of the Solomons. The Japanese sustained a great defeat, the first of many, at Guadalcanal.

This major battle turned the tide for the Allies in the Far East. In the centre of the Pacific Ocean, one thousand miles to the north, a major attack had been launched in the Gilbert Islands by the United States Marines, who, on one island alone, annihilated over 4,000 Japanese troops in an extremely ferocious battle.

On the Burma front, South East Asia Command had been created, with Lord Louis Mountbatten as Supreme Allied Commander. British, Indian, and American-led Chinese troops were fighting a tough battle in some of the most difficult country in the world. With the courageous help of the Chindits, operating well behind the enemy lines in central Burma, great damage and havoc had been caused to the Japanese. At the same time, the Allies had achieved complete air superiority, an important matter, and something which had been badly lacking from the start in the Far East.

Chiang-Kai-Shek's guerrilla forces were giving the Japanese cause for grave concern. The large net cast by the Allies in the Pacific was slowly but steadily beginning to tighten, against the cruel enemy, who had so callously attacked Pearl Harbour and invaded Thailand and Malaya without warning, killing and injuring so many thousands of innocent people in the process!

In Tokyo, a meeting was taking place at Imperial Army General Headquarters, with Hirohito, the Emperor of Japan in attendance, where this whole catalogue of Allied successes and Japanese defeats and losses was being considered. The War Lords were in much disagreement. It was true that the completion of the Siam to Burma Railway was a great achievement, but this was now overshadowed by their heavy losses and increasingly serious setbacks on land, sea and in the air. The emperor was again gravely displeased and was at a loss to understand why and how this should now be happening.

The War Lords argued that they had successfully stabbed Great Britain in the back, when she was fighting for her life in Europe. What, suddenly, was going wrong! There was also the difficult question of the Allied prisoners of war. However, that was quickly solved, with a decision being made to bring the fit survivors only across the sea to work in the mainland of Japan. These prisoners would be carried in the holds of ordinary cargo vessels, which would not carry any special identifying markings.

If the Allies chose to attack the convoys, well, who were they to argue. If they killed their own troops in the holds of Japanese ships, it would be good propaganda, anyway. In conclusion, the Emperor expressed himself strongly, feeling that not enough effort was being exerted to defeat the Allies. Finally the War Lords left the meeting in much disarray!

* * *

Back in the horrific jungle camp of Tamajao, life for the wretched prisoners of war commenced next morning, with the usual 'tenko' parade. Captain Suzuki was totally incapable of taking the meeting, still suffering from the previous night's drunken orgy. Major Toyoda was also not available, so it fell to the lot of Sergeant Yamanoto to climb Suzuki's sacred platform, to shout the orders and take the salute, all of which he did with great gusto and delight.

Various work parties were formed up, for outside work on railway maintenance and repairs, and also for quarrying ballast. Japanese troops were now travelling upcountry in trainloads and also along the dirt roads by lorry. There was much military activity towards Burma, whilst at the same time, the rice rations and other supplies continued to be brought upcountry by Thai river barges.

Desperately in need of information, the gang of four had made quite sure they would be on the ration run that day. Also included in the working party of ten were Nat Ruben, Alan Pottel, and four Dutchmen. Recently, there had been a new intake of fresh guards, but unfortunately many of the old enemies remained. This morning, however, it was a new guard who, with rifle and bayonet fixed, accompanied the party down the dirt slope to the river barges.

The whole work party rested on the bank, while the new guard went aboard to converse with the head Thai. It all followed a familiar pattern. Ayut, who could speak fluent Japanese, in reality held the rank of Captain in the free Thai underground movement. He stood talking to the guard with an impassive look on his face, a brave native of Thailand and a loyal friend of the Allies.

The usual bribery worked quite smoothly, thus allowing plenty of time to talk with the prisoners. It had been agreed that Ed would act as the spokesman again, while the rest of the work party covered for him.

Today there was much to discuss. Kneeling down behind a stack of rice filled sacks, Ayut had special information. The Japanese had brought up several anti-aircraft batteries, positioning them in areas on the outskirts of the capital, Bangkok, the railway marshalling yards and extensive sidings at Non Pladuk. Sites were also being established near the bridges at Tamakan and also on the outskirts of Kanburi.

Clearly, the enemy were preparing against Allied air attacks, which were obviously expected any time from now. As there had been none to date, this was an encouraging sign. It was also rumoured, but not confirmed, that the enemy were planning to take fit survivors from the railway to work in Japan.

From underground headquarters in Bangkok, Captain Ayut had been informed that three more loyal Thai agents had been captured. After being tortured by the sadistic Kempi-Tai, they were made to kneel with their hands tied behind their backs and beheaded by the sword.

From the same source, came news of four Australians and two British soldiers, who had made a brave escape from Konkuita, across the border into Burma. Trying to get water and supplies from a small village, they had been betrayed by natives, hunted down by the Japanese, recaptured and executed by firing squad. At this stage of his information, Ayut paused, and peered through a small gap in the rice stacks. He smiled in satisfaction. The new guard was busily engaged, the old ruse with a young Thai whore was working well.

"It is safe to carry on with our conversation" he remarked. "Every time we meet, you naturally ask about help for an escape". Ayut assured Ed, that the underground movement were still trying desperately to organise a safe escape route through the very difficult jungle to the coast of Burma. The plan was to travel downstream a few kilometers by boat, then return upcountry into Burma on the far side of the river. Due to the lack of enough agents, to date the plan had not proved to be successful. To escape into the Thailand jungle with nowhere to go would be a highly dangerous undertaking. After a constant diet deficient in both quantity and quality and lacking the necessary vitamins, most of the prisoners of war would be far too weak and physically unfit to attempt or to undertake such a formidable task.

Ayut was also able to tell Ed the latest world headlines, including the landings in Italy and the fact that the Italians had immediately surrendered to the Allies, although the Nazis were still fighting bitter battles against the Allies on Italian soil. At the conclusion of the meeting, Ed thanked Ayut for all his help and information.

Ayut then went on to inform Ed that in a certain sack marked with a small white cross at the neck was a small box of drugs for Captain Saunders, the Medical Officer. This sack along with several others, had at Ayut's instigation been stashed away in the undergrowth ready for the nightly collection. All was well.

"Time to go, Ed", said Ayut. "The guard will be returning from the bushes any minute now. One further matter, British, Australian and American Red Cross supplies have been arriving in Bangkok. Already, large quantities have been despatched to the Japanese troops in Burma. We thought you should know about this important matter. Go now, the guard is returning." Ed picked up a heavy rice sack, and placing it on his shoulders, rejoined the work party.

After darkness that night, the ration gang returned to collect their stolen food sacks. After the safe recovery, the small box of drugs was taken by Ed and Bill to Captain Saunders, who was, indeed, pleased to receive them. Among the most important were emmetine for dysentery, quinine for malaria, and a quantity of iron and vitamin tablets. A lengthy discussion took place on the news of the day. The vital information learned gave renewed hope to all that night.

Back in their hut, Ed and Bill, together with Morrie and Foxy, were talking over the world news, as well as what little information they had received from Captain Ayut. Ed said, "In my opinion, we need much more information about the enemy's movement of supplies upcountry." Bill agreed.

Morrie asked, "You're up to something Ed. What have you got in mind?"

Ed thought for a moment before replying. "Well", he began, "I was thinking two things: (a) Can we escape into the jungle and still survive, bearing in mind our physical condition, and (b) I feel sure that we could rob the bloody railway sidings and get away with it!"

Foxy's reaction was, "Quite honestly, I don't think we would survive very long in the jungle, but we would have to talk it out."

Morrie was much more to the point. "Have you gone out of your bleeding mind? Here we are, thousands of miles away from real civilisation, in some of the worst jungle in the world. We stand no chance mate! You've been reading too many bloody novels!"

There was silence. As an angry Morrie got his breath back, he continued, "This is for real mate, not the bloody movies." Bill retorted in amazement, "Don't we bloody know it!"

Morrie wasn't finished. He was determined to have his say. "Captain Ayut has told us clearly. At the moment, there's no chance of escape. It's as much as we can do to survive. Having gone this far, I don't suppose any one of us could even screw a good woman right now."

That upset Bill. "Speak for your bloody self, mate", he snorted indignantly.

"Well, you know what I mean", answered Morrie. Finally, with nothing solved, the conversation petered out. Exhausted, the men quickly fell asleep.

Across the vast camp in the 'New Amsterdam' area a young Dutch sergeant and a private soldier, together with two Australians, two British and an American G.I., had made plans and settled final preparations to escape that night. Captain Saunders had been made aware of the plan, and had bluntly told the Dutch sergeant that the odds were far too great for the attempt to succeed.

In his opinion, their chances of survival were practically nil, but in view of their determination to escape that night, he had agreed to fiddle the camp sick figures, so that the seven men would not be missed for two or three days. He also wished them the best of luck and issued them with the five precious hand grenades the medics had carefully preserved and hidden for so long.

It was after midnight when the seven prisoners made their way down through the undergrowth towards the river bank. Sergeant Paul Buuren led the way. They were armed with stolen knives and pieces of thin rope, but carrying little or nothing in the way of spare rice or other food. They were determined to live off the jungle to survive. They had heard that the fit survivors from the railway might be taken downcountry, en route for Japan. They knew the terrible risks and were only too aware of the consequences for them of failure. In their desperation it was now or never!

They finally arrived at a special place in the jungle, where in stages they had secretly built a huge bamboo raft, large enough to hold all seven of them. It had been safely hidden. In minutes, they had the raft launched and were all safely aboard. Moving quickly into midstream and using makeshift paddles, they finally made it safely to the far bank of the river Kwai, and disappeared from sight as they made their way deep into the unknown and almost impenetrable jungle.

Heading towards caves in the mountains, the group stumbled across a lone Japanese patrol. Using hardwood trees to shelter behind, they used the five hand grenades to good advantage. In the confusion among the remnants of the Japanese patrol, they managed to escape safely to the caves, where they rested before resuming their trek towards Burma.

Five days later, the Japanese back in Tamajao were still unaware that seven prisoners had escaped, thanks to skilful handling of the sick figures by Captain Saunders.

However, after morning 'tenko' on the sixth day, without any reason being given, the usual daily work parties were delayed. Suddenly the inmates sensed there was something wrong when they were ordered to remain on the parade ground. Suzuki had returned to his comfortable hut, and the POW's sat on the dusty ground in the morning sun just waiting. A small Japanese transport lorry drove into the camp and off loaded what appeared to be large mailbags, which were securely tied at the top.

Ed and Bill were at the front with Morrie and Foxy. They watched as the large sacks - twelve in all - were quickly dumped on the ground from the truck. Two armed Japanese guards stood by, preventing the prisoners from approaching. As the small truck drove away out of the camp, a buzz ran round the ground. Could it be mail?

The thoughts and rumours ran wild. Just imagine if they were letters from home - something they had never received!. It was just possible: excitement and optimism grew. Perhaps the Japs had finally had a change of heart. Perhaps pigs could fly!

Nearly half an hour had passed, when interpreter Atwai emerged from the commandant's hut, followed by Captain Suzuki, Major Toyoda, and Lieutenant Hiramatsu, who was among the recent new intake of Japanese guards. From the way he was lurching unsteadily it was obvious that Suzuki had again been drinking. The four men climbed the steps to the platform, dressed smartly in their tropical green uniforms, white open neck shirts and highly polished boots. The three Japanese officers were bearing oversized Samurai swords, which dangled from their waists.

The commandant gripped the handrail for support, and bowed to the Japanese flag, which hung limply above. The other officers bowed in their turn. Sergeant Yamanoto bowed low to his masters, then rapidly barked out orders to the other guards who sprang to attention, then bowed in turn. Swiftly, they ordered the bareheaded and barefooted POW's to attention in the morning sun.

Captain Suzuki commenced to speak. "Today, for the first time we have received mail through the International Red Cross in Bangkok. I must inform you all, we have received nothing else or any other help from that source. No doubt, many of you are wondering if there are letters for you amongst this mountain of mail. But it matters not, in view of a very serious matter which has come to my attention."

The commandant paused, looking around his vast captive audience, then continued. "In view of what has happened, it becomes necessary for me to punish the whole camp by destroying these mailbags." As the words sank in, an audible gasp of dismay went up from the POW's. Captain Suzuki beckoned forward two guards, who appeared with lighted torches and promptly plunged them into the twelve bags of mail, the POW's only possible link with home, making sure they were entirely destroyed in the roaring inferno.

The prisoners could only stand looking on in disbelief, as the letters from their loved ones were consumed in flames before their eyes. The flames burned fiercely, reaching full fury, before dying away, leaving only smouldering embers on the parade ground. Like so many others, Japanese prisoners of war who were upcountry on the railway were destined never to receive any mail or Red Cross parcels whatsoever during their captivity. This morning, they were puzzled to know the particular reason for Suzuki's familiar outburst of hatred!

They did not have long to wait. From behind Suzuki's hut marched six armed guards. Behind them, roped together in a chain like animals and with their hands tied behind their backs, were the seven prisoners of war who had so bravely escaped from 241 six nights earlier. Barefooted and bareheaded, and each wearing but a loincloth, they stood silent and alone. Following them another six armed guards marched menacingly.The pathetic escaped prisoners were brought to a halt a few yards in front of the commandant's platform.

From the tall bamboo gun posts surrounding the camp, the Jap machine gunners swung their deadly gun barrels round to point directly at the ranks of helpless POW's, lined up on the parade ground, reminiscent of the blood bath at Tonchan. The sun blazed down on the bizarre scene. The atmosphere was charged with danger. An uncanny and uneasy silence prevailed as Captain Suzuki arrogantly commenced to speak again.

"How stupid of you to think you could fool the Imperial Japanese Army. Fortunately, a loyal native reported the whereabouts of these seven prisoners, and they were hunted down and recaptured. They have been courtmarshalled for escaping. I have warned before, but my warnings appear to have gone unheeded."

He looked down at the seven Allied prisoners of war who, despite their present grim situation, their ordeals and sufferings in the jungle, and their natural fear of a vicious Japanese revenge upon them, still managed to hold their heads high. They glared back in defiance. If they were afraid, they certainly did not show it!

The whole grim episode would have provided a perfect setting for a Hollywood war film, except that this was actually happening.

Suzuki was speaking again. "The sentence is death by firing squad." No one moved. "The parade will remain standing until after the sentence has been carried out. Your bugler can collect his instrument and will be permitted to sound your 'Last Post'." Then, addressing the condemned prisoners directly in front of him, he continued, "You will now be taken from this camp and marched to a place of execution outside the boundary. You will each dig your own graves, or you can be left for the vultures. Is that clearly understood? There was no reply. The entire parade listened in total and absolute silence.

Two more guards then appeared, carrying seven spades between them. They were to accompany the firing squad. The new lieutenant, followed by the interpreter, descended the platform, and joined Sergeant Yamanoto on the parade ground.

The camp commandant had the last word."This morning's scheduled work parties will commence one hour from now". Atwai, the officer and the firing squad of twelve men all bowed low to Captain Suzuki, who saluted as they marched the seven doomed men, still roped together, off the parade ground towards the camp gates. The remaining prisoners of war stood tense and silent, sick in heart.

Captain Suzuki and Major Toyoda remained standing on the platform. Meanwhile, a young bugler from the Norfolks was permitted to go to his hut, collect his bugle and then return to the parade.

Completely resigned to their fate, the seven prisoners were marched a distance of 500 yards outside the camp boundary, to a small clearing in the jungle. Lieutenant Hiramatsu ordered the party to halt. The interpreter Atwai stood beside the Japanese officer. The prisoners were cut loose from their bonds and forced to dig shallow graves. When the task was completed, sweating and grim faced, the seven men were made to stand at the foot of each grave.

Through Atwai, the Japanese officer asked if they had anything to say before sentence was carried out. Each man had his own bitter feelings. With trembling lips and in perfect English, the young Dutch sergeant spoke for all as he replied, "As soldiers, it was our duty to escape. You are about to commit murder."

Sergeant Yamanoto spat out orders in Japanese. The firing quad took up their positions, six kneeling down on one knee, the other six remained standing upright. Lieutenant Hiramatsu gave the orders, "Prepare to fire." Twelve rifles were raised to firing positions, the safety catches clicked off. To the last, the seven prisoners never cracked. Sergeant Buuren called out firmly, "Look to the heavens, comrades", as the order to fire was given. In a flash, it was all over. Their crumpled bodies crashed to the ground. Their life blood gushed forth, staining the soil of Thailand.

Among the Allied nations, Australia, America, Holland and Great Britain could be justifiably proud of their sons who died so bravely, paying the supreme price demanded by the Japanese for attempting to escape.

Not for them to be mentioned in despatches, or to receive awards for gallantry. They would lie forever in the wilds of the Thailand jungle, a small statistic among so many others. These seven brave prisoners would form just a very small part of those thousands whom history would eventually record had 'died in the hands of the Japanese'!

Only when time had passed, after the war had finished, would their families learn of their deaths. They would never be forgotten. Their comrades on the railway would never forget and never forgive the enemy for the 'Siam to Burma Railway'. The Japanese inhumane treatment, bestial cruelty and brutality towards their helpless prisoners were almost beyond belief.

From his wooden platform back in the camp, Captain Suzuki bowed low to the Rising Sun and saluted as the volley of shots echoed eerily through the morning air. The young bugler from the Norfolks stood stiffly to attention, raised the bugle to his lips, and sounded the Last Post. The strains they'd heard so many times before, the sound that was to haunt everyone present till the day they died. Suzuki then dismissed the parade, ordering it to be reformed one hour later.

In the jungle, Sergeant Yamanoto gave the orders. The two guards who had carried the spades pushed the seven bodies into their shallow graves and covered them with the freshly dug soil.

The vultures circled above in the brilliant blue sky. Lieutenant Hiramatsu smartly saluted. Atwai looked on in stunned silence, the only independent witness to the murder. The firing squad was re-assembled under Sergeant Yamanoto. The Lieutenant gave the final order to march as they left to return to Tamajao 241.

Behind them in the small clearing, the seven graves lay beneath a frame of wild frangipani trees, their spreading branches covered in masses of small beautiful white flowers with deep yellow centres. A myriad of butterflies flitted everywhere. The most vivid multi-coloured tropical birds flew freely to and fro. The sun blazed down from the bright blue sky on to the whole scene. It highlighted the dark green jungle vegetation, and provided a background almost like giant green arms reaching out. In so short a time the area would be reclaimed and the seven lonely graves would be lost forever in the maze of the Thailand jungle.

One hour later, 'tenko' was once again called in the camp. On the parade ground, the prisoners were being divided up into various groups for the many varied and difficult daily tasks. Along with Foxy and Morrie, Ed, Bill and several others were on a party selected for work on the recently completed railway sidings, half a mile south of Tamajao.

Although the events of that morning had shocked and depressed them, they were glad to be going to the sidings. The gang had previously worked on the project, but not since final completion.

Assisted by Foxy and Morrie, Ed and Bill were particularly keen on carrying out a careful reconnaissance. In the main they were aiming to assess the possibilities of approaching the railway sidings by a different route alongside the river. This was for future reference, in order to ascertain whether a passable trail could be found from the water's edge.

They had a daring if somewhat ambitious plan in mind. If escape was too dangerous, then there had to be a way of stealing from the enemy to provide some comfort for the prisoners of war or, better still, of inflicting some kind of damage or hindrance on him, some way of causing havoc and destruction if at all possible, but without incurring his wrath or revenge in the manner just witnessed that morning!

Today's task was to re-lay some of the main rails which had buckled out of position, and to rebuild them with rock flint ballast and new wooden sleepers. It was difficult and tough in the blazing sun. At lunch-time 'yasume', the POW's were able to rest in the shade of the trees and take careful stock of the area.

Ed possessed a good memory, and imprinted firmly in his mind was the complete layout of the railway sidings. He felt confident that he could draw the site in the form of a map, once they had returned to camp.

During the break, they had observed a trainload of wounded Japs going downcountry, looking disillusioned and pathetic. They had also noted troops and supplies going upcountry.

At the sidings, there were several sets of hand-operated lever points, which could redirect trains in and out, so as to allow the mainline through traffic to proceed nonstop into Burma. There was even an engine turntable. It was an impressive setup, and provided the Japs with the facility to hold trainloads of good and supplies in the sidings while other trains full of troop reinforcements and ammunition could be sent straight to the Burma Front, where desperate fighting was now the order of the day as the Japanese were finally succumbing to the attacks of the Allied air and ground forces.

This was indeed an exciting and challenging situation, with the gang of four already planning things ahead. Despite the odds and the half mile journey in bare feet through the jungle, they were exhilarated and undaunted at the prospect.

As an ordinary work day on the railway nothing eventful took place. Although still severe, the pressure on finishing the stints of work did not seem to be as great as before the completion of the main track. That day only four men took beatings, and were forced to stand to attention in the blazing sun for hours. Their crime was that they hadn't worked hard enough. At the end of a long day's toil, the prisoners of war wearily marched back to Tamajao.

At the camp, there followed the nightly bathe in the river, with the usual rice and jungle juice meal. There was still a flavouring of tea in the boiled water, but no milk. The supply had now been exhausted. The four lads rested for a while, talking over the events of the day. Ed said that he ought to enter the grim details into his box of secret notes.

Morrie told him quite bluntly, "Bloodywell dump 'em!" Ed argued that with all the information gathered, it would prove a great help after the war.

Morrie was not convinced. However, Ed went ahead and added to his notes, returning the small box below the soil, hopefully for safe keeping.

Whilst he had been in the hospital hut, Ed had had a small painting given to him by the artist, George Bold. One day, he was holding a spare piece of paper and sat painting. "There you are Ed", he said. "Reckon that looks like you." Ed had thanked him and promised to keep the painting, which was about five inches wide and six inches long.

His mates agreed that it was first class, an uncannily true to life portrait showing how he looked at that time. He kept it safely hidden away on top of his precious notes.

That night, Ed decided to visit Captain Saunders to update him on the current situation and to find out if he had heard through Atwai the friendly interpreter of any new developments about the Japs. He did not have to walk far on that occasion, as the Australian medical officer was taking a stroll around the camp to find out if there had been any change in the general situation.

"G'day, Ed", grinned the tall officer, "Just the bloke I'm looking for." Ed was pleased they had met, and the two of them sat down by one of the large bonfires to talk. Ed quickly outlined all the events of the day. Captain Saunders listened in grim silence, only interrupting to ask the odd question here and there.

When Ed had finished, the M.O. commented, "I'm the last person in the world to say 'I told you so', but I warned those poor blokes. I know they used the hand grenades to knock out a Jap patrol. It was only when they made the mistake of trusting a native in a distant village that they were betrayed. They were trying for food and water, they were bloody desperate!"

Ed looked surprised. "How come you know so much about their recapture?" he demanded.

"Atwai got all the information from the Japs and passed it on to me this afternoon", came the reply.

There was a deep mutual trust between Ed and Captain Don Saunders. Ed confided, "Well, I have now come to terms with the fact that we could still escape, but today's events have proved that survival in the jungle in our present poor physical condition and with so little equipment will invariably end in disaster. The only real escape is death."

The Captain looked startled for a moment. "Hell, Ed, that doesn't sound like you."

Ed grinned. "I didn't mean it in the sense that there's no hope. Of course there's hope, but we've got to survive."

The M.O. nodded his agreement, "Having come so far mate, we will survive!"

They talked for a long time. Captain Saunders explained how he managed to confuse Major Toyoda over the number of sick in the camp, by doubling up and juggling the figures around. Ed told the officer that he and his mates were planning to raid the railway sidings when they had more information on supplies from the Bangkok underground. The M.O. was not surprised, but made Ed promise to put him in the picture, before the plans were put into effect.

As they prepared to go their separate ways, Captain Saunders' final word of advice was, "We've all been through a hell of a lot together. You don't need me to remind you and your mates of the risks involved. Hear me good, Ed, with these bastards there's no second chance!" He rose from the ground, bade goodnight, and strode off in the direction of the hospital huts.

Ed made his way back to the lads in his hut, who were eagerly waiting for news from the M.O. Late into the night they sat, talking over all the vital pieces of information. They decided they needed a lot more detail before carrying out the plan to raid the railway sidings. Exhausted, one by one they finally fell asleep.

Foxy dreamed. It was September time back home in England. He had been out all day helping with the harvest. The smell of fresh corn was in the air. The Suffolk countryside looked wonderful. It had been a perfect day.

He walked up the garden path to his parents' cottage. Dad had strolled off to his favourite pub in Needham. Mum was as cheery and bright as ever.

"Sit you down my son, and enjoy your dinner", she was saying.

Her broad Suffolk dialect was as great as her warm sunny smile. The meal was fantastic. A quick bath, a spruce up in the mirror, a kiss on the cheek for mum and he was gone.

He got out his old bike and rode through the tiny village of Creeting St Peter, free wheeling down the hill towards Needham Market. He knew that his pretty girlfriend Emma would be waiting for him by the river Gipping at Hawksmill. She usually cycled across the first bridge and sat on the old wooden seat by the river bank, feeding the ducks with pieces of bread while she waited.

He rounded the corner and pedalled towards the first bridge. Standing up, Emma spotted him and began to wave like mad. My God, she sure looks beautiful thought Foxy as he drew closer. Suddenly he applied the brakes, pulling up sharply. Throwing down the bike, he reached to his belt for a hand grenade. He had spotted a Jap machine-gun nest.

He yelled to Emma, "Take cover, the bastards are here." With his right hand, he pulled out the pin and threw the grenade with all his might.

He woke with a start. Ed was shaking him by the shoulders. "Wake up, Foxy. For Christ's sake, wake up. You're having a bloody nightmare or something. You've been yelling: Take cover, and punching me in the bleedin' side, you silly sod. Are you awake now?"

Foxy sat upright with a start. "Of all the strange things", he muttered. "Sorry Ed, I dreamt I was back home. Christ, it was bloody marvellous", he added wistfully. "It was all sort of mixed up. Then I saw a bloody Jap machine-gun, like the one we knocked out of action in the Chinese cemetery on Singapore. You remember that night, mate?"

Ed muttered, "I'll never bloody well forget it."

Foxy gave a sheepish grin, "Hell Ed, that was some dream, mate. Goodnight, Ed" Pulling up his rice sack, he rolled on one side and was instantly asleep again.

Ed lay awake in the darkness, thinking of his family back home. Times had always been extremely hard for his widowed mother. There had been a lot of mouths to feed. It was a long time before he dozed off again into a restful sleep.

CHAPTER 17

We'll Meet Again

Towards the end of November 1943, two landslides had occurred on the railway embankment, one to the north and the other to the south of Tamajao 241 camp. This was not surprising, since whenever the attention of the Japanese guards was diverted or they were simply not as observant as they should have been, then the prisoners of war, with much cunning and concealed malice towards their captors, cleverly sabotaged the construction work.

Captain Suzuki had been instructed to put the prisoners to work on repairs without delay. Across the border in Burma, the Japanese military situation had suffered a number of serious setbacks and this had prompted Lieutenant Colonel Yanagisa to send Suzuki urgent and abrupt orders to move his arse and get his finger out. The effect of these orders did nothing but infuriate and anger the camp commandant, who was still suffering from a hangover as a result of his previous night's drinking bout.

Captain Suzuki, of the Imperial Japanese Army, was not happy as he took his place on the platform for a very early morning 'tenko'. Dawn had just broken through as the guards commenced to check the POW's on parade. There was always a lot of pushing and shoving to avoid the front rank, who were required one after the other to shout out their numbers in Japanese. If you could keep out of the front line, then it considerably lessened the chance of a beating or a kicking, which was the reward for shouting the wrong Japanese number. This was quite likely, given the difficulty of the Japanese language.

Following the usual procedure, from the left the counting began. Ichi, Ni, San, Shi, Go....... (1,2,3,4,5). All was going well until the Jap with the check list, accompanied by two Koreans, got to Chalky White from Norfolk. In English his number was 122. Trying hard in Japanese, Chalky made the mistake of shouting the Japanese for 22. From his nearby platform, Suzuki was not pleased. He scowled, and barked out an order, waving his hands to the two Koreans. They moved closer. Chalky went down on the dusty parade ground like a sack of coals as he promptly received a brutal kick from a hobnailed boot which landed on one of his bony shins. At the same time he collected a hefty punch in the face from the other Korean. The guards glared at him as he staggered to his feet, the fresh blood running down on to his bare foot immediately attracting a multitude of flies.

The situation was not new. Morrie was standing next to Chalky and sensed that it was fast becoming another small but highly dangerous situation. The Jap with the check list was enraged. "You speak Japanese number, OK-ka?", he shouted. Chalky was in pain, afraid and distressed. Taking a chance, Morrie spoke up, giving Chalky's correct number - 122, followed by his own number - 123. This earned Morrie a sharp punch in the face, which sent him reeling backwards.

The camp commandant was fast becoming impatient. He shouted loudly to the guards, ordering them to hurry up. There was no time for games this morning. Abruptly, the incident was over.

The ritual of reporting back to the commandant then commenced. Bowing to the flag, to the commandant and to each other, it was nevertheless quickly completed. Various work parties were quickly formed and marched to the stores to collect tools. Rapidly leaving the camp gates behind them, they found themselves heading in two opposite directions, the largest gang going northwards.

The four mates, together with Nat Ruben, Doug Pardy, and another Londoner from Bermondsey Harry Strauss, were in the southbound gang.

Morrie muttered to Foxy: "Know where we're going?" Foxy grinned as he replied.

"Sure do, Morrie. Looks as if we're heading for the railway sidings." Bill, who was marching alongside with Ed, joined in the conversation.

"Bit of luck if we are.What d'you reckon, Ed?" He looked at Ed, who smiled.

"Damn right, it's a bit of luck. We all need to keep our eyes open today, fellows. I want to try to complete my map of the layout when we get back tonight!"

Execution squad officer, Lieutenant Hiramatsu, was in charge of the party. A Nippon corporal led the way with armed guards following at the rear. Three or four hundred yards before reaching the sidings, they had to form a single column as they left the dirt road and followed a narrow jungle path in the direction of the river. Then they took a second path to the left, which led them again towards the railway sidings. In the distance, they could hear the hissing of a large steam engine. Suddenly, they arrived at the track. Some three hundred yards short of the sidings the embankment had subsided. There was much work to be carried out.

The Nippon engineer in charge of the sidings and the adjoining tracks was Lieutenant Tarrimoto, most definitely not a friendly character. On his immediate arrival, the main work party was split into sections. Various arduous tasks were quickly organised and the POW's put to work rebuilding. It mattered not where the captives hailed from, the United Kingdom, Australia, the U.S.A., or any other part of the free world. In common with other Japanese and Koreans, Tarrimoto possessed an intense hatred for all Allied POW 's.

Soon the familiar shouts of "Speedo, speedo" and "Buero" (fool) were echoing through the hot morning air. Ed and Bill were made to stand to attention in the blazing sun for two hours, following a number of painful blows to the body with stout sticks for not working hard enough. Chalky White and Harry Strauss were receiving similar treatment. The railway might be finished, but nothing had changed. Around midday, 'yasume' was allowed. Weary and exhausted, the lads flopped down on the ground in the shade.

For his succulent midday meal, Lieutenant Tarrimoto decided to walk the three hundred yards downtrack to the sidings, where a Japanese cookhouse was in operation. The POW's eagerly ate the small portion of cold rice they had been allowed to bring in their messtins, and thirstily drank cold water from their army bottles. The Japanese officer in charge and a number of the guards were seated in the shade a few yards away. Three of them had gone to sleep, whilst the others were eating their field rations, smoking and talking among themselves.

Ed whispered to Bill that he had an idea to make an inspection of the river bank, to see if it was possible by night to get access that way to the railway sidings. "Let's take a chance, Bill", he urged. Together, they approached the Nippon officer. Duly bowing, as was required, Ed showed an empty water bottle, and posed the question: "Permission to go to the river to get more 'misuwa'? (water). Lieutenant Hiramatsu didn't seem to understand, his mind was on other things, as the Jap sergeant sitting next to him was busy explaining to the newly arrived officer the passions and delights of the Thai whores.

Ed demonstrated, pointing to Bill and himself, then in the direction of the nearby river, and again repeating "misuwa". To their surprise, Hiramatsu answered "OK-ka, speedo-ka." He informed the Jap sergeant that there would be no need for a guard to accompany the two POW's. He was well aware that they would not be able to escape into the jungle or swim across the waters of the river Kwai. He added, "Ni mae" (Two men only). Ed and Bill both replied, "Aringato" (Thank you), bowed low once more, and promptly headed off down a narrow twisting path towards the river.

The blazing sun filtered through the undergrowth. Overhead swung a tribe of chattering monkeys. Slimy snakes slithered away from their path. For a few brief minutes they felt elated and strangely free as their bare feet padded on the dry earth towards the river. As they got closer, Ed remarked, "Blimey, Bill, that officer wasn't very smart, thank Christ!" Bill grinned widely, knowing full well what Ed meant. Since the frightful cholera epidemic, all POW's would only drink water from the river that had been boiled. It was a ruse that had come off OK. What the two lads intended to do was to carry out a quick reconnaissance of the river bank in relation to the railway sidings, as well as to investigate the feasibility of getting to them by night along the river bank, a distance of approximately half a mile from Tamajao.

Moving swiftly along, they suddenly arrived at the fast southflowing waters of the river Kwai. Rapidly, they climbed down the steep muddy slope to the edge of the shimmering waters. The world seemed strangely different there, almost too good to be true. Looking downriver, they could see a sharp curve to the right, which allowed them to view a dirt road that led from mooring posts on the river bank up the steep slope to the sidings. To the north in the direction of Tamajao, the two lads penetrated fifty yards or more along the edge of the river bank.

Apart from the natural habitat of the jungle, and the distant noise at the railway sidings, the atmosphere was uncannily quiet.

"Bill", said Ed "I've got more or less a complete picture."

That pleased Bill. "OK, Ed. Reckon We'd better get back now."

"Well", answered Ed, "I know we won't drink it, but we'd better fill our water bottles in case they check." Together, they approached the water's edge, filled both bottles, then laying them on the bank, they returned to the water to wash their bodies in mud from the river bed as well as to rinse out their chopper covers. For a few brief precious minutes, they splashed at the water's edge before commencing their journey back to the railway line.

As they trekked through the narrow path, Ed grinned at Bill, who was in front. "I'm sure we can do it, Bill, but we need more information from Ayut. Also, we've got to do a lot of talking and planning to make the mission worthwhile." Bill turned his head round and laughed. "Couldn't agree more, Ed". Reckon we'd better get a move on." As they emerged at last from the green vegetation, the POW's were already being aroused to return to work.

Lieutenant Tarrimoto was just arriving back from the cookhouse at the railway sidings, suffering from acute indigestion, having scoffed a large meal of rice, chicken, salad and Thai beer in too much of a hurry. This did nothing but add to his dislike of Allied prisoners of war. "Speedo, speedo, all plucking prisoners must work hard, speedo", he snarled.

Within minutes, everyone was again slogging away at the tasks they had been allocated. As the afternoon progressed, it looked as though the line would soon be running again. If that was not the case, POW's would have to stay on until completion. Later in the afternoon a ten minute 'yasume' was called. Almost as one, the sweating weary POW's sank to the ground, thankful at last for a short break. As they lay looking up at the brilliant blue skies of Thailand, suddenly there was a drone from above. Instinctively, everyone looked upwards. The drone grew louder.

"Christ", exclaimed Ed. "I don't believe it, a bloody plane!"

Everyone could now clearly hear the roar of the engines, but no-one could see anything. Whatever it was, it sounded large and powerful, and must have been flying at a great height. Gradually, the engine sounds trailed away in the direction of the Thai capital, Bangkok. Coupled with the news they had already heard from the underground via Captain Ayut regarding the newly installed anti-aircraft batteries downcountry, the POW's were elated, confident that at last an Allied reconnaissance plane was surveying the entire railway link.

Lieutenant Hiramatsu looked around arrogantly at the hopeful POW's. "Nippon", he announced, waving his right hand to the sky. Harry Strauss, who was sitting next to Ed and Morrie, looked indignant.

"Bollocks", he muttered. "The stupid sods. That was one of ours, mate."

Morrie grinned in delight at the Eastender. "Sure it was, Harry. There's no two ways about that!"

* * *

Nearly two hours went by. The embankment had been repaired and the railway lines re-laid. The men were collecting up their tools in readiness for the march back to Tamajao camp. Then, once again, they heard a heavy drone in the skies. It grew louder and louder until the sound seemed right overhead. The many upturned faces could still see nothing. Steadily, the noise faded away in the distance towards the borders of Burma.

* * *

That night, back in camp, as usual the rumours ran wild. There was a lot of wishful thinking among the prisoners, although the Japanese did not seem at all concerned over the incident. Foxy and Morrie, together with Ed, Bill, Nat, and Harry Strauss were discussing the exciting possibilities of air attacks on the railway. Morrie's immediate reaction was predictable. "Bloody long overdue", he contended. This was an attitude shared by all Allied prisoners of war in the Far East.

"Better late than never", said Foxy halfheartedly, more for something to say than a wish to disagree.

"Late", exploded Bill. "That's the bleedin' understatement of the year." Bill, like so many others, was angry. "Someone should have told them in London about the much boasted 'Jewel in the Crown', the fortress that never was - only on paper - the Island of Singapore!"

For a moment there was silence.

Ed remarked bitterly, "What a bloody forlorn hope it was, throwing in thousands and thousands more ground troops, for a one-sided seventeen-day battle that the so-called military experts, thousands of miles away in London, must have known was already lost! With a total lack of air support, no tanks, sod all. You don't have to be a bloody general to know we hadn't a chance in hell!

Morrie interrupted, "Someone's got a lot to answer for when this bleedin' war is over! But no doubt they'll sweep it all under the carpet as usual. Must be bloody great giving orders, sitting safely on your arse ten thousand miles away from the battle front!"

Foxy summed it all up. "It was just a bloody face-saving exercise for someone, government or army, or both. We'll probably never know!"

Ed broke into the conversation again. "Look fellows, we've been through this a thousand times, and as I see it, we're the poor sods who are stuck with it. So let's give it a rest. While there's life, we've still got to give it a go, agreed?" At this, they all agreed reluctantly with his sentiments and changed the subject.

Ed had managed to complete his plan of the railway sidings and late into the night the lads discussed the layout and the alternative ways of approach. There was argument and differences of opinion as to which would be the safer route. They were all agreed that they must first contact Thai agent Ayut for more vital information before they could finalise a plan for a raid on the sidings. The daunting prospect of what lay ahead gave them a sense of excitement and a purpose to carry on.

Early the next morning, interpreter Atwai visited Captain Saunders. He had some important information for the rugged Australian medical officer, who was about to take his morning clinic prior to his hospital rounds. He asked Atwai into his hut for a quick talk in order to find out what the enemy was planning. It seemed that the fighting over the border in Burma was giving the Japs cause for serious concern in view of the heavy losses they were sustaining on the ground.

Atwai also confirmed that it was an Allied reconnaissance plane which had flown over the rail link to Bangkok and the Japs were now on the alert against the possibilities of air attacks. At the moment, his more direct news was to the effect that enemy officers were awaiting orders from the warlords in Tokyo with reference to an evacuation of the fit POW's downcountry via Chungkai and Kanburi to Bampong, and then back down the Malay peninsula to Singapore. There they would embark in cargo ships en route for Japan!

The interpreter left after promising to report back immediately he learnt any further news. Don Saunders, very pre-occupied, set about his morning tasks. To add to his problems, he was also deeply concerned over the condition of Padre Schofield. Always a tower of strength, 'Happy Harry', as the lads preferred to call him, had not been at all well lately. The M.O. was aware that the padre had beri-beri in both feet, but suspected it was an even more serious matter. However, the Captain had many other medical crises to cope with that day.

The gang of four had been out all day with a work-party, breaking flintstones in a nearby quarry. Nothing exceptional had happened. As on other recent occasions, however, they had noticed barefooted Buddhist priests, in deep yellow robes and with closely shaven heads, wandering about the area. No-one really knew where they came from or where they went. It seemed that they came from some isolated temple a few miles away across the Burmese border, beyond the Three Pagoda Pass. Passing close by the prisoners, sometimes these Buddhists walked alone, at other times they were in pairs. The Japanese were apparently completely unconcerned by their presence although the guards always kept on the alert. There was no conversation between the Japs and the Buddhists. On the contrary, they just tended to ignore the wanderers on the infrequent occasions when they made their appearances.

That night after all the chores had been finished Morrie, assisted by Nat, was busy doing the rounds flogging tea and coffee obtained by courtesy of the corrupt Japanese cookhouse sergeant. Foxy, Doug, Bill, and Les Ardwool were sitting in a group talking. Ed was on his way over to the hospital hut, to speak to Captain Saunders. As he approached the entrance the medical officer was just emerging.

"G'day, Ed", he said, smiling at the soldier. "I was wondering when you would turn up for a chat. C'mon over to the bonfire and we can sit and talk for a while." Purely by chance, just at that moment along came Morrie and Nat with the metal tea tank which Morrie had 'acquired' some time previously. They paused for a rest, handing out two teas with a 'no charge to you' grin. Following a short break, they continued on their rounds into the 'New Amsterdam' area. Don Saunders updated Ed on the latest information from Atwai.

"Looks like we may have some more headaches", said Ed. "How are you going to sort out the fit from the sick if it does happen that the enemy start to evacuate?" The captain thought for a moment before replying.

"That's a difficult one to answer. I guess it will be one of those situations where you can't judge till you actually are confronted with it. It's really a case of wait and see." He continued, "Have you and the lads got any more information from Captain Ayut?"

"No, but we're trying to get on a ration run in the near future, 'cause we need more details about the enemy supply situation. In other words, what are we likely to find if we do manage to mount a successful raid on the trucks in those sidings."

"Good idea", came the reply. "By the way, as I suspected all along, Atwai tells me that International Red Cross supplies are being taken from Bangkok direct to the Jap troops in Burma. It makes me feel very bitter to see our poor lads suffering and dying in their thousands, while those bastards are stealing Red Cross medical as well as other supplies, which were intended to aid prisoners of war."

"If it's any consolation", replied Ed, "We'll take all we can get off them, especially as it's only our own goods we'll be nicking."

The M.O. grinned. "Good on yer, Ed, but be careful and please keep me in the picture." Ed promised to do so.

Just then Bluey, the Aussie medic, came hurrying over. "It's the padre", he spluttered. "He's been singing all the evening with the fellows in the hospital hut and now all of a sudden he's gone quiet and he looks to be in a real bad way." Captain Saunders jumped to his feet and headed towards the hospital hut with all speed. Ed made his own way back to his mates, who were sitting round a bonfire. They began to discuss how to wangle themselves on to a ration run so as to be able to make contact again with Ayut, the Thai underground leader.

Over in the hospital hut, Captain Saunders was massaging Padre Schofield's heart. It was, as he had thought, a beri-beri cardiac arrest. His efforts were to no avail. In a short space of time the padre was dead. The medics covered his body with rice sacks and carried it on a stretcher out to the mortuary hut. There they placed it alongside four others who had died earlier. The railway was finished, the link up had been made, but the POW's in the camps were still dying. That night Captain Saunders looked down grimly at the padre's empty bed space. Major Boone sensed the way he felt.

"Bad situation, old chap", he remarked. "We're all going to miss him." Sadly, the Dutch medical officer nodded his head in agreement. Captain Saunders sat down on his own bedspace. With a sigh of despair he commented bitterly: "Well, God didn't do much for him. On the other hand, I suppose, he might just have done him a favour by taking him from this bloody hell!"

Early the next morning, in the brilliant sunshine, Padre Schofield was laid to rest with the four other young soldiers in the jungle cemetery of Tamajao 241. Captain Saunders had left the Dutch medical officer in charge of the hospital hut so that he could attend the funerals and pay his last respects to his Australian comrade and the four British prisoners of war.

On his return from the cemetery, he was informed that the Japanese medical officer, Major Toyoda, was to meet him that afternoon. Atwai felt sure that word had at last arrived from Tokyo concerning the movement of the POW's downcountry en route to Japan. It was a question of wait and see. Meanwhile, there was the daily clinic to take and hospital rounds to attend to.

Out on the daily work parties in the nearby quarry that afternoon, the enemy officer in charge had a visit from Lieutenant Tarrimoto, who arrived down the dirt track in a small open truck. He left almost as promptly as he had arrived, and Lieutenant Hiramatsu gave orders to the Japanese corporal responsible for breaking the rocks into flints. He was told to take ten POW's and two armed guards immediately and carry out a small repair job on the line south of Tamajao, about a quarter of a mile from the sidings.

In the quickly selected party were the gang of four, two Dutchmen and four Australians, including Sergeant Reg Farquel from Hobart who had struck up a great friendship with Ed and his mates. After half a mile march down narrow paths they arrived at the spot where Tarrimoto had decreed that repairs should be carried out. In actual fact there was very little wrong. However, the lads were put to work in the blazing afternoon sun. An hour later, 'yazume' was called by the Jap corporal, who seemed in no hurry to do anything. The POW's quickly sat down to rest in the shade of the trees. Conversation was sparse.

Ed whispered to Bill and they got up, and approached the Nippon corporal in charge. Bowing to good effect, they then asked permission to 'benjo' (toilet) in the bushes. "OK-ka", came the reply. When out of sight, Ed and Bill quickly went in opposite directions. After three or four minutes, they met up again and emerged from the undergrowth and returned to rejoin their mates, still resting on the ground.

"Excellent", whispered Ed to Morrie and Foxy. "There is a rough path along the river bank. We'll talk about it tonight."

Meanwhile, back in camp, a meeting had been taking place with Major Toyoda, Atwai, Captain Saunders and Major Boone. It was mainly to inform the medical officers that higher authorities had ordered the evacuation of all fit men downcountry. No secret was made of the fact that they would be taken eventually to the islands of Japan, probably by ships sailing from Singapore. The M.O.'s had been loaned scales from the Japanese ration stores to weigh the fit men - in effect, anyone weighing above eight and a half stone! No sick were required. Anyone with amoebic dysentery or other complaints was to remain at Tamajao for maintenance work on the railway line.

Captain Saunders asked for further details. In reply, Major Toyoda stated that, commencing in twenty four hours time, the men would be taken downcountry by train in batches of 200 at a time, until only the sick were left. Major Boone was informed that he would be taken down to Tamuwang, where his services as a skilled surgeon were required. This would leave Tamajao without a surgeon.

Furthermore, it was ordered that, except for a skeleton maintenance work party, all the POW's were to remain in camp next day so that the selection of POW's could take place. Captain Saunders was to supervise, subject to the final approval of Major Toyoda. The returning daily work parties heard more details at 'tenko' that evening. Captain Suzuki was clearly uneasy as he addressed the vast parade. The messages received from Tokyo to evacuate so-called fit prisoners of war were not to his liking. After all he had become next to God, second only to his beloved Emperor. To envisage the possibility of remaining camp commandant of such a reduced number was unthinkable, but it had its compensations. He would of course still be serving his Emperor. He could still have a lot of amusement with the POW.'s under his brutal command. And then of course there was the unlimited amount of drink in which he could drown his sorrows, while as a bonus delighting himself with specially selected passionate whores sent up by barge for his ultimate pleasure. Yes, on reflection, Suzuki would still be of much importance to his lord and master Hirohito, Emperor of Japan.

As night fell and the bonfires blazed, the whole camp was agog with rumours. Morrie and Nat were still busy doing the rounds whilst Ed, Bill and Foxy were holding a serious discussion. It was an uncertain future. The gang of four had been mates a long time. Did the news mean that they were now about to be split up? No-one would know until after the weigh-in and medicals had been held the next day.

Harry Strauss returned from the hospital hut where he had been visiting another Eastender mate, Ron Smith, popularly known as 'Smithy' from Dag. (Dagenham). He was recovering from malaria and amoebic dysentery. "Christ", exclaimed Harry, as he sat down beside Ed and Bill.

"How's Smithy from Dag?" asked Foxy. "He's getting on OK", replied Harry. "But I mean to say, it's his mate Geordie Dunlop from Newcastle. He's a great bloke, a bloody good laugh, but when he talks so bleedin' fast I have a job to understand him."

While they were talking, Morrie arrived back with Nat Ruben. "How's business?" laughed Ed. Morrie grinned. "Well, like they say on the seafront back home, not good but not too bad, although things look like being bad in the future if they're sending hundreds of blokes downcountry." Foxy laughed. "It's all in the lap of the gods, Morrie my old mate. We'll all just have to wait and see what happens after tomorrow."

Ed and Bill were concerned that they hadn't made the ration run. They needed desperately to contact Ayut for vital information. Despite the uncertainty, they were still planning to go ahead with their raid on the railway sidings. After a lot more discussion they all returned to their huts, exhausted and too weary to talk any more. A while later most of them fell into a restless sleep.

The next day, following the morning 'tenko', all POW's had to report in batches of fifty to be examined and medically assessed. It was late afternoon when the gang of four were finally checked by Captain Saunders and his team. Major Toyoda was present with a checklist, which was divided into two columns, headed 'To remain' and 'Downcountry'. Ed was first up, weighing in at just over eight and a half stone, with a medical history of chronic malaria, amoebic dysentery, beri-beri, and a host of other tropical complaints. Toyoda ordered him to remain upcountry, as were Bill Slatoe, Foxy and Morrie. That was a relief. At least for the present they would be staying together.

Smithy from Dag, Harry Strauss from Bermondsey, and several more of his mates including Geordie Dunlop were also ordered to remain. Ed and Bill's friend, Reg Farquel, the Aussie from Tasmania and a number of other Australians were declared unfit and marked to remain upcountry, too tainted with tropical diseases to be considered for transportation to Japan. Unfortunately, Nat Ruben, Doug Pardy, Les Ardwool, and hundreds of others were selected to move downcountry, whenever the Japanese decreed to move them out.

They hadn't long to wait. Two days later, at an early morning 'tenko', the camp commandant announced that the initial batch would leave that afternoon. The first selected were two hundred Dutch POW's from the New Amsterdam area of the camp. They were to march to the railway sidings half a mile away. They would be followed in turn by another two hundred every twenty four hours until the evacuation was complete.

Four days later, in early December 1943, Nat Ruben, Doug Pardy and a number of other friends, were informed by Atwai that they were to report next day ready to move out in the early morning, with a mixed bag of British and Australian POW's. They sat around the bonfires that night, their last night in the horrific Tamajao 241 camp, talking amongst themselves. They tried in a futile manner to assess the grim problems that lay ahead.

Morrie Finestein was particularly upset. His mate Nat Ruben would be going downcountry early the next morning. The cheerful lad from Bethnal Green would be sorely missed. Nat was philosophical about the general situation. "Sure, I'm gonna miss you, Morrie, and your business enterprise. Then, there's Ed and Bill, our old Suffolk pal Foxy Wright, and all our other pals, but you know, mate, we've made it so far. Somehow, some day, I'm sure we'll meet again."

The young POW's looked at one another in the flickering glow of the bonfire. For a moment there was a strange sort of silence. Then Bill tried a more cheerful line.The best he could come up with was, "Just think, lads, what a glorious piss-up we'll have when this bleedin' war's over." Doug Pardy came over to sit beside Ed and Bill. "OK, Doug?" asked Bill.

"I'm OK", replied the fair haired youngster from Southend. "Just been thinking, though, about my wife Doreen. Wonder if she's still waiting for me. Maybe she thinks I'm already dead. You know, we hadn't been married many weeks before I left for overseas. Just wish I could see her again." Doug gave a big sigh, then he carried on talking quietly. "Mind you, I wouldn't want to stay up here in this bloody hellhole. Things could be getting very dodgy, I reckon. Still, we don't have a bleedin' choice anyway." He gave a weak grin. "Been wondering about the journey to Japan by sea. Christ Almighty, any bloody thing could happen! You know, with the Allies, they're bound to attack the Jap convoys in the Pacific. Reckon that could be dodgy an' all."

Les Ardwool, one of the Suffolks, who hailed from a little village near Wickford in Essex, spoke up. "Tell you what, lads, I've got an idea. There's an old pub on the Runwell Road going towards Woodham Ferrers. It's called the 'Quart Pot'. You all remember the name.When this bloody lot is over and we're all back home again, then I'll get in touch, and we can all meet again.What d'you reckon, fellows?"

"Sounds like a damn good idea, Les", replied Ed. "It's not far from Southend." Everyone present liked the prospect and all agreed.

As they sat talking and gazing into the fire, they suddenly heard the sound of singing drifting through the night air. Young Jock McCabe was strumming his old battered guitar. In the background, they were singing to the tune of 'I'll be seeing you, in all the old familiar places', a great favourite amongst the POW's. In turn, round every bonfire, young POW's joined in, until the whole camp became alive with the sound of their young voices, trying to escape their desperate plight and keep their spirits burning. The impromptu musical interlude ended with 'Should auld acquaintance be forgot, for the sake of auld lang syne.'

As the last notes faded away, Les was gazing rigidly into the dying embers of the fire. He looked at his friends, then remarked, "There is one important thing we should all remember, though." He paused for a moment thoughtfully, and continued, "Well, let's put it this way. The old 'Quart Pot', if some of us don't make it back home, we will expect the others to gather there and drink one for us. Agreed?"

Ed pondered over Les's words. It seemed a little uncanny, him saying that. It was as though he knew, in advance, that several of them gathered around the bonfire that night were destined never to return, never to meet again!

The lads remaining upcountry in the camp had said that they would bid a final farewell to their mates early the next morning, before they left for the railway sidings to commence their hazardous journey. Wearily, they made their way back to their bug-ridden bamboo slats.

Pulling up their filthy rice sacks for cover, most of them fell into an uneasy sleep. Several more, like Ed, and Morrie, lay awake for a long time on their uncomfortable bed spaces. They were thinking of their loved ones thousands of miles away. Tomorrow was another grim day. Who the hell knew what it might bring. In their strange and frightening situation anything could happen. Meanwhile for a few brief hours, sleep was the only possible means of escape!

CHAPTER 18

The Sidings

The day of departure for those due to travel downcountry dawned forebodingly. A brilliant early morning tropical sun blazed down relentlessly from a cloudless blue sky on to the dusty parade ground of Tamajao 241. Apart from a small party of some fifty POW's sent out to work on railway maintenance, all other POW's were ordered to remain in camp for the day. This proved to be useful since it enabled young comrades, who had fought and suffered together, the opportunity to say their farewells.

The two hundred men scheduled to move out were instructed to report on the parade ground for 'tenko' in small groups at various times during the early morning. Gradually they began to arrive with their precious few belongings. Suzuki's sacred platform was, as yet, still vacant. Even the camp guards did not appear alert or in a hurry. This would change rapidly on the arrival of the camp commandant, but for the moment, all was quiet and relaxed.

Ed and Bill, along with Foxy and Morrie, had gathered at the parade ground early. They were followed by Harry Strauss, Smithy from Dag, Geordie Dunlop, and scores of others from all over the United Kingdom. Many Australians and Dutch arrived also with the remaining four Americans at the camp. All had one thing on their mind. They had come to say goodbye to their departing comrades.

The gang of four were busy talking to Doug Pardy, Nat Ruben, Les Ardwool and several other mates of theirs who were leaving that day. Suddenly, the first shrill whistle sounded for the downcountry batch of prisoners to form up. This meant it was time for all the others to leave the area. Out from the commandant's hut strode interpreter Atwai, followed quickly by Major Toyoda and finally Captain Suzuki. They mounted the steps on to the platform. The guards commenced their customary bowing and saluting and then began the shouting, pushing, screaming and bashing of the prisoners, to get the parade into order for their lord and master. For a few minutes, amidst the confusion, the last swift handshakes and good wishes were taking place.

Morrie put a friendly arm around Nat's shoulders, his eyes were moist as he tried to contain his tears. "Ta-ta, Nat", he said. "See you in Bethnal Green." Nat swallowed hard and produced a false grin on his handsome young face. "So long, Morrie mate. It'll soon be over and I'll be down to Westcliff to see you!" Unbeknown to them at the time, they were destined never to meet again, as proved to be the case, sadly, with so many others gathered there that fateful morning!

Les Ardwool and Doug Pardy shook hands with their mates. It was a sad moment as Les spoke to Ed for the last time. "Had a thought, Ed, about my mother. She's the greatest. If for some reason I don't make it, will you go and see her. Tell her it wasn't my fault. Give her my love, please." Ed nodded his agreement. He knew the address all right. She lived at Wickford, not far from Southend.

He grasped Les's hand firmly, and trying to sound cheerful, replied, "By the same token, mate, will you call on my ma and tell her I'm sorry. I love her, and she's the finest mum in the whole wide world." Les nodded, too choked to reply. Deep in his heart, he was convinced that Ed and his mates staying upcountry on the railway had absolutely no chance of survival.

The Japanese guards were shouting and punching. Ed gripped his old friend Doug Pardy's hand. There was no further time to say anything, save: "Good luck, Doug, see you back in Southend one day." The whistles shrieked. Suzuki bellowed instructions from the platform. Only the downcountry party were to remain on parade. All others prisoners were to go back to their huts immediately!

The commandant was getting impatient. Captain Saunders shook the hand of Major Boone. "Thanks for all you've done in this camp, major." The surgeon from Suffolk smiled as he replied with a cheerful "Good luck, old chap." Then he lined up with his loyal team of medics, ready for the counting and checking before being marched away.

Those remaining watched from the far side of the vast parade ground, as the two hundred marched forward, barefooted in the morning sun. Goodbye to George Bold, the popular camp artist, to big Billy Foster from down under, goodbye to old friends! Led by Lieutenant Osato, who bowed and saluted Captain Suzuki, and escorted by armed guards the party marched briskly through the tall bamboo gates of Tamajao, heading south in the direction of the railway sidings.......

The men in the camp continued to wait and watch until the column disappeared from sight. Young Harry Strauss remarked to Ed and his mates: "I wonder if we'll ever see them again!" At that point in time, little did anyone realise the true significance of his words. It would not be until after the war was over that anyone would learn the fate of their friends.

There was a strange feeling of having lost something that morning. Ed and Bill followed Morrie and Foxy back to their huts. "Sod the expense", said Morrie. He decided it was time for a brew up on nicked tea. For a long time they sat in the shade of their hut and talked about their families, their hopes, and their very uncertain future.

Finally, they determined that life must go on, and somehow they must get on the ration run in order to make contact with Ayut in a desperate bid to obtain vital information. The rest of the day passed quite uneventfully. Atwai came by to inform them that normal work parties would resume on a reduced scale the next morning after 'tenko'. He went on to spend a long time talking to Captain Saunders, who questioned him at length in an effort to obtain every scrap of information that he had learned or overheard from the Japanese officers.

* * *

Two mornings later, the opportunity that Ed and his mates had been seeking came their way. Following 'tenko', sergeant Yamanoto ordered the last ten men to report as a separate group for the ration run. Among them was the gang of four, Taffy Jones from Tonypandy, Harry Strauss, and four Australians, including Sergeant Reg Farquel. The Korean guard was Kumdiet, better known as the 'Bombay Duck' because of his stocky build and his enormous protruding rear end, which waddled like a real duck. In keeping with his kind, he was not very bright, but, like his cronies, possessed the same cruel streak and special kind of hatred for all Allied war prisoners.

Fortunately, he had been on the ration run on many previous occasions, and was eagerly looking forward to his free fags and the bonus of a young Thai whore for his lustful satisfaction. In the event, this was to prove useful to the POW's. They were marched across the parade ground between the two cookhouses and steadily down the steep dirt slope until they reached the mooring posts on the banks of the river, where as usual, four barges were tied up.

"All men yasume", grunted the 'Bombay Duck, as he climbed aboard the first barge to converse with the head Thai. The ten POW's rested on the ground in the shade, waiting patiently for the guard to reappear. The old Thai women on the barges chewed the blood red betelnut and two younger women in their gaily coloured sarongs waved and giggled from the fourth barge. Nothing had changed.

A few minutes later, Korean Kumdiet reappeared, clearly unable to contain his excitement at the familiar prospect of spending time with a Thai female. This enabled the gang of four to board the first barge. Captain Ayut, who was standing quietly there, looked unmoved and as impassive as ever. According to the pre-arranged plan, Bill, Morrie, and Foxy set to work unloading the heavy sacks of rice.

Ayut indicated the number of sacks they could stash away in the vegetation, ready for collection after dark. He beckoned to Ed to kneel down behind a pile of sacks out of sight while they conversed. Ayut spoke first. "The enemy are bringing up two anti-aircraft batteries, which are to be sited near the railway sidings. They are anticipating heavy air attacks soon." Captain Ayut signalled a pause in the conversation, while he made himself seen, directing the unloading operations. Satisfied that the Korean was now pre-occupied with the young Thai whore from the fourth barge, he returned.

Kneeling down beside Ed, Ayut spoke again. "All is well. We shall not be disturbed for several minutes." He continued, "The Japanese losses in Burma are heavy. They will shortly be bringing down trainloads of wounded. They are also desperately pushing up supplies to their troops. It is a fact that they are intercepting International Red Cross supplies in Bangkok, which were intended for Allied prisoners of war. These parcels of food and medical supplies are being sent directly up to their troops in Burma. I hope you will be able to recover some of these goods, which were sent by the Allied nations for the benefit of all of you." Ed listened intently, as Captain Ayut paused and then carried on speaking.

"According to one of our agents, there are twelve open-topped railway trucks, the last two covered with tarpaulins. When they left Bangkok for Burma, they contained Red Cross supplies. We have estimated that they will arrive in the sidings at Tamajao on the day of the 23rd December, where they are to remain for three days in order to allow down trains with wounded to pass. I hope this news will be of some help to you. I wish we could do more. Remember, it's the last two which contain the Red Cross medical supplies."

Ed asked Ayut the correct date. "Today is the 21st of December, 1943."

"Christ", muttered Ed, "Only two days to go." He thanked the loyal Thai, and then posed a number of other questions, promising to convey all the information to Captain Saunders. Ayut looked out again and observed that all was still safe. Korean 'Bombay Duck' had disappeared into the bushes with the girl. He turned, smiled, and spoke yet again. "My good friend, Ed, be warned. The situation is now changing. As always, it is highly dangerous. If the Japanese should cease to bring rations upcountry by barge, then I have planned other means of contact. Please be patient." Ed then asked about today's extra rations. Captain Ayut gave a white-toothed grin as he replied, "Your friends have already safely hidden in the undergrowth all the spare sacks we have. All is well. Be very careful, my friend. The Kempi-Tai have recently raided the camp north of Konkuita. Many were tortured as a result. Several more have since died."

He looked out once more."Ah, the guard and the girl are leaving the bushes. Go now. We will make contact again. Good luck, my friend." Ed shook the Thai warmly by the hand, then bending low, he staggered up with a heavy sack of rice, swung it up on his shoulders, and rejoined his mates struggling up the steep dirt slope to the cookhouses.

Later that night, under cover of darkness, the stolen rations were recovered and fairly shared out. When this task was completed, Ed left his mates and went over to the hospital hut to talk with Captain Saunders, who listened carefully to all the news that Ed had managed to obtain. "It all ties up with the news that Atwai has overheard", the M.O. confided. "It looks as though the Japs intend to reduce the size of this camp to some five or six hundred only, for work on repair and maintenance on the railway line. Guess we'll have to wait and see what really happens. Either way it looks a grim situation." Ed agreed.

He then outlined details of the plan that had been drawn up by the gang of four. "If Ayut's information is correct, we'll be able to get hold of some of our own Red Cross gear." Don Saunders felt that, although he liked the prospect, the risks involved were really too great to warrant getting caught and paying the supreme penalty. He conveyed his thoughts to Ed, whose reaction was predictable. "Sorry, Captain, our minds are made up. It's what you might call a calculated risk, but it's a chance we have to take."

The medical officer knew only too well that the Pommies would go ahead anyway, and failed to see the point of arguing over the matter. He stuck out his hand to shake. Ed gripped it firmly. "Don't worry, Captain. We fooled 'em before, and of course, we'll be careful, OK?" At that moment, Bluey arrived to ask the M.O. to attend a young Australian who was dying from amoebic dysentery. The M.O. said, "Sorry I've got to go, Ed. Good luck, and take care!" Then he hurriedly headed for the appalling stench of the hospital hut.

Back with the three other members of the gang, Ed was holding a serious discussion. There wasn't much time to lose if the trucks were due in two days' time. By the light of the large bonfire, with the aid of a small stick Ed outlined in the dust the exact position of the sidings, working from a small map he had completed on stolen Japanese paper. A feeling of excitement crept over them, something they had not experienced since the night of their attack on the river barges.

Late into the night, the four thrashed out a plan of action for the twenty-third. Finally they agreed to a dummy run the next night after darkness. Especially pleased at this, Foxy added that it would give them an opportunity also of pinching a couple of chickens from Suzuki's farm on the way back. It gave to all the gang a degree of anticipation and, despite the serious risks involved, a sense of hope. They lay awake a long time that night before they were finally overtaken by sleep.

After darkness had fallen the next evening, the four lads held a lengthy final discussion, making preparations for a 'dummy' run to the sidings in order to assess the feasibility of attempting a raid on the following night, the twenty-third of December, 1943.

Before they left, Ed dug up his small tin box and updated his precious brief notes on recent events. He grinned to himself as he carefully replaced them, with the small portrait of himself by George Bold on top. It was still intact, His mother would like that. He shut tight the lid, and reburied the box in the ground safely out of sight below his bedspace. As a final precaution, he smoothed the loose earth over it so that the soil appeared to be completely undisturbed.

The dummy run was planned to commence at around eleven o'clock. As on other special occasions, on his left wrist Morrie was proudly wearing the watch Bill had nicked. He was armed with just a three foot length of thin rope, identical to that carried by Ed. Morrie tried hard to appear nonchalant and completely at ease but deep inside himself he was filled with misgiving and terribly apprehensive. Having committed himself to the scheme, however, there was no way he was going to back out now. For a moment he had a strange thought. His Jewish momma, back home in Westcliff, would have bloody killed him if she knew what he was up to, taking such risks!

Foxy shook him out of his reverie. "Ready, Morrie boy?" the Suffolk lad grinned.

"OK", replied Morrie. "Ready when you are."

Foxy and Bill were both armed with short knives, which had been painstakingly made razor-sharp on a slab of rock near the river when no-one was about. Carefully sheathed, these were hanging round their waists on belts made of tough jungle raffia twine. From Ed's belt hung his carrier bag, also made of the same jungle raffia, for they never knew when a chance of scrounging something in their travels might come up.

Dressed in best 'Foxy' tradition, with merely one rough rice sack as a kind of pullover to keep out the cold night air, a simple loincloth, and nothing else they may not have looked like tough commandos with all their modern equipment going into action, but their burning British spirit was still the same. By day they were just ordinary Japanese prisoners of war, but by night they became desperate men prepared to take enormous chances and, if need be, to pay the supreme price for their courage!

Harry Strauss and Reg Farquel were made aware of the plan and agreed to try to take care of anything unusual that might occur back in camp during their absence. A whispered "Good luck, mates", and then the four men left the attap hut. Moving quickly from hut to hut in the darkness, they reached the undergrowth in a few minutes. Keeping low well out of sight of the guards, they got to the river bank without any trouble. Everywhere appeared deserted. It was indeed fortunate that the Japs seemed to be afraid to be alone in the jungle at night, contrary to what they had all been told in the early days of the battle for Malaya and Singapore.

They made their way stealthily along the river bank and in no time at all reached the animal stockade, popularly known as 'Suzuki's Farm'. By now the four were so familiar with the area that they looked upon it as a ration-free zone. As they bypassed the stockade Foxy grinned and could not resist the temptation of muttering to himself, "We'll be back later for supper, chick-chicks." Morrie heard him and murmured, "Bloody idiot." Bill and Ed indulged in a soft chuckle together as they all padded barefoot along a difficult and rough narrow path which followed the natural sweeping curve of the river.

At times the thick undergrowth gave them problems. With no protective clothing to speak of it was very tough going. In the odd patches of bare ground, the silver rays of the bright tropical moonlight filtered through and formed uncanny and apparently moving patterns. From the bank the fast flowing river seemed to stretch onwards for ever, curving and twisting like an enormous silver snake. Not a word was spoken. In the distance they could hear the hissing of a steam engine. They were approaching their objective. Drawing closer, they suddenly reached a dirt road leading up from the river directly into the sidings.

Ahead there was a great deal of noise and activity. The four POW's paused for a brief whispered conference. Having come this far they decided to carry on and investigate further. Keeping well into the undergrowth they made their way along the edges of the dirt road towards the distant sounds. As they approached, the hissing of steam engines grew louder. They could hear voices shouting in Japanese. At last they reached a spot where the jungle suddenly stopped. Safely hidden, beyond the undergrowth edge they could carefully observe the whole chaotic scene, which was bathed in brilliant moonlight.

About fifty yards from their place of concealment no less than three steam engines, similar to the old tank engines back home, were standing in the sidings. Two were hissing and puffing out clouds of steam, whilst the third stood silent. Tamil natives were busy loading its tender with sawn wooden logs ready to fuel the engine. A Jap signalman was pulling at one of the hand levers which operated the points. He signalled with a makeshift white flag - in reality a piece of white cloth tied to a stick. Puffing furiously amid great clouds of steam, the first engine slowly moved forward over the points and on to the main line pulling fourteen goods trucks behind it. Ten of these were large containers with huge tightly closed sliding doors. At the end of the train, the last four trucks were open-topped, with tarpaulin covers tied down with rope. Chugging northward towards Burma, it disappeared into the distance.

Asking the other two to stay put, Ed and Bill proceeded further into the undergrowth skirting the edge of the sidings. Five long minutes later, and much to the relief of their mates they returned breathless but smiling. "OK lads", whispered Ed. "Let's get back. We've got all the information we need for the moment." Stealthily they made their way back to the river bank and returned to Tamajao by the same narrow twisting path that they had come by.

Eventually, they reached the jungle stockade - 'Suzuki's Farm'. Foxy called to the others, "Hang on just a minute, lads. Supper time, by courtesy of Suzuki." In a flash he was inside the stockade. Five minutes went by, and to the other three it seemed like hours. Just as they were beginning to get impatient, Foxy re-appeared carrying three dead chickens. "No noise, no trouble. I just wrung their bloody necks." Ed loaded the chickens into his carrier bag and the party continued on their way back to the camp via the river bank. At the mooring post, there was nobody in sight. Silently and swiftly they re-entered the camp, making their way up the side of the dirt road past the Jap cookhouse. Well contented with their night's work, they safely arrived at their hut.

Pausing only to bury the dead chickens below their beds until the next evening's feast the four lay down to sleep. Morrie announced that it was now 2 a.m. and he was 'bleedin' knackered'. Ed felt very restless. His thoughts were in a whirl. The actual evening of the raid seemed only a few hours away. The mission they had planned had got to succeed without any casualties to any of them. It was a formidable and daunting task that they had embarked upon. Suddenly, he fell asleep.

To all intents and purposes, the next day was just like any other. The lads went about their usual routine with no outward sign of the excitement and turmoil inside them. The evening came finally. The four young lads sat around the bonfire for a last-minute briefing before the planned raid. The chickens had been quickly disposed of and they all felt better after the meal, which they had shared with their mates. Morrie posed the question "What if the trucks haven't arrived when we get there?" Without hesitation, Ed answered "In that case, we'll have to abandon the mission and get back to camp as fast as possible." Bill said that it would be a safer bet for Foxy and Morrie to hide and observe from the undergrowth, whilst he and Ed went for the two goods trucks. Foxy thought deeply about the problems which might confront them at the sidings.

He spoke about certain possibilities, concluding "We won't really know until we arrive at the sidings and see for ourselves. Then we'll need to make swift decisions and act accordingly." Morrie snorted "You sound like a bleedin' general, Foxy." The Suffolk lad replied with a grin "Not really, Morrie. I doubt if you'd get a general to risk his bloody neck the way we do." Morrie smiled "Well, you know what I mean." Foxy nodded, he understood perfectly. Finally, all was ready. Morrie announced the time "Eleven o'clock, lads." This was the real thing. The four lads made ready to leave.

Once again, Harry Strauss and Reg Farquel wished them good luck as they disappeared from sight, making their way carefully down to the river. Moving swiftly and silently past Suzuki's stockade they were soon on the trail which led to the sidings. In the distance they could again hear the hissing of steam engines. They had travelled the half mile and were fast approaching the railway sidings. They emerged from the undergrowth to find themselves by the side of the dirt track which led up from the river into the sidings. Keeping well concealed, they made their way steadily forward until they reached the spot where they had been the previous night.

From a cloudless sky the brilliant moonlight seemed to illuminate the whole area of the sidings. To the right there was one solitary engine steaming and puffing, making ready to pull away at any moment. The four men gazed anxiously down from their hiding place, straining their eyes to take in every detail. Ed gripped Bill's arm excitedly. Less than fifty yards slightly to the north were stationed twelve open-topped goods wagons covered with heavy tarpaulins which appeared to be well fastened down.

Ed recalled Captain Ayut's words. The last two trucks were the ones containing the Red Cross medical supplies. The four looked hard at the stationary trucks. "That's it", whispered Ed. "It's the two at the back that contain the gear. Let's move in a bit closer." A feeling of exhilaration and tense excitement rushed through their veins as they stealthily moved further along in the undergrowth, to arrive at a position where they were directly opposite the two end wagons.

From this point, there was a distance of forty or fifty yards to be covered in the brilliant moonlight without any protection from the undergrowth. The four men paused for a whispered conference. This side of the line appeared deserted although they could plainly distinguish Japanese voices in the distance, possibly on the far side of the truck! The large steam engine was now making much more noise, puffing its way slowly out of the sidings. It headed northwards pulling a chain of heavily loaded sealed metal trucks which the watching POW's presumed contained ammunition for the enemy troops. They waited patiently until the noise of the train died away. Listening intently, they could still hear the odd Japanese voice in the distance. The railway sidings suddenly seemed strangely deserted. They held a final brief whispered talk. It was agreed that Bill would go first with his knife ready to slash the ropes holding the tarpaulin down. Ed was to follow close on his heels with his killer rope and raffia carrier bag. Foxy and Morrie to remain on the alert in the bushes in case of an emergency.

The plan was to steal as much as possible in two runs. Once they had the gear back in the undergrowth hopefully all would be well. In the event of unexpected danger Foxy would give out the wild cry of the gibbon ape. With a final look at the siding all was set. Bill led the way with Ed close behind him. Sprinting, they quickly made the fifty yards to the first wagon. Bill slashed rapidly at the ropes. Ed climbed up the side of the truck, pulling back a corner of the rough tarpaulin. He dived in and almost shrieked with joy at the large bundles he could see in the brilliant moonlight heavily marked with blood red crosses. They seemed too heavy to lift. Ed beckoned Bill to come aboard. With a quick furtive look round,

Bill clambered over the side of the wagon. No word was spoken. His knife glinted in the eerie moonlight as he quickly slashed open the first bundle with astonishing speed. Ed commenced to fill the carrier bag with the various small packages and sealed bottles until it was loaded to capacity. "Back to the others" hissed Ed. Grabbing the bag, Bill swung down on to the ground. He ran swiftly across the open space to where Morrie and Foxy were watching and waiting. Ed stayed low in the goods truck. His breath was coming in short spasms as he waited for Bill's return.

In a few short minutes Bill was back. Ed filled the second bag that Morrie had been carrying and Bill again made it safely back to the undergrowth. Ed was about to pick up a parcel and leave the wagon when he was alarmed to hear the plaintive cries of the gibbon ape. "Christ!" Something had gone wrong. His reaction was instinctive. Unknown to him, Foxy and Morrie had spotted a lone Japanese guard walking along the side of the trucks nearest to them towards the one that Ed was concealed in.

In the undergrowth, Foxy and Bill gripped their knives. It was a dramatic and tense moment. Ed could hear the footsteps of the guard's hobnailed boots on the track below. The adrenalin was pumping fast as he instinctively reached for his short length of rope. His knuckles were white beneath his tanned skin as he prepared to kill barehanded if need be.

Back in the bushes Morrie gripped his rope in both hands. The three lads held their breath, remembering Ed's words "If anything goes wrong there must be no panic. Wait calmly or our fate will be sealed if shooting starts." Each man waited anxiously. The guard reached the wagon in which Ed was crouching. He paused, looking at the cut ropes dangling down in the moonlight. He hesitated as if puzzled. Ed tensed himself, his thin rope clenched tightly in his two hands. The other three were too far away to help. Leaning his rifle against the wheel of the wagon, the Jap began to climb the side, using both hands. Ed crouched low, waiting until the Jap's head appeared over the side of the truck, looking down to where the tarpaulin had been turned back.

The surprised enemy soldier had no chance against the desperate prisoner of war. In a flash the thin rope encircled his neck, tightening with such force and speed that he died instantly without a murmur. Foxy and Morrie watched anxiously as Bill dashed from his cover over to where the crumpled body of the Jap lay beside the track. His first instinct was to load the body into the truck. Ed shook his head. There was no time to lose. "What the hell?" questioned Bill."He's got to go with us" whispered Ed. "They'll find him in the truck." Rapidly he pulled the tarpaulin back into place. Grabbing the dead Jap by the neck of his tunic Ed started to haul him towards the undergrowth. Bill picked up his rifle and bayonet and together they manhandled the body across the line back to where the others were waiting. "OK lads, I had no choice. It was him or us" said Ed. "He's a good Jap, well bloody dead!" he added grimly.

"What the hell do we do with the body?" asked Morrie. "Into the river fast" came the reply. "We can't sod about!" Quickly they gathered up all the medical supplies, two raffia carrier bags in all. Bill carried the rifle, Ed slung the dead Jap across his shoulders and they headed for the river. Minutes later they arrived at the bank. "Stay in the undergrowth" whispered Ed to Morrie and Foxy. They nodded. Ed and Bill slid down the bank, hauling the dead Jap between them. They waded out some distance before the fast flowing waters of the Kwai swept the body into midstream and downriver. His rifle and bayonet swiftly followed, sinking rapidly to the bottom. Even if he was washed up lower down, it might look as if he had slipped and caught his neck in the rocks, which jutted out at irregular intervals. Soon there was nothing to see but the moonlight on the waters. The two men waded back to the river bank, joining up with their two mates in the undergrowth. Together they began their difficult journey back to Tamajao along the narrow twisting path. It had been quite a night. They had a good quantity of medical supplies. They'd also had a near go. Ed grinned in the dark. Captain Saunders would be well pleased. Silently they padded on, bypassing Suzuki's private farm. They were getting closer to the camp. In the dark shadows of the undergrowth near the mooring posts, they stopped for a few brief moments to get their breath back.

There was no sign of any guards. All was well. They climbed along the edge of the dirt road, keeping well out of sight. Safely they re-entered the camp, silently making their way back to their hut. It had been a long day. Once inside, they had a short whispered conference and agreed it would be wiser to deliver the stolen Red Cross supplies direct to the hospital hut that night, just in case there was a sudden search. Morrie and Foxy flopped out on the bamboo bedspaces. The other two men carried the loot in the raffia bags across the grounds, arriving at the hospital hut in the early hours of the morning.

The two Aussie medics were still on night duty. "G'day, Ed and Bill." they greeted the two late visitors."Bloody oath, you blokes are late. What have you been up to?" The lads laughed. "Well", said Ed ruefully, "We've been for a bit of a stroll. You could say, about half a mile each way. Got some presents for the sick. Our own Red Cross gear, nicked from the Japs." Bluey and Joe looked in amazement as the lads emptied out their loot on the spare bedspace. "Streuth, Joe!" exclaimed Bluey. "We'd better stash this lot away out of sight until the morning." In the dim flickering glow of the coconut oil lamps, Bluey gave a big grin. "Captain Saunders will sure be happy about this lot tomorrow morning."

Ed and Bill both laughed. "We've sure had a rare day, Bluey. Guess we'd better turn in now. G'night fellows." They got up to leave. "G'day, Ed, g'day Bill", replied the medics. "Thanks a million. Guess we'll see you blokes tomorrow, OK?" Ed had a sudden thought. Will you tell Captain Saunders I'll see him tomorrow night." With that, the two lads left to return to their hut. Everyone seemed sound asleep when they arrived. In a matter of minutes Ed and Bill had joined them. It had been a busy day at Tamajao!

CHAPTER 19

Target: The Siam-Burma Railway

Christmas 1943 came and went, with the prisoners hardly noticing it. On Christmas Day they had a day's 'yazume', held their traditional sing-song in the evening, after burying two men who had died that day.The first of January 1944 arrived with no regrets, only a thankful goodbye to 1943 - a black year in all the young prisoners' lives!

It was the night of January 10th. that the prisoners of Tamajao were awakened from their sleep by the heavy roar of bombers passing overhead. By the stolen watch it was roughly half past two in the morning. My God, they sounded heavy and frightening. Some of the lads rushed to the door of the hut, but there was nothing to see. "They've just got to be ours", commented Bill to Ed. "Wonder where they're heading?" Ed thought for a moment before he replied, "Bangkok, I reckon. They got large railway marshalling yards there, as we know." Bill grinned, "Sure hope they knock the shit out of 'em." As they spoke, there were voices everywhere. The whole camp seemed to have come to life.

The men in captivity were delighted. At long last a strike against the cruel enemy. In the darkness of the small hours they talked and argued excitedly. Perhaps our lads would destroy the many bridges that crossed the river and clung to the sides of the mountains. Perhaps in time to come they would destroy the whole bloody railway! About two hours later the bombers were heard returning from the raid. Ed lay back on his uncomfortable bedspace just thinking and hoping. The others were all wide awake. Morrie had got so bloody excited that they had a job to restrain him from rushing out of the hut and cheering.

Thankfully, there was no sign of any guards. "Just imagine", said Ed, "they're really our own fellows up there flying free above this hell on earth." Bill replied, "Makes you think Ed. Wish to Christ we were up there with them flying free!" Morrie had calmed down and was quietly thinking. He spoke to Ed. "If we could get on a ration run soon, we could find out from Ayut what's really happened." It was with considerable difficulty that the prisoners fell back into a fitful sleep.

That night Morrie dreamed he was back home in Westcliff, near Southend. It was summertime and he had a day off from the markets. Being young and fit, he was always an early riser. His mother knew his habits well. He would be back from his morning run for his breakfast in about an hour. He was her only child. His father had died from consumption at an early age and Minnie Finestein had vowed never to marry again, despite the many offers. Her son Morrie was her life, her reason for living, and he was a good Jewish boy, not religious, but a good son. Morrie strode briskly from Preston Road, through into Hamlet Court Road, over the bridge crossing the railway and down Palmeira Road on to the seafront. It was one of those rare beautiful English summer mornings. He loved his walk along the promenade in the direction of Southend Pier. A few more yards and he would turn back and head for home, where momma, as he affectionately called her, would be busy dishing up crisp bacon and fried eggs. He grinned as he relished the thought. Nearby was a wooden seat and he sat down for a moment to enjoy the tranquil scene.

Little sailing boats painted in bright colours bobbed up and down in the calm shimmering sea. Looking across the estuary of the river Thames he could clearly see the outline of the Kent coast in the sunlight. To the left lay the long pier of Southend. Morrie decided it was time to return home, following the same route, before the early morning crowds arrived. At that moment the seafront looked almost deserted. Jauntily, he walked on. The sea air was exhilarating. He continued past the Westcliff swimming baths and unexpectedly the whole magic scene faded from sight. The morning sunlight became bright tropical moonlight.

In the river were his mates Ed and Bill dragging a dead Jap soldier between them. Suddenly they let go of the body and it rapidly floated away downstream. Instinctively he yelled out "Get a bloody move on before the bloody bastards catch up with us." Ed and Bill quickly returned to the thick undergrowth where he and Foxy were anxiously waiting. Both his mates were soaking wet. He felt bloody cold. He awoke with a start. Bill was shaking him. "For Christ's sake, Morrie, shut your bleedin' row up. What the hell are you shouting about?" "Bleedin' hell", muttered a sleepy uncomfortable Morrie, "it was all a bloody dream. I thought I was back in Westcliff. Momma was making breakfast. Wonder if I'll ever see her again." Foxy reassured him. "Sure you will, Morrie. They were our boys up there tonight. They'll be back and we'll be free one day. That's for sure, mate! I know only too well what bloody nightmares we get out here." Morrie pulled up his filthy rice sacks but was totally unable to drop off to sleep again. That dream, it had all been so real. He lay awake until the sound of the Japanese reveille jolted him and his mates back into the grim reality of yet another long day in the hands of the enemy.

The fifteenth day of February, 1944 arrived. They had now suffered in captivity two long cruel years. Mercifully, unbeknown to them, they still had almost another two years to survive before the unconditional surrender of Japan. There had been more nightly air raids down south and the military situation was slowly but surely changing. On the morning of February 21st., they were again on the ration run at long last.

It was another hot sunny day in the jungle. The ten men were marched across the grounds and down the dirt slope to the river. They were escorted by a single

Korean guard, who immediately went aboard the first barge, as was customary, to confer with the head Thai. In the meantime, the prisoners' work party rested in the shade on the grass. Apart from the gang of four there was Harry Strauss, Geordie Dunlop, Reg Farquel and three more Australians. They all sat about patiently, looking up at the cloudless blue sky. On the barges, the old Thai women were still chewing the dark blood red betel nut. Over on the fourth barge two younger Thai girls aged around twenty, dressed in bright check coloured sarongs, waved and giggled at the prisoners, who laughed and waved back.

Being a Suffolk countryman at heart, Foxy took a particular interest in the wild flowers which grew in colourful abundance on the hillside. Among them were sprays of beautiful wild orchids, some of the rarest and most striking in the world. He was also fascinated by the wildlife amongst the birds and animals, which flew and roamed so freely. As he watched, one multi-coloured bird came to rest only a few yards away. It was a majestic specimen, with a short curved tail, displaying a magnificent deep crimson and white plumage, a king of his breed, with tiny bright eyes looking almost inquisitively at the prisoners. Suddenly, it spread its beautiful wings and, flying swiftly and freely away, it disappeared into the distant hills.

The Korean guard emerged from the barge complete with his free evil smelling Thai fags. In accordance with their plan, the gang of four pushed forward, making sure they boarded the first barge. The Korean gestured to the other prisoners to follow him as he allocated them to work on the other barges, before moving on to barge number four to be entertained by the Thai whores.

Captain Ayut was waiting aboard without any signs of nervousness. He nodded an acknowledgement as Bill, Foxy, and Morrie commenced the heavy task of unloading the heavy rice sacks, leaving Ed to converse with him. Ayut knelt down beside the sacks, signalling to Ed to follow suit. "It's safe to talk now." He spoke quietly in his excellent English. "From time to time I will observe what's happening with the Korean guard. If it runs true to form, we will have no problem." Ed listened intently as Ayut continued, "A Jap body was washed up on the riverside at a remote spot downstream. It looked as if he had a broken neck. We made sure the body was disposed of on the far side of the river."

Feeling somewhat relieved, Ed thanked Ayut and quickly explained what had happened. Ayut was pleased and he went on to give Ed further information. "The goods trucks have now been sent upcountry from the sidings and the enemy are installing the two anti-aircraft batteries I told you they were expecting. They are to be positioned one to the south and the other to the northwest. You will have noticed Buddhist priests in the area. They wander miles from the border, through the Three Pagoda Pass into our country. The Japanese do not like them. They keep well away."

Ed nodded that he understood. "Wait there one moment while I make myself seen and observe how the unloading is going." Ed remained in position, crouched low behind the stacked rice sacks. Ayut went and had a brief word with Bill and Foxy. Morrie was still coming back down the sunlit hill with Harry Strauss. They were both sweating like hell. The underground agent quickly explained to the lads what sacks were safe to steal and stash away in the undergrowth as usual, and informed them that a small box of drugs was concealed in one of them, bearing a special mark. This was to be handed to Captain Saunders, the medical officer in charge of the hospital. Bill and Foxy replied "OK!" They fully understood and thanked Ayut. He smiled and waved them on their way.

Returning, he knelt down beside Ed. "All is well, my friend. Our young decoy has lured the guard off the fourth barge and into the bushes. It is safe to continue our conversation." He smiled at Ed, displaying his perfect set of white teeth. "For your information there is now a small force of Thai guerrillas operating mainly at night from across the river. Their objectives are the same as yours, to sabotage the enemy wherever possible. They are led by Major Bulpakdi, an important member of the Thai underground movement. He speaks perfect English as well as Japanese and other languages." Ed listened in amazement as the quietly spoken Captain Ayut continued "Before the war he was a student at Bangkok University. His young wife was raped and murdered by the Japanese. He has killed many times and will show no mercy to the enemy. At night he is supplied from a sampan with ammunition and explosives at certain points on the river where the Japanese are afraid to go. Last week a number of his guerrillas wiped out a complete Japanese patrol a few miles north of Tamajao."

Ed remained silent, trying to absorb all this news. Ayut continued "We rely a great deal on Major Bulpakdi for information. Although under the yellow robes he has been well armed, on occasions he has passed himself off as a Buddhist priest in order to fool the Japanese." Ayut stood up abruptly looking to make sure that the Korean guard was still in the bushes with the Thai girl. He was. He squatted down again beside a very excited Ed. "You and your small band of comrades have already wrought much destruction and hindered the enemy, despite your own cruel suffering in captivity. If it becomes necessary, Major Bulpakdi will contact you. In his own way he will help you if it is at all possible."

Ed replied that he now fully understood the current situation. Could the Captain provide him with details of the recent Allied bombing raids down south. The Thai agent answered his question."Several raids have taken place on the outskirts of Bangkok, on the marshalling yards and railway sidings. Many enemy anti-aircraft batteries have been in action. The Japanese have no fighter planes in Thailand. Many Japanese troops have been killed and wounded. So far, no Allied aircraft have been brought down. It is now only a matter of time, my friend. The tide is turning." Taking another quick look at the river bank, Ayut hissed "Ah, the guard is returning, Go, now. We will meet again."

Ed rose to his feet. elated by the information he had gained. Struggling with a sack of rice, he staggered off the barge up the dusty dirt slope towards the two cookhouses. The rest of the day passed without anything unusual occurring, just a continuous hard slog unloading the barges. That night under cover of darkness the POW gang returned surreptitiously and retrieved the stolen food. As always, this was divided up and shared equally among the prisoners. Captain Don Saunders gratefully received his small box of lifesaving drugs. He was delighted to hear the latest news from Captain Ayut, relayed by Ed. The gang of four discussed the information in great detail. They also felt the news was good and it was just a matter of time before the enemy would be beaten!

*   *   *

Seven more monotonous and cruel months passed however for the luckless and unfortunate inmates of Tamajao 241. It was now late September 1944. In those seven months nothing had changed. There had been further contact with Captain Ayut, but no meeting with the Thai guerrilla leader. Like many other prisoners, Ed began to wonder, deep in his heart, if perhaps it had just been wishful thinking after all.

The monsoon season had come and gone once more. Life and warmth were returning to the jungle with the renewed fast growth of the luxuriant vegetation. The wild animals roamed freely again. The prisoners of war had regularly heard Allied planes going over at night, to return again two hours later, heading back into Burma. As usual on these occasions a vast number of rumours had run wild throughout the camp, but nothing positive transpired.

The four pals who had come this far through their captivity together had taken several more calculated and daring risks. Their very survival seemed to depend upon the excitement generated by these escapades. Their most recent operation had involved the dangerous task of a reconnaissance to locate and map out the exact position of the two Japanese anti-aircraft bases to the south and to the northwest of the railway sidings.

The map was drawn on stolen Japanese paper and hidden away for future reference with Ed's secret notes. Morrie had already warned Ed not to get any bloody stupid ideas, like having a go at blowing the AA guns up or something equally crazy. Stealing explosives would prove more difficult than before. Ed discussed the possibilities with Bill, who liked the idea, but also thought it was too dangerous. "Nice idea, Ed, but too bloody risky" he said. Despite this opposition, deep down Ed still nursed his secret ambitious feelings, but for the time was forced to keep such thoughts to himself.

Towards the end of November '44 Ayut had brought bad news. There had been a disastrous Allied air attack downcountry. The various prisoners of war camps remained unmarked and vulnerable, as most of them were situated close to that most important of military targets, the railway, with its bridges, sidings, and attendant ammunition dumps. In one night, 100 helpless Allied POW's had been killed and 400 others badly injured. The news was received with dismay by the inmates of Tamajao. Realising that air raids were a vital part of the Allied plan to cut off the enemy's main supply route into Burma, the prisoners fully understood the dangerous position they had been placed in by the Japanese. Nevertheless, it seemed an ironic twist of fate that, having suffered and survived so far, the POW's should be subjected to bombing by their own forces. Each blow delivered against the enemy was received with joy. At the same time it brought a natural fear of death or injury during every attack.

Christmas 1944 was nothing to celebrate. POW's still died, the daily situation seemed to deteriorate further. The camp commandant Captain Suzuki's temper and rantings became even worse, following the increased Allied air raids. The helpless POW's were sent out to work, many of them very sick and weak, still being treated as starving slaves, repairing the damage that had been created by the air attacks. There were many occasions when they were transported further upcountry by lorries through the Three Pagoda Pass into Burma to work on urgent rail and bridge repairs.

During this period, both Ed and Bill had bouts of sickness with chronic malaria and recurring amoebic dysentery. Along with Foxy, Morrie and so many others the brave young Australian medical officer, Captain Don Saunders, had himself been struck down several times. Somehow or other he had always managed to rally round and struggle on to save the lives of others. Many times, in scenes reminiscent of Tonchan, his heart was filled with despair and pity for his fellow prisoners of war.

Desperately short of all types of medical supplies, the M.O. argued and pleaded but was repeatedly beaten for his efforts by the well-educated Doctor Death. Captain Suzuki had been observed on many recent occasions smoking American Camel cigarettes. It was a cruel situation with so many men still chronically sick. Many died for the lack of the necessary drugs and medical supplies, which the POW's were now well aware were being confiscated for use by the Japanese.

On the night of the fifteenth of January 1945, shortly before 2 a.m., the roar of Allied bombers were again heard in the skies approaching Tamajao. Ed was awake in a flash. He had a strange intuition that something dramatic was about to happen. The other three of the gang were also awakened, along with many others.

"The first wave seemed to have passed over" said Bill. Ed agreed.

"Can't sleep, mate. Got a strange feeling something's up." Morrie sat upright on his rough bedspace.

"Christ, Ed", he exclaimed, "What d'you reckon is gonna happen?" Morrie could always be relied on to get worried.

"Damned if I know", replied Ed. Foxy rose to his bare feet.

"Gonna take a look outside", he said.

"I'll come with you", replied Ed. A few minutes later all four men had vacated the hut and were standing a few yards away, talking quietly, when suddenly they heard the roar of what appeared to be a lone aircraft. The lads stood up and strained their eyes as they stared up into the brilliant tropical moonlit sky.

Excitedly, Bill gripped Ed's arm. "There he is, mate. One of ours", he shouted. The four men were spellbound. Silhouetted against the moonlight was a lone four-engined bomber, fearful in size and casting an uncanny shadow as it flew towards Tamajao, following the route of the river Kwai. As it reached the area over the giant curved wooden bridge only a few hundred yards from the POW camp, a series of strange whistling sounds grew louder and louder into an alarming shriek. Six single explosions rocked the earth. As if by magic the whole area was floodlit by the harsh brilliant glare of the incendiary bombs.

The giant curved bridge was visible for miles. In seconds, another series of explosions rent the night air, as the railway sidings half a mile away were also lit up by incendiary bombs. The anti-aircraft battery to the northwest went into action against the Allied pathfinder aircraft, who had completed his mission by lighting up the whole area and starting many fires. Round after round was fired into the sky without success. Shrapnel was falling all round as the giant pathfinder banked overhead, gaining height rapidly. He flew safely back in the direction of Burma.

The POW's stood as if riveted to the ground. "Christ" yelled Ed. "Here they come." Instinctively, the four men threw themselves flat on the ground. From where they lay, they could clearly see a formation of nine Liberator bombers. flying relentlessly towards the POW camp at a surprisingly low level. The formation suddenly changed, widening and forming behind each other into a single file. As they swooped over the camp approaching the railway sidings, the first stick of bombs was released, screaming down and blasting the sidings with a number of violent explosions. The earth trembled below the POW's, as they lay tensed on the ground. The target was not the bridge, but the sidings. The two Jap anti-aircraft guns blazed into action as the second, third and fourth bombers dipped their noses towards the target. The incendiaries still burned brightly, illuminating the whole area. With fine precision, the bomb-aimers released their deadly loads. As they whistled down the huge four-engined aircraft flew through the flak unharmed gaining height rapidly, before circling over the broad river and heading north towards Burma. The fifth, sixth and seventh planes dived in turn amidst the violent eruptions. The northwest anti-aircraft battery was blown out of action sky-high. Lying flat on their bellies, the prisoners of war cheered each time another explosion took place. In between bangs, a jubilant Ed called out to his mates "Bloody good job it's half a mile away." Morrie answered for all as he replied "You can bloody say that again, Ed!" Plane number eight dived, putting the other anti-aircraft battery out of action. Two of its bombs fell short of the target and much too close for comfort as far as the captives were concerned. They felt the earth shake violently beneath them. From where they lay, it looked as if all the goods trucks were ablaze. Silhouetted against a blazing skyline, the final bomber went into a dive, his bombs scored a direct hit on a line of loaded ammunition trucks waiting to go upcountry.

The prisoners of Tamajao, shaken up but excited, watched in fascination as the last plane circled high above, heading in the direction of its home base in Burma. A chain reaction continued from the ammunition. Explosions were taking place one after the other. Vivid red, green, orange and multi-coloured flashes shot hundreds of feet, high into the night sky, as the last compartments of the all-steel trucks blew themselves apart. Strangely, suddenly an uncanny silence was all that was left.

In the distance, all that remained were flames and dense smoke belching upwards. Conversation returned, as the POW's realised that the raid was all over. "Christ Almighty!" said Foxy. "Did you ever see anything like that."

Morrie was collecting his scattered wits. "Bloody hell, fellows, put the fear of Christ up me!"

Bill laughed. "Bullshit, Morrie. You're a bleedin' heathen, like the rest of us."

"You know what I mean", said Morrie with a smile.

"Sometime in the not too distant future they'll be back to have a go at the bridge", said Ed.

"I think they'll have a bloody job with that one", chimed in Bill.

"Why's that?" interrupted Foxy.

"Cos it's not across the river, is it? It just edges the water as it winds round the side of the mountain" replied Bill.

"It'll be soddin' difficult to hit with the bleedin' mountains in the way", added Morrie. "Just hope we're not around when they attack it 'cos it's much too bloody close for comfort."

It was a long time before they got back to their bedspaces and could doze off into what was left of a long and exciting night.

The next morning the prisoners were aroused from their uncomfortable sleep by the non-musical tones of a Japanese reveille. Their rude awakening was assisted by the fanatical screams and kicks from the ever hateful guards. The POW's lined up for their meagre ration of boiled rice and drinking water. Shortly after breakfast there was a special early morning 'tenko'. The shrill whistles sounded. The guards, clearly in an ugly mood, pushed, shoved, punched and kicked until at last all the prisoners, except for the sick in the hospital, were lined up on the dusty parade ground.

At this time the commandant's hallowed platform was still vacant. The POW's were alive with conversation. King rumour, accompanied by wishful thinking, reigned supreme. After some delay the interpreter Atwai, followed by Lieutenant Hiramatsu and Major Toyoda, emerged from the commandant's comfortable hut. Walking briskly, they covered the few yards to the steps and mounted the platform. Much bowing and saluting was taking place as the resplendent Captain Suzuki walked from his hut. Sergeant Yamanoto leapt to attention, and bowing low to his lord and master, screamed "All men 'kijoski' (attention)!" The commandant was smartly dressed in his dark green uniform, clean white shorts, polished boots, his ceremonial samurai sword dangling from his waist. His beady eyes glinted behind his thick horn-rimmed glasses as he unsteadily climbed the four steps to join the others already on the platform. They all bowed low but he pushed them rudely and brusquely to one side before catching hold of the handrail for support.

He then proceeded to question Yamanoto concerning the rollcall numbers and the sick in hospital. The 'Pig' bowed yet again to the commandant before reeling off in rapid Japanese a complete report on the captives. This formality completed, and with the interpreter Atwai at his side, Captain Suzuki turned to address the 700 prisoners of war who were still standing barefooted on the parade ground.

"Last night, as you are aware, Allied aircraft brutally attacked our railway sidings, killing and wounding many brave Japanese soldiers. Nippon planes have taken their revenge and shot down every aircraft involved in this cowardly action. If your forces dare to continue these attacks, then we will make examples of you prisoners of war and you will pay the price with your lives!" Suzuki was enjoying every minute. He looked around at the POW's, who showed no response, no emotion. They just continued to stand to attention and stare straight ahead, almost as if he didn't exist. He then went on, "Today all prisoners will work first of all on repairing the main line and then on the sidings. This work must continue until the railway is in service again."

"Any prisoner who laughs at the situation, or does not work hard enough will be severely punished. As from now there will be no night bonfires in this camp.

Guard strength will be doubled. Any prisoner who attempts to escape will be shot without warning. There is no time to be lost. There is much work to be carried out. Long live our beloved emperor." With that, Captain Suzuki bowed low to the Japanese flag flying above him and then dismissed the parade.

Work parties were quickly formed up, tools drawn from the stores. In a short space of time they were being marched through the gates of Tamajao, down the dirt road towards the sidings. In charge of all the work parties that day was the Executioner, Lieutenant Hiramatsu, and under him were Sergeant Yamanoto, Koreans Kaneshiro and Chiba as well as several others. All were well known for their brutality to the prisoners. As they marched, Harry Strauss remarked "I've heard some old bollocks in my life, but the crap that Suzuki was rabbiting on about tops the lot!" Geordie Dunlop was walking beside him.

"Couldn't agree more, mon. He's a bloody raving lunatic!"

Ed muttered to Bill and Foxy, "Better watch out today, mates. Reckon we're in for a rough time."

On a more cheerful note, Morrie added, "At least, we won't have to worry about blowing up the bloody anti-aircraft guns." Foxy grinned in agreement.

The half mile distance was quickly covered. Scenes of devastation greeted them. There was not much remaining of the sidings. Where the turntables and points had once stood, there was a vast hole. All around were giant craters. Burnt out goods trucks were strewn everywhere, with twisted metal wrapped round them like bands of steel. The ground rails had completely disappeared. The surrounding forest area looked half bare as if some giant had lopped off all the tops and upper branches from the teak trees. The remains of two Jap soldiers could be seen hanging from a tall tree, some thirty feet or more from the ground.

The early morning troops had removed most of the bodies, and the wounded had been taken away. Japanese engineering officers were out in force, busily directing repair operations. Transport lorries were arriving from another marshalling yard a few miles away bringing in fresh steel railway lines and other essential supplies. There was no time to survey the scene.

The labour gang included the four pals and several more of their mates.They were all hard at work on the main line, digging out mounds of earth and stone and filling in the bomb craters. The tropical sun grew hotter as they slaved on, urged to work harder by the heavy sticks wielded by the guards accompanied by the all too familiar cries of "Speedo, all men must hurry, speedo." Eventually a 'yazume' was called. Almost on the point of collapse, the POW's lay down in the shade to rest and drank thirstily from their water bottles.

As they rested everyone could hear the drone of a high flying reconnaissance aircraft, although the many upturned faces could see nothing in the blue sky above. Bill said, "Reckon they've come back to take a look at last night's results."

Morrie replied, "I don't care a bugger what they've come to look at so long as they don't drop any bleedin' bombs while we're here."

Foxy thought for a moment, then added, "Don't think they'll attack in the daylight, but you never know for sure."

All too soon they were back to work. As the day dragged on it was surprising to see what had been achieved by slave labour. As bomb crater after bomb crater was filled in and levelled over, another gang laid the new sleepers and spiked in the rails. As the normal time for finishing approached a small open top truck arrived from Tamajao 241. It stopped amidst a swirl of dust. Down from the truck stepped Atwai the interpreter. He bowed and spoke in rapid Japanese to Lieutenant Hiramatsu, who called for a 'yazume' period. Sergeant Yamanoto gave orders for all working parties to cease and attend a brief meeting. The prisoners of war wondered what was up. They were soon to learn. Atwai addressed them "Captain Suzuki has given orders that the main line must be restored tonight. The rest of the sidings can wait. Two of the cooks have brought along your evening rations of rice and veg. as well as boiled water for drinking. You'll have to work until the job is finished. Form a queue for your food and water."

Wearily, the men queued up to receive their meagre rations. They had no choice, anyway. Even the guards looked disinterested and disenchanted with the prospect of working on late into the night. The evening sun was still hot as the POW's and the guards sat down in the shade to eat, scattered in small groups along the edge of the section under repair. As they ate, they idly noticed four Buddhist priests with close cropped shaven heads, in flowing deep yellow robes, walking steadily and boldly in their bare feet towards them.

It was not an unusual sight. The guards totally ignored them as they wended their way past the sitting groups of POW's. Ed and Bill watched with keen interest as the four disappeared into the undergrowth in the direction of the river. Ed walked over to the chargehand Korean and duly bowed. "Benjo-ka?" (Visit latrine), he requested, holding his stomach. The Korean was busy stuffing rice into his mouth. Without even looking up he muttered, "OK-ka." In a flash, Ed vanished into the undergrowth.

What he expected, he wasn't quite sure. He'd acted on a sudden impulse. He looked in vain at the wild foliage around him, remembering what Ayut had told him months ago. He had never given up hope. In desperation something urged him to call out quietly the words that Ayut had instructed him in. "Nai phan tri" (major). There was no answer. He didn't really expect one and was about to return to the work party when a sudden rustle from behind caused him to turn round quickly. To his utter surprise, a yellow-robed Buddhist priest appeared almost from nowhere. Holding his hand to his lips, he beckoned the POW to follow him behind the base of a large teak tree, where he squatted down.

"Major Bulpakdi?" stuttered Ed. The priest smiled, as he spoke in perfect well-educated English. "Ed Warton? Captain Ayut has spoken often about you. There is no time to lose. Things are going well in Europe. Germany will soon be defeated. We are making great efforts here in Thailand. The Allies are closing in towards Japan in the Pacific theatre." Ed listened almost in disbelief as the major continued. "When the time is right, there will be an uprising in Thailand. As the British Fourteenth Army draws nearer from Burma, we will contact you. Do nothing at all until then. You must be prepared to overpower the guards, seize their weapons, shoot and kill and we will join forces with you!"

He smiled again, "Do you understand?" Ed nodded that he did. There were a million questions flashing through his mind but there was no time. The major had the last word. "All is well, my friend. Help is coming. You have all suffered so much. Do not be downhearted. Do not speak about me for several hours. It is not safe. Go now, we will meet again." In a flash, he suddenly vanished into the deep undergrowth.

Ed's brain was reeling with the information received. He collected his thoughts and returned to the work party, sitting down beside Bill and Morrie, who were just finishing off the last precious grains of rice. A few minutes later the guards started shouting. "Speedo!" The men resumed their hard labour which, with the aid of kerosene flares, lasted until the early hours. Exhausted, they stumbled back to Tamajao to sleep.

CHAPTER 20

The Bridge at Tamajao

Several days had passed before Ed was in a safe position to explain events and give the vital information he had received to Captain Don Saunders. The railway sidings had been repaired and temporarily at least the extreme outside pressure on the prisoners of war had been lifted. At last, a lengthy meeting was now taking place between the two men in the medical officer's small room adjacent to the main hospital hut.

The Australian M.O. respected his fellow POW's and in particular Ed Warton and his mates. Without their help in stealing medical supplies and food, many more prisoners would have died. The last three years in captivity had changed the young doctor from Melbourne into a toughened man. Now gaunt and thin in features, with premature grey hair, he still retained his handsome looks and rugged balanced sense of humour. He smiled almost boyishly at Ed. "Hell, man", he said, "D'you realise that we're going to survive, mate! We'll be out of this bloody hell before long."

Ed laughed, "Like to think you're right, captain."

"Sure I'm right", came the swift reply. "I've got a feeling deep down in my guts which leads me to another problem, you and your mates!"

Ed looked puzzled.

The M.O. continued, "I've tried talking to you blokes many times before about taking unnecessary risks. OK, they've always paid off, and we're all very grateful for the things you've provided which we would not have had otherwise! So far, you have been extremely lucky to get away with it, but I've been talking to Atwai about the current situation. As we all know only too well, Suzuki and his mob are an evil bunch of war criminals, murderers would be a far better and more accurate description! They are getting jumpy and desperate, now that the tide has turned. Obviously, Allied air raids are increasing. Daily, it is becoming more dangerous for them, and as I see it, anything could happen!".

"Meaning?" asked Ed.

"Meaning", replied the young Australian officer, "simply from a physical point of view, more than ever must I stress.....Aw, shit, for God's sake, man, don't take any more chances. They could prove your bloody last, OK? I'm serious about this!"

Ed thought for a moment about what the doctor had said; then his face broke into a huge grin. "OK, captain. I'll tell the lads we've got to lie low for a while." Don Saunders held out his hand. Ed shook it warmly. The Australian laughed with relief. "Hell, why don't you come on down and live in Australia when this bloody war is over. We could sure do with some Poms like you."

"Might just do that, captain. Goodnight."

Don Saunders rose to his feet. "G'day, Ed. Remember what I told you."

Over in their hut, the gang of four had several long discussions on the action suggested by the Thai underground leader, Major Bulpakdi, when he had met Ed in the jungle. The prospects of succeeding in overpowering the armed guards, seizing their weapons, liberating the whole camp, and joining up with the Thai guerrillas did not seem to be very high, given the general physical state of the prisoners. If and when the call came, it would prove a challenging and daunting task, one that was full of exciting possibilities which gave them hope, The third anniversary of the fall of Singapore had passed. Three long years during which they had slaved and suffered in captivity. How much longer would it continue? The spirit still burned bright within them, although no-one knew the answer to this difficult question.

* * *

Beyond the jungles of Thailand, in the outside world the wide net cast by the Allies in the Pacific was fast tightening around the Japanese. After some of the bloodiest battles of the war, at a cost of thousands of lives, the United States of America had recaptured the important islands of Guam and Saipan. This had brought the war much closer to the homeland of Japan. Following extensive bombing and more bloody fighting, the Philippine Islands had also been retaken, as well as the Midway Island group.

Daily, Allied aircraft and submarines were attacking Japanese convoys and warships. Cargo ships bearing the Japanese flag were sent to the bottom of the Pacific Ocean. Regrettably, there were no other markings on some of these vessels which, unknown to the attacking Allied planes and ships, were in fact carrying our own men, on their way to Japan. Battened down in the holds of these unmarked enemy ships were trapped helpless Japanese prisoners of war, survivors from the horrendous infamous Siam to Burma Railway of Death. Among them was the Hofuku Maru. which was sunk on 21st September 1944 by American bombers off the coast of Manila. Below decks, she was carrying 1,300 British prisoners of war.....

May the eighth 1945 brought the official end of the war with Germany. As Europe celebrated, in the jungles of Burma the British Fourteenth Army fought on regardless. They had the enemy on the retreat. The Japanese prisoners of war were still being brutally and cruelly illtreated. Hundreds were dying from malnutrition and from every conceivable type of tropical disease, whilst the enemy still plundered the International Red Cross supplies, refusing to give anything whatsoever to the unfortunate prisoners of war.

During the third week in May, at Imperial Army Headquarters in Tokyo, the warlords were holding a long and serious meeting. The Prime Minister and Emperor Hirohito were in attendance. Faces were long. The staggering amount of losses in troops, equipment, ships and aircraft, and the loss of vast territory were the cause of much bitterness. For Japan, total defeat was not far away!

The warlords, dressed in resplendent uniforms, were in complete disarray, blaming each other for lack of co-operation and the many defeats. Open quarrels had broken out!

A humiliating feature was the rage of God Hirohito. Just like that other megalomaniac in Europe, Adolf Hitler, he had declared one day he would rule the world. He was angry beyond reasoning. His war lords had completely misjudged the situation and the real strength of the Allied nations. The unconditional surrender of Japan was but a few weeks away. The Emperor made his anger and grave displeasure plain to all. Finally he left the meeting, a disappointed and badly disillusioned man!

* * *

Meanwhile, in the grim jungle camp of Tamajao, nothing had changed. Together with Ed and Bill, Elmer Baker had badly miscalculated. An apparently easy opportunity had proved more difficult and they had all been caught stealing dried salted fish from the Japanese cookhouse. After the expected beatings, they were strung up to trees in the camp for five days and nights before being cut loose. Sergeant Yamanoto and Korean Kaneshiro were responsible for this inhumane and cruel punishment.

On release, Bluey and Joe, the two Australian medics, carried the three of them into the hospital hut for treatment. They lay semi-conscious alongside Morrie and Foxy, who were recovering from another recurrence of chronic malaria and amoebic dysentery. None of them felt very good but they were pleased to be together again. Captain Saunders sensibly didn't say, 'I told you so', but simply went about his daily heartbreaking tasks with the same tremendous dedication and courage he had shown throughout his captivity. Captain Suzuki and Major Toyoda still refused the medical officer and his brave team of medics the amount of drugs and supplies that were so urgently needed, and which would have saved hundreds of prisoners' lives.

* * *

It was now early June 1945. Despite the great odds, Foxy and Morrie had made good recoveries. Ed and Bill were soon making remarkable progress, whilst the Australian M.O. was doing his best to keep them in the hospital hut away from the Japanese.

Feeling sore and badly bruised, they lay talking to their mates. Each evening brought many visitors. Smithy from Dag. and Harry Strauss always came by with Geordie Dunlop and Reg Farqual. Somehow, between them they managed to keep their spirits up. Morrie was very upset at the cruel torture his mates had undergone. "Fuckin' evil bastards!" he raved. "Just hope we get out of this alive and watch the bleeders hang slowly. No, on second thoughts, that's much too bloody good for 'em!"

Ed grinned though his bruised lips, although even that was painful. "They sure beat the shit out of us this time, Morrie. Feel sorry for that poor bloody G.I. who was caught with us." There was an uncomfortable silence for a few moments. They all knew what a painful death Elmer had suffered. When they had all been brought into the hospital hut, he had lapsed into a coma and had died without regaining consciousness. During his beating, the unfortunate American had received some vicious blows to the head, his skull had been fractured and internal bleeding had caused his inevitable death.

It was obvious that Ed and Bill had escaped death by the narrowest of margins. It was only after Captain Saunders' persistent pleas for their lives that Major Toyoda had relented and obtained permission from the camp commandant to release them from their bonds. Ed had expected the final punishment to be the cooler. This time he had been lucky. Never, as long as he lived, would he forget or forgive how they had punished him on the island of Singapore. Bill was feeling better. His two black eyes and battered face bore the hallmarks of a Japanese beating.

"Hell, Ed", muttered Bill, "Reckon when we get out of this, we should spend the rest of our lives hunting down these bastards and throttling them with our bare hands."

Ed turned his aching head painfully towards his mate. Trying to smile, he replied, "I'll promise you one thing, Bill. I will remember these bloody animals till the day I die. Their ugly faces will remain with me wherever I go in this world. If we ever should meet up again" - and here he paused to get his breath back - "I will kill them regardless, with my bare hands, with a knife, or with anything else I can lay my hands on at the time. That's my promise, mate!" He laid his aching body back to rest on the uncomfortable bamboo slats. Foxy leaned over and patted him gently on the shoulder.

"You're gonna be all right, Ed boy. So is Bill. This bloody lot'll soon be over, that's for sure." The group fell silent. The two medics gently lifted the body of a young Scotsman they called Hughie from the bamboo on to the rice sack stretcher and then swiftly carried him from the hospital hut. He had died from starvation, malnutrition and dysentery. He would suffer no more. His Scots mate Jock, also very ill, was quietly weeping. Tears ran down his hollow cheeks as he lay beside Hughie's empty bedspace. There was nothing at the time that could be said to comfort him.

* * *

At the end of the first week in July, Doctor Death had compelled Captain Saunders to send a number of sick men, including Ed and Bill, to report back for work breaking up flintstones in a quarry on the side of the craggy mountain overlooking the river and the long sweeping curved bridge at Tamajao. Foxy and Morrie had been back at work for two weeks, despite the fact that they were all totally unfit and horribly thin. There was no mercy shown by the Japanese and

Koreans. The four lads quickly got together again. In spite of their suffering, the spirit still burned bright.

The Allied airforce was continuing its relentless bombing of the railway. Daylight raids were now commonplace, and had become dangerous and terrifying. So far, the bridge that hugged the base of the mountain had not been under attack. Downcountry, two other bridges at Tamarkan had been pounded and wrecked, as was also the case with the Wang-Po viaduct. Many Allied prisoners had been killed and wounded during the raids. By now, the Japanese had no aircraft at all in the area and all their anti-aircraft batteries had been silenced.

Major Bulpakdi and his small tough team of guerrillas had successfully ambushed several lone Japanese patrols and completely annihilated them. Steadily and relentlessly the British Fourteenth Army battled on through the swamps and jungle of Burma, pressing towards Malaya and Thailand. The Allies were preparing for an invasion of these territories. Tough jungle paratroops were on standby ready to be dropped at strategic points. Patrols had already been dropped as advance parties and had moved into hiding, some of them not far from the appalling POW camps scattered along the railway.

One evening near the end of July, the four mates were called to see Captain Saunders. His news was bad. Atwai had learned from the Japanese of the cruel murder of Captain Ayut of the Bangkok underground movement. They were deeply shocked and saddened. The brave Thai had finally been betrayed by one of the local natives, who had received a cash reward from the enemy. After torture by the Kempi-Tai, they had bound his hands behind his back, forced him to kneel down in front of them while they beheaded him with a sword. This dastardly deed had occurred on the river bank north of Brankassi.

Each day those prisoners remaining in camp were forced to dig large deep trenches outside the boundary. Atwai learned with dismay that if the Allies did not stop bombing the mainland of Japan, then all prisoners of war would be stood in these newly dug trenches and machine-gunned. The grim news received a mixed reception. The POW's were delighted to learn that the Allies were bombing the Japanese mainland, but not a bit excited at the prospect of being executed by machine-gunners!

Out on the railway, the devastation caused by the bombing meant urgent repairs were required to be carried out daily. Despite their poor physical condition, the POW's slaved away beneath the tropical sun. Work in the quarry was also continuing without serious incident until just before the end of July. The four mates were working there in the heat, when the guards called a 'yasume' period. They left the quarry and wearily lay down in the long elephant grass on the hillside. It was late afternoon.

From where they were resting, there was a perfect view of the valley below. The prisoners drank thirstily what little water was left in their bottles. The ten guards lay smoking and idly talking some fifty yards away. Foxy looked down at the river. Shimmering in the afternoon sunshine, the broad river Kwai twisted and turned, banked on either side by the dark green tropical undergrowth.

"Seems a rare peaceful sight down there, boy", he remarked to Ed and Bill. They nodded in agreement. For a few moments Morrie gazed down the mountainside. "Blimey", he said, "Foxy's right. It looks almost too peaceful. You'd never think there was a bleedin' war on." The sun blazed down from a vivid deep blue cloudless sky. Butterflies fluttered to and fro, flashing rare beautiful colours. Tropical birds winged their way freely across the valley. Amidst the green foliage on the hillside lay patches of wild bright tropical flowers, shining out from the dark green like coloured stars of unbelievable beauty.

Down below, a few hundred yards to the south, lay the enormous curved wooden bridge of Tamajao, the monstrous creation that had cost so many innocent prisoners of war their lives. Thinking back to early conversation, Ed recalled it would be a difficult target to hit, tucked into the base of the mountain, half in the water and half out. From afar, there was a drone in the blue skies. At first, no-one seemed to take any notice. It was not unusual for Allied aircraft to make low flying attacks in the daytime. As the roar of the engines grew louder, however, some of the POW's jumped to their feet. Everyone was staring upwards into the blue skies. From where they stood on the green hillside, they had a perfect view.The first nine camouflaged four-engined bombers passed swiftly overhead. As the last one roared onwards downcountry, a stream of leaflets poured out, floating down towards the ground like millions of pieces of confetti.

"Christ Almighty", yelled Ed, "Look at those!" The others stared as if mesmerised. almost in disbelief. With the sun behind them, rapidly approaching in the distance came a second formation of nine Liberator bombers. They were following the natural course of the river, flying low in the centre of the valley. The excitement of the POW's was tremendous. Abruptly, all that changed as the formation suddenly fanned out, banking and circling overhead.

"Bloody hell", yelled Bill, "they're gonna attack the bridge!"

"Run for the rocks", bawled Ed.

The guards were running fast, back towards the quarry. "Christ", shouted Morrie, "Bloody hell, dive for cover!" The POW's flung themselves flat between whatever craggy rocks they could find in a hurry on the hillside. The giant aircraft circled again, almost as if hovering above them. Ed raised his head to look. It was an inspiring and fearful sight, as the first stick of bombs whistled down, missing the bridge and exploding wildly on the mountainside where they lay in fear. Six almighty explosions took place. Shrapnel, tons of rubble and earth shot high into the air. The second and third aircraft released their bombs much nearer the difficult target, without scoring a hit. There was no time to escape out of range. The shocked POW's lay on their bellies as the earth rocked and trembled beneath them. As they lay between the craggy rocks that jutted out on the hillside, the next stick of bombs screamed down. Two of them landed on target, hitting the northern section of the bridge, where it entered a tunnel. Four more bombs exploded violently on the side of the mountain, causing avalanches of rocks and rubble to crash down on to the bridge. It swayed dangerously under the sudden impact, but amazingly still held.

The last attack aircraft circled once more, flying in again from the sun. Three bombs fell short, hitting the mountainside where the prisoners lay in terror. The remainder landed solidly in the centre of the wooden monster, causing it to collapse instantly like a splintered matchbox into the fast flowing river below.

Following the path of the others the plane gained height rapidly and flew triumphantly away into the sun, heading over the border into Burma.

High on the hillside lay a series of bomb craters. Amid scenes resembling a battlefield, seven of the Jap guards had been killed outright. The remaining three were wounded. At the same time an unknown number of prisoners of war had been killed. Several more had been wounded and shocked. Cries of pain and pleas for help could be heard from various different places. Many POW's were staggering about in a daze trying to assist each other.

The last thing Ed remembered was an almighty blast as he and Bill were hurled through the air by the force of an explosion, landing some distance away. Foxy and Morrie had dived together into a small rock gully which undoubtedly saved their lives. By some miracle they were uninjured. In a state of shock they tried to search among the dead and wounded for Ed and Bill without success.

The camp at Tamajao fortunately escaped the bombing. The commandant ordered out all the spare guards to the scene. Major Toyoda gave permission to Captain Saunders and his team of medics to race to the mountainside to search and assist the shocked and wounded back to the camp hospital hut. By nightfall, most were accounted for. Five were still missing, among them Ed and Bill.

The interpreter returned from Captain Suzuki's hut, after a desperate plea from the medical officer. He found him in the hospital hut, working by the dim light of coconut oil lamps. Interrupting the M.O., Atwai said, "The camp commandant and Major Toyoda have given permission for you and a team of volunteers to search for survivors early in the morning. You are also instructed to bring in the dead and bury them." Atwai continued. "All general workparties have been suspended for one day."

Captain Saunders expressed his thanks to the interpreter, who in reply, added, "There will be no escorting guards. Japanese engineers will inspect the remains of the bridge tomorrow and assess what rebuilding is necessary." Don Saunders asked Atwai a number of searching questions. The interpreter replied, "From the information gathered, the Allies are definitely bombing the mainland of Japan. Therefore this will clearly create many difficulties for you." A distraught Morrie and his mate Foxy begged to go on the search party next morning. There was no shortage of volunteers. Harry Strauss, Smithy from Dag., and several others all wanted to go.

Deep down inside, Captain Saunders was very upset. He had known Ed Warton and his mate Bill so well. They had done much to help the M.O. and his patients. He readily agreed to take all volunteers with him and what medics he could spare from the hospital. They would start as early in the morning as the enemy would allow.

Later that night, Morrie and Foxy recovered from the initial shock of the air raid. They were both distressed and worried. "I can't help it, mate", said Morrie to Foxy, "but I feel something terrible has happened to Ed and Bill." Foxy thought for a minute and then replied, "Must be honest, Morrie, so do I. It's not like Ed not to turn up with Bill, still, they weren't among the dead the lads found this evening, so there's a good chance that we'll find 'em in the morning!"

It was a long time before they finally dropped off for a few hours restless sleep. As dawn was breaking through, they were both wide awake. There was a quite a while to go. Suzuki had decreed that the search party would not be allowed to leave the camp until eight a.m.

Captain Don Saunders had organised the hospital routine pending his return, leaving reliable Sergeant Les Thomas, RAMC, in sole charge, with only two medics to assist him. The Dutch medical officer, Major Van Gazell, had been sent down to Chungkai base several months earlier, thus leaving the Australian M.O. to struggle on his own.

The camp commandant had decided that two armed guards should escort the party after all. They were all lined up and ready to go as eight a.m. approached. The tall bamboo gates of Tamajao swung open. Barefooted, the rescue party marched through, carrying their bamboo poles and rice sack stretchers, with additional rice sacks to cover any bodies. Passing the large jungle cemetery, they took the path which led them in the direction of the mountain.

Back in his hut at the camp, Captain Suzuki and his fellow officers were listening intently on the powerful shortwave radio set. The broadcast was coming direct from the Japanese capital of Tokyo. The news was very bad. With the Allied bombing of the mainland of Japan, their many dramatic defeats in the Pacific and in Burma, it seemed as if the whole Japanese Empire was about to collapse around them. Suddenly, they were very worried people!

* * *

The rescue party climbed the side of the mountain until they reached the quarry. The first thing they discovered were the remains of the seven guards, which made a ghastly sight in the morning sun. One section stayed to lay out the bodies whilst the medical officer, accompanied by Morrie, Foxy and four others, searched further afield on the hillside overlooking the valley amongst the bomb craters and piles of rubble for the five missing POW's.

The warmth of the morning tropical sun slowly revived Ed Warton. How long he'd lain there he didn't know. Painfully he turned his aching head to one side. The brilliant sunlight dazzled him. His throat was dry and his back ached horribly. There was a feeling of dead weight and numbness below the waist in his legs. He appeared to be caught up between two small pieces of jagged rock. A few yards away was the unconscious body of his mate. Ed tried to move his legs. They felt trapped. In desperation he cried out, "Bill!" The words came clear enough, despite his dried up throat. There was no response. He called out again. "Bill, are you all right?" There was still no answer. Exhausted, Ed fell back. Weak and in pain, he tried to collect his scattered thoughts. Was Bill dead? The question flashed through his mind. He couldn't be, not Bill. He's too tough! The last thing he remembered was the almighty blast. Then it all returned to him. The air attack! The approach of the fearful four-engined bombers. He dozed off in the morning sun. Was he dreaming, or could he really hear voices in the distance calling out?

"Is anyone alive? Answer me, shout out if you can hear!" Ed recognised the Australian voice.

"Help", he shouted. "I'm trapped here."

Captain Saunders grabbed Morrie by the arm. "Down there quickly", he said.

They scrambled down the mountainside some thirty yards, with Foxy close on their heels.

"The other side of the crater", said Morrie. They tore round. Foxy tripped over a small piece of rock. Quick as a flash, he picked himself up and ran to join the others.

"Ed", yelled Morrie, throwing himself down beside his mate. "You're alive!" Ed gave a weak smile.

"Sure, Morrie. I'm OK, but I don't know about Bill over there."

Captain Saunders was glad to find his Pommie friend. Kneeling down beside Ed, he ordered, "Don't try to move." Morrie grasped Ed's hand in his own. He was overwhelmed to discover his mate was alive. Suddenly, Ed could feel life returning to his legs. The medical officer had pulled off a dead body from his lower half. It was the remains of Taffy Evans.

"Stay where you are. Don't move yet!" ordered the Captain. "Stay with him, you two!" Morrie and Foxy nodded. It was good to know their mate had survived. The M.O. reached the spot where Bill was lying. Bluey and Joe were with him. As one, they knelt down. His breathing was steady. He had an ugly bruise on his right temple.

"Stretcher", ordered the medical officer. "Get him back to the hospital as soon as possible!" he added. "Hopefully, he's only concussed.We won't know for sure until later." The officer returned to Ed. "Your mate's going to be all right. How do you feel now?"

Ed was drinking water from Morrie's bottle. "A helluva lot better", he replied.The medic Joe Langton returned. "Found the other two, Captain. Both dead, I'm afraid." Silhouetted against the morning sun, Captain Saunders looked grim. "Two alive and three dead. Guess they're the five we were looking for. OK, fellows. rally everyone together. Get the wounded back first, then bring in the dead."

They gently lifted Ed out from the two rocks where he had been trapped all night. The M.O. rolled him over on to his belly while he made a quick examination of his back. "Guess you hit the base of your spine real hard when you landed on the rocks, Ed, but hopefully it will be OK. Helluva bruising, though. Afraid you'll have to ride back on our deluxe stretcher."

"Thanks, Captain", replied Ed. "Before we go, can we see down the valley?"

Morrie and Foxy looked down. "Sure you can, Ed. Look down to the left as we lift the stretcher. You'll get a perfect view of what was the bridge of Tamajao." They raised the stretcher. Ed gazed down on the scene below as they staggered up the hillside. The broad river still shimmered in the morning sun. Round the base of the mountain where the bridge had once been there was nothing but a few beams sticking out of the river. It was as if by magic some giant had plucked the long curved monster from the edge of the mountain and river.

"Did a good job, didn't they?" remarked Ed, as the lads reached level ground at last. They put the stretcher down and paused to rest for a few minutes. "They certainly did that", answered Captain Saunders, who was still with the stretcher bearers. "The Air Force did a grand job on a bloody difficult target. It was a legitimate military objective. The sad thing is, as far as we are concerned, that the enemy forced our lads to work so close to a danger area. The score to date is eighteen POW's killed and forty-seven wounded. Ironically, only seven bloody Japs were killed. Strange sort of war, mate!"

The party then commenced their trek back to Tamajao 241. It had been a tough heartbreaking morning. After the midday meal of boiled rice and jungle juice, with boiled drinking water, the dead were buried in the cemetery beyond the camp gates by permission of Captain Suzuki. Since the death of the padre, the duty of burying the dead had fallen to Captain Saunders. He led the procession of stretcher bearers to the graveside. The eighteen POW's were buried in a communal grave, which had been prepared by an earlier work party. A simple ceremony, a few words from the bible, the strains of the 'Last Post', and it was all over. The procession wended its way back into camp. It was now the last day of July, 1945. A reconnaissance plane was heard droning in the sky above Tamajao late in the afternoon. From that time onwards, there were no more air attacks by the Allies. The POW's wondered why.

In the hospital hut Captain Saunders and his medics had done their best to patch up and make the wounded as comfortable as possible in the circumstances. Ed suddenly felt a whole lot better. No bones were broken. Despite the pain at the base of his spine, he was able to walk slowly around the hospital hut.

Bill regained consciousness. He was also lucky. No broken bones. "Concussion and shock", announced the medical officer. "You got real lucky, mate." Bill gave a grin and said, "Guess they need me and Ed back in Southend after all!" Morrie and Foxy were sitting on the bamboo platform next to them. Morrie spoke up indignantly, "So they don't need me in Westcliff, or Foxy back in Needham Market?" he questioned.

Bill laughed. "Course they do, Morrie. Pitsea market would never be the same without you. As for Foxy, well his mum would never forgive us if we went back without him!" They all laughed together. It was a short relief, an escapism. Just the good feeling of having survived so far and still remaining together.

The dim lights of the coconut oil lamps were flickering after dark, causing strange shadows to appear within the hospital hut. Patients and visitors were lying down or sitting talking when Captain Saunders entered to talk with the patients. He stood in the centre gangway and announced, "I've got some good news I'm sure you'll all be interested in!" There was an immediate silence. The medical officer himself was excited. "The interpreter Atwai has managed to steal one of the leaflets that was dropped by our aircraft. The Jap troops have been collecting them up and handing them in." Don Saunders paused a moment to look around his attentive audience, then carried on speaking. "Obviously, the enemy are very upset at the moment. It follows that they don't want us to know what's really happening. They've still got the guns in their hands at present. In our poor physical state, we are at a grave disadvantage, so I don't want to risk anything happening that could only result in our slaughter. We've come too far for that! As I read this leaflet out, don't cheer out loud. We don't want to attract any attention from the guards, OK?"

The men quietly agreed.

"The message is one of hope, real hope, It reads: Hold on! We are coming! Underneath is a map in brief showing how close our forces are. I'll pass the leaflet round, but then please return it to me for safe keeping."

After the excitement had died down, Captain Saunders collected the leaflet. "Better keep this out of sight, lads. The message is clear enough. It'll soon be over now. Hold on! G'day, fellows!" Amidst a spontaneous burst of applause Captain Don Saunders left the hospital hut. Speculation raged all that night. Could it really be true? Was help that close? Among the many unanswered questions, the patients finally fell asleep......

CHAPTER 21

Liberation

Like all others, the tenth day of August, 1945 commenced with the ear shattering sound of the Japanese reveille, arousing the POW's in the jungle camp of Tamajao 241 to an early morning start. The routine did not change but, completely unknown to them at that time, the end of World War II and freedom were just a few days away!

The same old breakfast of boiled rice and drinking water was hardly over when the guards started blowing their whistles, shouting, shoving, and bashing. Despite their many other troubles, those who could still walk, hobble, or limp, lined up on parade for the morning 'tenko'. The counting and the cursing continued till the guards were satisfied that everything was in order. Surprisingly, in the last few days work parties had been getting smaller and more men were left in camp each day for 'yasume'. It was the first positive sign of something unusual being afoot.

As the POW's waited for the arrival of the camp commandant the morning sun blazed down from a blue cloudless sky. The machine-gunners in their tall bamboo gun posts looked down on the dusty parade ground, the barrels of their deadly weapons glinting uncomfortably. Ed and Bill were quite well and feeling a lot better, although Captain Saunders had decided that they should stay in the hospital hut as long as possible.

Foxy, Morrie, Harry Strauss, Smithy from Dag., and many others were in the front ranks idly talking, waiting for the shouts of 'kioski' (attention), which always heralded the appearance of the commandant. They had not long to wait. Atwai and Major Toyoda were mounting the four steps of the platform, with Captain Suzuki strutting arrogantly behind them. Following him was Lieutenant Hiramatsu (the Executioner). Sergeant Yamanoto bowed low, saluted to the flag, and began barking out his orders. The other guards all bowed low in turn.

Suzuki had been drinking again. Clumsily, he returned the salutes and acknowledged the bowing, as he gripped the wooden handrail for support. His ugly face was grim. He launched into his usual propaganda speech, which had no effect on anyone. They were all well accustomed to his ravings and obvious lies. "The reason the Allies have stopped bombing the railway is simple. Japanese fighter aircraft (there were none) have shot down all the enemy aircraft in Burma!"

Glaring around the parade ground, his beady bloodshot eyes glinted behind his large hornrimmed glasses. He continued to rave for the next five minutes, and went on speaking. "Senior Japanese engineers will soon be arriving to commence rebuilding the bridge at Tamajao. When this happens, you will all have to work very hard in order to get the railway line operational again. Today many of you will be on maintenance work at the sidings." Captain Suzuki, the camp commandant, bowed low to the Japanese flag, and concluded with: "Long live the Emperor!" He then dismissed the parade and left his hallowed platform.

The general parade was then divided up into work parties. As they prepared to draw tools and march out of the camp, general conversation broke out again among the POW's. "What a load of old bollocks!" exploded Foxy. "Guess we've heard it all now, mate!" He was talking to Morrie, who was grinning broadly.

"It's bleedin' pathetic", replied Morrie.

"Almost bloody hilarious, I'd say", Harry Strauss joined in, "A load of old cobblers, mate. Bleedin' Jap tripe as usual." Five minutes later they were marching through the camp gates towards the sidings half a mile away.

Back in the hospital hut Captain Saunders and his medics were pleased at the remarkable recoveries amongst the wounded, in particular at the progress of Ed and Bill. The two lads were sitting outside the hut in the morning sun talking. "Every day is a bonus, Bill". I'm bloody sure it won't be long before it's all over. We're all gonna make it, mate". Bill gave a satisfied smile. He shared Ed's enthusiasm and never-failing determination for survival. "Damn right, Ed", he replied, "we're winning, that's for sure!"

That night Foxy and Morrie visited the lads in the hospital hut. The old gang of four sat talking on the bamboo platform. "Updated my notes", said Ed.

Morrie replied, "I still think you're bloody daft. It's too risky. I should dump 'em Ed, just in case."

Ed laughed at his mate. "Don't worry, Morrie, it'll be OK, you'll see!" Morrie was not convinced.

Foxy exclaimed, "Don't know what it is, but there's certainly something strange going on!"

Bill looked at Foxy. "How do you mean?" he demanded.

"Well, it all adds up, Bill. All of a sudden the air raids seem to have stopped. Makes you think, don't it?"

Morrie nodded his head. "You don't think the bleedin' war's over and we don't know nothing about it, do you?"

Ed laughed, "That's wishful thinking, Morrie. No way yet, mate! Suzuki's still there, the guards and machine-gunners are still at their posts, and the poxy rice rations are still being dished out. It's not over yet, I don't reckon."

Captain Saunders came by to talk with the lads. "G'day, you blokes!" The M.O. grinned as he sat down beside the men on the bamboo platform. "Guess you're all thinking the same as the rest of us. Something's going on all right, but I'm sure I don't know what the hell is happening. I'm just hoping that Atwai will be back shortly with some news. Reckon we'll have to keep our fingers crossed and hope for the best!"

"One thing's for sure", said Morrie. "They can't send any soddin' trains up from the sidings. There's no point, 'cause the bleedin' bridge has gone. Tell you what, though, there's a long trainload of Japanese wounded stuck in the siding. Must have been there five days now. They're in a terrible state. It looks like they can't get them downcountry.

Foxy added, "Must say the guards seem very much on edge and bloody badtempered. Ah, here comes Atwai."

They all looked at the Thai interpreter, who had just arrived in the hut from seeing the camp commandant. Captain Saunders rose to greet him. Finding a spare space on the bamboo platform, he squatted down beside the medical officer.

"Not a lot of news, I'm afraid", he said. "Suzuki told me there has been a violent shoot-out with guerrillas north east of Konkuita. A lot were killed and the Japs claim to have shot their leader, Major Bulpakdi. A sniper got him with a bullet in the back, but of course I don't know how true that is." He continued, "The news from Tokyo is bad, but all of a sudden they seem suspicious of me and I can't get near their radio set. One piece of important news is that Captain Suzuki has stated that he has to personally report to Lieutenant General Ishida, chief of staff in Thailand, at a camp somewhere downcountry. He expects to be away a few days and will be leaving by lorry transport early tomorrow morning. In his absence, Lieutenant Hiramatsu will assume the duties of temporary camp commandant. Major Toyoda is remaining as the chief Japanese medical officer, so I guess we will have to wait and see what develops. If anything interesting happens, or I hear more news, I'll keep you all posted." Bidding everyone goodnight, he left the hospital.

* * *

The fifteenth day of August, 1945 arrived. The prisoners of war in Tamajao 241 were not informed that the war had ended. The only unusual feature was that the Japanese had halted all outside work parties. 'Tenko' was also cancelled. Everyone was on an official Japanese 'yasume'. Still no-one knew the reason why. For two days the POW's sat about in small groups talking, arguing, waiting and hoping. For what? They weren't altogether sure.

* * *

August 17th. dawned. As usual, the prisoners queued for their meagre rice ration. The tropical sun blazed down over the distant hills, shedding glorious colours intermingled with the dark green vegetation of the jungle. Wild animals were stirring to roam for prey. To the weary men, it was but another day to survive......

In the intense heat of the midday sun, the Thai interpreter hurried towards the hospital hut to speak to the medical officer, who was requested to attend the commandant's hut immediately. The two men walked briskly across the vast dusty parade ground to Captain Suzuki's residence, where Lieutenant Hiramatsu and Major Toyoda were anxiously waiting. They entered and were asked to take a seat. The Japanese lieutenant looked grim as he outlined to Captain Saunders the latest news, nothing less than the unconditional surrender of Japan!

Outside in the grounds of the camp, speculation amongst the POW's rapidly grew. The rumours spread as fast as ever. It had to happen one day, why not now? Ed and his three mates were seated on the ground in the shade of a clump of bamboo trees close to the hospital hut. Morrie was idly recalling the time when Ed had nicked a stick of dynamite from under the nose of a guard and had promptly stuck it in the small hollow of a sawn-off log, which was being loaded on to the fuelling tender of a steam train. "Christ", laughed Morrie, "I'd have liked to have been near enough to see what happened when it was thrown on to the fire under the boiler." The other three lads joined in the laughter. In any event they never did find out what had really happened.

Bill was wistfully thinking ahead. "Just reckon we could all be going home soon", he remarked.

"Can't be soon enough", answered Ed. As he spoke, from where he was sitting, he noticed Atwai entering one of the POW huts, emerging shortly after with the young camp bugler from the Norfolks. They quickly disappeared in the direction of the parade ground. Ed thought it was strange. Turning to his mates, "That's bloody funny", he said. Wonder what's going on?" He explained what he had seen.

Foxy smiled as he replied in his pleasant Suffolk manner. "It's a rum old do, boy. Reckon we'll all find out soon enough." Minutes later, for the first time in captivity, a British bugle call was sounding out from Suzuki's platform: "Fall in A, fall in B, fall in all the companies." It was repeated again and again. The entire camp was alerted as the notes echoed in the midday sun. In the excitement that followed, there was no time to grasp the significance of the call.

Like wildfire, the POW's rose to their bare feet and stampeded towards the parade ground. As they arrived, by force of habit they lined up in some sort of order. Breathlessly they waited. On the platform was Australian medical officer, Captain Don Saunders. Beside him stood British Sergeant Ray Porter. Next to him was Atwai, the Thai interpreter. The noise of the crowd died down into a murmur, and then complete silence as the Australian began to speak in a strong clear voice.

"Don't move from where you are. We are still under armed guard. Gentlemen, this is the happiest moment of my life! The war is over and the Allies have won. In a minute, I'll give you more information. It's all over, lads!"

For a few brief seconds silence prevailed, then as the words sank into the captives, suddenly someone began to cheer and cheer. It grew louder as everyone cheered and cheered. The excitement was tremendous. It was several minutes before Sergeant Porter managed to restore order. Silence fell again as Captain Saunders proceeded to explain the difficult situation that had been created.

"All Japanese POW commandants have been instructed by radio from our

Supreme Allied Commanding Officer, South East Asia Command in Burma. They are to remain on guard in the camps until Allied forces arrive to liberate all prisoners. It is feared that the rapidly retreating and now totally demoralised Japanese army might attempt to kill us. The camp commandants will be held responsible for the safety of us and the other prisoners." In the event this proved not to be the case as many hundreds of thousands of Japanese troops laid down their arms and surrendered.

The Australian officer went on to say that each camp was to lay out on its open parade ground the letters 'P.O.W.' as large as possible. This was to make identification easier for Allied aircraft to locate the numerous camps in order to drop paratroops, food, and emergency medical supplies.

Almost immediately, the men began to cut down dark green bushes and lay them out in the shape of the letters required. The dark colour would show up well against the light dusty parade ground.

Many seemed in a daze. Was it too good to be true? Each man was preoccupied with his own thoughts and problems. From a secret hiding place appeared an Australian and a British flag, whilst the few remaining enterprising Dutch and Americans skilfully made up their own national flags out of old bits of bedding and cloth. Proudly, four bamboo poles were quickly erected next to Suzuki's infamous platform and the four Allied flags prominently displayed. The machine-gunners still looked down on the display in an awkward and uneasy manner.

The Japanese officers remained in the commandant's hut. All POW's had been led to believe that the Japanese, particularly the officers, would prefer to commit ceremonial hari-kari rather than submit to surrender. Throughout their captivity, the impression had been given to the prisoners of war that no Jap would have surrendered as the Allies had done at Singapore, but would have killed themselves first.

Noticeably, but perhaps on reflection, not surprisingly, none of the Japanese officers and guards at Tamajao 241 took this much publicised way out!

The gang of four were so excited that at one stage Bill thought that they'd all gone barmy at last. None of them really seemed to know what they were talking about. After a while they calmed down and decided to spend the time visiting sick mates in the hospital hut. As they jubilantly entered the sick bay, the excitement there was as great as everywhere else in the camp. Despite their pathetic state, it was clear that the spirit still lived on. Ed and Bill stopped to talk to Johnny Lorell from Nottingham. Sadly, death was not far away. He asked if the lads could carry him ouside to see the flags and know it was really true. Ed went across to Captain Saunders and made the request.

The M.O. replied that unfortunately there was nothing that could possibly be done to save him. Bitterly, he commented, "Sheer bloody malnutrition and starvation. It'll make no difference, Ed. He might as well die happy. OK, let him see our flags." Ed and Bill took one end of the rice sack stretcher and Foxy and Morrie the other. Carefully they carried his body, weighing only six stone, to the edge of the parade ground. There they gently lowered him to the ground and knelt down beside him. Johnny looked up with pride in his sunken eyes. Teardrops appeared running down his hollow cheeks. He gripped Ed's hand with his bony fingers, whispering hoarsely, "We made it, Ed. We bloodywell made it. We're going home!" Those were his last words, as he choked and died in his moment of freedom.

Sadly, the lads returned his body to the mortuary hut. Two hours later he was laid to rest in the cemetery beyond the gates of Tamajao. His four mates escorted him on his last journey. On return to camp, the lads were subdued.

"Bleedin' ironic", remarked Morrie, "Robbed in his hour of freedom!" Bill reached out and patted him on the shoulder.

"C'mon, Morrie. We've seen it all before." Ed tried to smile. "Just think, Morrie, you'll soon be back down Hamlet Court Road in Westcliff. Won't be long, now. It's for real, mate!"

Morrie cheered at the thought. He grinned at Foxy. "D'you reckon they'll know you back in Needham Market?"

Foxy's face was wreathed in smiles as he replied, "Soon as I get out of that bloody station in Ipswich, boy, I'm back in Suffolk and I'm on my way home. Needham, that's real country, brother!"

Just before four o'clock, there was a loud roar in the skies. The lads looked up into the vivid deep blue. There they were flying low, a flight of four-engined American bombers fast approaching the area of Tamajao 241. Circling overhead, they levelled out as they reached the camp. As they watched, like magic the paratroopers jumped one after the other in rapid succession. The parachutes billowed out as they made a swift descent towards the camp. The first ten landed directly on target, in the vast dusty parade ground. As others landed in different parts of the camp, excited POW's rushed to the parade ground just as the paratroopers were releasing their harness.

Immediately they went into action, aiming their short deadly sub-machine guns at the guards in the gun-posts, who were ordered to surrender or die! In minutes, it was all over. The Japanese were lying flat on the ground, begging for their lives.

The ex-POW's were held back as the American commander ordered all Japanese, including the officers, to be isolated into one hut under armed guard, well separated from the former prisoners. An American master sergeant approached the ex-prisoners of war. "Christ", he exclaimed. "You guys Limeys? Hell, what have these bastards done to you guys? Goddamn it, you look like skeletons!"

By now, several more paras had begun to arrive. "Wait till you see the cemeteries on the line!" shouted the ex-captives. Although well-toughened by the war in the South Pacific, the American paratroopers were clearly shaken by what they saw and learned that day. When some sort of order had been restored amidst the excitement and the chaos, the American commander stood on Suzuki's former platform to inform the ex-POW's that he had been alerted by radio that within the next few minutes, the first patrol of British commandos would arrive in the camp on foot. They had been dropped from the air two weeks earlier and had been hiding in the hills close by. They had linked up with Thai guerrillas in preparation for an Allied invasion of Thailand and Malaya which was to have been launched within the next two days. Due to the sudden surrender of Japan by the God Emperor Hirohito, the invasion was no longer necessary and had been called off.

The American continued, "The Japanese surrendered unconditionally to the Allied nations on the 15th. day of August." Whilst he was speaking, spontaneous bursts of wild cheering broke out as through the now open camp gates marched a platoon of tough British commandos. Sweating in the heat, they had trekked miles to reach the camp. Well armed, dressed completely in camouflaged jungle green lightweight battledress, they were led by a young major. The prisoners learned later that he had been dropped with his men no less than seven times behind enemy lines in the jungle, and had fought his way out.

Marching proudly alongside the British patrol were the tough Thai guerrila fighters, led by Major Bulpakdi, whom the Japanese had claimed only recently to have killed. The ex-POW's cheered themselves hoarse. It was several minutes before any sort of order could be restored. There were so many questions to be asked and answered.

Amidst the excitement, another squadron of planes arrived overhead. The men gazed up in wonder as many different coloured parachutes opened up supporting containers of food and medical supplies. Swiftly they descended to the ground. Captain Saunders happily addressed the men, informing them that they might have to remain in the jungle camp for several days yet before motor transport could be organised to take them downcountry to the capital Bangkok.

As he was speaking, the Japanese officers and guards were being escorted away to another camp, where they were to be held prisoner, pending their eventual trial for war crimes. There was news of the cruel and sadistic Captain Suzuki. Along with many others, he had been captured at his old infamous camp at Tonchan, and was also now a prisoner awaiting his fate.

The paratroop commander resumed speaking. "A few words, you guys. Just to bring you up to date, it's all quite crazy here in the jungle, with the Japs surrendering in thousands. Our forces recently dropped atom bombs on the mainland of Japan, compelling the Emperor to surrender his country unconditionally to the Allies, thus ending the war they started when they attacked Pearl Harbour, Thailand and Malaya." At that stage, none of his audience knew what an atom bomb was, but whatever else had happened, they were grateful that it had stopped the war so suddenly. Many felt that these so-called 'atom' bombs had indeed saved their lives!

That night outside the boundary of Tamajao 241 a small group of wandering priests gathered in a circle to play their weird instruments. Round large bonfires, the ex-prisoners of war sat talking. There was so much to talk about. The strange music drifted through the night air. It seemed to Ed and his mates the same sort of music they once had heard a long time ago, in the grounds of a Thai temple on their enforced march to the jungle hell. It had been a sort of warning not to enter 'Death Valley'!

Ed and Bill sat with their two mates. It was all over now. So many of their friends had died. Sitting there in the jungle camp it seemed hard to believe it had all happened. The bonfires blazed brighter as the deep tropical darkness descended. Accompanied by Captain Don Saunders, their two Australian mates Bluey and Joe came over to join them. They'd been through a lifetime together. They all sat on the ground, their thin faces lit up by the flickering flames. They were both sad and happy.

"Came by to say thanks for everything. We're going to miss you blokes", said the medical officer.

Bluey added, "We reckon all you Poms should come and live in good old Aussie." The British lads laughed. "Maybe one day, some of us might just do that", replied Ed. The others all agreed. Ed felt a little embarrassed. "How do we say thanks fellows for our lives?" he asked.

Captain Saunders held out his hand for all to shake. "Aw, shit, Ed. We were all in it together, mate." Morrie and the others all shook the Australians' hands, a token of their true friendship.

There was a momentary silence. Morrie spoke up: "Wonder what will happen to those bastards who have killed so many?"

"D'you reckon they'll be punished?" asked Foxy.

"They should all hang bleedin' slowly", added Bill.

"Wonder if they'll keep Japan disarmed?" commented Ed. There was so much to ponder over that night.

"What sort of deal will we get back in the U.K.?" asked Morrie

"Only time will tell", answered Ed.

Liberation was about to present the survivors with a whole new world full of surprises.

Strangely they were going to miss their mates. In a few short days they hoped to reach Bangkok and leave Thailand en route for home, wherever that may be. For the British, home lay some ten thousand or more miles away. In the heavens above the tropical stars shone brightly. The music of the priests could be heard no more. Farther away in the hills, densely covered by jungle, the night cries of the wild animals grew less and less.

Suddenly all was still. Peace had come to Thailand. Hundreds of miles from civilisation, they all sat talking. Sleep was out of the question. Slowly the dawn broke through, the dawn of freedom!

It seemed like a wonderful dream. They just sat and talked and talked and talked......

THE END

EPILOGUE

Below is a small selection of the more widely known Japanese war criminals, familiar to almost every unfortunate Allied prisoner of war who was forced to slave on the construction and maintenance of the infamous Siam to Burma Railway. It is not possible to publish a complete list due to limitations of space. It will suffice to name but a few of the cruel and sadistic war criminals mentioned in this book.

Railway cases tried and sentenced by the Allied War Tribunal Committee, as follows:-

Captain Suzuki - Commandant of Tonchan Camp
- Death by hanging

Sergeant Yamanoto . Tonchan Camp
- Death by hanging

Korean Chiba - Tonchan Camp
- Death by hanging

Korean Kaneshiro - Tonchan and Tamajao Camps
- Death by hanging

Lieutenant Hiramatsu - Tamajao Camp
- Death by hanging

Major Toyoda - Tamajao Camp
- Death by hanging

Major Mizutani - Commandant No.5 POW Group Siam
- Death by hanging

Many of the other enemy POW camp officers and guards got away with life imprisonment or even a few short years in gaol. Some were even pardoned!

The chaos after the war meant that so many of the enemy who had committed terrible atrocities against Allied prisoners of war escaped without any retribution at all.

Lieutenant General Ishida, chief of staff in Thailand, received only ten years behind bars for his responsibility for war crimes in connection with the railway!

The characters you have met in this book faced many more trials and tribulations before they were finally rescued from their jungle camps and taken to Bangkok, the capital of Thailand. For the British, it was then an air journey to military hospitals on the outskirts of Rangoon in Burma, en route long-term for the United Kingdom and home!

Whilst undergoing treatment and recuperating from their ordeal, the four heroes of this book were stunned and deeply saddened to learn of the death at sea of so many of their young comrades. Nat Ruben, Les Adwool, and many other prisoners of war were among those believed to have gone down when the Hofuku Maru, a Japanese cargo vessel carrying some 1,300 Allied POW's, was sunk by American bombers off the Philippine capital of Manila on the 21st September, 1944. Doug Pardy and several others were more fortunate to survive the terrible journey to Japan in the holds of unmarked Japanese cargo ships.

Today, in very many different Allied countries there exists a special kind of Association called FEPOW - Far Eastern Prisoners of War. In the United Kingdom this Association has many branches. The author is proud to be a member of the Southend-on-Sea branch, in Essex.

Forty-two years on, now in their late sixties, several of the survivors from the railway still meet with their many friends and other ex-POW's on the first Tuesday in every month at the Royal Naval Association Hall in East Street, Prittlewell, Southend. At 9 o'clock in the evening, the chairman calls for silence and proposes a toast to absent friends. Ed, Bill and Morrie, white haired but still upright, stand together in silent tribute to their comrades of yesteryear who are no more. Their thoughts race back through the years to the jungles of Thailand and to their courageous fellow prisoners of war - pals whom they will never forget! Foxy still lives in his beloved county of Suffolk, and once in a while the old comrades visit him for a real reunion.

Each year in the province of Kanchanaburi, situated in the west of Thailand, is held a 'Bridge on the River Kwai' week of fairs and festivals to commemorate the end of World War II.

With such poignant reminders spread throughout the province the main objective is to remind all peoples of the awful horror and cruelty of war and the joys of peace! History records that, during the construction and maintenance of the infamous 'Siam to Burma Railway' alone, 16,000 young Allied prisoners of war - predominantly British and Australians - and over 100,000 Chinese, Malays, Indian, Thai and Burmese all died in the hands of the Japanese!

Amongst the many other thousands of Allied captives held by the enemy throughout the Pacific and the South East Asian theatre of war, over one third were already dead when the atom bombs fell on Japan and led to unconditional surrender to the Allies! Thus came the end of the war started by the Japanese in their unprovoked and vicious attack on Pearl Harbour - when, beside the partial destruction of the American fleet, many thousands of innocent Americans were killed!

The grim facts reveal to the world an appalling waste of lives and are a shocking indictment of Japanese inhumanity to man.

E. Warwick
1987

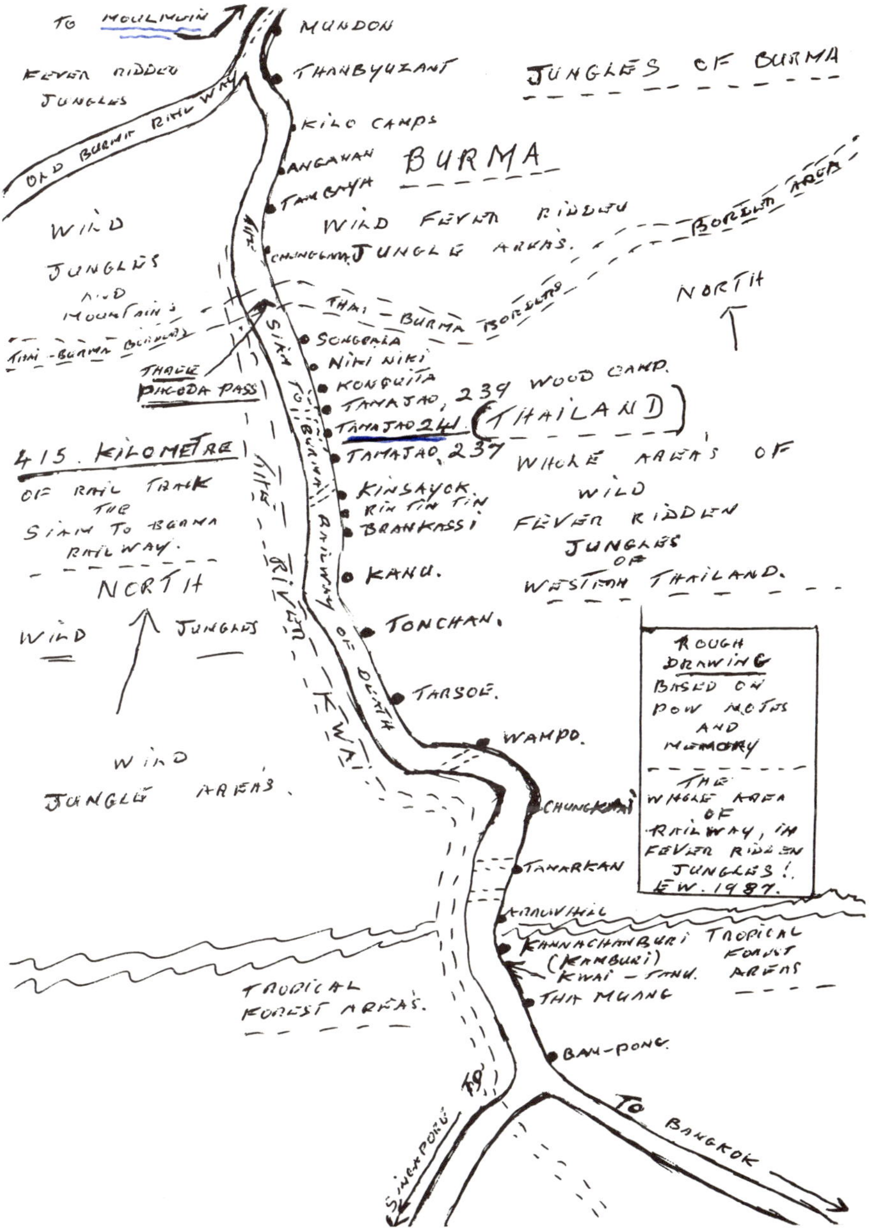

(FIRST DRAWN IN CAPTIVITY, 1943)
E.W. 1987.